THE

Erie Canal

BRIDES

COLLECTION

7 Romances Develop Along Manmade Waterways of New York and Ohio

THE
Erie Canal
BRIDES
COLLECTION

Johnnie Alexander, Lauralee Bliss,
Ramona K. Cecil, Rita Gerlach, Sherri Wilson Johnson,
Rose Allen McCauley, Christina Miller

BARBOUR BOOKS
An Imprint of Barbour Publishing, Inc.

The Way of a Child ©2019 by Lauralee Bliss
Wedding of the Waters ©2019 by Rita Gerlach
Digging for Love ©2019 by Ramona Cecil
Return to Sweetwater Cove ©2019 by Christina Miller
Journey of the Heart ©2019 by Johnnie Alexander
Pressing On ©2019 by Rose Allen McCauley
The Bridge Between Us ©2019 by Sherri Wilson Johnson

Print ISBN 978-1-68322-867-7

eBook Editions:
Adobe Digital Edition (.epub) 978-1-68322-986-5
Kindle and MobiPocket Edition (.prc) 978-1-68322-987-2

All scripture quotations are taken from the King James Version of the Bible.

This book is a work of fiction. Names, characters, places, and incidents are either products of the authors' imagination or used fictitiously. Any similarity to actual people, organizations, and/or events is purely coincidental.

Published by Barbour Books, an imprint of Barbour Publishing, Inc., 1810 Barbour Drive, Uhrichsville, Ohio 44683, www.barbourbooks.com

Our mission is to inspire the world with the life-changing message of the Bible.

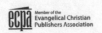
Member of the
Evangelical Christian
Publishers Association

Printed in Canada.

Contents

The Way of a Child

by Lauralee Bliss

Dedication

With grateful thanks to:
Little Falls Historical Society, Little Falls, NY
Louie Baum, my tour guide extraordinaire in Little Falls
Jas. Townsend for the cheese making video and wardrobe ideas
Ramona Cecil, fellow critiquer
Rose McCauley for the collection idea
Tamela Hancock Murray, my agent
Steve Bliss, fellow critiquer and encourager

Chapter 1

Melanie O'Neil paced about the bedroom with her thoughts flying from one to the next. Her dress of pale green with an empire waist and tied with a moss-green ribbon swept the wooden floor, stirring up dust. How she wished she could calm the prickles dashing down her back or stop her fingers from twisting a handkerchief into a large knot. The day had finally come. If she chose to go, he would be waiting for her at the crossroads, the wagon loaded with possessions and provisions, ready to find the reverend and begin a new life in a strange land.

Sam told her how Ohio was ripe for farming, far away from this place that had seen many troubles, from poor weather to enemy invasion. The area still bore the scars of war in scattered piles of rubble. The village of Little Falls had to be rebuilt when renegade tribes decimated it twenty years previous. Yet her heart remained fixed in this place. She had grown up here. Buried her mother here. Worked beside Father in his business dealings. Inwardly she hoped Sam would have a change of heart. That he would arrive on his handsome bay horse, ready to say he'd been too hasty in his decision to abandon everything for a new place. He would acknowledge that Little Falls was his home too.

Melanie looked out the window, envisioning him riding up with a new desire to remain here. They would have a simple ceremony overlooking the river where she often went to pray, serenaded by the rushing sound of water over the rocks. They would build a home adjacent to the land owned by his family. And she would learn how to be a wife and then a mother. It seemed perfect.

But no. Sam wanted adventure and a new life. Ohio was calling his name.

A knock on the door interrupted her thoughts. Her hands shook, nearly dropping the handkerchief. The door creaked open and a familiar voice greeted her. "Are you all right, daughter?" her father, Raymond O'Neil, gently asked. He appeared strong and immaculate, dressed in tailored breeches and leather boots, a waistcoat fastened by brass buttons overlaying the broadcloth shirt. His reddish-brown hair that Melanie inherited reflected the sunlight streaming through the window.

"Sam is leaving today," she announced.

He stepped back as though the words had delivered some unseen blow. "I didn't know it would be so soon."

"We visited yesterday while you were away on business with Mr. Mader. He said if I agreed to leave, to meet him at noon at the crossroads. We will find the reverend to marry us and then make our way to Ohio."

Father's eyes widened and began to glimmer. Were those tears in his eyes? She prayed not. "He told me of his intent a few days ago," he said grimly. "Though he did not ask my permission, nor did he tell me it would be so soon." He straightened, his head held high, hands clasped behind his back in a picture of authority. Would Father now ask that she forsake Sam's proposal? "And what did you say?"

"I—I told him I would go if that's what he wanted." Father's hands slowly tightened and the veins began to bulge in his neck. She avoided the look on his face and turned to the view out the window, beyond the lay of the village and the river below, to the long mountain framing the valley. She must settle the anxiousness in the air. "He is desperate to head west. He's read all the tales of adventure, of Daniel Boone and stories of frontier life. He's grown weary of this place." She heard a shuffling across the wooden floor and then the aroma of tobacco mixed with the scent of the study where Father spent many long hours at his desk. She turned to face him. No longer did he portray a picture of anxiety, with the lines now softening on his face and large blue eyes that spoke compassion. There had only been the two of them since Mother's passing from the influenza many years ago. Maybe that's why hesitation also gripped her this morn with the thought of leaving him alone, possibly never to see him again.

"It's difficult to make such a change," he said. "I won't keep you here against your will, you understand. But I would be uttering a falsehood if I said I wouldn't miss you or that I didn't need your help in our work."

The work entrusted to Father's good hands was negotiating with the farms in the valley to purchase lands for constructing the Grand Canal. The project would allow an all-water route to transport goods and livestock and people from the Hudson River to the western regions. It was good for commerce and for Father's reputation, to be a part of securing the land so the canal could become a reality. But for Melanie, consumed by her affairs, she wondered if any of her involvement mattered. Especially when it came to her happiness.

Melanie inhaled a deep breath to gaze once more at the scenery. The view of the distant river meandering over the rocks proved comforting. She did love this place. The thought of leaving it for some wild territory she knew nothing about frightened her in many ways. She had tried to relay her fears to Sam—the difficult journey, finding a place to call home, the strangeness of it all. He only brushed it aside with tales of adventure and excitement.

Finally she turned from the window, moving to the large satchel to inspect the contents she packed in haste. Father looked on, saying nothing as she noted her other good dress neatly folded, a linen petticoat, night clothing and undergarments, some stockings, and then her dark blue pelisse for those chilly days.

"I will ready the carriage," he said softly. "I hope you will allow me to accompany you and bear witness to the marriage."

Melanie glanced at him. "Of course. I'm sorry, Father. I know you want me to stay. But I can't help but think this may be my only opportunity to marry and have a life. There are sure to be children too. You would love a grandchild."

Father said nothing, but from the way his lips twisted and his shoulders began to curve inward, it was as if the storm clouds once more descended. She tried to shake the thought away, instead thinking on scripture and how one plans his way but God wisely directs the path. While there appeared to be obstacles of the heart in place, if this was not meant to be, God would surely show her the way.

Melanie glanced around the room once more for anything to slip into the satchel. Sam had been firm that she not take much. She tucked in her Bible, a mirror that once belonged to Mother, and a shawl Grandmother knitted during the long journey from Ireland. The room began to shimmer under the flow of tears as she thought of her life here—of picnics and merriment by the pretty falls that gave the village its name, of Father's hearty laughter and the seriousness of the business as they traveled the valley, greeting the farmers and talking about the new canal. Now uncertainty and fear took over.

Father fetched her bag to load into the buggy. Puffiness encircled his shiny, red eyes. She tried to stem her own emotions, wishing now he had remarried after Mother passed on, to fill the void in his heart. But Melanie must consider her future and Sam's wish. Despite Father's sadness, it was her duty to marry and have a family. Even if it meant living far away in a strange new land.

They said little as the carriage pulled away from the humble home for the last time. She tried not to look at anything in particular for the emotion of having to bid farewell to a place she had known all her life. They crossed the narrow bridge spanning the river that flowed over rocks large and small. Along the shore were many fine places to romp on a hot summer afternoon and have Sunday picnics. She caught sight of a boat moving slowly through the old lock built around this rocky part of the river. It reminded her of Father's work and the Grand Canal project that would see a new and larger canal bypass the area.

"At least you will have many things to do," she offered.

He shrugged. "The commission's work has always been our work, and it is nearly finished."

Melanie winced. "Father, this is *your* work. I am but the lowly daughter, and. . ."

"Lowly indeed. You are my only child, my daughter, and my joy. Because of that, I will not keep you here against your will. I give you my blessing, even if my heart breaks for missing you."

The ride became enshrouded in silence, except for the sound of the wheels on the hard-packed earth and the snort of the horse, Hagan, prancing along. Soon they came to the crossroads where Sam said he would be waiting with his wagon and team. Father brought the gig to a rest at the junction and pulled out his timepiece. "When did your Sam say he would arrive?"

"Noon."

"Then it should be soon." He sighed as his gaze swept the clear blue sky without a hint of clouds. "It's certainly a lovely day to wed and begin a journey to Ohio."

The words held hope, though Melanie wondered at his sincerity. She shared in the view of the rolling countryside with farms scattered among the hills. Irish and English farmers had settled these parts, with large holdings for raising cattle. She considered what life in Ohio held. What would she see? What kind of people lived there? Would she be homesick?

Time passed slowly. After a while she shifted in her seat and gazed about, only to see another wagon rolling along the road. Hope stirred until she recognized the wagon's markings. "It's Mr. Thomas, Father. Sam's neighbor. Maybe he has seen Sam."

When the wagon came to a stop beside them, Father tipped his hat in a greeting. "Good day. Have you seen Mr. Winston on his way here?"

"Sam? Why he left at sunup just as I was headed to do some chores. Said he was going to Ohio. Gave me some nice things too, things he didn't want to take with him. Said the wagon was already full."

Melanie's mouth fell open. "I'm sure he didn't mean it."

The man shrugged. "I can only tell you what I saw. Then he left."

Melanie shook her head. "I don't understand. Sam said he would meet me here at noon. I'm certain of it. What time is it now, Father?"

Father looked at his pocket watch. "Nearly one o'clock, daughter."

Melanie tried to steady the beating of her heart and wiped her damp palms across her skirt. Just a few days ago they sat beside the river where Sam had taken her hand in his and told her his plans. Perhaps something had delayed him. Like gathering provisions or completing whatever errands needed to be done. "We will wait a bit longer," she said, though anxiety began to creep in. "He—he may be buying supplies for the journey. Or. . .or he is delayed for some other reason." She couldn't help the wavering of her voice that betrayed the escalating anguish.

They continued to wait quietly with private thoughts consuming each. She sensed Father's concern but didn't know what to do. Until suddenly Father flicked the reins and turned the gig about.

"Father?" Melanie began questioningly, trying to stem the flow of tears welling up in her eyes as they headed back down the road. The scenery around her blurred.

"I'm sorry, dear one. Sam has had a change of heart. The neighbor said as much."

"No! Perhaps his errands took him longer than expected." *Or maybe he no longer wants to go to Ohio*, she thought, suddenly excited at the possibility. Hadn't that been her prayer—for a change of heart? They could still marry by the backdrop of the river where she had lived all her life. They could set up their home, raise a family, and live in God's goodness and mercy. "I'm sure there's an explanation why he isn't here." She sat up straighter. "He may be home even now. We should go right away, Father." Hope brought the tears to a standstill and quieted her heart as they made their way toward the place where Sam grew up. As they drew nearer, she thought she recognized his horse behind the fencing. "See? There's his horse."

Father offered his hand to help her alight from the buggy. She lifted her skirt and walked up to the door, just as it opened. Sam's mother stood in the doorway, wearing a frown.

"Please, Mrs. Winston. If you may, I must speak to Sam."

"He's gone," she said shortly, without emotion.

"I see his horse is here. We were to meet at the crossroads at noon, but it's long since passed." Melanie glanced beyond the woman, hoping to see the man's sheepish face, his hands thrust inside the pockets of his breeches, an apology waiting on his lips.

Father strode up behind her, removed his hat, and bowed. Sam's mother obliged by opening the door wider. "What happened to your son?" Father asked weightily.

The woman stepped back and looked at the ground. "I beg your forgiveness, Mr. O'Neil, but Sam felt it unwise to take Miss O'Neil to such rough territory. I must agree with him. It is far too dangerous for a young woman, with enemies roaming about and danger underfoot. Maybe once he has settled and then returns for a visit, which he plans to do come the New Year. . ."

Melanie shook her head as the tears came once more. "Why didn't he tell me? Why did he leave without saying goodbye?" Her questions remained unanswered as Father slowly took her arm and gently guided her back to the carriage.

Melanie's hands fell limp in her lap, her shoulders heaving as tears slowly dripped down her face. "Why?" she blurted. To be left at a crossroad, with no sign of the one she loved and whom she presumed loved her. How could this be?

Father shrugged. "I don't know, daughter. But it's for the better. God is guiding your steps."

Melanie tried to believe that, even as doubt bubbled up within. "Is the Lord truly guiding me?"

He looked over at her and patted her hand. "Our blessed Lord does not waver in His care for us. He did not want you to be alone in some forsaken place. Or in danger. I held little peace for this situation. I must admit, I'm glad."

You may be glad, but my heart is broken. Melanie began to gasp.

Father shook his head. "Do not fuss so, daughter. There is a time to weep."

Melanie bit down hard on her lip, forcing the emotion of her breaking heart inside. When they arrived home and Father left the gig, she remained in the seat and picked up the reins. "Do not unhitch Hagan, Father. I must go for a drive."

He looked at her. "Do not go after him."

"I have no such intention. Sam left without saying goodbye. He broke his promise to me. I must seek God to find out what to do next. And to forgive him. It's all I can do." Her voice trailed off. With a click of her tongue, Melanie ushered the horse onward along the dusty road. She cared little where the gig took her as she passed the junction where she was to meet Sam, find the reverend to marry them, then journey on to a new land. A thick lump formed in her throat.

Melanie tried to concentrate on the peaceful fields despite the sorrow. She continued to ride along until she spied two small figures trudging down the road. "Whoa, Hagan," she said, bringing the buggy to a stop before two small boys, barefoot in the dirt. Dust covered their young faces as they peered up at her. Their books, bound by a leather strap, were tossed over their small shoulders. "Where are you off to, young ones?"

"Goin' home," said one.

"Are you a queen?" inquired the other, staring up at her with large brown eyes as his small lips parted in awe.

Melanie laughed. "Certainly not. I'm out for a ride. Have you finished your lessons so soon? It's very early."

"Teacher was sick."

"Well then, come ride with me. I would like the company."

"Hooray!" the boys said in unison and climbed aboard, nestling in the cushion seat beside her. It didn't bother her in the least that the boys left dirty markings on the cushion and on her new skirt. The gown was to be her wedding garment, but no longer. She focused on the gleaming smiles on their dirty faces and the joy in their voices that eased her sadness.

"What's his name?" one of the boys asked, pointing to the horse.

"Hagan. It means young one. He loves to run. He's quite swift. What are your names?"

"I'm Matthew. I'm the oldest. I don't know why. We have the same birthday. But that's what Papa says. This is Luke."

"Ah. So are you a good older brother then, Matthew? Protecting Luke from strangers?"

"Ha ha. You're a stranger."

"No she isn't," Luke protested. "She's a queen. You can tell."

Both boys stared at the simple carriage that bore them up, which to Melanie appeared no different than any other cart. Though it did have some nice trimmings, like wood carvings and a padded seat cushion made of fine velvet. Father liked the rig as it was quick on the road yet elegant when calling on people. As they rode along, Melanie recognized the farm and property they passed as belonging to a client of Father's. They had recently called on the owner there with regard to acquiring property to build the Grand Canal. In fact, the man had been most agreeable to the compensation offered and even liked the new water route for transporting goods. "Isn't that the Mader farm?"

"Yes," Matthew acknowledged. "Papa's farm isn't far from here."

"You both have such a long walk to town."

"Papa usually takes us. But he had to wait for the calf to be born." Matthew suddenly jostled her arm. "Go down that road!"

Melanie ushered Hagan onto another road laden with stones, hoping they wouldn't break a wheel or toss one of Hagan's shoes. Before her stood several buildings and plenty of acreage where black dots of cattle grazed peacefully in the distance. To the right stood a two-story framed house, surrounded by land that extended to the river. She presumed one day that land, as well as the Maders' land, would be dug for the canal. "Do you like boats?" she suddenly asked.

"Yes, I like boats," said Matthew.

"I do too," piped up Luke. "We go fishing sometimes."

"Well you will soon see lots of boats on their way west to the Great Lakes." She decided not to say much about the canal, unsure if Father had yet called on the boys' father to inquire of the land easement.

As she brought the gig to a stop, a man came running from the barn, wiping his hands on a piece of cloth. "Matthew? Luke? What happened? Why aren't you at the schoolhouse?"

"There was no school, Papa!" Matthew called out. "Teacher was sick."

"A queen brought us home!" Luke declared. "Just look at the fancy wagon, Papa!"

Melanie felt warmth invade her face, which grew even warmer as the man acknowledged her with a nod. He then looked down at his own clothing smeared with blood, which Melanie tried to ignore. He turned aside, his voice faltering. "Please excuse my appearance. I just birthed a calf. . . ."

"Yes, of course. The boys told me. I'm Melanie O'Neil."

He offered his hand then quickly retreated when he saw his bloodstained fingers. "Beg pardon, Miss O'Neil. I'm David Marshall. Thank you for bringing my boys home."

"Oh, it was no trouble at all. They are delightful." She gazed about the place to note the house with flowers in the front and a well with a bucket nearby. Just then two additional family members descended the porch steps, sporting salt-and-pepper-colored hair and faces beaming with curious smiles.

"See what a grand carriage she has, Grandpappy!" Luke called out to the older man.

"Very fine," he replied with a wink. "I'm sure David has already thanked you for bringing home our grandsons, madam."

"And you are just in time for tea," added the older woman.

Melanie looked upon the gathering and in particular, the faces of the boys who smiled and nodded as if thrilled to have her here. Never did she feel so welcome and on a day that had seen such sadness and confusion. Maybe this was the Lord's way of bringing hope and healing.

"Thank you. This helps me greatly. More than you could know."

Chapter 2

W e were brought home by a queen. . . . "The words reverberated in David's mind as did her last remark—that the offer of tea helped her in her time of need. Having washed away the offense of birthing the calf, he now assisted the fine woman from the fancy carriage. She placed her gloved hand in his, lifting her skirt of light green, which appeared far too regal for a simple drive in the countryside. Where could she be going, dressed so fine? he wondered. Despite her plans for the day, she thought to look after the welfare of his boys—an act of true selflessness and a tender heart that warmed his own. He hadn't known many women like that. Or if there were, he'd been too busy in life to notice. Until now.

"You have quite a large farm," she observed. Her blue eyes swept pasture-lands of green as far as the eye could see, marred only by the cattle grazing in the distance and several small groves of trees.

"It was passed down to me by my father." He couldn't help the pride in his voice. Not only did he own vast acreage but also the house, several barns, and other small structures. With his herd of cows, he'd forged a profit from cheese making that began with his pa on the advent of the war with England. The venture had succeeded beyond his wildest expectations.

"Welcome," greeted his father-in-law, extending his hand, which the young woman grasped.

His mother-in-law curtsied and offered a smile. "To whom do we owe the pleasure?"

"Miss Melanie O'Neil."

"Hiram Boice, and this is my wife, Louise."

Louise waved her hand. "Please come in. The tea is ready."

Miss O'Neil nodded and smiled before setting her sights about the place. The room where they took their seats wasn't much to look at, with simple furnishings and some treasured pieces from England. What type of home did she live in? he wondered. Likely one of the fine brick residences in Little Falls with a view of the river below, complete with woven floor coverings and fine furniture. He could envision a coat of arms hanging above the fireplace, perhaps even a suit of armor or other weaponry on display. But then he recalled her last name of

O'Neil, denoting an Irish ancestry, and the idea of money aplenty and a coat of arms vanished from his thoughts.

Now as he watched her sitting there, prim and proper, with her back straight and hands folded in her lap, he tried to recall the last time a young woman had graced their humble home. Perhaps his cousins from New York City. Then he caught the eye of his father-in-law and the smile on the older man's face. It surprised him that Hiram and Louise would be so captivated by Miss O'Neil's presence. He thought the mere image of a young woman would evoke sad memories of their daughter Leah, his wife, who departed this life after giving birth to the two rambunctious boys that now chased each other around the room. He saw no discomfort or sorrow but only smiles. *Perhaps time does heal and makes a heart ready to receive new blessings.*

"I hope I'm not intruding on your family devotions," Miss O'Neil said.

"Certainly not," said Louise. "We always gather in the afternoon for tea and prayer. Isn't that right, David?"

All eyes focused on him, expecting him to welcome the woman and make her feel at home. "Yes, of course. We're glad you can stay for tea and whatever else Louise has made. She is an excellent cook."

"I made some lovely doughnuts," Louise added with a smile. "Matthew and Luke, come help me serve our guest."

"Hooray, we get to serve a queen!" Luke said loudly.

David saw a deep flush seep across Miss O'Neil's high cheekbones. Such a reaction told him she was not some highfalutin woman of means but rather appeared embarrassed that Luke would address her with such regality. He listened as Hiram asked questions, eager to hear about her life.

"Your name sounds Irish," Hiram ventured.

"Yes. We came here after the War for Independence and settled in the village."

"We have been here that long as well."

David watched her twist her gloves in her hands and shift in her seat. Her eyes began to shimmer with tears. "I only hope I never see a day like this one again," she declared. "I thank the Lord for sending me your sweet boys today. They were a pleasant distraction for me."

The comments nearly brought David to his feet, wondering what happened to make her so melancholy. "Are you well?" he asked, hoping she would explain further.

"I always presumed a man would keep his promise. . . ," she began then straightened in her seat, her frown replaced by a smile when Louise entered the room, carrying a pot of tea. Luke followed, trying to balance a plate of doughnuts. Just then Matthew leaped up to snatch one, upsetting the platter and sending doughnuts tumbling to the floor. A hound rose from the corner of the room and began eating them.

"Oh dear!" Louise cried. "Scat now," she scolded, trying to shoo the dog away.

"Boys, you know what I've said about being greedy," David reprimanded in a stern voice as he rescued the plate.

Matthew and Luke looked at David, who held the plate holding the few remaining doughnuts. "Please forgive their actions," David directed to Miss O'Neil and offered her a doughnut.

She chuckled in amusement as her long fingers slowly picked up one of the treats. "Oh, I do understand. When I saw this plate of delicious doughnuts, I wanted one right away too." She winked at the boys, who laughed in return. Miss O'Neil gently nibbled on a crusty exterior before exclaiming, "How excellent. You must tell me how you made them."

"Why, I never presumed a fine woman like yourself would cook or bake," Louise remarked.

Hiram shook his head. "What a thing to say to our guest, Louise!"

Louise's worn face took on a reddish hue. "I meant no disrespect. It's just that a woman of your means. . ."

Miss O'Neil looked at the fried treat in her hand. "I've cooked many times. We sometimes hire in a young woman to help on occasion when it's busy or we have been traveling and are too tired. But actually, I'm quite a good cook. With simple things, that is. But I would love your recipe."

"You must come again, and I will show you." She paused. "I miss teaching a young woman how to cook." David saw a faraway look in his mother-in-law's stark gray eyes and knew she was thinking about Leah.

The offer sent a broad smile filling Miss O'Neil's face. The sight brightened the room as if touched by the sun's rays. Everyone smiled and laughed with a joy he had not heard in a long time while they ate doughnuts and drank the soothing tea.

"This is very kind," Miss O'Neil finally said, looking over at David. "God knew I needed this gift of hospitality."

"The Lord cares," Louise agreed. "And He loves." She bustled over then and sat right beside Miss O'Neil, patting the woman's hand. "All of us have been through terrible things. Heartache, sorrow, sickness, pain. He is able to carry it all. I know."

Melanie O'Neil looked down at Louise's wrinkled hand. David expected her to draw away, but she did not. "I believe you. I never thought a simple ride in the country would bring me to such kind people." She glanced at the two boys fighting over the last doughnut. David intervened to split the doughnut in two so each could take half. The boys stuffed the goodness in their mouths then went to play with their tin can of soldiers. David watched Miss O'Neil stare fixedly at the scene as Luke stood each soldier one by one in a row while Matthew took the other half and stood them in a line opposite Luke's. Her eyes were a lovely shade of blue, with eyebrows drawn together in careful concern. Her reddish-brown hair was caught in a bun, with delicate ringlets framing a set of high cheekbones.

"You can't take our land!" Matthew now shouted as Luke advanced his row of soldiers.

"We come in the name of the king!" Luke responded.

"We've been talking about the war with England," David explained when Miss O'Neil flashed a look of concern. "The boys were too young to remember much of it."

"It only ended two years ago," Hiram piped up. "May there be no more aggression so we can live in peace, as God would have it."

"That's why Sam wanted to go to Ohio," Miss O'Neil said wistfully. "I was to marry today, you see." She looked away with a smear of red flooding her cheeks. "I'm sorry. I shouldn't be bothering you with such things."

"Of course you should," Louise said, patting her hand. "It's important."

"I was to leave with him today for Ohio," she continued, the sadness evident in her voice. "But he never came to meet me at the crossroads. His mother thought it unseemly for a woman to go. Why he couldn't tell me himself, I don't know."

Louise sighed loudly. "How thoughtless and uncaring. To make a promise and then leave without saying a word."

"I should not concern you with my sorrows," she repeated, bowing her head.

"Nonsense. The Lord directs us to bear one another's burdens."

David sat silently as Miss O'Neil continued to tell of this man who left her with no word of his intentions. Who could abandon such a lovely woman? He must be a scoundrel with no heart. Except a journey into the unknown did hold many dangers. "Perhaps he was considering your safety—" David began.

Miss O'Neil whirled, her blue eyes blazing. "He knew me well. If he didn't think I should go, he might have said as much. But even after he promised to marry me, he left."

David fell silent. A battle now raged at their feet between the boys, with several of the soldiers falling over from verbal gunfire noises. Seeing the soldiers lying there on the floor, David wanted no more pain or death. Just life. Only life. And God's peace.

"Maybe it's just as well," Louise continued. "If the man could not keep his promise, he would not be able to lead the way in a marriage. The Lord directed your steps for the better, my dear."

"That's what my father believes." She took out a handkerchief from the tiny bag hanging over one arm and dabbed her eyes. "He's happy I didn't leave.

There's only the two of us to look after each other. I must believe all this will work out for the best."

"It will, my dear. I'm certain of it."

Miss O'Neil smiled and stood to her feet, stuffing the handkerchief back into the small bag. "I should be going. Father will worry. Thank you for your kindness."

"Before you go, we must pray for you, dear," Louise said.

David watched every person close their eyes, and he did too, while Louise offered a simple but gracious prayer that God would heal the hurt in Miss O'Neil and fulfill her every need. When his eyes flicked open, the woman was gathering her wrap and putting on her gloves. He went over to open the door for her and escort her to the buggy. "I hope you're not leaving on my account," David suddenly remarked.

Her blue eyes flashed in his direction. "Why would you say that?"

"I didn't mean to upset you when I said the gentleman may have been seeing to your safety. Though I do believe him dishonorable for leaving without a word."

"Thank you. I'm glad I came here and could release the burden into the Lord's care. If not, it would have been a very sad afternoon."

David trusted her words though he could plainly see the pain lingering in her blue eyes. Usually he never thought himself an observer of inward emotion. He never read such emotion in Leah until she told him outright what she was feeling. Nor did he exhibit it himself. For now he set the observation aside to assist Miss O'Neil into her carriage.

"Thank you for having me to tea," she said, gathering up the reins.

"Thank you for bringing my boys home." He thrust his hands into the pockets of his trousers, watching her skillfully maneuver the horse to a fast trot down the lane. He wondered how any man could leave one so brave and beautiful at a lonely crossroad without explanation. But neither would he wish her the trials of a new life in a far-off place like Ohio. If he were that fellow, he would have taken Melanie O'Neil into his home right here in the valley and called her his own.

David froze. Chills darted through him, wondering how he could think such things, especially after such a brief encounter. Unless the time had come for him to consider taking a new wife and a mother for his boys. The sound of youthful chatter confirmed his thoughts as Matthew and Luke raced out of the house, satisfied by the doughnuts and milk and eager to knock around a leather ball with sticks. Though they had all gotten along quite well these many years after Leah's passing and thrived under the watchful care of his godly in-laws, David believed they needed more. Someone to read to the boys, to teach them how to respect and love all living things, to impart a certain tenderness and care that he could not.

David glanced down the road as the dust clouds dissipated from the wheels of Miss O'Neil's carriage. He could hardly wish for her, from a stately upbringing, perhaps with a lawyer as a father, a life here on his farm. Just as her former beau must have realized, Melanie O'Neil was on this earth for finer things.

Pushing the encounter from his mind, David headed to the barn to retrieve a hammer and nails to fix some fencing broken by an ornery bull. He sauntered out to find Luke dashing up to meet him.

"The queen was sure pretty, wasn't she, Papa?" he asked breathlessly.

"She was very nice."

"I hope I get to ride in her carriage again. Maybe when we go to school tomorrow we will see her."

David had to wonder if their paths might cross again. For now he whistled for Matthew and instructed the boys to help hold the wooden post in place. They huffed during the job, their small faces bright red from the effort, as David nailed the fencing.

"Mama was like that, wasn't she, Papa?" Matthew asked, breathing hard.

The hammer froze in midair before landing squarely on the nail head. "Like what?"

"Pretty and nice and all."

He hesitated, his thoughts flashing to the beauty and simplicity of Leah, though it had been many years. "Yes, she was."

"I know. I seen the painting of her."

The painting of Leah, commissioned by her parents long ago, still hung in the hall near the boys' bedroom. He did his best to tell them about her, with stories of her kind heart and hard work and love, though they never knew her. The boys had her characteristics in their brown hair and eyes. She liked to laugh, but she also had a mind of her own, similar to Melanie O'Neil. Leah once talked of moving from here to a safer place. When she was expecting the twins, she told David she wanted her babies to grow up in peace. There must be somewhere safe to go, like out west where many were headed including a few of their friends. David objected, telling Leah that travel in her condition would be far too difficult. God would watch over them. And he was determined to work the land passed down to him.

He pounded in the nails as he recalled the night of the boys' birth—the terrible struggle, and Leah's strength quickly leaving. He could do nothing but watch her pass into eternity. Then he faced a different battle, with no mother for the babies and trying to make a living on his farm. He often wondered how all this could be God's mercy and love. He spent many long days and nights thinking, reading the Bible, and praying, but received little in the way of answers. Finally he came to accept it as God's will, like everything else in his life. Even if he didn't understand, God did, and he had no choice but to trust. Now looking at his twin boys, full of life and happy as the birds that flew about the fields, he knew that God had indeed watched over them with kindness and strength.

David looked up to see another dust cloud stirring from the road. He thought Miss O'Neil might be returning, having left some sundry inside the home or wanting to talk more. For a brief moment the thought made him glad.

Instead the rider on horseback was his neighbor, Oscar Mader. *A shame he's not bearing a basket of good cooking, like homemade strudel from his wife.* He set down the hammer and went over to greet him. "Hello, Oscar. How is Henrietta?"

"*Ja*, she's *gut*, very gut indeed. But I had to come show you dis." The stocky man dismounted in a flourish and strode up, pulling a paper out of his pocket. "I did it, David."

"You did what?" He took the paper from the man's outstretched hand.

"I bargained, I did. Wit dat gentleman from the village."

David nearly dropped the paper. He knew who Oscar meant. He'd heard of the businessman in his fancy rig, traveling from farm to farm, looking to buy up land. He glanced at the agreement Oscar had made to sell sixty acres to the Grand Canal project. "I can't believe you sold your land."

"He made me a gut offer. And we need the money. What's a few boats coming by my home? I could use dose boats to take my apples west."

David shook his head and handed the paper back. "It's fine for you. . ."

"And for you. They will come here next."

David felt the muscles in his neck and shoulders tense. "There is no need for them to come here. I have no intention of selling."

Oscar scratched his head, covered with thin strands of brown hair. "It's gonna come whether you want it or not. You canna stop it."

"I can if I say no. Then how will it work?"

Oscar shook his head. "Why would you do that? They will take it for the common good, and you will get nothing. I hear the talk. Better to sell and make some money than be angry and have other folks angry at you too. And I will tell you, being angry is more tiring than a day's work plowing a field."

David turned to gaze at the very land the highfalutin folks wanted for their Grand Canal project. He tried to imagine water cutting through the prized grazing land for his cattle. The shouts of boatmen transporting their wares. His herd scared by strangers and the boats making their way through. The peace of the land forever disturbed by man's progress.

"Yer a hard man, David Marshall. And maybe foolish too, ja? I hope you will think about your family. You need to decide soon." He returned to his horse.

David knew he should ask more about the meeting, to find out the final price Oscar negotiated and other details. But disgruntlement outweighed knowledge. Instead he returned to the work of shoring up the fencing, despite Oscar's words that pounded him like the hammer he wielded.

Then he saw Hiram heading his way. "What did Oscar want?"

"He sold off some of his land for that canal they're planning to build."

"He did?"

David nodded, adding a decisive blow to the nail to match his irritation. "He says we're next."

"Hmm." Thankfully Hiram offered no further comment. The farm and land belonged to the Marshall family, and David had inherited it when Pa died. He had been instructed to keep it in the family and not give any of it away to strangers to use as they pleased. Besides, no one knew the future. Land like Oscar's could go to ruin. Or suffer the effects of strangers roaming about. "And it will," he pronounced.

"What will?"

"If they come, they would tear up my land and scare my cattle and decrease milk production. If the cheese production fails, then we become paupers."

Hiram shook his head. David did not expect the man to understand. No one understood, save God alone. But he remained firm in his decision. If that businessman came seeking his land, David would have plenty to say, along with a rifle by his side.

Chapter 3

O my God, my soul is cast down within me. . . . Deep calleth unto deep at the noise of thy waterspouts: all thy waves and thy billows are gone over me.

Melanie reflected on these words in Psalm 42 since Sam's abrupt departure for Ohio. She tried to understand why he had left her here. How could he think she was not capable of enduring the rigors of a journey and a new land? Did she appear like one who could not do what was expected of her? Did he not trust her to be by his side? Or was God simply guiding her steps as everyone claimed?

As she gazed at the water cascading over the rocks that gave the village its name, the sound soothed her hurting heart while she prayed for a new purpose. Father, of course, was glad she remained in Little Falls. He said how much he would hurt by her absence. There was plenty to do with the housekeeping, particularly since Father had let go the girl who came to help. No one remained to make a good meal or care for the chickens and other stock or do the wash. Or be company in a lonely house. Still, Sam was her last hope for a meaningful life, lest she become the spinster daughter of a businessman who worked for the canal commission. Would the future now hold nothing but the work here at home, Father's business, and visits with women in town where she was expected to gather and socialize?

Melanie opened the Bible but only saw blurred words before her as if a fog had descended over her eyes. It had been happening more and more lately, something strange with her sight. At times her head would ache, for which she partook of white willow bark and a cool cloth on her brow. She hoped all the excitement of the past few days had not brought on some strange illness. Just the thought of sickness carrying away loved ones without warning, like her mother, worried her. *Lord, I pray that whatever is ailing me will soon be gone.* What better way to release worry than to put it in the hands of the living God who numbered the very hairs on her head.

Melanie sighed and jumped to her feet. Enough with this melancholy. She gripped the Bible close to her and squinted at the dusty road with several men driving wagons, intent on their errands. It reminded her of Father's work with the canal commission, traveling to and fro in the buggy, meeting families and discussing the coming of the canal. He thought of her as a sweet touch and calming influence in the business dealings. Melanie would be glad, though, when this came to an end. Just a few outstanding parcels remained, and Father was readying himself for the final meetings. So far everything had gone well, with most farmers eager to be a part of this new enterprise. The last one, a Mr. Mader, had brought them much relief when he agreed to sell the land. His smile went from ear to ear over the idea of a canal for transporting his goods.

Melanie lifted her skirt with one hand to begin the walk home, glad for the time spent in prayer by the river to renew her strength. The wind caressed her face as she paused to tighten the strings of her bonnet around her head when she heard young voices call out.

"Look, look, it's the queen!"

"It's us!"

Melanie squinted against the rays of piercing sunshine to make out two figures waving frantically from the back of a wagon. The man holding the reins drew the wagon to a stop beside her. They were none other than the twin boys and the father who introduced himself as David Marshall. He stared at her from a face boasting beard stubble, his hat set low over his head of wavy brown hair.

"Hello, Miss O'Neil. Can we offer you a ride?"

"I'm just heading home. It's not too far. I like the walk."

"I have a few errands to see to. The wheelwright and the blacksmith. One of my horses may need a shoe."

Seeing the boys smiling broadly and hearing the distant sound of water playing over the rocks, an idea came to her. "Would your boys like to visit the river? We can go exploring. Then you can do whatever needs to be done in the village."

"Oh yes, can we, Papa?" the boys said in unison.

His eyes widened at the suggestion. "I'm not sure. They can be mischievous and—"

"I do understand," she assured him with a smile. "I have watched over Mrs. Lindon's boys. I also know boys love adventure and the river."

Mr. Marshall nodded, his face cracking a smile. The twins jumped off the cart and raced to her side, their faces beaming. "Hooray!"

"Mind Miss O'Neil now," their father said. "I will return here soon."

When the cart moved off, both boys eagerly grabbed hold of her hands. Melanie obliged, allowing the sturdier youth, Matthew, to carry her Bible as she enjoyed the feel of small hands in hers, each so trusting and filled with expectation. Dare she think they longed for motherly attention? Not that their grandmother, Louise, did not give womanly affection. But there was something in the feel of the hands that told her how much they needed more in their lives and how difficult it must be. "How are you this day? Any news?"

"We named the calf Star."

"What a grand name. Let me guess. He has a star on his forehead."

Luke bellowed with laughter. "Yes, yes! Papa said you were smart. He talks about you all the time."

The mere notion of David Marshall complimenting her sent warmth rising in her face. "I can't imagine I've done anything worth remembering."

"No fine lady has come to the farm," Luke said.

"He likes having a queen see us," Matthew added. "And anytime you want us to go in your carriage, Papa says we can."

Melanie laughed. "Well for now, the Lord gave us fine feet to take a lovely walk and enjoy the day and the falls along the river." Yet learning that their father had talked about her made her curious as well as pleased, even if they'd only seen each other for a brief time. The two adorable boys jumped up and down as they came to a wide-open place where they could view the cascades tumbling over rocks of different sizes, framed by the backdrop of a stately mountain ridge. Melanie never tired of this place but found peace in the roar of the water where she often prayed and read from the Bible. Now with the boys by her side, she wondered if God was answering her prayers in unexpected ways.

"Maybe we can go fishing?" Luke wondered.

"What a lovely thought. We can find a calmer place on the river to fish. My father has a pole we can use." Father used to enjoy fishing on a fine day like this. Maybe once his work with the canal was finished, he could exchange the anxieties of it all for the peace found in the flowing river and the expectation of a fine catch for dinner.

The boys grabbed her hands to return to the road, both talking at once of all the fish they would catch and how they couldn't wait to see her house. Melanie smiled under their youthful exuberance, all the while hoping they would not be disappointed when they saw the modest brick house in the village. It was no cabin but neither was it a castle.

Once they arrived, the boys examined everything with glee—from the braided rugs on the floor, to the tapestry of the Irish countryside on the wall, to the stylish desk and bookcase and other Federal furnishings. They threw themselves into a set of twin chairs, exclaiming how they were princes upon their thrones and then began ordering around pretend servants. While they were busy, Melanie located the fishing pole and glanced at the clock to see time ticking away. "Come, we will take Hagan and the buggy to the river," she decided. "We have little time left to fish before your papa returns." She gestured them outside to the stable and hurried to hitch up Hagan with the boys assisting. They exclaimed their joy at having another ride in the "fancy wagon," as they called it. To Melanie it was but a rig to take her from place to place, but the boys felt like nobility.

"I hope Jimmy sees me!" Luke declared. "He hid my slate the other day."

Melanie glanced at him as she climbed aboard the rig. "Why would he do that?"

Luke shrugged. "Dun' know. I wanted to hit him. Papa told me no. It's bad."

"Your papa is right. We don't repay evil for evil. Say a prayer for the boy instead, that he will have a good heart."

Luke and Matthew nodded as if they were used to their father saying such things. "We say our prayers every morning and before we go to bed," Matthew said. "And we pray before we eat. And Granny Louise reads from the Bible."

Melanie motioned for them to climb into the gig, which they did, each occupying the same place when she last took them to their home. She flicked the reins and headed down the dirt road. "So tell me, who is your favorite hero from the Bible?"

"David!" Luke chimed. "The one who threw a stone at the giant!"

"David!" Matthew echoed. He then lowered his voice. "But I'm not supposed to say Papa's name."

Melanie couldn't help but chuckle. When both twins uttered the name David, if she closed her eyes, she was quite certain she couldn't tell them apart, though they possessed different characteristics. Matthew was stouter and taller than his brother. One had lighter brown hair, and the other, a mark on his left cheek. She'd heard of twins who looked exactly the same and often drew the attention of everyone around them. But not these two.

Arriving at the river in a matter of moments, the boys jumped off the gig in glee. Their father had not yet appeared, giving her hope they still had time to do some fishing. Melanie took out the pole and asked the boys to use the small wooden spade she'd brought to dig for worms. The boys took the tool and busied themselves with harvesting bait when Mr. Marshall rode up in the wagon. *Oh dear*, she thought.

"We're going fishing, Papa!" Luke exclaimed as Matthew held up the pole.

He stared first at them then at Melanie, the reasons why they must hurry home no doubt on the tip of his tongue. Instead he slid off the cart to the ground below. "I suppose we can fish for a bit."

"Have you found bait?" Melanie asked, thankful their father allowed the boys to continue with their adventure. Just then she caught his eye and the crook of a smile on his face. Did he find her too outspoken? Or headstrong? Instead he went to help the boys harvest bait, finding plenty of worms in the soft soil near the river. "Will you show them what to do next?" he teased.

She returned his smile of amusement. "Of course. My father was a good teacher." She picked up a long, moist squiggly worm, drew in a breath, and baited the hook. "There."

"Hmm. You did well." He gave the pole to Matthew.

"I want it!" Luke protested.

"You each get a turn. First Matthew, then you." Mr. Marshall showed the boys how to fling the line into the river as Melanie imagined a scene long ago with Father, hearing his words about the importance of fishing and providing for the family during the war that crisscrossed their land.

But now new tingles came when David Marshall sat down beside her, watching his boys take turns with the fishing pole. "A fine idea," he mused. "I haven't taken them fishing in a while. I feel sometimes I'm neglecting certain things in their lives."

"You have plenty of work in keeping up the farm, I'm sure. One can't be expected to do everything."

He eyed her with a look of appreciation that suddenly made her flush. "It's difficult, but I'm glad Hiram and Louise are here to help. I don't know what I would do without them." He paused. "But I know there's a lack in their lives, having no mother." He paused, his face taking on a reddish hue, and faltered. "Not that I'm suggesting anything. . .that is not my intention."

Melanie suddenly liked this man for his caring concern. "You're looking after their happiness as any father would. My father felt the same way after my mother died. It shows your love for them." She added, "And they are fine boys."

David Marshall now stared at the river, his hands cupping his knees. Melanie imagined those hands that had seen much toil suddenly taking hold of hers. And then his firm strong arms, clothed in simple homespun, coming to hold her. She caught her breath, chastising herself for thinking such things and so soon after being introduced. Yet she felt a need stirring within her—the need to feel wanted and loved.

"I guess it's good then you saw them on the road. At least they now have the attention they've been wanting for a long time." He went on to talk about how busy it had been on the farm but how eager he was for a prosperous future. Melanie listened carefully, hearing words of hope but sensing a hole remained. Could it be that God had plans to fill that empty place? She blushed at the thought. Yes, she liked the boys, but any thought of a kinship with their father must to be put aside. It wasn't proper.

"You've told me so little about yourself," he remarked.

"There's not much to say, really. I've lived here all my life. My mother died when I was young. I'm an only child. It's always only been Father and me, and we do a great many things together. I also help him with his work—"

Suddenly Luke yelled that the line had caught on something. They both came to their feet and approached the boy, his face red as a tomato, struggling to maintain control of the pole. David yanked on the line and a huge, wiggling fish plopped onto the shore.

"Hooray!" the boys cried together.

He stared in surprise, first at the fish then at Melanie. She couldn't help but quip, "You seem astonished they could catch one."

"You're right, I am." He baited the hook and returned it to Matthew's care. He then grabbed a pail he had in the back of the wagon and scooped up some water for the fish. "Could it be that you're good luck for us, Miss O'Neil?"

"I'm happy to be a blessing, if that's what you mean. And perhaps I did bait the hook well." She managed a smile before gathering her skirt and walking slowly up the hill. She glanced over her shoulder and saw David staring after her as if he liked what he saw. Just the idea of another man taking notice of her after Sam's rejection sent a wave of pleasure flowing through her.

"I don't understand why your beau would leave you," he suddenly said, coming up behind her. "But it's for our joy. I've never seen the boys so happy."

She considered the life he had described as a farmer, a life she'd never experienced save for the small garden and the few livestock she tended. Father was a businessman, and his primary work was the Grand Canal commission. Their lives were very different. Maybe this was the reason Sam decided she would never thrive on the frontier. It could not compare to a sheltered existence here in the small village, beside the great waters of the river.

"You seem distressed," he noted, pulling her away from her thoughts.

"I'm thinking of the Lord's workings in my life. When we plan our way, it's difficult when the Almighty suddenly takes us on a different path."

"I understand that well. Life changed very much for me after my wife's passing. But there wasn't time to think about it, with babies and the farm. Louise and Hiram help greatly."

"They are your wife's mother and father, correct?"

"Yes, but I worry about them. Hiram had a bad bout with the ague last season that left him weak. Louise says her legs and arms ache. Life is fragile and unpredictable."

He appeared ready to say more when shouts sent them to the shore once again and to the two boys fighting over possession of the fishing pole. "Matthew and Luke, I think we're done fishing for today. We have chores to do." The boys started to fret until a stern look from their father sent them into silence with downcast faces and protruding lower lips. "You must thank Miss O'Neil for all she did for you."

"Thank you," they both said. Then Luke asked, "Can I ride in the fancy wagon?"

Melanie glanced over at David, who shook his head. "Miss O'Neil has a good many things to do. As we all have." He lifted his hat to bid her farewell. "Thank you again."

Melanie smiled, watching him carry the pail and place it in the wagon while the boys found places to sit near the large wheel fixed by the wheelwright. When they drove away, waving, she thought about the abrupt entrance of the Marshall family into her life. For some reason she felt a part of the family, even if it was just for a season.

Melanie ushered the carriage the short distance to her home where she saw Father's tall form standing in the doorway, looking quite dignified in his short waistcoat, fall front trousers, and top hat.

"Daughter," he greeted, nodding as he grabbed the reins. "Out and about, visiting friends?"

"I visited with the father and his two boys, the same boys I offered a ride to the other day." Father went ahead of her as he guided Hagan toward the stable. "We borrowed your pole and went fishing," she added.

He glanced back at her and laughed. "I'm surprised. I had no idea you knew where the pole was. Or that you knew anything about fishing."

"You'd be surprised what I remember from childhood, Father. You taught me well. As David, um, Mr. Marshall says, he doesn't understand why Sam wouldn't want me with him on the frontier. I know a good many skills."

Father sighed as he began unhitching Hagan. "Maybe in God's infinite wisdom, He knew you should be here helping others instead. Like your father."

"You seem to be doing quite well," she said with a laugh. "And how was the meeting with the representative from the commission? You said last night he was stopping by on his way to meet those getting ready to start the dig."

His grin melted into a serious expression. "Tiresome, but we are nearing the end of the final land acquisitions. I have but two parcels left to acquire in the area. In fact. . ." He paused as Melanie ran her hand over the horse's muzzle. "One of the tracts belongs to a farmer named Marshall. Didn't you say the man and sons you met today were called Marshall?"

"Yes." She remembered the river that ran through a far corner of David's land and how the area would do well for a canal route. She said nothing more about it but fed Hagan some hay before following Father into the house.

He drew out several parchments from his satchel. "Here it is. The land is owned by a David Marshall."

Melanie felt her face heat at the mention of his name.

"I acquired his neighbor's property. Mr. Oscar Mader. The Marshall land adjacent to the Maders' is quite a sizable parcel."

Melanie wondered what David would think of giving up his land for the sake of the canal. She had not yet told him of her father's involvement in the project. Not that it mattered. Most farmers where happy to help the cause while lining their pockets with extra money. They were promised bridges, docks, and other items of interest to obtain their consent. Surely David could use the money to help his darling boys. And who knew but the access to the canal might help him sell grain or whatever his land produced. He was a God-fearing soul. He would understand the need. "When do you plan to see him?"

"Soon. The commission is eager to have this settled quickly so the digging may commence on time."

Melanie went to the cupboard to take out some doughnuts she had made the other day. After meeting Louise and enjoying her delicious baking, she'd found a recipe to make a batch. Now the thought of returning to David's home, not for a visit but to ask for his land, made her apprehensive. It shouldn't after all. Mr. Mader was most agreeable to it. Yet she couldn't help a nagging feeling that worried her. While she prayed for the good in all things, she realized she must also pray against the bad.

Chapter 4

David couldn't help but smile as his boys chased the new calf around the pen, hoping to catch the creature like it was a new game. They'd decided on the name Star for the unique pointed markings on the calf's head that reminded him of watchful nights when he would think and pray as he gazed into the starry skies. There had been much to pray about in the last week since he first laid eyes on "the queen," as the boys called the fair Miss Melanie O'Neil. No doubt the family had money, but she possessed none of the airs of one christened with royalty. Instead she gave attention and sympathy to others, like the kind things she had done for his children. It fascinated him that she'd so readily wanted to entertain the boys and take them fishing while he went about his errands. He'd never known a woman to do anything of the sort, though his mother-in-law had been rumored to pick up a fishing pole now and then. But mostly Louise kept to the house, engaged in the tasks of housekeeping and making meals. He could not imagine someone like Melanie O'Neil performing such earthly tasks. She must have help to maintain the fine brick home described by the boys. Those homes were the few that survived the devastating raids of twenty years ago. He had little memory of it, being a small boy when war parties ravaged the area, seeking revenge. Pa and he had hidden in the woods up on the mountain to escape the danger. From a lookout, Pa described seeing smoke and flames from the town opposite the river below. Thankfully their home and farm had been spared, being downriver from the village of Little Falls. Now, many years later, Pa's farm was his to care for and take pride in. It had succeeded beyond his expectations, so much that he even hired on extra hands to assist in the cheese production.

David left his sons playing with the newborn calf and walked over to another large barn where much of the cheese making took place. Shelves held an assortment of cheese resting on salt, at various stages of curing. Workers were busy warming the milk or working the presses that would yield cheese after careful effort and patience. David looked on with satisfaction at what had been accomplished since Pa first dabbled in making cheese. His father would be proud to see how far he'd come these last few years. The business flourished, with local farms and villagers eager for cheese to add to their meals.

Yet, despite the success of the work, he still sensed a void once pushed aside with the busyness of life and now made apparent by the appearance of the interesting and beautiful Miss O'Neil. The idea of taking a new wife, a mother for his boys, and the joy of companionship and love, all came in like a flood of new emotion. He thought of her many times, walking about the farm, the wind and sun catching the fire of her hair, a smile brightening her otherwise waxen complexion. He liked how she had been in command that day on the river and never shirked when it came to baiting the fishing pole with a wiggling worm or helping the boys enjoy a fishing expedition. The mere thought spawned a deep interest in knowing more about her and asking the Lord if this fair woman might be the answer to life's lonely tide.

Just then David heard the children yell in the direction of the main house. He walked out of the cheese barn to see the familiar carriage of Melanie O'Neil arriving at the farm. The boys circled the carriage, jumping up and down with glee at her arrival. This time she was accompanied by a distinguished gentleman wearing a top hat, fashionable waistcoat, breeches, and boots. For a moment the joy that surged in his heart abruptly ceased, replaced by a cloud of concern. Who was the gentleman? Had she already found a suitor and so soon after being abandoned at the crossroads?

The man removed his hat and bowed while Melanie said, "I'd like you to meet my father, Mr. Raymond O'Neil. Father, this is David Marshall. We have met on several occasions."

David blew out a sigh, grateful but also a bit embarrassed to have thought the man a suitor. Mr. O'Neil now offered his hand, which David shook. "You have impressive holdings here," he noted with a smile.

David was happy the gentleman approved, even more so when he thought of Melanie and a wife in the same instance. Impressing the father was important. "Thank you. My pa did a good deal of work here, and I inherited it after his death. Including the cheese making."

"A cheese farmer, eh? Delightful. I've heard of a few such farmers in these parts. I would very much like to see what you do, if I may."

David could hardly contain his eagerness to share all he could and make a name for himself in the man's eyes. He led Mr. O'Neil and the graceful Melanie on a visit of the farm, including the livestock, crops, the vast acreage that extended to the river, and the numerous outbuildings. They paused at the cheese barn where he showed them the cheeses curing on the shelves, the large wooden barrels, some covered with cloth during the process, the wooden cheese presses, and a young man prying newly formed cheese from a circular mold. Out of the corner of his eye he watched Melanie's reaction to it all. Her face appeared impassive, her hands clasped before her, her stature straight and dignified. She hadn't uttered a word since introducing her father. He wished then she was the same as that day by the river—happy, carefree, and enjoying the fine day while his sons fished at the river's edge. He wondered at the change.

"You must need many workers for your cheese business," Mr. O'Neil noted.

"One can always use more help. The cows are producing well, and I'm thinking of increasing production if I'm able." He noticed Melanie and her father exchange glances, and he thought he caught a twinkle in her eye. Hope stirred within him. No doubt they were happy to see a prosperous place. Perhaps God had sent them here as a sign that he ought to consider the fair Melanie O'Neil as a possible wife. As soon as it was practical, he would speak privately to her father and see if the door to courtship lay open. For now he followed them outside and watched her father stride through the grass, his head high, heading toward the river that served as the boundary for the property.

"Yes, this is excellent." Mr. O'Neil whirled about and clasped his hands behind his back. "Mr. Marshall, I can find the workers you need and anything else you require for your farm. You could increase your production twofold."

David could hardly believe what he was hearing. His heart began to thump loudly in his ears. This was better than anything he ever expected. "You can?"

"Most certainly, and if you desire, your cheese can be transported right from here."

David blinked. "I—I don't understand."

"It's quite simple. Fine men of the state have come up with an excellent idea of helping farmers in the valley, especially in the area of transportation. A proposed canal from east to west would meet those needs and bring prosperity to the region. We only require a small piece of property to help make the plan a reality."

David was trying to understand while watching Melanie step away and look off to the river and beyond. "I'm not sure I understand."

"I'm part of a commission ready to give you a fair sum of money for one hundred acres of land to build the canal. Just think of vessels going from the Hudson River all the way to the lakes and beyond to Ohio. The ease of transportation will bring increased profits far greater than anything we can imagine. And you could be in the forefront of it all."

David's mouth fell open. His hands began to twitch. "I—I don't believe it. You. . .you're the one Oscar talked about? He sold you his land for. . .for that ditch?"

"A very useful and necessary canal. Your neighbor was eager to make good money and happy with the idea of transportation. Naturally he was concerned about a canal dividing his property. We assured him we'd build a bridge over the canal. However, it appears your boundary ends at the river."

David stared in disbelief at what was unfolding before his very eyes and ears. He caught another glimpse of Melanie who remained distant, her attention seemingly focused on the river, though her face had taken on a reddish hue. How could she be a part of this? All this time, even during the visits with his boys, her father was the one taking the land in this area. It kindled an anger he fought to contain. "My answer is no. No, sir. I will not sell."

"I understand there might be concerns and—"

"There is nothing more to be said," David interrupted. "Good day." He whirled and walked away, refusing to acknowledge either of them. His fingers tightened, his feet swift, his face feeling like it had been burned in the embers of the fireplace. *How can this be? Melanie O'Neil held an affection for my family, or so I thought. Now she is here, agreeing to this scheme to take my land. Dear Lord, how could I have been tricked into thinking she could be the one? That she cared?*

"David, what's the matter?" Hiram called.

"Those people came here to take my land," he burst out, swiping off his hat and batting his leg with it.

"What do you mean?"

"Those people. The O'Neils. They want my pa's land for that fancy canal. I won't have it, not while there's breath in me." David continued walking fast, back to the main barn where the boys had been playing with Star. They came running up to him, only to stop short and stare with deep brown eyes and trembling lips.

"Papa?" Matthew began.

"I'm sorry, but Miss O'Neil will no longer be visiting us."

The boys stared at each other. He wished he had the words to explain why. Then he heard something he never thought he would. Wails erupting from their young throats. And his heart began to tear in two.

◆•————•◆

Melanie felt the sticky dampness of her dress clinging to her. The air grew thick with anger and hurt. They stood where David had left them, in the midst of a green and beautiful field under the glow of the sun, yet it felt dark and dreary at the same time. She could not believe David would be so quick to say no. The money would help his children, and the canal would provide a way to deliver his cheese. Instead of gratefulness like Mr. Mader had for the canal, she witnessed David's raw anger. Maybe it was good this had come to light before she allowed other emotions to direct her path. "Father, come. We must leave at once."

"I don't understand," Father murmured while Melanie hooked her arm through his and swiftly guided him toward the carriage. "Everyone I've met has been most agreeable. You recall Mr. Mader, who was happy to sell. We work tirelessly on the details to make folks happy. But this Mr. Marshall appears to have made up his mind before we even arrived."

Melanie sighed. "I don't know, Father." She said nothing more as they approached the main house and the buggy resting before it. She tensed when she spied Hiram and Louise on the front porch. She tried not to catch the looks on their faces but guided her father to the carriage.

"I do hope you will stay to tea," a voice called out.

Melanie whirled to find Louise drifting down the porch steps. She glanced at Father, praying he had other business to tend to. She did not want another confrontation with David.

"How delightful," Father said with a smile. He took off his hat and bowed with a flourish. "We would be happy to accept, thank you."

Melanie issued a nervous sigh and whispered, "Father, I don't know if this is wisdom. . . ."

He patted her arm. "Of course it is," he answered softly, smiling toward the older couple. "We are not the enemy but people with good intentions." He nodded to Louise and followed her into the house.

Melanie kept her eye trained for David but saw no sign of him as they took seats in the main room.

"I'm Louise Boice. This is my husband, Hiram. We enjoyed talking with your daughter the other day." She smiled. "Our grandsons say the most wonderful things about her. She is good to them."

"My daughter has a good and kind heart. She is always thinking of others."

Melanie said nothing, preoccupied with the thought of David suddenly materializing in the doorway, angry lines crisscrossing his face, his eyes but mere slits, his words poised to accuse. Louise poured the tea and passed a plate of apple fritters. Melanie could hardly eat or drink but only wanted to leave as quickly as possible. And then, to her chagrin, Father began expounding on the canal project.

"I hear talk of it in town." Hiram finally spoke up after sitting quietly in his place. "We have the original canal, you know, the one they built many years back for boats to navigate around the large rocks."

Father straightened in his seat, his excitement for the project visible. "Yes indeed. The plan is to build a newer and better one, with a system that will extend across the state. I offered your son good compensation if he would allow the canal to be built on his land."

"Oh, David is not our son," Louise corrected. "Our daughter was married to him for two years before she died."

Father sat back in his seat and placed his cup on a nearby table. "Oh, I am so sorry to hear of your loss."

"Leah went to heaven when the boys were born eight years ago. Since then it has been just David and us, caring for the farm and the boys. God has blessed us in many ways, but I believe He wants to bless us even more."

Melanie felt hope stir within as Father leaned forward. "Maybe you can convince Mr. Marshall of the canal's necessity, madam. I too understand loss. And how we need help. I lost my wife many years ago, but we live as best we can in this world until we can join them in the Lord's presence."

"Oh, I agree."

They spoke for a brief time further, enjoying the tea, until Father stood, set his hat on his head, and offered his thanks for their hospitality. When they exited the house, Melanie caught sight of a dark figure standing on a hill in the distance, observing them. The figure never moved but stood his ground, unwavering. She followed Father to the carriage, ready to climb on board, when a small voice issued a tentative greeting. Matthew stood nearby, a fistful of yellow flowers from the field in his hand, which he thrust toward Melanie.

Joy and wonder coursed through her. "Sweet Matthew, are they for me?"

He nodded shyly. Her heart burst out in a song of thanks for the thoughtfulness of the little boy, despite what had happened. She glanced once more to the hill and the silent figure who witnessed it all. Prayer now filled her being for the man, that the Lord would touch his heart as He had others in the family. Not for the sake of a canal, but for the sake of peace and joy instead of anger and fear.

"Thank you, Matthew. I will put them in a cup of water when I return home. Where is Luke?"

Matthew shrugged. "He ran off when Papa said you can't ever come back."

Melanie felt her lips part in astonishment and reached out to steady herself on the side of the buggy. "I'm sorry for that. But do tell your papa, please, that I will obey his wishes."

Matthew shook his head and stepped forward. "But I want you to come back. We can run and go fish and play with Star. Please?"

Melanie gently patted his hand. "We must honor your father. But you can always pray for him."

Matthew nodded. Just then she saw David striding down the hillside. Quickly she climbed into the buggy, ordering Father to make haste before David could reach them. Father turned the buggy around and headed down the road, just as David came alongside Matthew. Melanie gripped the flowers given by the little boy as a newfound symbol of peace and hope. What appeared hopeless could still bring fruit for the future. Matthew and Luke, Louise and Hiram, and yes, David, were all worth much in God's eyes. If only David would open his heart to allow new things inside. Maybe he dreaded the coming of the canal, the strangers swarming his land, digging up the earth that had been a place of solitude and source of strength for his family for over a generation. Maybe she needed to see all this from his eyes and not just her own.

"You seem quiet," Father observed.

She stared at the symbol of sunshine and love in her hands. "We must consider Mr. Marshall, Father."

Father gave her a sideways glance, his eyebrow raised.

"When someone is forced to give up something that's theirs, it's bound to stir up harsh feelings. Like Mr. Marshall, being forced to give away land to mere strangers."

Father sighed. "I do try to understand the landowners, but there is little time left, daughter. The commission grows impatient. Already the men are set to begin digging the canal west of here. This parcel is a critical link once that area is complete." He paused. "Perhaps if I ask the neighbor to encourage Mr. Marshall."

Melanie looked at the flowers. Was it possible that God could change a situation by way of a child's touch? Already Matthew had helped her understand David's circumstances. Maybe a child could also work on David's heart in a miraculous way before it was too late.

Chapter 5

Sleep eluded David once again as he glanced out the window to see the moon set the fields aglow. Ever since the arrival of Melanie and her father, a myriad of thoughts replaced the peace of sleep. His father-in-law tried to broach the subject of the canal and the O'Neils' proposal, but he pushed it away quicker than Luke did a plate of vegetables at the dinner table. What disturbed him also was how his expectations of that visit had been squelched. After all, he'd been summoning the courage to see if Melanie was destined to become a part of their family, with her sweet ways and sharing their lives at the river's edge. Hope had filled him.

Now anger replaced any faith for the future. Anger too that what he had witnessed, perhaps since the first day she brought the boys home from school, may all have been a way to win hearts and ultimately his land. He paced before the window, sweeping back his hair. His fingers scratched at the beard stubble that had not seen a straight razor in a while. It made no sense trying to make himself presentable. He wanted to control everything, from the farm to the home to his appearance. It matched well the turmoil brewing in his heart.

David wished for the dawn so he could begin the day's work. Staying busy was the only way he could think of to squelch the memories of Melanie's stark blue eyes staring at him or the way her father asked about his land. Just the other day he stood on the very piece of ground where they planned to dig the big ditch. He pictured the scene of shovels chewing up clumps of earth to carve out a place for the canal. Water would fill the passage, and boats would make their way westward. Then he envisioned boatmen arriving at the new dock and people flocking to buy cheese. And he would transport the cheese to distant towns and bring in a handsome profit.

David shook his head. Maybe he wanted to believe a canal in the middle of his land would be good for business and good for him. If he said yes to it, Melanie was sure to visit, wearing a smile, playing with the boys and sharing in long conversations with him and his in-laws. Life would be very different. Except he could not forsake a promise in exchange for possible happiness.

He drew on a pair of old breeches and a shirt, and thrust his feet into the leather boots. He lit a lantern and walked out to the still fields, with the distant mooing of the cows to remind him of milking time. He walked to where the canal would exist, paralleling the river beyond. The mere thought of it sent strange chills racing through him, and he turned cold. How could he allow this after what he promised Pa on his deathbed? He had promised to care for this land, to pass it on to his sons, to not sell it to anyone.

Suddenly he was transported to that sad scene in the same room where his in-laws now slept peacefully. His father lying there in bed, a mass of skin and bones to the disease that ravaged him. The physician said it might be a tumor, but he couldn't be sure. Whatever the illness was, it had eaten up the man. Pa called him to his bedside and reached out to him with a bony hand. "You're all I have," Pa had said in a choking voice. "I leave this farm to you, son. T—take care of it."

"Of course I will." David forced away the tears. Pa never wanted to see a son of his cry over anything. Pa wanted him to remain strong and unemotional.

The man coughed and in a raspy voice added, "You must keep it. Don't give it to anyone or sell it. It is ours. Promise me."

"Yes, Pa."

David winced as the scene built in his thoughts, sending his feet shuffling and forming a lump of sadness in his throat, which he tried to swallow away. He never shed a tear over anything, no matter how difficult the situation. Not even when Leah died in childbirth, leaving him with infant sons and a farm to care for. Soon after, Louise and Hiram came to help. Hiram often encouraged David to do his share of weeping, that even the King of kings wept. But David would not. In his mind, strength won out over difficult times, the same strength he now summoned this day when confronted by buyers for a land he promised never to sell. But inwardly he wanted to let out the emotion. To beg the Lord to send forth His light and tell him what to do. To shed tears, not for sadness but to release the burdens he had carried for so long.

He continued in this early morning sojourn of thought, finding his way to the cemetery and the silent stones marking the places where loved ones slept, awaiting a better resurrection. Several of the Marshall family were buried there—his grandparents, a brother Clarence, his ma and pa, as well as Leah's grave, all silent, even as the rays of the rising sun slowly began to fall on them. But gazing on the slabs of rock with the names and dates of their births and deaths chiseled in the stone, he felt no tears or even a semblance of sorrow. He only wished they were alive to speak words of encouragement, to listen, to share in an embrace, to feel the sun together and enjoy the harvest. To watch the boys grow up to manhood. And suddenly David wished everything had worked out with Melanie O'Neil. He wanted a woman to share his life with and experience the wonderful things of marriage he dearly missed. He wished her father had not come seeking his land, and that he could have asked to court her. It would have all ended in joy and not anger. But he knew there was nothing he could do, especially as he gazed at Pa's grave and the name *Henry D. Marshall*. He had made a promise to keep this farm in the Marshall name for generations to come. And he would be no man of honor if he broke his promise to a dying man.

✦•———•✦

Melanie paced about, restless over the conflict at the Marshall farm a week previous. Since then, Father had left for an important meeting with the canal commission in Albany. At first she wanted to dismiss what happened and only look forward. But on the day he left, Father told her he must have the Marshall land to finish the acquisition process. Pressure from the commission would come to bear. Since that terrible day at the Marshall farm, Father walked about the house hunched over as if bearing the great burden placed upon him. Patches of graying hair had begun emerging among the locks of reddish-brown. There was little doubt the recent events weighed heavily on him, and now he would have to face the men that demanded action. Melanie worried what this might do to Father in the end.

If only she knew how to convince David to change his mind. To realize that this canal would benefit his family and many others. It was not a selfish proposition but a selfless one. She sighed, trying her best to concentrate on her tasks for the day. It all seemed pointless, considering what was happening. Life had once been exciting, visiting and engaging David and his sons in the fishing expedition, until the meeting at the farm changed everything. The flowers Matthew had given her had long since wilted, but she kept one dried flower in her Bible to remind her that God's ways were not her ways. Kindness still prevailed, even from the least of them. She must continue to have faith.

Melanie glanced at the timepiece on the mantel and thought of the boys and their schooling. They would soon be dismissed at noontime for dinner and play in the warm sunshine. Dare she go to the schoolhouse to see them? It might do well to discover how things were going with David since the meeting and if anything had changed.

She picked up her wrap, checked her features briefly in a mirror, and slid her reticule over her arm. She strode to the one-man buggy to hitch up Hagan and made her way to the small mercantile in the village. It had little in the way of sundries there, but she did find some children's toys, a ball and cup toy and a drum with sticks. She then picked up a decanter of fine rosewater, inhaled the fragrance, and tried to read the description. The words appeared as if she were looking through a bridal veil. She brought the bottle closer and finally was able to make out the fine print, describing the scent and where it came from. Shrugging, she put back the decanter to save it for another day, perhaps when she wasn't so preoccupied.

Melanie then made her way to the schoolhouse, a small structure that also was the teacher's home. The school had only seven families of students, but she could hear the joyful shouts of pupils set free from learning for a time to run in God's creation. She paused to see David's twin sons chasing each other. Suddenly they noticed her, gave a yell, and raced up to the buggy.

"Look, it's the queen!" Luke said breathlessly. He pointed to the gifts she carried, his deep brown eyes widening. "What's that?"

"Aren't you the curious one," she said with a laugh. "Something odd yet interesting that I found and—"

"Hooray!" Luke grabbed the drum set and Matthew the ball and cup. The *rat-a-tat-tat* sound of the drum being played sent children scurrying over to inspect the ruckus. Melanie was happy to see Luke showing off his drum and even allowing a pupil to play with it.

"How is your father these days?" she asked Matthew.

He shrugged as he tried his best to scoop the ball into the cup. "He doesn't say much. Grandpappy asks all the time why he's so quiet." Matthew concentrated on capturing the ball and when he did, let out a shout of glee.

"Did your father say what's wrong?"

Matthew shrugged. "No. He doesn't say anything. He doesn't take us anywhere either. I wanna go fishing sometime."

"I'm sorry. You know, you can come fishing with me anytime you want. Whenever your father gives his permission, that is."

Matthew looked at her, his eyes widening and a smile on his lips. "Thanks. Maybe I will ask him today."

The teacher rang the bell. Matthew and Luke took off with their new toys, eager to show them to the others. Melanie waved at the teacher who waved back. She was happy to have made the boys happy, but sad to hear of David's melancholy. Why the idea of selling land would leave him in such a state did not make sense. The only way to change the man's heart, she felt certain, was for God to intervene in a miraculous way. How that would happen, she didn't know.

❖—————❖

Melanie busied herself with her embroidery for the next few days, trying hard not to think about the boys or their father. It proved impossible. With each passage of the needle through the fabric, she thought of the stitches needed to create a beautiful work in another's life. Maybe that's why she felt the need to buy the boys a few gifts. To let them know she was thinking of them. To show them that she cared and hoped David would realize it too.

Just then Melanie heard the front door open and shut. She stood to her feet as Father walked in, exhausted by the long and tiring journey from Albany. He flung his tall hat on the table and raked his fingers through his hair.

"Are you all right? Has something happened?"

"The word has been given. The committee demands the acquisition be finalized or they will acquire the land by force."

Melanie tensed as a disturbing image of David raced through her thoughts, a rifle in his hands, ready to defend his land. "Surely they can't just take his land from him. We are a free country."

"They are claiming the ground for the common good. The canal is for the good of the people, and Mr. Marshall is standing in the way of progress and people's livelihoods. They will do whatever they must, even take it to a courthouse."

Melanie shook her head. Something must be done. Maybe God would grace her with the words to say. Not that she had any influence, but a friendly visit might allay concern, especially after giving the gifts to the boys. A door could unexpectedly open, but first she must knock.

Melanie announced she was leaving on an errand and Father grunted from the open door of his study. He sat at his desk, a hand cupping his head in a picture of dejection. How she wanted to ease his anxiety over the situation and lessen the burdens he carried. Hurrying out to the stable to hitch Hagan to the small carriage, she wondered what she was doing. Or if anything could be accomplished. At the very least, she would not see others burdened by this any longer. There must be a remedy.

The ride proved peaceful to her heart and soul as she felt the brush of the early summer breeze on her face, carrying the scent of wildflowers. Birds appeared ready to give chase to her buggy as Hagan held his head high, the wind ruffling his mane. When she entered the next road, she caught sight of a man lumbering along, gnawing on a reed. Melanie brought the buggy to a stop and greeted him. "Mr. Mader?"

He lifted his hat. "Hallo. Yer with the fancy man from the village, eh? His daughter?"

"Yes, I am. Melanie O'Neil. We came to talk about the Grand Canal."

"Do you know when they're gonna start digging it?"

Melanie shook her head. "I do not. Especially now that your neighbor has refused to part with his land."

Mader took the reed out of his mouth. "You mean David? Ja, he told me."

"We offered similar to what we did for you. For him it was good compensation and a dock."

"He's a hard man, miss. Never saw a harder man, and I'm German. Though I know da gut Lord can work on a hard heart and make it. . .what? Like dis soft ground, eh?" He kicked up earth in a small spray of brown.

Melanie appreciated the scripture that imparted hope. "Yes."

"Ja, I went over there with the paper and told him about it. He wasn't happy, no. And I did hear you and the fancy man paid David a visit not that that long ago. Louise told my wife Henrietta about it."

Melanie inhaled a deep breath. "Yes. I realize it takes time to come to a decision as important as this one. But time is also short. They are starting construction on the canal very soon. I thought I might stop by and speak to him again."

"You're mighty brave. I don't believe I would do that if I were you." Mr. Mader waved and continued along the dirt road that led to his farm. Melanie wondered if she should heed his warning and give David Marshall more time. But she remembered Father's stricken face. She had no choice but to try and reason with him.

When she turned the buggy into the lane, the jarring of pointy rocks sent the buggy jostling and her teeth chattering madly in her head. Finally she rode up to the house to be met by Louise, who offered a smile, much to Melanie's relief.

"Why, good day, my dear. Aren't you the sweet thing."

Melanie was taken aback by the greeting until she saw the boys emerge, one playing the drum, the other tossing the ball into the cup. They both waved and ran over to pet Hagan.

"How are you?" she asked Louise, gathering up her skirt and slowly dismounting.

"Well, the men are out in the fields, the boys are playing with your fine gifts, and I am quite lonely in the house. So please come in and keep me company."

Melanie accepted with anticipation. Years had passed since she'd enjoyed a nice chat with an older woman. She followed her inside and into the kitchen area where Louise hung the kettle on a hook over some glowing embers in the fireplace. On the table was a new batch of freshly baked biscuits with a scent that made her mouth water and reminded her she'd not eaten her noonday meal.

"Come sit at the table here, and we'll have some nice biscuits with jam."

"Will the men be joining us for afternoon tea?" she wondered, remembering the last time they took tea.

Louise shook her head. "Not today. It's just the two of us. There's too much work to be done. But I must say how delighted I was to hear how you bought the boys some presents. That was kind of you."

"Has David seen the toys?" she wondered.

"I don't believe so. They've been very busy with cheese making and getting ready for a delivery. I don't expect them until sundown." While the tea steeped, Louise talked of the gardening she had done and the flowers planted in the front bed. She then poured two cups of tea. They sat companionably at the small wooden table in the kitchen area. For a time they ate biscuits and chatted about the fine weather and the many chores that must be done this time of year.

Melanie shared about her new embroidery, and Louise smiled. "Oh, let me show you mine." She went to another room and returned with a pattern of yellow wildflowers on fine muslin.

"How lovely," Melanie said. "Just like the flowers Matthew gave me after our last visit." She paused. "I hope you don't mind me asking, but has anything else been said about the canal? My father is most anxious to hear."

The older woman's forehead crinkled, and her eyes drew together. "If you mean is David still angry about it, the answer is yes. Hiram and I believe your father's offer is a gift from God. The boys would have fun meeting people in the boats, and the canal would help in delivering the cheese."

"That's what my father believes. The canal is meant to help, not hurt. We never meant to hurt anyone."

"Of course not. But for some reason David insists he cannot let go of any of the land. I don't quite know why. There must be a reason, but he won't talk about it." She took a lengthy sip of tea.

"I would be happy to speak to him," Melanie said.

The older woman's gray eyes widened. "My, my, you're brave. I suppose someone needs to find out what is burdening him. I can't imagine this is all because of Leah," she said repeating Mr. Mader's observation.

Melanie leaned over the table. "Please tell me about her."

Louise straightened, her lips curving into a smile, her cheeks taking on a rosy tint as if delighted by the request. She poured out her heart about her daughter and ended with, "I know she is in a better place. I had hoped, perhaps, that one day we would have a new daughter and a mother for the boys. We would not have to live alone anymore. We could taste the fine spring sun in our house and share laughter once again." A tear slipped down her craggy cheek. "I do not want to put any of this on you, of course. It's only a confession. But if by some miracle God does provide in ways we think not, who are we to argue?"

Melanie thought of the miracle she also needed. But none of it seemed possible with this impasse. Even with the lovely day by the river when she and David talked, and the possibility that God might be doing something special in their hearts, the canal project had taken it all away. She confessed this all to Louise.

"I understand." Suddenly Louise looked aside, her face taking on a reddish hue. Melanie followed her gaze to see the dark figure of David standing in the kitchen doorway, the hat he wore sitting low on his head, his hands holding something, though she didn't know what. Had he overheard their conversation? Her feet began to shuffle beneath the table, her hands feeling moist, her mind fighting for something good to say. Except a plug of emotion in her throat kept the words at bay. The only thing she could do was pray. *Dear God, please help me.*

Chapter 6

He couldn't help but admit how lovely Melanie O'Neil looked, sitting at the table opposite his mother-in-law, appearing as if she belonged there. The two had been sharing tea and conversation, which he listened to for a moment before Louise noticed him in the doorway. "Good day," he said stiffly, walking into the room, refusing to look Melanie in the eye. He headed for a small preparation area to cut into the wheel of aged farmer's cheese he had brought up from the barn. The cheese would pair nicely with the biscuits Louise had made. With his mind on Melanie sitting there watching, he cut a few more slices to share.

Melanie straightened in her seat with wide eyes and parted lips when he offered her a creamy slice. "Thank you. That is very kind." He watched as she nibbled daintily on the cheese. "This is very good."

"Is it?" he asked. The question sent her spinning about in her seat with the same look of surprise.

"Why would I speak a falsehood?"

"I'm not sure. Maybe you can tell me why you're here. And why you suddenly decided to buy my boys presents."

She did not shirk. "Because I wanted to. And because we're friends, or I thought we were."

"Now, David," Louise said gently, "she is also here because, like me, we're concerned about you."

David stared, first at Louise then at Melanie. "There's no need to be concerned. I'm quite fine."

"Are you?" Louise wondered. "Are you being truthful before God?" With a smile she slowly pushed the Bible across the table.

He winced at the sight of the Holy Book and the words in it that could slice sharper than the blade used to cut the cheese. The last few days he'd thought of nothing but Melanie O'Neil. He could not understand why, as much as he wanted to think that all her sweet ways were a means to take his land. Yet he could not shake their past encounters. Especially the remark he made while they spent time by the river as the boys fished. *"Could it be that you are good luck for us, Miss O'Neil?"*

"*I would be happy to be a blessing,*" she had responded.

"I am fine," he said again. "But you do know why Miss O'Neil is here, don't you? On behalf of her father, no doubt. And the ditch they want to build, right through the heart of my land." He saw Melanie tense, her lips press into rigid lines, the creases on her face marring an otherwise flawless complexion.

"Yes," Melanie admitted. "That is part of the reason."

David's mouth fell open. Never did he think she would admit it, convinced instead she would deny everything.

She continued, unflinching. "I am here too, because my father made you a very good bargain, as he did with Mr. Mader. He understands how difficult it is to part with land that has been in the family. But there are important people in the commission above my father who will get the land they need, come what may."

David bristled. "So you came here to warn me?"

"And to see if anything can be done to allow the work to begin. The canal will be built, whether you want it to or not." She paused. "And my father is very burdened by this. His heart is tender toward the woes of a farmer. He doesn't want anyone's land taken against their will. He wants the land freely given from the heart."

David gritted his teeth at this description when he thought of the burden placed by his father over the fate of the land. "It is never my free will if the end result is still my land in the hands of some commission. I promised my pa on his deathbed I would never part with it. How can I go back on my word? It would be like taking back a deed from the grave. Once it's buried, it is buried. There is no changing it." Now he saw her eyes widen once more and her lips part in wonder.

"I had no idea Henry said that to you," Louise piped up, looking over at Melanie.

"Yes, he did. I never told anyone, though I never thought I'd find myself giving up land belonging to the Marshall family."

Louise exhaled a sigh, and he saw both women exchange glances. Melanie stood to her feet and pushed a small embroidered ladies' bag over one arm. "I don't think there's anything more to be said on the subject. Except that I would like to talk about something else, if you please." She nodded toward the rear of the kitchen where the cheese block rested on the wood table. "Like your fine cheese and how you made it. I'm quite good at cooking, but I've never made cheese."

David blinked at the sudden turn of conversation. Caught off guard, he wondered what to do. Until a passing glance at his mother-in-law's favorite Bible, with its tattered edges, spoke loudly to his heart. He chose then to embrace peace. His neighbor, Oscar Mader, had been right about one thing. Being angry was much more tiring than a day's work plowing a field. "I'll show you how it's made, if you wish."

Melanie remained silent as they walked through the tall grass. Even when they passed a rise overlooking the distant river and the land her father wished to purchase for the canal, she said nothing. At the barn he invited her in where several young men from the village were hard at work in the cheese making process. He showed her the steps in creating the product, from the heating of the milk, to the mixing of the rennet and separating the curds from the whey by hand, and then using the presses at various stages to form the blocks of cheese. He scooped out some freshly made curds with a wooden paddle, salted them, and offered her some.

Her voice sounded like a song when she said, "Delicious! I had no idea all the work that goes into cheese making."

One of the men brought the wagon to the entrance, ready to load the bed with aged cheese. "Where are they going?" she asked.

"To the towns and villages west of here. These blocks of farmer's cheese have completed their aging."

"And we are behind schedule, Mr. Marshall," said Abe, a youthful man with curly brown hair and bright eyes. "I was supposed to have this there in two days. But it's gonna take longer than that, I expect."

David scratched his head. "It can't be helped. That's the way things are." He paused, with a sideways glance at Melanie. She was observing the long rows of cheese sitting on the shelves. Some had been there a good while. The longer the curing process, the sharper and drier the cheese. He half expected her to whirl about, her blue eyes flashing, ready to tell him how good it would be to have the canal nearby to help in transporting the cheese. "Do whatever you can," he told the young man before retiring to Melanie's side. She asked a few more questions about cheese making, though he remained preoccupied about the delivery. A part of him desired to know how this Grand Canal might help in his endeavors. If it did, it would become part of the farm's workings, and this canal, part of the farm. Or would the whole idea of a ditch running through his land be a nuisance and an eyesore?

He turned toward her. "Tell me. Are you happy with what you do for your father? Going to farms, seeking property for the canal?"

Her eyes widened in surprise. "I do like to visit. I also like to help Father because I'm his daughter. Anything less would be sinful. Just as I'm sure you helped your father."

"Actually I never wanted to," he admitted. "But when he became ill, things changed. And I know times change too." He watched the last of the cheese blocks loaded into the wagon. "I do wonder about that canal of yours and what it can do."

"It's not my canal, sir. It belongs to everyone. I know many are happy it's coming. Would it be helpful if you had access to a water route for transporting goods rather than the unpredictability of road travel?"

David wanted to speak the truth—how his heart yearned to say yes, not only to the workings of a canal to move his goods but to the working in his heart, stirred by her presence. A part of him wanted to make her happy, to see a smile on her face and her lips thanking him. If she only knew how he'd tried to work up the courage to ask to court her that one day. Until the canal brought a halt to everything.

An object suddenly caught his eye, and he reached down to pick up a book he had inadvertently left behind. *Robinson Crusoe.* It was a tale he'd read long ago as a lad and still read to this day for encouragement. Now he began flipping through the pages. "Miss O'Neil, you must read this one part. It is excellent." He found the page he was looking for and handed the book to her.

Melanie stared, a puzzled look on her face. She brought the book so close to her face that her nose nearly touched the page, and then she began reading—

" 'Call upon me in the Day of Trouble, and I will deliver, and thou shalt glorify me.' " And then she read, " 'Wait on the Lord, and be of good Cheer, and he shall strengthen thy Heart; wait, I say, on the Lord.' It is impossible to express the Comfort this gave me. In Answer, I thankfully laid down the Book, and was no more sad, at least, not on that Occasion."

"It brought back memories of the hardship I've had," David admitted, "but also that God will strengthen us, no matter what trial we face. It is a good lesson to learn." He paused at the pained look on her face as she continued to stare at the book. "Your eyes are not well, are they, Miss O'Neil?"

Her hand shook as she returned the book to him. "What? I'm only tired, and the printing is far too small."

"I fear it's more than that." He took a pair of spectacles from the pocket of his breeches, ones he wore on occasion when he had difficulty reading. "Try these."

Melanie stepped back. "Oh no! I think not."

"Please put them on, and then try to read. They will help, I assure you. Trust me."

Slowly she took the spectacles from his outstretched hand. Her eyebrows drew together and her face wrinkled up. He nearly laughed at the sweet look as he showed her how to put them on. She struggled to position the frames over her petite ears then took back the book he handed her. "Oh my word! I—I can see!"

"You need spectacles, Miss O'Neil. Then you will see everything."

Suddenly her look of amazement disintegrated into tears. "I don't know what to say. I thought. . . I thought I was ill. I thought I was losing my sight. I know people who have. I prayed, but. . ." Their gazes met, and he reached out to gently wipe a tear from her cheek. "Forgive me." She hiccupped and pawed for a handkerchief inside her tiny bag. "I don't know what came over me."

"I felt the same way when I got these spectacles. I felt like Jesus had healed me of my blindness. I wish at times I didn't have to wear them, but they have done well for me." When she took the spectacles off and tried to return them, he pushed her hand back. He liked their brief touch. "Keep them. I can use Hiram's."

"I—I don't know what to say," she murmured in a soft voice. "It. . .It's like the sun has come out from a cloudy day."

David could think of many words that filled his mind at the moment. With the look of the woman before him, her blue eyes shimmering and her lower lip trembling, he dearly wanted to take her in his arms to soothe away the distress and give her a kiss of affection. But he forced himself to remain still.

"Thank you again. I—I should be going home. The hour is late."

"Of course." He led the way out of the barn and to the main house where Hiram stood on the porch, chewing on a reed, a questioning look on his face. David didn't dwell on it. The only vision he saw was Melanie's tear-stained face thanking him for the gift of sight.

✦— —•✦

Melanie felt reborn, as if she had entered a new world, now clear as glass. The last time she felt this way was the night she gave her heart to Jesus. It had been a difficult night, filled with the memories of her mother and the loneliness she felt. During that time she reached out to God, read the passages of love and compassion in the Bible, and prayed for His guidance and peace to fill her life. After that night she knew her life would never be the same. The next day everything appeared different. She saw the cross everywhere, in the way the sticks had been formed to support the vegetables in the garden, to the tree branches to the doorframe of the house. Birds chirping away were like the music of angels around the throne. Everything was new.

Since the day David gave her the spectacles, she felt the same new birth. Perhaps her heart was likewise clearing of muddy waters left from Sam's abrupt departure, leaving her unable to envision the future. Maybe this was a new start, without the anger or disappointment. Yes, David was angry over the land. But he'd reached out with compassion to help her when she needed it most. He had moved beyond his discontent to offer the gift of sight. She felt her heart pound in her chest. Maybe he was also seeing her differently, his face softening when she shed tears of gratefulness for the spectacles, the tear he brushed away with the stroke of his finger. Not that she had much to offer in return. In fact, the only thing she had brought to his world was Father's request for his land to create the Grand Canal.

Despite the doubt, Melanie felt like singing as she went about her daily chores. After a time she took out the wire spectacles. They were a simple contraption of metal stems that went over the ears to anchor them. They attached to small pieces of glass that sat on the bridge of her nose. She wondered how such a thing could make the words appear so clearly. It was like a miracle. Slipping the spectacles on her face, she took one of her father's books from the library and began reading aloud.

"I had no idea such books were to your liking."

At Father's deep voice, she whirled to see his distinguished form. His eyes narrowed as he surveyed her face. "What on earth are you wearing?" he asked.

"They are spectacles, Father."

"I can see that, but where did you get them?"

She closed the book and returned it to its rightful place on the shelf. "I went over to the Marshalls the other day."

"You did? Whatever for?" He drew closer and dropped weightily into a chair.

"I'm not certain, exactly. I guess I wanted to see if David, I mean Mr. Marshall, was truly angry about the land, or if God might be at work. I visited with his mother-in-law, Louise. You remember her. She's a kindhearted soul. And then suddenly David was explaining cheese making to me. He talked about having to take the cheese by wagon and how tedious it was. I think, Father, he is beginning to understand the importance in having a canal for transportation."

The comment brought a smile to his weary face. "My clever daughter. I knew you would find a way to communicate what I could not. You have a gift. But I still don't understand how it is you are wearing those spectacles."

"I've been having trouble seeing. I didn't want to worry you. David wanted me to read something from a book, and I could hardly see the words. Even things far away have been troubling for me. He then took these out of his pocket and insisted I try them. Now I can see!"

Father continued to stare, even as he shook his head in wonder.

"He also insisted I keep them."

"Well, we can't accept such a gift. We will replace them as soon as we can."

"He is very generous, Father." She paused, wanting to tell him how things had changed, that the hard stone in David Marshall was slowly changing to one of flesh, by the grace of God. She wanted to share how hard David worked with his profitable cheese making business. And who could forget his adorable sons that she wanted to bless with whatever came to mind, be it toys, or carriage rides, or fishing. *Dear me*, she thought, *is my heart changing too? Am I falling in love with this man and his family?*

"You look as if you've seen a ghost," he mused. "What is it?"

"I don't know yet, Father. I'm overwhelmed by everything. But we can surely say that God is with us."

Father exhaled a sigh. "I hope so, my dear. We must finish this work for the Grand Canal. Time is running out, and somehow we must have this man agree to sell his land."

She heard the words of desperation. God knew what was required. He knew what needed to be done. And she would go at once and give these circumstances in prayer. It was the only thing left to do.

"I am going to the river," she said.

Father nodded as his eyelids drooped and his head began to sink to his chest in sleepy fashion. She grabbed for her wrap and Bible. The wind of promise carried her feet down the road, and she felt happy as she waved at passersby in the streets of Little Falls. Soon she came to the familiar sound of the river rushing over the rocks. She stopped short to see a family at her usual place of prayer, with a picnic spread out, sharing in conversation. She felt a brief sense of disappointment until she saw two young boys scurrying about. They saw her and squealed before telling the occupants on the blanket who it was. In an instant a man lurched to his feet. And suddenly Melanie felt a mixture of both joy and dread.

Chapter 7

The tall stature. The pale brown riding boots. The wavy brown hair. Even if she could not read his mind from the look on his face, Melanie still felt gratitude at the sight of David Marshall. Though he may carry an inward disagreement over the canal, none of that mattered. He had given her the gift of sight. "I'm glad to see you again," she said, striding up to him. "I can't begin to tell you how much the spectacles have meant to me." She took them out of her pocket.

"I'm glad you're finding them useful." He nodded at the Bible she carried. "I see you also like to come to the river. This is not far from where we took the boys fishing."

"Yes. And you too have discovered it." She followed him to the blanket, where Louise and Hiram greeted her with joy and invited her to share in their biscuits and apple butter. The boys raced up, showing her the new fishing poles David had made for them.

"You have done wonders with the boys, my dear," Louise said with a wink. "Hasn't she, David? They are so happy and full of life now. It's a joy to see."

Melanie gave him a quick glance, only to see him pick up a biscuit. "They do love fishing," he admitted. "We have been several times since that day we talked and they shared your pole by the river."

Louise offered her a biscuit, to which Melanie shook her head. "I'm sorry I can't stay long."

"Business?" Hiram inquired. "The canal?"

She darted a glance toward David, who said nothing. "I will say the commission is desperate to finish the land acquisition, and Father is unsure what to do. It must be settled, as they are beginning construction west of here."

"I think a canal is a fine idea," Hiram announced, ignoring the startled looks directed at him by both David and Louise. "The canal here in town is a necessity with the rocks in the river. We need one that can provide quick transportation westward. Roads have too many obstacles to overcome. We need a trustworthy and smoother way to transport our cheese, don't we, David? I believe this is an answer from the Almighty."

"I'm not sure we should be talking about this right now," he began.

"If not now, then when, pray tell? You heard Miss O'Neil. There is no time left."

Melanie could feel the joy of the picnic suddenly darken under a cloud and knew she must bring everything back to the light. "I do love being by the river," she said. "The Bible shares much about life by a river, you know." She donned the spectacles and opened the Bible. "Your dear son-in-law is letting me use these, and they work wonders." Louise smiled and nodded while Hiram winked. Melanie cleared her throat and read, "Behold, I will do a new thing; now it shall spring forth; shall ye not know it? I will even make a way in the wilderness, and rivers in the desert."

"How lovely," Louise said. "And quite fitting."

Melanie wished she knew what lay in David's heart. He was a godly sort, she believed. This was God's Word after all, planted to do a good work. How she prayed that God would speak to him about embracing new things, like a river in the desert. One that could make a difference in a time that had seen dryness and uncertainty.

The boys returned from the shore, set down their fishing poles, and delved into the biscuits and jam. With their mouths full, they acknowledged Melanie. "Look at the queen in Papa's glasses!" they said, laughing.

Melanie took them off. "Your father is very generous."

Luke took a large bite out of a biscuit, swallowed, and then thoughtfully announced, "Papa, you should marry this nice lady. Then we would have everything."

"Yes!" Matthew echoed. "Can she be our mother? Please?"

Melanie's face heated, unable to believe what she was hearing. She dared not look at David but could imagine his face. He might even take to his feet and hurry away, unable to remain under the shadow of such things as her and the canal and the boys' statements. But he remained seated in his place, still and silent.

"Now, boys, that is for grown-ups to decide," Louise reprimanded.

Matthew and Luke laughed as if they had not a care in the world, then took up their fishing poles and returned to the water's edge. An awkward silence fell over them. Melanie knew she must take her leave before things worsened. "I'm sorry for interrupting your picnic like this," she said softly. "I didn't mean to."

"You did not," Louise said.

Melanie refused to say anything else for fear of further anxiety. She held out the spectacles to David. "Thank you for their use. My father will buy me new ones."

David shook his head. "Keep them until you have a pair."

"But how will you see?"

"Please don't worry about that. I will see just fine."

Can you see? And not just with your eyes but also with your heart? Melanie wondered before offering her thanks and hurrying away. Her mind was a mass of jumbled thoughts. *Oh God, I don't know what is happening. Please help me,* was all her heart could pray.

＊━━━━━━＊

David knew something miraculous happened since giving Melanie the spectacles and then seeing her once more at the river. He felt a stirring in both heart and spirit he could not ignore. While she could not physically see without them, neither could he see without God to show him the way. He still struggled to accept this idea of the canal. Now he stood several days later, staring at his farmland, watching the cattle peacefully graze with the river lazily running by, trying to envision the changes. There were good things to be said about a canal, he reasoned. Not only the ease in transporting the cheese he made, but Luke and Matthew could fish as much as they wanted in a secure and safe place, when the canal was free of boats. It may not be a hindrance but rather a great benefit, as Melanie and Oscar Mader tried to tell him.

It pained him he had treated her like he did, as if she were only interested in her private affairs. She cared for her father and David's family and business, as he once cared for Pa and the promises made. She also cared for his sons. This was his land now. Pa was dead. The dead must bury the dead. Now was the time for life and God's will be done, whatever that might be.

He heard his name then and turned to find Hiram lumbering toward him through the tall grass. "A fine place to think," his father-in-law commented.

David nodded.

"Have you given any more thought to that canal project?"

David knew his in-laws appeared willing to have this business of the canal on the land. They also liked Melanie, even if it must be hard to see a young woman about the farm, with the memories of their daughter who was now parted from them.

Hiram sighed. "I know this is your land, David, and you have the final say in it."

"You have a say also, Hiram. You are family."

He smiled. "I do think of you as a son in many ways. But also, I think of you as a man looking out for his family. And I think God's been trying to get you to see things differently."

"What things, in particular?"

"That maybe He's chosen to give us a gift when we thought it could never happen. The gift of this young lady. There's a kindness and strength about her much like Leah. But she is good-hearted to the boys and honest with us all."

David inhaled a breath, wondering if he dare speak of the thoughts he'd had these many days. In particular, the day Melanie and her father came here, and how he'd contemplated courtship before news of the canal silenced it all.

Hiram went on. "The boys are right. Miss O'Neil would make a fine addition to the family."

David recalled how easily the words came forth from the children's mouths. Then there was Melanie's reaction and how she abruptly left. "I'm not sure she feels the same way."

"Have you asked her?"

David saw his father-in-law eye him with a grin. "At one time I thought of asking to court her, but then her father talked about the canal business and. . ."

"Love of land gives nothing. Love for each other is the greatest gift one can have. You might consider giving that gift, David, and see where it leads. It may surprise you."

David nodded. If only he could be certain love was in command and not just the want of land or anything else. If only he could read a heart. But how could he know unless he asked?

An hour later David arrived at the O'Neil home in the village of Little Falls. The boys often described the fine brick house and furnishings fit for a queen, as they liked to call Melanie. Now he wondered if he, a simple farmer, was doing the right thing. He thought of leaving, but if he didn't face what was before him, he knew peace would take flight and he could be left mourning what might have been.

David thanked Mr. O'Neil, who invited him in and presented him with tea. The mere act of this man pouring tea for them set his mind at ease. The O'Neils were not of noble birthright. They were simply a father and daughter making the best of what life had given them. "I will be brief, sir. I know you are interested in a portion of my land for the canal. I have thought long and hard about this. I prayed and sought the wisdom of others. And I must tell you now, as hard as it is for me, I will sell you the land you need."

Mr. O'Neil nearly dropped his cup of tea. Just then David heard a gasp, and he whirled in his seat. Melanie stood in the doorway, lovely in a blue dress accentuating her reddish-brown hair, rosy cheeks, and blue eyes. She covered her mouth with her hand. "Forgive me for listening," she said and turned away.

"Please wait!" David's voice rang out, and she paused. "I—I have something else I must say. I've been wanting to ask this for some time but other things got in the way. Things that have since been resolved to the good of all, I might add." He then faced Mr. O'Neil. "Sir, if you would permit me, I would very much like to court your daughter. She has been a gift to my family, my boys, and to me. I would like to learn more about her and see where God leads us in the end."

David watched the gaze of the father meet his daughter's. The man stirred and stood to his feet, as did David. "And what does my daughter have to say about this?" Mr. O'Neil inquired.

For a moment no one said anything. Tension gripped David, and he feared he had made a dreadful mistake. His heart quickened, and his palms turned damp. Until he heard a soft voice say a bit breathlessly, "Yes. I—I accept."

David could not believe it would be this simple. When he saw the smiles appear on both their faces, he knew he had heard God's voice. Tears began to fill his eyes, which he no longer tried to contain. The Grand Canal had not only opened his eyes to see the grandness and beauty in Melanie O'Neil but to see God's love too.

◆——·——◆

Joy filled Melanie over what she had witnessed in their humble home in Little Falls. Did David Marshall just agree to a land acquisition? And on the heels of it, ask Father if he might court her? She shook her head, wondering if it had all been a dream. The looks on both their faces and the way David regarded her spoke of a changed heart. She lay awake the night before, thinking about their various circumstances and David's reactions, from the meeting at the river while his sons fished, to his anger when Father first broached the subject of David's land, and then the tender way he had given her the spectacles so she might read. Everything had changed for the better.

"Would you care to go for a walk?" David now inquired, offering his arm. She glanced questioningly at Father, who nodded. His arm felt strong beneath her fingertips, with the ripple of muscle evident under the cloth from the heavy labor of the farm. The sunshine was bright and warm as he led the way down the road, saying how happy his sons would be to hear their news.

"But you must tell them once and for all that I'm most certainly not a queen!" she said with a laugh.

"You are to me." His voice was serious. "You have always shown concern for us. Especially my boys. They need that in their lives. Direction, a steady hand, motherly love." They came to a grand view of the river before them, carrying white foam from the rocks farther upriver. "A canal will have no barriers," he noted.

"No. It is easy to navigate. It will help boats sail far and fast. We will see God's blessing in this place."

She felt his hand tighten around hers. "He is already blessing us, in ways I never thought possible."

"Yes," she agreed. "I never thought after Sam left me that day, I would meet a father and sons who captured my heart. But the Lord is in the difficult and the good. In the sorrow and the joy. We only have to walk out our journey, and He will lead us."

David turned, the brim of his hat lying low over his head, the shadow crossing his face. He swiped the hat away, revealing eyes that gazed intently at her. His head tilted, his lips finding hers in a soft and gentle kiss. It was perfect, just as all this had been made perfect in time. Though she laughed now as a thought crossed her mind. She tugged on his hand and they continued walking. Melanie knew where she was going, even if David did not.

He smiled. "I hear you laughing. What is it?"

"God used my poor eyesight and the sweet ways of little boys to make everything clear."

David took her hand in his. "I believe the next few weeks, months, or however long the Lord has for us will be interesting, Queen Melanie."

She laughed again. "So long as you remain the king of the home and our lives."

"By God's grace."

Suddenly they were at the crossroads, one road leading west, the other east. "This is the place where I was to go to Ohio," she said.

"Are you saying goodbye?" he asked quietly.

"No. I am saying. . .I'm home."

Melanie entered David's strong embrace. Good things lay ahead of her on the road of life. And the land could not have been made any sweeter, graced by God, and flowing with its own milk and honey. A perfect place to call home.

Lauralee Bliss has always liked to dream big dreams. Part of that dream was writing, and after several years of hard work, her dream of being published was realized in 1997 with the publication of her first romance novel, *Mountaintop*, through Barbour Publishing. Since then she's had over twenty-five books published, both historical and contemporary. Lauralee is also an avid hiker, completing the entire length of the Appalachian Trail both north and south. Lauralee makes her home in Virginia in the foothills of the Blue Ridge Mountains with her family. Visit her website at www.lauraleebliss.com and find her on Twitter @LauraleeBliss and Facebook at Readers of Author Lauralee Bliss.

Wedding of the Waters

by Rita Gerlach

Chapter 1

August 1819

The small village of Goshen Creek, an afternoon's ride from the Erie Canal in Rome, New York, with a population of no more than two hundred men, women, and children, astounded Charlotte. Summer brought with it a multitude of birds, butterflies, and honeybees. A pleasant change from the coarse existence of city life. Seedlings from the cottonwood trees shook loose from their moorings and floated like snowflakes in the fragrant breeze.

Her uncle, Henry Verger, had acquired a ministry. Called to serve the good people of Goshen Creek as a physician, he held his leather bag upon his lap as the wagon drew into the heart of the village. From under her bonnet, Charlotte glanced at him to see his reaction to the simple dwellings and the people who paused to stare as they passed by. Chickens and spotted geese wandered along the dirt thoroughfare. They passed a well and then a smithy shop where the blacksmith pounded his hammer against an anvil. The man hesitated, the air suddenly silent from the heavy clink of his tool. He nodded, and Uncle Henry raised his hand to him. Charlotte returned the nod, and soon the sound of his hammer hitting iron returned.

Anxious, she looked ahead. "Goshen may be small, but it's pleasanter than town. I wonder if they have a milliner's shop."

"You have a new hat packed away, don't you?" her uncle asked.

"For Sundays, I do. A lady cannot have enough hats, Uncle."

"Hah! You'll find out soon enough that isn't the case. The women of Goshen are likely to own a day bonnet and another for Sundays. You'll fit right in."

Charlotte wished to ignore that fact, for she loved the wearing of a good bonnet, made of the best straw or linen, with broad colorful ribbons. "I suppose I'm vain on that score," she said. "Do you think the house will have feathered mattresses?"

"You'd love to have a feathered mattress, wouldn't you?"

"Indeed, I would. And a copper soaking tub. This journey has me very sore and dusty."

He laughed. "There is always the nearby creek."

"You don't expect me to bathe in it, do you?"

He nudged her chin. "Of course I don't. I was joking."

Charlotte smiled. "I was right to assume you were. Now that I think of it, I'd like to try wading in a creek. I bet the water feels wonderful."

"Charlotte, you do make my heart rise. I cannot imagine all I would have missed if I hadn't taken you under my wing after your parents went on to paradise. I hoped you would wed a man of my profession, but I've come to realize a man with a sense of humor—in good taste—would be the perfect match for you."

Marriage was the last thing on her mind. She could not wait to see the home they would live in and set up housekeeping and her uncle's surgery. In her dreams, she saw a saltbox building with a green door and tall mullioned windows. There'd be a garden in the back rife with vegetables, and roses in the front.

She loosened her hat's ribbon beneath her chin. The driver reined in the mules. It had been the most uncomfortable ride of her life. She had been accustomed to a carriage with velvet seats. The wooden bench of the wagon and the constant dips and sways made her body ache.

The driver turned his head. "This is the place, Dr. Verger."

Charlotte drew off her hat and looked at the small house settled on a knoll. The front faced the late afternoon sun, which sparkled in the blown window glass. A pair of elms sheltered it from the wind. A rude wooden fence lined the front. The gate, of the same design, sat open as if to say they were welcomed to cross into the yard.

The driver alighted and held his hand out to Charlotte. "Ah, look there on the porch, miss. Someone's left a basket of victuals."

Charlotte smiled and stepped down. "Oh, how good of them. I'm starved."

Uncle Henry fumbled with his specs. "Don't rush, Charlotte. Rushing will work you into a sweat and cause a faint."

"Yes, Uncle. I'll try, but I'm so hungry, and can't wait to see our new home."

She raised her skirts and headed up the porch steps. There she scooped up the basket and stepped to the door. She couldn't wait for Uncle Henry, so she opened it and walked inside. The room smelled of lye soap and linseed oil. Sturdy oak wainscoting lined the plastered walls, and she could see the places where the oil had brightened the wood. To her disappointment, there were no carpets or mats on the floors, and the windows were shut, making the interior hot and musty.

Fanning her hand in front of her face, she walked across the planks, stopped, and looked down. Bewildered by what she found, she pinched her brows together. "Uncle, there is sand on the floor."

"It's the way country folk keep their floors clean, Charlotte."

She threw her hands over her hips. "I'll not have sand on our floors."

"Well, there must be a broom in here somewhere."

"Didn't Dr. Neely have someone other than his poor wife keep house?"

"How should I know, my dear?" Uncle Henry brushed the sole of his shoe across the floor. "It's not so bad."

"It may be the custom, but it shan't be mine." She pulled up the window sashes and the breeze flowed inside. The fragrance of lilacs came with it. She leaned out one of the windows. "There's a lilac bush growing on the side of the house, Uncle."

"I can smell it," he said. "I think this place will do nicely."

Charlotte pulled away from the window and glanced around the room. The fireplace had been swept clean. Spindle chairs stood in front of it. An oak table with two pewter candlesticks caught a streak of sunlight. It looked barren to Charlotte. She was accustomed to much more than this. "It's nothing like we had in the city," she said.

"We're in the wilderness, where you don't need to impress anyone. People here only have what they need. Wants are secondary."

"It's a small village. Who is here for me to impress?" She walked over to the fireplace. "Look they left a butter churn." She grabbed the handle, raised the lid, and looked inside. "It's empty, but something I can try, if I can figure out how it works."

"I'm sure there will be many new things for you to try, Charlotte."

She looked at him. "We'd need to buy a cow."

Uncle Henry's stomach gurgled, and he slapped his hand over it. "Pardon me, Charlotte dear."

"You're hungry." She headed over to the basket on the table. "It certainly was nice of the person who left this."

"Some may not be so nice when they find out I'm half blind without my spectacles." He pushed them back up his nose when they slipped. "If I ever lose them, it will make your work doubly hard."

"Don't you have a spare pair?"

He pursed his lips and tapped his finger against his chin. "Hmm, I think so somewhere in my bags. I should hire an assistant, Charlotte. You'll have enough to do with keeping house."

"I'm sure you won't need extra hands."

"Well, we shall give it time and see how it goes."

A red-and-white-checkered cloth lay over the basket. Charlotte drew it back. "Apples!" she cheered. "A pot of butter, a jug of cider, a pint of cream, two loaves of bread, and a meat pie." She handed him an apple.

Adjacent to the front room off to one side of the house, she found a stocked kitchen. A stone fireplace along one wall and a baking oven delighted Charlotte.

Copper pots hung from the rafters and a hutch stood against the opposite wall. On its shelves were flow blue china plates, cups, and saucers. Charlotte wondered why Dr. Neely and his wife had not taken them with them. Had they been the wife's wedding present, or had they belonged to another family?

Uncle Henry stood by the table and bit into the apple. "I hope you aren't disappointed, Charlotte. This kind of living won't be what you are used to."

"I like what I've seen so far," she replied.

Her uncle looked around the room. "Look at all the stuff in here. Must have been too much to pack. I do wish Dr. Neely and his good wife all the best. I daresay I am not as brave."

"Imagine, Uncle, the challenges they will face as medical missionaries. We must keep them in our prayers."

Charlotte took down two plates from the hutch. Uncle Henry looked at the pie and rubbed his hands together. Charlotte cut into it and put a slice on a plate. "I must thank the person who gave us all this. There was no note saying whom. But I'll find out."

Her uncle took a bite and rolled his eyes. "Hmm, this is excellent. Kindness is but bread upon the waters."

Charlotte watched him finish off three-quarters of the meat pie and all the cider. She sat in a ladder-back chair with her chin cupped in her hand and wondered why he had never married. Deep commitment to his profession may have been the cause, but a broken heart that had never mended spoke the loudest. She had asked him once, and he told her of a ladylove he courted in his youth. A beauty and an heiress, she had many beaus, and ended up choosing the wealthiest among them, a man from a prominent Philadelphia family with deep roots in the Revolution. A doctor's life turned out to be rewarding but lonely.

An orange tabby leaped through the window near the table. He gave the newcomers a squint and a soft mew. "Look, Uncle. Oh, isn't he lovely!" Charlotte reached out and the little creature rubbed against her hand. She cuddled the cat and it licked her cheek. "If no one claims him, I will. I'll call him Robin."

"Why that name, child?"

"After Robin Hood. One of my favorite legends." She poured cream into a dish and the cat lapped it up.

Someone knocked on the door. Charlotte stood. When she opened it, there on the porch stood three women. "Good day, ladies. The doctor is not ready to receive patients yet."

"Oh, we haven't come because we are sick," said the tallest of the three. "We've come to welcome you to Goshen Creek."

Charlotte smiled. "Thank you. Please, won't you come in?"

"We prefer to sit out here on the porch," said the lady closest to the door.

"It is such a fine day," said another.

"We won't keep you but a minute." The last to speak moved Charlotte to the steps. Upper-crust city ladies would have been shocked to see these women hike their skirts above their ankles and plop down on bare wood.

A middle-aged woman with steel-gray hair spoke. She pointed to her friends. "This is Mrs. Schmidt and Mrs. Vance. I am Mrs. McKenna."

"We know your name, dear," said Mrs. Vance. "You're Charlotte Verger, and you've come with your uncle, Dr. Verger. Where is he?"

Charlotte sat on the upper step. "My uncle is enjoying a helping of meat pie. Which of you ladies left the basket?"

Mrs. McKenna wiggled her head. " 'Twas me. I hope he likes it."

"Your gift is greatly appreciated," said Charlotte. "Our provisions were dry by the time we reached Goshen Creek, and there were no carriage houses nearby to stop for a meal."

"All of us in Goshen Creek want you to feel welcomed."

"We've only been here an hour or so and believe me, we feel most welcomed. I doubt I'll be able to match your meat pie, Mrs. McKenna. Uncle Henry has had a look of jubilation on his face from the first bite."

"My husband, the Reverend W. T. McKenna, looked euphoric at mealtimes when we were first married. I guess he's bored by my cooking now. I've been wedded to him for forty years."

The name held Charlotte's attention. "I once knew a family by the name of McKenna."

"The reverend has family roots in Philadelphia, Boston, and New York. Our nephew was born and raised right outside the city you hail from. Perhaps you knew him. Blaine McKenna."

Charlotte's heart skipped a beat. "I. . .remember him, yes."

Mrs. McKenna's eyes widened. "Really? What a fascinating coincidence. Neighbors? Schoolmates? Or was there something, if you don't mind me asking, something more, you know, something. . ."

"If you mean something of an intimate nature, we were friends," Charlotte said.

Not another word could she get out. Her hesitation to tell more halted her speech, for her heart had been attached to Blaine seven years ago, and broke when he left to fight the British as far south as Washington City.

She stretched out her legs and changed the subject. "So your husband is the minister here?"

"Indeed he is. We don't have a proper church building yet, so we have Sunday services in the town hall. . .little as it may be. Sometimes on warm days, we meet out in the field near our house. There's nothing like hearing him preach under a blue sky."

That sparked Charlotte's interest. "I should like to attend. I've never been to an outdoor service."

"Then you have something to look forward to," said Mrs. Schmidt.

"We have picnics afterward," said Mrs. Vance.

"Goshen will grow even bigger with the canal," said Mrs. Schmidt. "I just hope not too big."

Mrs. McKenna frowned and clicked her tongue. "That canal has caused hardships that won't be remedied."

Charlotte grew inquisitive. "What kinds of hardships?"

"Some men working on the canal are ruffians, drunkards, and plain wicked. Then there are the orphan boys searching for work. They are mistreated and cheated out of their pay. Clergy, such as my husband, have preached against these transgressions, but not every man working on the canal listens. 'Tis a sad state of affairs."

Mrs. Schmidt looked up at Charlotte. "And then there are the fevers. Oh, some people do get the malaria something fierce. Dr. Neely went out to the workers many times. Lord knows how many passed on. The village has been very grateful to him for keeping it away from our little community."

Charlotte did not speak immediately but paused to think about what she was hearing. The letters her uncle had received from Dr. Neely gave a glowing account of the village and surrounding area, and praised the progress of the great canal being dug from where Albany met the Hudson River to Buffalo and the great lake called Erie. Not once had he mentioned fever, let alone ruffians and abused orphans. She ran her palms over her skirt, nervous about what she and Uncle Henry were there to face.

"We heard nothing but good things from Dr. Neely," she said. "Never about these hardships."

Mrs. McKenna nodded. "Well, don't let them frighten you, Charlotte. I promise you'll be safe here."

The looks on the other women's faces told Charlotte differently. Each had lost her smile and had a look in her eyes that made Charlotte question Mrs. McKenna's word. If fever spread to this part of the state, the likelihood of it spreading to Goshen Creek seemed high. Philadelphia citizens were not spared from influenza, typhoid, and malaria outbreaks. Could Mrs. McKenna be right that living more isolated protected them?

"You must tell my uncle everything you know about the ailments people have in these parts. That way he'll be prepared for every contingency."

Mrs. McKenna patted Charlotte's hand. "Don't worry, Charlotte. Surely Dr. Verger knows what to anticipate. Before Dr. Neely left, he told us Dr. Verger was one of the most talented physicians he's known. He said they were in medical college together."

"That is true, they were." Charlotte stood from the step. "I must go back inside and unpack our trunks. I haven't even seen the upstairs part of the house or the surgery."

"Well, we won't keep you," said Mrs. McKenna.

Mrs. Schmidt stood and shook out her hem. "Don't forget to tell her about the reception on Friday night, Ruth."

"Oh yes. It's to celebrate your arrival. We shall have musicians, dancing, and a bounty of food."

Charlotte's spirits lifted. This was grand news. Goshen Creek was not the backward hovel she'd expected it to be. She and her uncle would meet all the residents of the small village. "I'm delighted! Should I bring anything?"

"Only yourself and Dr. Verger."

Unable to contain her excitement, Charlotte clutched Mrs. McKenna's hand. "Thank you, Mrs. McKenna. Thanks to all of you ladies. I thought I wouldn't be able to wear the ball gown I bought in Philadelphia, but I shall."

The women giggled and looked at one another with raised brows. Mrs. McKenna said, "We aren't that fancy hereabouts. No one wears silks and satins in Goshen Creek. Wear something like you have on today."

Followed by her friends, she strode off the steps and crossed the grass to the dirt road. Charlotte stood stunned, seeing them as a clutch of hens that clucked and strutted as they passed the humble dwellings lining the thoroughfare.

She looked down at her dress and sulked. "Wear something like this to a dance?" Then she lifted her eyes to the older women striding down the road in their muslin bonnets and homespun frocks. Robin circled around her legs. She crouched down and stroked his ears. "Well, Robin, I suppose I have a lot of changing to do."

Chapter 2

Friday evening could not have come fast enough. In the upstairs bedroom, Charlotte shook out the folds of her silk lavender gown. She hated to put it back in her trunk. Such beauty should not be wasted, but to overdress for a welcoming would be an insult to her neighbors. One thing she did not want to do was to appear high and mighty, an impression she did not aspire to.

With care, she laid the gown over a sheet of rice paper and picked up her gloves. She hesitated before slipping them on, but the silky feel of them made her wish she could wear them to the reception. Like the gown, they had to be stored away for another time.

Mrs. McKenna had hinted that the women of the village were not like wealthy Philadelphian ladies who wore stylish fashions. The idea of wearing one of her day dresses to an affair made her cringe, but she accepted it. She chose the one she would wear to church on Sundays. It surprised her Goshen Creek had not built a church like the ones she had seen in country towns—bright white with tall steeples and bells and high windows that opened in the summer.

The empire dress made of white summer muslin turned pale yellow in the candlelight. Yellow—the color people turned who were sickened with fever. She'd seen it in Philadelphia and dreaded the thought such suffering could waylay a small village like Goshen Creek. When her uncle told her he intended to take Dr. Neely's offer to replace him, it was like a breath of fresh air. To move away from the hustle and bustle of the city seemed dreamlike, exciting, and new. Were her expectations misplaced? She held the dress in front of her and sighed.

"Charlotte Verger," she said to her image in the mirror, "you're assuming too much."

"If it is your beauty you question, you are in the wrong, Charlotte."

She whirled around. Uncle Henry stood in the doorway. How smartly dressed he looked. She set the dress aside and went to him. With nimble fingers, she adjusted his neckcloth. "You look handsome tonight. I'm sure it will please all the single ladies and widows."

He laughed. "It's the suit, and I'm an old man in it."

"You are still young enough to attract the ladies. You'll have them hanging on your arm before too long."

He pulled his watch from his waistcoat pocket and looked at the time. "We'll be late if you don't hurry. Why aren't you dressed and ready to leave?"

Charlotte stepped away. "I couldn't help but hesitate." She closed the lid to her trunk. "I am used to wearing ball gowns to dances. I don't suppose the women in the village will ever do so."

"I'm sure they will not. These are godly, modest people. They do not have the money to spend on silks and satins. Sunday best is what they will wear."

Charlotte's eyes brightened. "Actually, I'm glad."

"You want to fit in, don't you?"

She nodded. "I am hoping to."

"Dear girl, you are wise in your choice not to be overdressed. It would be like a peacock strutting in a barnyard. The hens would not accept you as one of their own."

"I agree, Uncle." She sat on the edge of her bed. "Every ball I went to in the city was held in a stuffy room. All the ladies were finely dressed, but there was so much rivalry it drove me to distraction." She shook her head. "You would not have believed the gossip, and if you wore an out-of-season style, your family's financial situation was called into question."

"All that is true, I'm sure. Ever wonder why so many older gentlemen chose to sit in another room?"

"It was always obvious to me." Charlotte stood and picked up her Sunday dress. She held it in front of her, while facing Uncle Henry. "I shall wear my muslin dress. I like it very much. It's pretty, simple. No frills. What do you think?"

"It is very appropriate," he replied.

Charlotte looked up at him with a smile. He closed the door, and Charlotte slipped out of her day dress and into her muslin best. A breeze blew through the window and through the fabric. She wondered if there'd be any handsome gentlemen at this affair—as handsome as she remembered Blaine.

She drew her dark hair up and brought wispy curls down along her neck and shoulders. She then added a thin band of braided gold ribbon and baby's breath. Turning from the mirror, she looked over at Robin as he lounged on the windowsill.

"I'll dance far into the night, Robin, and sleep until noon." The cat crossed his paws and squinted. "It cannot be much different from the cotillions back home. Well—maybe just a little."

◆━━━●━━━◆

Charlotte laid her hand on her uncle's arm as they made their way toward a building made of whitewashed clapboards. The only beings on the street were the wandering chickens and a sow with her piglets. Charlotte laughed. "Are they not adorable? I should like a piglet as a pet."

Uncle Henry laughed back. "A foolish notion, my girl, for they do grow, you know."

"Where is everyone?" Charlotte said with a glance farther down the road.

"They're all inside. It is customary for guests to arrive before the persons honored."

"It seems like a lot of bother to me."

"You mean this is troublesome for you? That is quite ungrateful, Charlotte."

She shook her head. "Oh, I did not mean it in that way. It just seems the ladies have gone to so much trouble to greet us. I hope we have not put them out, that is, if they feel obligated."

Uncle Henry moved on with Charlotte. "They are friendly folk here. Think of how it would be if they ignored us."

"Hardly a thing to happen, you being a doctor."

The sow hurried across the road. Her piglets squealed and followed. A boy with a lengthy stick chased after them. He stopped, drew off his cap, and bowed. "Excuse me, Dr. Verger, Miss Verger. She got out of the pen again. Pa wants me to round them up."

He ran off in his pursuit of the frisky swine, swinging his stick and making unusual sounds Charlotte had never heard. She put her hand over her mouth and giggled. "Should I help him, Uncle?"

"What? Oh, you are a sprite, Charlotte Verger. That you would joke of such a thing. I doubt you'd know how to catch one if your life depended on it. Put your mind on the reception instead. We are almost there."

She squeezed his arm and looked ahead. The doors to the meetinghouse stood open, and laughter and talk could be heard coming from inside. "You think there will be enough gentlemen to keep me occupied?"

He nudged her chin. "It is difficult to say."

"Well, I hope they aren't all of an age to be my father or you, Uncle Henry."

"If there is a shortage of young fellows, surely they will have invited people nearby."

Her smile fell. "Good people, I hope, otherwise they would be men working on the canal, and Mrs. McKenna told me they are lawless ruffians."

"Well, if that is so and they behave badly, good men will take care of them. If things get too rough we will leave. I'm up for an early night anyway."

◆—————◆

All heads turned when Charlotte entered with her uncle. Conversations died down and the silence made Charlotte uneasy. Mrs. McKenna rushed forward. She wore an empire dress made of dark brown homespun and a huge goose feather in her hair, the largest Charlotte had ever seen. The feather fluttered over

Mrs. McKenna's forehead, and she blew it back with a wave of her hand.

"Welcome, Dr. Verger, Miss Verger."

She bent her knees and wobbled. Charlotte took her arm. "It isn't necessary to curtsy to us, Mrs. McKenna," Charlotte whispered.

"Ah, I suppose not. Yet one mustn't be rude to the newcomers of our community. Punch?"

"I'm not thirsty, thank you."

"Be sure to visit the food table. The ladies have gone all out to please you, Doctor."

"Thank you, Mrs. McKenna. We'll be sure to."

"The men linger by the table, anxious to meet you. My husband would come right over, but as you see, he is occupied in comforting Mr. Vance. The poor man's leg prevents him. Gout is his constant enemy."

Uncle Henry nodded. "I shall be happy to attend to him, Mrs. McKenna, with an easy remedy."

"Oh, it's so good of you, sir." Her bright face darkened. "You won't bleed him, will you? I don't believe in that kind of thing."

"Nor do I, madam. Has he a wife or a daughter that cares for him?"

"Alas, he is widowed."

"Perhaps you could persuade him to keep free of alcohol and meats, and give him a mixture of water and black cherry."

"I shall," she said excitedly. "I'm always willing to lend a helping hand. I think I have some black cherry cordial in our cupboard, you know, for medicinal purposes."

Mrs. McKenna looped her arm through Uncle Henry's and moved him in the direction of the refreshment table. Charlotte hesitated to follow. She looked around the room and soon found herself surrounded by a group of village girls. She realized the friendliness of the people in Goshen Creek was superior to the snobbery of upper-class city folk. It put her at ease to be herself, for the girls were as chatty as roosting hens.

"We're so pleased to have you, Miss Verger."

"Is your gown the latest fashion in the city?"

"What a pretty pattern."

"Was your journey terribly long? Did you meet any trouble on the way?"

"You must think us behind the times. Your dress is much more appealing than ours."

Charlotte looked down at her dress. "Oh, but I disagree. Your dresses are very pretty." There were better things to talk about than clothes. Charlotte attempted to change the subject. "Do the ladies in town have a quilting bee, or a Bible study I could attend?"

"We have both of those."

"I wish we had a sewing group where we could make clothes like yours, Miss Charlotte." The girls would not let go of the subject of clothes. "It's been awhile since we saw the latest fashions or had a peddler come by with patterns to sell."

"I brought some patterns with me, if any of you wish to see them," said Charlotte. Every face lit up another notch.

"Are they easy?"

"Indeed they are, and very pretty."

She did her best to answer each question that followed. The girls gave their names and presented invitations for Charlotte to visit their homes.

"Our quilting group meets on Mondays, if you'd like to come."

"Where?" Charlotte asked.

"Just down the road. We meet in Mrs. McKenna's sitting room."

"Have you met our minister?"

"I have not, but Mrs. McKenna told me about him. Is he a good preacher?"

One of the girls, Ethel, giggled. "I'll put it this way, Miss Charlotte. No one falls asleep when Reverend McKenna preaches."

A trio of musicians struck up a country melody and young beaus drew up to the group. Plainly dressed, hair past their ears, and boots instead of dancing shoes, they each bowed and asked if she would dance with them first. She graciously declined after seeing the anxious looks on the girls' faces. They were whisked away and she watched them whirl out onto the dance floor. None could be beyond the age of twenty. Charlotte was twenty and three—unattached and unmarried.

"You're being kind to us, Charlotte," one of the girls said over her shoulder as she was led away. "Don't decline the next offer."

Charlotte smiled back with a nod.

"Charlotte, don't you like the Scottish reel?" asked another.

"I adore it," she said. "But I shall be happy to watch how the ladies of Goshen Creek preform it."

"So you will not be out of step with us?" laughed Ethel.

Charlotte felt the urge to tap her foot in time with the music. So lively was the tune, so lively the dancers. They held hands, swung, and whirled. Charlotte was delighted. The quadrille had always bored her. But here, a country dance had the air of the romantic.

From the far side of the room, Charlotte saw a familiar face. He stood in front of a window where the light brushed over his flaxen hair. Not wanting him to see her reaction, she lowered her eyes and remained isolated in front of the stone fireplace swept clean of ashes. 'Twas a warm night, and she batted her fan to cool her face. She looked back at him. His attention was somewhere other than her. But when their eyes met, he put two fingers against his temple and saluted her. His brown-eyed gaze, the slight lift of a smile, caused her heart to thump. There was a time when she thought she'd never look into those eyes again.

Ethel drew beside Charlotte. "I am all out of breath," she said. Her wire-rimmed glasses enlarged her eyes to the size of half dollars. "The gentleman I was dancing with stepped all over my feet. I'm not willing to walk away from here limping." She shook out her hem and looked at Charlotte. "Are you all right, Miss Charlotte? You look flushed, and I don't think it is from the candlelight."

Charlotte fixed her eyes on the brown ones across the room. "Someone just saluted me."

Ethel glanced in the direction of Charlotte's gaze. "Oh, that is interesting. No wonder your cheeks are so red."

Charlotte put her hand on her cheek. "Am I really that flushed?"

"You are, but it will fade."

"Indeed, I hope so."

"A touch of rose to the cheeks is attractive, Charlotte. Don't wish it away too fast."

"I'd rather be pale. . .like the tablecloth over there."

"And look sickly? Do not wish it." Ethel clicked her tongue. "I wonder who he is. Do you know him?"

Could Charlotte pretend she did not? The more she glanced over at him, the more familiar he became. How could he be the one she imagined? Many a man had flaxen hair and dark brown eyes. Many had broad shoulders and a handsome face. Still, those eyes were like the ones she'd seen long ago, at a time when love was new and seemed everlasting—when she would have her heart broken for the first time.

"Not your type, hey?" Ethel sighed. "He certainly is mine. Just look at those eyes. They're as brown as a basket of Christmas chestnuts. And the cut of his jaw is so masculine. I like the way his hair brushes over his collar, don't you?"

Charlotte looked away. She realized if she kept her eyes on him, her emotions would rise higher. "I suppose such a man is easy to single out, Ethel."

"He should come over and properly introduce himself," Ethel said, seeming not to have heard Charlotte. "He's most likely one of the workers on the canal. Strong arms—and a bit of a rascal, I'd say, after the way he hailed you."

"Surely there are some workers who have decent manners."

Ethel placed her hand over her heart. "Oh, he's looking over here again. You think this time *I've* caught his eye?"

"It is possible."

"Oh, he's coming over. If he should ask for a dance, I shall give it."

Charlotte swallowed a lump in her throat as he crossed the room toward her. Mrs. McKenna hurried in front of him. He stopped. She wound her arm through his and brought him over. With great enthusiasm she said, "May I introduce you ladies to my nephew?"

Both girls gave a short curtsy.

Charlotte studied his face. There—on his right brow—a tiny scar practically invisible in the candlelight. *I wonder if he ever forgave me for throwing that rock at him. It was so wrong of me.*

"Blaine, this is Miss Ethel Stocklittle, and this is Miss Charlotte Verger, newly arrived to our little community, like you."

He gave Ethel a short bow and then gave one to Charlotte, keeping his eyes on her.

Ethel said, "The Reverend McKenna says he has family from Philadelphia. Are you one of them, sir?"

"It is where I grew up." His glance went from Ethel to Charlotte. That he was her first love caused a pang. "That is where I got this." He pointed at the scar and grinned at Charlotte. Mortified, she lowered her eyes.

"Oh," said Ethel, taking a closer look. "I would not have noticed unless you had shown it to me."

"I refer to it as a trophy, Miss Ethel."

"I dare not ask how you got it."

One corner of Blaine's mouth lifted. "A stone. A little girl threw it at me."

"Oh, she must have been a very bad child."

"No, she was a very good child. I was a very infuriating lad."

At least he admitted to his failings, thought Charlotte. Still, she had injured him, and it caused her much regret. Charlotte lost her smile along with any idea they would have an amiable reunion.

"Are you planning to settle here with your aunt and uncle?" Ethel put her hand on his arm.

Charlotte took a step forward. "Perhaps Mr. McKenna is visiting for a short time and not settling, Ethel."

"Oh, but he is settling," said Mrs. McKenna.

"As a worker on the canal?" Charlotte's eyes engaged his.

Ethel guffawed. "Oh, you are being a busybody, Charlotte." She tapped Blaine's arm with one finger. "You don't have to answer if you don't want to, Mr. McKenna."

"Oh, but I do," he replied.

Ethel's mouth fell open. "Oh, I do apologize for calling you a busybody, Charlotte, now that Mr. McKenna is agreeable to discussing his arrival."

"I took no offense," said Charlotte.

Ethel wiggled her head. "Good."

Blaine placed his hands behind his back. "My aunt told me your uncle will be the doctor in Goshen, Miss Charlotte. I'll be glad to make his acquaintance. Medicine is quite an undertaking."

"But a worthwhile one, sir, and he won't have as many patients as he once did in Philadelphia, which will be easier on him at his age."

Mrs. McKenna took Ethel by the hand. "Dear oh dear, we've left the gentlemen to themselves. My husband is shaking his head at me. And, Ethel, you mustn't neglect your fiancé."

Ethel frowned. Within a group of older gentlemen, a short stout man wiggled his fingers at her. "Oh yes. Albert. I forgot about him. Let us carry on, Mrs. McKenna."

Off they went, and Charlotte stood beside the cold hearth enjoying the cool draft coming down the chimney. "I've never met people as lively as these." She looked at Blaine. "Have you, Mr. McKenna?"

"I'm too distracted to notice." His eyes offered a friendly, quizzical smile. "At the moment—I'm remembering you."

Heat flooded her face and she dropped her closed fan into her palm. "Me?" she whispered.

"Yes. Don't you remember me, Charlotte?"

"How could I forget?"

"You just didn't recognize me."

"You look older and. . ."

"And you look prettier since last I saw you." He stepped closer. "I hope I did not embarrass you, pointing out my trophy."

"Why do you call it that?" she said.

"To see if you remembered me without my calling out your name and gathering you up in my arms."

"I am glad. An outburst and embrace from you would have been awkward."

"See, I've grown into a gentleman."

"I suppose you married that girl you left me for."

He looked aside. "I never left you for another, Charlotte."

"Your departure held every indication that you did."

"We were children."

"Sixteen is not so young. Plenty of people marry at sixteen."

"Not I, but I do regret losing touch with you. Did you know your father forbid me to speak to you?"

She lowered her eyes. "Yes, I remember."

"I was not up to his standards. He didn't want his daughter associating with soldiers."

"And that is what you've been all this time?"

"Not entirely." Disappointment flooded his eyes. He moved beside her close enough to whisper, "I'm sorry if I hurt you."

She glanced away. "It is in the past. I got over you quickly."

"Hmm, that tells me something."

She glanced up at him. "May I ask what?"

"It tells me I did not court you the way I should have. I was a boy, immature, and not at all experienced in wooing a girl. I wager I can win you now."

She held back a laugh and gave him a sidelong glance. "That is an interesting challenge."

He smiled. "Do you accept it?"

Charlotte shifted her gaze to the group of dancers out on the floor. "I shall have to think long and hard about it."

Chapter 3

He was not at all like the men in Philadelphia she had as dance partners. It had nothing to do with his good looks, his dreamy eyes, and the masculine tone of his voice. His clothes were not made of the fine combed cottons and lightweight wool the upper-class gentlemen wore, nor were they tailored to fit his physique. Instead, he wore buckskin pants, a cutaway jacket, and black military boots. The boots needed polishing, and his neckcloth was too loosely tied. Yet his hair and neat sideburns, his eyes and firm mouth, made all the difference in the world to Charlotte. In this case, it was not the clothes that made the man but the complete opposite.

"Do you still dance?" he asked, holding his hand out to her.

"I do, but I'm not familiar with this reel."

"Come, I'll teach you. It's easy."

"I can see it is. I'm just not sure I—"

"You're not afraid, are you?"

"Of a dance? Certainly not."

She huffed and moved to turn. He took up her hand and stopped her cold. "It's been a long time, Charlotte. I've missed dancing with you. The last time, my heart was in my throat. Take a chance, won't you?"

She turned her head. "I don't know if I should."

"Are you afraid of risk? I never knew you to be."

"You are still incorrigible, Blaine McKenna."

"Incorrigible, yes, but only when I need to be." He drew her closer, caught her up in the strength and warmth of his grasp.

"I lost my heart. . .once," she said. "I dare not lose it again."

"If you do, allow me to be the one to find it."

He looked down into her eyes. She tried to avoid his gaze, but it proved useless. He still made her heart reel. His hands holding hers, even after so long, felt right as he took her out onto the dance floor. The more Charlotte turned and moved with him, the more she began to feel no time had passed since they'd seen each other last. When the song ended and the musicians set aside their instruments, she dipped in a curtsy, as did the other women, and then took his hand.

"I enjoyed that. Did you?" he asked.

Her reserve weakened. "Yes, very much."

"They'll start again after they've had a rest." He pulled her hand through his arm then walked over to the punch table and handed her a cup. She tasted the sweet liquid as a group of children ran by. "It's hard to believe we were like that once," said Blaine.

Charlotte's smile broadened. "One childhood memory I have of you is when you climbed the tree in front of my father's house and he shouted you down."

"Ah, yes, the big elm. I skinned my knees more times than I can count climbing up and down that tree. My father built a platform in an oak in the woods behind our house to keep me and the other lads out of trouble. I loved that place. All the boys in the neighborhood did."

Charlotte drifted back to a day when she sat on her parents' front-porch step. It faced the woods, and she could hear Blaine shouting to her afar off. He would climb to the top of an evergreen, and she'd raise her hand to him. Then he would disappear into the boughs and she'd wait, hug her knees, and keep her eyes fixed on the road, until finally there he was, in his grass-stained knees and dusty clothes, jogging toward her.

Setting her cup down, Charlotte folded her hands in front of her. "I have something to confess."

"I'm all ears."

"I was jealous of you."

He frowned. "For what?"

"I was jealous I wasn't allowed to climb trees and you were."

Smiling he leaned toward her. "There's no one stopping you now."

She shook her head. "Indeed there is. My uncle, for a start. It would be unseemly of me to climb anything but a kitchen chair. Besides, I have no idea how to climb a tree. It is different for you."

"I disagree. Come with me." Blaine took her arm and led her out the door. There were other couples milling around on the lawn. Some had spread out quilts and were eating cake and drinking punch.

With her curiosity piqued, Charlotte widened her eyes. "Where are we going?"

"To the back. You'll like what you see."

She walked with him to the rear of the meetinghouse. Evening light spread over the path, and a haze of magenta skimmed over the sky. Within the hour, night would fall. She looked back over her shoulder to see the distance between the meetinghouse and the ancient oak he brought her to. She measured her steps in case they lingered and darkness fell. Charlotte dare not be caught alone with him after sunset.

When she saw the enormous oak, she looked up through its branches where starlike silver twinkled. The trunk looked as wide as a canal boat, its branches broad as the roof of the building.

Blaine pulled off his coat and set it on the ground, then he leaped up and grabbed hold of a thick branch. With ease, he pulled himself up then swung one leg over and sat down. Smiling, he looked down at Charlotte. "Are you coming up? Nice view up here."

She shook her head and laughed. "I cannot."

"Are you worried you'll tear your pretty dress?"

"That is partly the reason."

He held his arm out to her. "Grab hold. I'll pull you up. You don't have to go any higher than this."

Hesitating, she put her lower lip between her teeth. Then she looked up at him. His eyes caught the light. They compelled her to reach up and wrap her fingers around his strong ones. "You'll hold tight to me? You won't let me fall?"

"I promise," he said. "I bet you're as light as a feather."

She stepped closer and held up both arms. Before she knew it, her feet were off the ground. She shut her eyes. *I can't look down.* Blaine's other hand moved to her waist and in a moment, she was seated next to him. She hugged the trunk and glanced down. She drew in a deep breath. "This is higher than I thought."

"We can go higher if you want."

She looked at him with a start. "Oh no. This is just fine."

"Tell me if you change your mind."

"I won't change it." She tightened her hold. "Do you think anyone saw us?"

"Who cares if they did?"

Charlotte listened to the laugher and joviality coming from the meeting-house. She felt something she had never felt before. Calmness in a place that oozed with it. Absent were the clatter of carriages and horses, the cries of street vendors, even the slamming of doors.

"Who would have thought we would meet again after all this time." Blaine's hand moved close to hers. "Do you still have that little birthmark on your palm?"

She held her hand up. "Still there, under my glove."

Could he have been any more gentle or bold in taking her hand and slipping the glove off finger by finger? She knew she should pull away, but her heartbeat rippled with renewed love. Indeed, long ago she loved him. Now love returned with a more mature feeling.

He turned her hand over. "Ah, there it is. God must have had a reason to place it there."

Charlotte drew her hand away and put her glove back on. "I hate it."

"No one else in the world has a birthmark like yours. A tiny heart no bigger than the tip of your finger."

"You teased me about it when we were children."

"I'm sorry. I was an uncouth boy then." He turned to her. "I've had my ideas about that mark for a long time, Charlotte. It means you can hold a man's heart in the palm of your hand."

She swallowed. "I never thought so."

"It's true. You've always had mine."

"But you haven't seen me in years. You should have forgotten me by now."

"Not an easy thing to do."

"I heard you joined up, and I wondered what had happened to you."

Blaine looked back toward the meetinghouse, and Charlotte followed his eyes. "I packed up and joined the army when the Brits returned. I was a lad eager to route them out of America once and for all."

"Was it as terrible as they say?"

"The backwoods fighting was the most dismal. The Battle of Baltimore not so much, but it was spectacular."

Charlotte gasped. "How can war be spectacular?"

"A bad choice of words on my part."

"You are forgiven, Blaine McKenna."

"I thank you. I should have written to you. I'm sorry for that too."

"A letter would have put me at ease. . . . I would have known you were safe. What happened after the war?"

"I apprenticed as a surveyor and a geologist."

Charlotte smiled, glad to be moving away from the topic of soldiering and war.

"So you examine the lay of the land and rocks. How interesting. I don't know how surveying is done exactly, but I've heard it is important for the completion of the canal. Is that what you'll be doing?"

"I've the paper that says I will."

"Is it the reason you didn't go back to Philadelphia?"

He glanced at her with a corner of his mouth lifted in a sad smile. "My only living relatives are here in Goshen, and it is my duty to watch out for them in their old age."

"I feel the same about Uncle Henry."

"I'm not surprised. You were compassionate as a child."

"I've always loved him. He's been a father to me. What about your parents? I don't remember them very well, except your mother had blond hair and was petite."

"They've been gone many years now. I avoid the subject."

"I understand. I don't talk about my mother and father's passing either.

If I do my heart aches."

He touched her shoulder. "Then we won't talk about it."

"Have you any other reason for coming to Goshen Creek?"

"Yes. My aunt wrote and told me about the new doctor and his pretty niece. I saw the name Verger."

Charlotte was at a loss for words. She shut her eyes and reminded herself not to presume too much. Perhaps she and Blaine were only meant to be friends. Anything beyond it would be the grace of God.

"I see. But you must have another reason."

"I accepted a surveyor's job. I really couldn't believe my luck. A good position making a lot of money, my aunt and uncle, and then. . .you, Charlotte."

She smiled. "Frankly, I am amazed at the course of things. We were good friends once. I never thought we would be again."

Blaine nodded. "God does work in mysterious ways, as the preachers tell us."

Charlotte sighed. "You are a mystery to me, Blaine McKenna."

"How so?"

"That you would stop doing whatever it was you were doing, for digging a ditch in the mud. Surely your aunt and uncle told you the stories about the workmen, how they are lawless and vile."

"They can't all be as wicked as you say. I've heard there are godly men and preachers among the boatmen."

"Thank God for those men. I hope they can help the poor orphan boys that come for work. I've been told they are terribly mistreated."

He nodded. "I've heard the stories too. If I should meet any, I will do what I can to help them."

"Bring them here to Goshen Creek. I wager there would be families here that would take them in, or tradesmen that could apprentice them."

Blaine agreed. "I think that is an excellent idea."

A group of people headed their way over the dewy grass. Uncle Henry's stride was forceful, and a lump formed in Charlotte's throat. Could it be he'd give her a tongue-lashing in front of all those people?

"Charlotte Verger, why on earth are you in that tree?"

Charlotte looked down to see her uncle's worried eyes. The McKennas stood beside him. Mrs. McKenna held her hand over her mouth and kept saying, "Dear me. Dear oh dear me."

"I'm admiring the view, Uncle."

"View? There's nothing to see up there that you cannot see from down here."

"I'm also talking with Mr. McKenna. We were childhood friends in Philadelphia."

"Mr. McKenna, I am appalled you would allow my niece to climb a tree."

"He didn't allow me to climb it, Uncle," Charlotte said. "He pulled me up when I asked him to."

"Disgraceful."

She leaned forward. "Have I caused a scandal?"

"You've caused me and the McKennas to worry. You could fall and break a bone." He shook his gray head. "And besides, it is unseemly. A grown woman your age up in a tree."

"I suppose it is, Uncle. The view is quite nice though." She giggled and her uncle's stern face softened. He stared at her a moment as she kicked out her feet. Then a smile crept slowly over his face and his anger relented.

"You think it's funny, Charlotte?"

"I mean no disrespect, Uncle Henry. But how you put it is. 'A grown woman your age up in a tree.'"

Uncle Henry waved his hand at her. "Come down from there at once."

"I can't," she said. "I'm afraid I might tear my dress."

"Charlotte, you are being an imp."

"Don't be harsh on Charlotte, Dr. Verger. I blame my nephew." Blaine's uncle stepped forward. "Blaine, bring the lady down. You should know better than to engage in such folly."

Blaine swung under the branch and landed on his feet. He held his arms up to Charlotte and she dropped into them. Strange, how comfortable she felt with him. Once more, it seemed as if they had never separated.

Uncle Henry shook his finger at her. "Do not do that again, Charlotte."

She put her head on his shoulder. "Never?"

"Besides a broken bone, you could have fallen and been made black and blue. And yes, you could have torn your dress, and don't think I would have put out good money for another." He held her at arm's length. "What convinced you to do such a thing? You know it is dangerous for a girl."

She blinked up at him. "I cannot say, and why is it dangerous for a girl?"

"Strength, Charlotte. Strength. Besides, it is a show of poor conduct."

Although his face had softened and his anger abated, Charlotte knew her uncle meant every word. "I'm sorry. It was unladylike of me. I will try to be more restrained."

Uncle Henry huffed. "Poor Mrs. McKenna is wrecked by this nonsense. And you, Blaine, can you not see what this has done to your aunt?"

Blaine kissed his aunt's cheek. "No harm done, was there, Aunt?"

She shook her head. "None to you, Blaine. As for Charlotte, tongues have already started wagging."

Charlotte walked over to the frazzled Mrs. McKenna. "Try not to feel distressed, dear Mrs. McKenna."

Mrs. McKenna blew into her handkerchief. "I can't help it. My nephew drew you up into a tree. We may be rustics, but we are civilized."

Charlotte glanced over her shoulder. Blaine gave her an apologetic grin. Then he went over to Uncle Henry and held out his hand. Uncle Henry took it, looking a bit reluctant.

She heard him say, "Sir, I'll never give Charlotte aid to climb a tree again. Please accept my apology."

"No more adventures of this sort, Blaine McKenna?"

"No, sir."

Uncle Henry strode off with the others, but Charlotte lingered and shot Blaine a frown. "How disappointing. No adventures at all?" she said. "How can anyone live without some adventure from time to time?"

A corner of Blaine's mouth curved into that mischievous grin she remembered. Not even a yard away, she pledged she'd put him to the test.

Chapter 4

The daily routine of Charlotte's life changed from the leisurely pace of the city to collecting eggs in the chicken coop behind the house, early mornings making breakfast, and sweeping and cleaning. A week had gone by since that night at the dance when she met Blaine again. They had seen each other every day, always in the presence of others, and she felt Uncle Henry had been keeping a keen eye on her, that she would act like a lady and not endeavor to find adventure in childish ways.

A new dawn rose with a heavy breeze, and she woke to a red rooster sitting on her windowsill. He crowed and flapped his wings. She rubbed her eyes, stretched her arms over her head, and yawned. Sitting up on her elbows, she frowned at the disruptive fowl. "Go away," she said. "Haven't you something better to do than to wake me?"

Robin scampered into the room and leaped up at the bird. It fluttered off with a squawk.

Charlotte lay back and thought on the dream she'd had. Blaine—it had been about him, and she could still see in her mind his handsome face.

"Lord, I never would have thought to see Blaine again, especially here in Goshen Creek. I thought he had gone away forever. I still love him, You know. So, if this is Your will, then I accept this love with great joy."

Outside the window, she heard someone whistling. She rose and donned her robe then looked out beyond the lilac tree. The same boy who had rallied the sow and her piglets the night of the dance raised his hat to her and smiled. "Good morning, Miss Charlotte."

"Good morning to you, Bobby Blakely. On your way to the schoolhouse?"

"Yes, ma'am, but I was given a penny to bring you this note." He handed it up to her, tipped his hat, and scampered off.

Blaine's handwriting had not changed. She recognized it immediately. Her heart quivered as she read the note, which was not what poets would call a love letter. Simple words said much to Charlotte.

Don't leave home.

You left your shawl at the house and I'm bringing it to you.

She sighed happily. Then she scolded herself. She'd left the shawl on purpose when she'd been invited to make apple jam with Mrs. McKenna and her friends. She left it on the table as she exited the house, knowing Blaine would be returning that night after surveying the land for the canal the last few days. Mrs. McKenna had called out to her that she'd left it. "Would you mind asking your nephew to return it to me?" Charlotte replied.

Mrs. McKenna gave her a perceptive look. "He's expected home tonight. I'll ask him first thing in the morning."

Charlotte had walked home with anticipation. President James Madison's war had torn them apart, but the years since seemed merely a flash of time. Had Blaine truly been in love with her, the kind of love where a man is swept away with a fierce passion that gives him no rest, or had she just been a fancy?

That morning, she waited on her front porch step with Robin beside her. She missed the scent of the lilac bush. The blooms had faded and the bush was now bright green and sprouting new branches. The hens made a racket in the small yard in the rear. Charlotte, chin in hand, looked up at the slow-moving cumulus clouds and sighed.

Her hair blew around her face as the wind picked up. There were no storm clouds in the sky, not the ones of deep grays and blues. Only the mounting white thunderheads against a cobalt sky.

The wind whirled translucent billows of dust off the road that tarnished leaf and blade. She raised her hand above her eyes when a figure came through it. His clothes were grimy. His untidy hair, tied back with a leather cord. His beard hung down his chest. He had an unsteady gait, although he held a walking pole for balance.

Many a woman would have fled inside the safety of their home. But not Charlotte. She remained where she was, set her hand against a post, and watched with a curious mind this person who looked like no one she'd ever seen.

When he reached the house, he looked at her and swept off his hat. "Pray, is there an inn or tavern hereabouts where a poor fellow like me might find a place to lay his head for the night?"

"There is a miller's house a mile south on the road, sir, whose good wife offers rooms to travelers."

"Ah, with my leg the way it be, another mile 'tis too far for me to walk."

Charlotte glanced down at the twisted foot. "How did it happen?"

"Born with it," he said, his scraggly brows lifting high on his forehead.

"How far have you come?"

"I cannot say. But I know it be miles and miles."

"From where have you come?"

"I've been wandering all my life. I don't know where I was born."

"I would guess you are a workman on one of the canal's boats, or on the building of it."

"Aye. Grown tired of the diggin'. I'm looking for another way to acquire money." He scratched incessantly. Fleas. Maybe a rash.

"I'd say you are in need of a bath and a good barber, sir."

He combed his fingers through his beard. "I'll not have a barber touch this lovely beard of mine. Took a long time to grow. But a scrubbing of me skin with grit and lye, I agree I need."

Charlotte tilted her head. "Who are you?"

"Don't matter. Besides, I suppose you've never heard of me. Name is Hatch."

Charlotte shook her head. He pulled at the shoulder of his coat and coughed. Compassionate and one to see the best in people, Charlotte stepped forward. "Are you unwell? My uncle is the doctor here."

"It's the dust."

"Are you hungry, Mr. Hatch?"

His eyes were glassy. He glanced around the empty street then back at her. "You wouldn't have a crust of bread to spare, now would ya?"

"I've more than a crust," she said. "Wait here." She headed to the front door. When she pulled it open, Hatch had come up the steps.

"Is the good doctor in, miss?"

"He is visiting a patient but will be back any minute now. And I'm expecting a visitor. Wait here and I'll get you a plate of food."

Hatch gripped the brim of his hat. She saw his face more closely. Deep wrinkles crisscrossed his cheeks and the corners of his eyes. Sparse hair hung in threads about his head. His lips were thin and cracked, with stained teeth widely spaced. All from being a hungry vagabond, thought Charlotte.

He slapped his hand against the door and moved in. She moved back.

"It be so hot, I'd welcome the shade of your home. You wouldn't want a poor stranger to eat on the steps or sit on the street to eat in the hot sun, would you? The Christian thing would be to let me sit at a table in a proper chair."

He walked past her into the main room and looked around. "Anyone else here with you, a husband or father?"

She hesitated. A sense she had made a terrible mistake overcame her. "I'll get some bread for you. You sit over there." He glanced at the chair and hobbled over to it. Charlotte placed two slices on a plate and poured cider into a tin cup. She brought it to him. He snatched the bread and devoured it as if it were his last meal.

Wiping his mouth with his sleeve, he looked at her with his head bowed. A dark light filled those eyes—salacious desire flooded them. "So you've no man here?"

"I live with my uncle."

Hatch looked around. "I don't see him."

"I told you, he will be back soon."

Hatch set the mug down and stood.

"You should go now," Charlotte told him.

She turned to the door. Hatch reached out and grabbed her arm. "I'm in no hurry."

"Let go of me!" She shook free of him and hurried behind one of the ladder-back chairs.

"Don't be a'feared."

"Go away!"

"I can't. It's been a long time since I saw somethin' as pretty as you."

"I don't doubt it. You look like you've lived in the forest most of your life."

"Don't be cruel. Give this poor fellow a kiss."

"You really think I would?"

"I've had women tell me I kiss best." He followed her around the table.

"I doubt what you say, Mr. Hatch."

He placed his hand over his heart. "You cut me to the quick, missy. Still, I'll have that kiss. Give it to me, and I'll go."

Hatch rushed at Charlotte and she ran to the door. Laughing, he twisted her around to face him. His hot heavy breath reeked.

"On my word, you need a bath and some toothpowder."

"If you got toothpowder, I'll use it and then kiss ya."

A shadow fell across the floor, and when Hatch pressed his pursed, cracked lips on Charlotte, a hand grabbed him from behind and tossed him back. Hatch rolled over the floor. Dazed by the blow, stunned and blinking up at Blaine with small beady eyes, he rubbed his jaw and scrambled to his feet. Placing his boot on the man's backside, Blaine pushed Hatch out the door.

Hatch stumbled across the porch and down the steps. He glared at the pair in the doorway, squashed his hat down, and then hurried away.

Blaine turned to face Charlotte. She pressed her back against the doorjamb, her breath heaving, one hand against her throat.

"Did he hurt you?"

"He frightened me some, that's all."

Blaine touched her cheek. "You might want to wash that kiss off."

Charlotte touched her cheek. She turned back inside and splashed water over her face. Then she dried it with her apron. "I'll never trust another vagrant for as long as I live. I fear to think what would have happened if you hadn't come when you did."

"You would have made him sorry, I'm sure."

"I was prepared to, if I could have gotten my hands on something."

"There'll be other homeless people in your lifetime. You don't have to trust them all, just treat them well. . .and have me with you."

Blaine reached inside his waistcoat and pulled out her shawl. Charlotte thanked him with a smile as he wrapped it over her shoulders. "You look pretty in this color," he said.

"For your service to me, sir, you will stay for dinner, won't you?"

"I'll stay for as long as you wish me to."

They looked at each other for what seemed several seconds.

"I will not feel at ease if you leave," Charlotte said, her voice soft and quiet.

"He won't be back, Charlotte."

"Will you go again tomorrow?"

"Yes. This time for two days."

"Two whole days. I'll be waiting here for you when you get back."

Blaine's gaze softened, and he lifted her hands to his lips and kissed them.

Chapter 5

Charlotte strolled out onto the porch and glanced up at a pale moon as it rose above the treetops. Two days had gone by, her longing for Blaine growing with each tick of the clock.

Goshen Creek flowed on the east side of the village. Smooth round stones made up the bottom, and the current swirled over deep pools. The bank had grown thick with grass and moss. Weeping willow trees shaded the water, their leaves moving like bird feathers in the breeze. Charlotte set her hand against one and listened to the water tumbling over the rocks. With another hour until nightfall, she had no reason to hurry home. The day's chores were over. Her uncle had no need of her.

She sat on a patch of grass above the creek, slipped off her shoes, and dipped her feet into the water. Footsteps broke the twigs over the path. Instantly, Charlotte turned her head. Her emotions rose higher when she saw Blaine drawing near. He had yet to see her. She pulled her feet from the water and pushed the hem of her dress over them.

"Here I am, Blaine," she said. "Have you been looking for me?"

He smiled and pulled off his hat. "I have, you dear girl."

"Aren't you the smart one to have found me?"

"Nothing smart about it. I asked your uncle, and he said you were out for a walk by the creek."

She drew her shoes back on. "It's all right if you want to sit beside me."

"Good, because I have something I want to give you." He stretched out on the grass and reached inside his pocket. Then he reached for her hand, held it a moment, and placed the gift in it.

Charlotte stared at a radiant cluster of purple crystals surrounded by white ones. "What is it?"

"An amethyst geode."

"I've never seen anything so beautiful."

"It's yours to keep—if you want it."

She looked at him wide-eyed. "Of course I want it. Purple is one of my favorite colors. I bet it looks lovely when sunlight falls on it. Thank you, Blaine."

"I hoped you would like it. It came from Uruguay."

"Surely you did not go all that way to find this."

He smiled. "No, I bought it in the city. That's what geologists do, you know. We collect rocks."

"But this is more than a rock. It's a gem, isn't it?"

"The amethyst, yes, but it's nowhere near as valuable as a diamond or ruby. Amethyst would make a pretty ring, don't you think?"

Her heart pounded. "Yes, a beautiful ring."

He drew her close. "Charlotte, I have to leave soon."

That old sensation of missing him returned. It began with a thud in her chest then a chill up her arms, and her throat tightened. If he were to go, she feared he'd never come back. He might be led somewhere else—or he could fall victim to the fevers that befell the canal diggers. Mud, water, infestations of mosquitoes and flies, poor living conditions, and bad food.

"You'll be back, won't you?"

"Of course I will." He kissed the top of her head.

She looked away, her eyes filling with tears. "Why leave at all?"

"I must make a living. It's not forever. The canal will be finished, and I'll settle here."

"Goshen is a good place to live—a good place to raise a family."

"Are you crying?" He turned her face to his.

"I cannot help it." She wiped her eyes.

"I promise I'll come back." He got on his knees and took her hands in his. "Stand up."

"Why?"

"Please, Charlotte."

Shakily, Charlotte stood. "What are you doing, Blaine?"

"I'm proposing."

She drew in a breath and waited.

"I'm not good at words. I'm no poet. But I can say, Charlotte Verger, I adore you. I love you, and I want to spend the rest of my life with you. Will you be my wife?"

His words gave her pause to consider—to reflect on how in love with Blaine she was, and how deep the secrets of love were.

"Blaine. . ."

"Will you?"

"Yes. Yes, I will."

He leaped up, leaned in, and kissed her. "You think that geode was all I'd give you? Here." He slipped a ring over her finger. "Will this do?"

She gasped at the cut amethyst stone set in silver. "Oh. . .it is beautiful." She held her hand out to catch the moonlight. "There are no craftsmen here. How did you. . . ?"

"I had the whole thing planned out."

She looked up into his face. "For how long?"

"From the day I left for the fighting. I didn't have the courage then to ask you to marry a soldier, and your father would not have allowed me through the door, let alone approved of my asking for your hand. I might not have come back, and you would have been left a widow."

She put her arms around him and pressed her cheek to his. "I would have married you then if you had asked me."

"I still have to ask your uncle for permission," he said. "I'll prove to him that I'm making my fortune and will take good care of you."

She looked up into his eyes. "I know he will be pleased. My uncle likes you. . . even through you made me do something unthinkable."

He gave her a questioning look. "And what was that?"

"You haven't forgotten you pulled me up into a tree and sat me next to you, have you? And you promised my uncle you would never to do it again. Uncle Henry respects a man of his word."

When he wrapped her in his arms and held her close, Blaine kissed Charlotte long and soft, causing her to dream of more.

◆———◆

The following morning, Charlotte waited outside the gate for Blaine. He rode his horse up to her and drew rein. "Take this, Blaine." She handed him a sack. "No one can tell me that camp corn bread is better than mine."

Blaine's eyes, bright with hope for their future, held Charlotte's, as if to burn her image in his mind. Her heart warmed, returning the emotion she read in them. "We are always parting," he said. "One day, it will not be so."

"Can't I go with you? I could cook and wash your clothes. I've been told there are women among the laborers."

"A few, but it's no place for you, Charlotte. Trust me."

"Why? Because of all the mud and that I'd have to live in a tent? I'm not afraid of those things. I can handle it as well as any man."

"Must we argue as I'm leaving?"

She kept her eyes engaged on his with the desire to keep this moment of parting fixed in her mind. He looked noble upon a horse, and she wished he would reach down and pull her up behind him.

"It is the last thing I want to do."

He leaned down in the saddle. "Come here. Take my hand."

She went to him, and he did as she had hoped.

"I'll take you with me as far as the bridge."

Content, Charlotte wrapped her arms around Blaine's waist and laid her head against his back. He clicked his tongue and the horse walked on.

Neither spoke as they rode away from the village, over the dusty road, and then onto a path that ran alongside the creek. A bridge made of birch logs crossed it, and Blaine reined in his horse.

Blaine turned in the saddle and kissed Charlotte goodbye.

"Be safe," she said. "Come back to me."

He kissed her hand and then helped her down. With her heart aching, Charlotte watched him tuck his heels into the horse's ribs and ride off. She stood silent and motionless until she could see him no more.

Uncle Henry patted Charlotte's shoulder. "Don't worry, dear girl. Blaine will be back."

"Yes, I know he will. Time will go by quickly if I keep busy."

"I will give you a list of summer herbs to gather. That should keep you occupied."

She turned to him. "Blaine says he should not be gone too long before he visits home. Fall will come and then winter. Surely they cannot dig the swamp when the snow comes."

"You are so right, Charlotte." Uncle Henry walked with Charlotte toward the front door. "It all depends on that wearisome canal. If it gives them trouble, the work will take longer."

He checked his watch. "I haven't had breakfast, and my stomach is making enough noise to make the hens nervous."

"Oh, my poor uncle." Charlotte slipped her arm through his. "Forgive me. I was so focused on seeing Blaine away, I delayed breakfast."

"And so you should. You love him, don't you?"

"You know I do."

"Well," he said, "we shall have a doozy of a wedding when he returns. Mrs. McKenna told me she is anxious to make wedding plans with you."

Charlotte breathed a sigh of gladness, leaned up, and kissed his cheek. "My life would be empty without people like you and Mrs. McKenna."

"Not as empty as my stomach." He laughed and patted his belly.

Chapter 6

Charlotte strolled along the road toward home. In her hand, she carried a basket filled with herbs. A chilly October caused them to wither and dry in the open meadows and along hedgerows. Wild chamomile. Burdock. Hyssop and goldenrod.

A man on a mule came around the curve and lifted his hand to her. He kicked the mule's sides to hurry it along, which did no good. The wretched animal staggered back and then forward again at the same lazy speed it had before. He turned the mule to the side of the road and doffed an old tricorn hat to acknowledge her.

"Good morning, miss."

"And to you, sir." She stood back, not forgetting the stranger that had been so bold to accost her.

"Mighty hot today. Would you have a cup of water to spare?"

"I have plenty, sir, but if you would prefer some cold cider, we have a small barrelful."

"Sounds delightful. I'd be most grateful for some."

He dismounted and looped the reins of the mule around a tree limb. "I shall remain here with my mule. It's only proper, and my boots are caked with mud."

Charlotte left him and returned with a pitcher. She filled a tin cup with the cider and handed it to him. "You're kind, miss. My throat is near parched." He drank it down at once then wiped his mouth with his sleeve.

Charlotte held out the pitcher. "More?"

He held out the tin cup. "Thank you, miss."

"Your poor mule looks the worse for wear. There is a watering trough over there."

The man glanced in the direction of her eyes. "Poor ol' beast. I forced him to a gallop more than once today, which he loathes, being bred to pull a wagon and a plow."

"Where are you headed?"

"This is Goshen Creek, isn't it?"

"That's right. Do you have family here?"

"Nope. Got a wife up there along Nine Mile Creek. I've come to find a doctor. Is there one here?"

"Yes, he's my uncle. Dr. Verger."

"I need to speak to him right away, miss."

Uncle Henry's shadow spread over the grass near Charlotte's feet. He stopped and looked at the man, drawing off his spectacles and then looking at the sooty mule behind him.

The man gave a slight bow. "Dr. Verger, I presume?"

"I am he, and you are?"

"Ralph Blaylock, sir. I need to speak to you. It's urgent."

"Certainly. Come into my surgery, and I'll treat whatever ails you."

"Nothing ails me, sir, except my heart." Blaylock slapped his hand over his chest.

"Your heart? I am concerned, Mr. Blaylock. Are you in pain? Are you out of breath?"

"Sir, my heart laments for my friends working on the canal at Montezuma Swamp. I've left my shovel and pic to bring you a message, then I'm on my way back to my wife, like I was telling this young lady. I'm done with digging Clinton's Ditch."

A thrill claimed Charlotte's heart that he had brought a letter from her beloved. She took a step forward, anxious and holding out her hand to take hold of the missive. "Have you brought a letter from my fiancé Blaine McKenna? He is working as a surveyor there."

"I'm not a mail carrier, miss. Can't say I remember hearing your fella's name."

Her heart sank to the soles of her shoes. "Please, will you look just in case you've forgotten he gave it to you? If he knew you were coming here, I know he would not have missed the chance to send a letter. It would be addressed to Charlotte Verger at Goshen Creek."

"Sure, miss. I'll do it only to satisfy you. Maybe he slipped it in and I didn't notice."

Blaylock rummaged, with brows bent, through his saddlebag. He looked at her. "Sorry. As I said, no one gave me any letters. I'm not a mail carrier."

Charlotte lowered her eyes. "I'm sorry to have troubled you, Mr. Blaylock. If there is nothing else, I'll go inside. I wish you well on your journey home."

She glanced at her uncle. He looked worried. His brows were pinched together and his mouth turned down. His eyes were fixed on Blaylock. "I think you should stay and hear what news this man brings, Charlotte."

Charlotte looked curiously at Blaylock as he searched his pockets. She set her hand over her uncle's arm. He took in an impatient breath. "Well? We haven't all day, man."

Voices and footsteps drew their attention. A crowd of men walked toward them. Alongside the men were their wives and children.

"Word gets out fast around here," Blaylock said. "They must think like you, miss, that I'm a mail carrier."

"Do you blame them? Letters and news are not a daily occurrence," Charlotte said.

Blaylock shook his head. "Sorry to disappoint them."

Charlotte frowned. "This is exasperating."

"Is someone sick from our village?" Uncle Henry asked.

Blaylock continued to search his pockets. Charlotte wished she could set aside all ladylikeness and shake his news out of him. Instead, she grabbed the mug from his hand and set it on the gatepost. "Not another drop until you tell us what has happened."

Uncle Henry pulled Blaylock forward. "Tell us before the people reach you, Blaylock. If it is bad news, I'll be able to calm them along with our minister. Stop delaying."

Blaylock shoved his hat on and kept his eyes fixed on the crowd. "There was a man down the road a piece. I spoke to him, told him I was looking for the doctor hereabouts. He said he was from Goshen and that a doctor resided in the village. Must have told his wife I was coming into town to find you, Dr. Verger."

"You told me you are not ill or injured. Why do you need me?" Uncle Henry's tone grew more and more stern.

Blaylock drew a paper from his pocket and handed it to Uncle Henry. "There's an outbreak of fever in Montezuma Swamp. Lots of men are very sick. It says so on that paper."

"How many men?"

"Hard to say. Hundreds it seems. Some threw down their shovels and pics and left out of fear. The ones that stayed are doing what they can to help the sick."

Uncle Henry thrust out his hands. "God help them. Why did they wait this long to send for help? The fever has spread to proportions I cannot imagine. Even if you find more doctors, this is an epidemic that is out of control."

Charlotte drew back and looked at her uncle. Her mind reeled with images of the man she loved lying sick in some awful place of dirt, mud, and foul water, stricken with fever, sweat pouring over his face, his body trembling with chills.

She turned to her uncle and set her hand on his arm. "I must go to Blaine, Uncle."

"Charlotte, you must try to be calm."

"How can I? I must go to him at once."

"I will not have it. You are to stay home."

Blaylock gave Charlotte a sympathetic look. "I'm sorry if I've caused you distress, Miss Charlotte."

She glanced at him. "My distress is not your fault. I'm grateful you've come to tell us what has happened and to find my uncle."

What else could she say? Raging thoughts poured through her mind, and visions of Blaine and the others suffering—even dying. She wanted to burst into tears and cry out, her eyes burning for release. Yet, for her uncle's sake, she strove to do as he asked. To stay calm. Staying home was a different matter.

Blaylock put his hat on and pushed back the brim from his forehead. Before he could say another word, the crowd overwhelmed the poor fellow. They all began talking at once, asking for letters, for word elsewhere, for news.

"Check your bag, man."

"Yes, look for a letter from Syracuse. It'll be for me."

"I'm not a mail carrier, people." Frustrated, he slammed his hat onto the road. "I've got nothing for any of you folks."

"Well then, have you news to tell?"

His face paled. Charlotte could see he was truly afraid to speak the truth to the anxious citizens of Goshen. She too wondered how they would react. The women would cry, causing their babes to cry with them. The men would be distraught and look to Uncle Henry to save their friends and relations working at Montezuma. Her eyes shifted to Reverend McKenna. His gaze spoke of knowing ill news had come, mingled with compassion and the need to comfort the people.

"News? Well," Blaylock began, "it's nothing like what's going on over there in Europe. Or what ails the king in England. I don't suppose folks in this neck of the woods care about those sorts of things."

"No, we don't!" a man cried.

One of the oldest citizens said, "We fought a revolution and another war that put kings and lords out of our minds."

Blaylock stuck out his bristly chin. "Good, 'cause I ain't got any news on them to tell. I've come to talk to Dr. Verger, but I guess since you're all here, I might as well tell you people, work has slowed on Clinton's Ditch. If you've got menfolk out at Montezuma Swamp, don't expect them home anytime soon."

With creased brows, Reverend McKenna stepped forward with his wife. "That's where our nephew has gone. He told us it'd be rough going."

"You're right about that." Blaylock spread out his arms. "Twelve long miles by eight of nothing but swamp water and mud. Sometimes the mud is up to the men's knees, it's so deep. I've seen skeeters the size of bumblebees out there."

"Mosquitoes the size of bumblebees? That's impossible," said the reverend. Everyone agreed with a nod.

"It's true, sir." Blaylock squinted. "I've seen them with my own eyes, the bloodsuckers."

"Tell them, Blaylock, what has happened. Stop this stalling, or I'll speak up," Uncle Henry said.

"Yes, be plain, man," said Reverend McKenna. "You keep beating around the bush."

Charlotte slipped beside Blaine's aunt. Mrs. McKenna looked at Charlotte and grabbed her hand. Blaylock crinkled his face. "Hmm, I'd frighten the ladies if I were to say."

Uncle Henry picked up Blaylock's hat and smacked it against the man's chest. "You cannot hide the truth from the people here. What you would tell me, I would soon need to tell them. So tell us all you know."

The crowd moved closer. Their faces were as anxious as Charlotte's. Were their hearts beating as fast? Her uncle looked controlled, cool, and put his hands on his hips. The rooster from the coop fluttered with an effort up onto the branch of the tree and crowed. The sound startled a few women, and for no obvious reason, it brought tears to their eyes. Charlotte knew they'd heard bad news before, and that their nerves were on tenterhooks. Mrs. McKenna drew out a handkerchief from her sleeve and wiped her nose.

Blaylock put his boot up on a stump on the side of the road. "I've this paper here written by one of the supervisors—gave it to the doc. Says they need doctors right away. The men are sick." His expression turned serious, his mouth curved down. "Several days ago, some fellows started feeling poorly. By the time the sun went down, they started having chills and fevers. They complained their heads hurt. After two days, some men turned the strangest color yellow you'd ever see—almost like the color of cornmeal. When night fell, men were laid up and having the worst troubles. Excuse me, ladies, for the details, but I got to tell it like it is so the good doctor knows."

Charlotte gripped her hands tight. With this many men sick, Blaine had to be among them.

"What other symptoms do they have?" Uncle Henry asked.

"They can't keep anything in their stomachs. They're plagued with fever and pain. Some have gone into a deep sleep. Some have passed on, though I can't say how many."

Uncle Henry looked somber. The crowd watched him, their faces wracked with worry.

"What does this tell you, Henry?" asked Reverend McKenna. "Could it spread here?"

"Could it be yellow fever?" Mrs. McKenna asked.

The crowd gasped and murmured. Uncle Henry looked around at them.

"Chances are it is malaria, which is rampant along the canal. You must all take precautions."

"What kind, Doctor? This man may have already exposed us to the sickness."

He held up his hands for calm. "You mustn't panic. What I recommend is that you keep your skin covered and apply a repellent. I have a supply of eucalyptus and lemon ointments in my surgery. My niece will give it out to each family."

An elder shook his head. "I've seen malaria. Bad business."

A few women began to weep.

"But, Dr. Verger, aren't we far enough away from such an epidemic?" asked a mother with her four children huddled around her skirts.

The reverend spoke. "Do not fear. We are miles from the swamp and surely in no real danger. However, we must listen and follow the good doctor's advice. We can thank Almighty God for it, and pray for the afflicted."

Uncle Henry thanked Reverend McKenna. "Ladies, take your children home and carry on as normal. Men, come to the surgery, and Charlotte shall give you a supply of ointment for each family."

Charlotte turned to Uncle Henry. "Will you go?"

He glanced at her, his eyes keen and intense with a worried light. "I will." He turned to Blaylock. "Mr. Blaylock, it would be best for you to go home to your wife. Send word to every town and village you pass that doctors are urgently needed at Montezuma."

Blaylock nodded, got into his saddle, and rode away. The mule moved slow and weary until the reins stung his hide and caused him to pick up his pace.

Uncle Henry moved into the crowd. They parted for him. Desperate looks were on their faces.

"I won't shield any of you in Goshen. This is serious. Men will die. I won't be able to save them all. Hopefully other doctors, though we are few in this part of the state, will go to the camp."

He turned to Charlotte and the McKennas. Charlotte stood in front of him, inwardly shivering and frightened for Blaine. She clutched her fists and pressed them against her stomach in an attempt to quiet her breathing. The people were volleying more questions at her uncle. She strained to listen to his replies. Finally, he took her by the shoulders and turned her and the McKennas aside.

"If I find Blaine, I'll get him home. If he is sick and cannot be moved, I'll do my best to bring him through the illness." He looked at their worried faces. "All I ask is that you be patient. . .and pray."

Reverend McKenna held his wife's hand. "I will go with you, Henry."

Uncle Henry nodded. "I'm glad for it. There will be men in need of you."

Chapter 7

U ncle Henry, please wait." Charlotte followed him up the steps and into the house. "I want to do something to help. I want to come with you."

"Give out the ointments, Charlotte." Inside the house, he headed up the flight of stairs to the small room that held his bed and trunk. "I'll only need one change of clothes. Help me pack."

She opened the trunk lid. "No, niece. I must use the leather valise."

Charlotte closed the lid and slipped the valise out from under the bed. She went to his dresser and pulled out two shirts. "You will need more than one shirt, Uncle, and a pair of woolen socks."

"Pack what you see fit, my dear, but not too much." Uncle Henry went to the bedroom door and stepped out into the hallway. "I'll be in the surgery, gathering what I need."

"I think there is plenty I could do if you just let me come with you," she said.

Uncle Henry looked back at her. "You cannot change my mind, Charlotte."

"Why not?" She shoved the socks into the valise. "I've helped you in the surgery, and I have skills."

"This is different."

"I need to go with you, Uncle."

"You need to stay home. I've told you, Montezuma is no place for a woman."

She went to him and put her arms around his neck, hoping her charming demeanor would soften him. "Please, Uncle. You know how capable I am. Besides, who will look after you?"

He sighed and brought her arms down. "Try to understand, dear girl. If anything were to happen to you, it would break my heart. I made a promise to your mother and my brother that I would protect you at all costs. Now, be a good girl and do as I say."

"Blaine might be among the sick, and I should go to him."

"Charlotte."

"I'll follow you on foot if I have to."

"No, you will not."

She made a swift turn, her back to him. "How can you refuse me?"

"I must be firm, Charlotte."

"If I were a man, you'd let me come, wouldn't you?"

"But you're not a man. You will stay with Mrs. McKenna. Be a comfort to each other."

He left the room, and Charlotte slipped the strap through the valise buckle and secured it. Then she carried it to the top of the staircase and paused to see his shadow disappearing into the surgery. When she went down the steps, Robin sprang ahead of her. She set the valise by the door and bit her lip, determined to change her uncle's mind. She stepped through the surgery door. Bottles and powders lined a cupboard. The door to it sat open, and on his desk were the remedies for the village. She stood silent and watched him fill his medical bag.

"This should be enough to go around," he told Charlotte. "You will see to it that each family is provided for, won't you?"

She nodded. "Yes, Uncle."

"I doubt the fever will reach this far, but in case there is an outbreak, I'm leaving a portion of Peruvian bark to treat the symptoms. You know how to mix it?"

"Yes, I know how, Uncle." Charlotte could not help but speak soberly.

"You see. You are needed here."

"The women know how to care for their families better than I."

He straightened up and let out a long breath. "All right, Charlotte. If for some reason I should need you, I promise I will send for you. But for now you will stay in Goshen with Mrs. McKenna."

Charlotte stood with her hands at her sides. All the sounds she'd normally hear had hushed and there was a cool breeze coming through the open window. She stared at the floor. She had no thought for anything but Blaine.

Outside the crowd was as her uncle had left them—fixed upon him with somber expressions. One of the villagers held a pair of horses by their bridles. "You take my mare, Dr. Verger, and you my roan, Reverend. Both are strong beasts. They'll get you there and back. You've got some rough places to go through to reach Montezuma."

Reverend McKenna set his hand on the man's shoulder. "Thank you. We'll take good care of them."

"No doubt you will, sir," the man said. "You'll have to take the road to Rome. Then take a packet boat down to Utica. You'll need to continue on horseback from there."

Charlotte sighed. "Such a long journey. Isn't there a faster way?"

"It's the route Blaine McKenna took, miss. He told me himself."

"It is true," said Reverend McKenna. "It is the best route."

Mrs. McKenna stepped up to Uncle Henry. "Be sure my husband eats properly and gets the rest he needs. He tends to go for hours without nourishment or sleep."

"Not to worry, Mrs. McKenna," Uncle Henry replied. "I'll see to it he does."

"And take good care of my nephew. Tell him his aunt is praying for him."

Reverend McKenna climbed into the saddle. "I'm a blessed man to have a wife who cares so much, but worry you should not, my dear. The Lord shall watch over us as He did the children of Israel when the angel of death came upon the Egyptians." He leaned down, took up her hand, and kissed the top of it.

Mrs. Schmidt handed Uncle Henry a sack. "Food to sustain you both on your journey."

Uncle Henry thanked her and then went to Charlotte. He set his hands over her shoulders and she lowered her eyes. "You shan't be angry with me that I've made you stay in Goshen. It is better this way."

He kissed her cheek then set his boot into the stirrup and climbed up into the saddle. He pulled the reins through his hands and moved the horse out onto the road. Helpless to do anything, Charlotte watched the two men ride away under gray clouds. Mrs. McKenna wept, and when Charlotte turned to her, the people walked soberly away.

"Don't cry," she said.

"I cannot help it, Charlotte. Blaine is like a son to me, and if anything should happen to him. . ." She put her handkerchief against her eyes. "I shall waste away with grief."

"As will I. I love him so much."

"I know you do. He has told me his feelings for you, and I am so happy you accepted his proposal." She pulled Charlotte into her arms. "Oh Charlotte. We must pray, and pray hard."

"With every breath, I will." She looked into Mrs. McKenna's face. "And we must think of what Uncle Henry said, that matters may not be as bad as we are thinking. I am worried too, but just because some men have come down with fevers does not mean Blaine has."

Mrs. McKenna nodded. "This is true. But until we receive news, we will be left in the dark."

Charlotte could not prevent the waves of unease that struck her. Released from Mrs. McKenna's hold, she walked with her to the small clapboard house on the edge of the village.

She set her shawl on the table beside the door, the place she had left it before when she hoped Blaine would return it. The windows in the house were open on the first floor. The day had begun hot and muggy. Thunder rumbled to the west. The wind strengthened and the curtains blew back. A soft rain fell.

Mrs. McKenna wrung her hands. "Dear oh dear. They'll be soaked to the bone with this rain. This was not the time for them to go. Dear me, they shall catch their deaths even before they make it to Montezuma."

Charlotte began to shut the windows. "You forget my uncle is an experienced doctor. They won't fall ill."

"I hope you're right, Charlotte. I worry so. I don't know how I shall sleep tonight."

"A mug of warm milk will help you."

Charlotte moved to the next window and shut it tight. For some moments, there was silence in the house save for the tapping of the rain on roof and window. Mrs. McKenna gazed out at the rain.

"It is a hard thing, to wait," Charlotte said.

"It is all we can do, Charlotte. That, and pray."

"Uncle Henry should have let me go with him."

"He was afraid for you."

"He knows I am capable of nursing anyone."

"That may be, dear girl. However, you must think of what you would be exposed to in that camp. So many rough men there. Some would not treat you kindly."

"I've nursed rough men before."

"I doubt you have of this type. You've heard the stories. Some of these canal people are godless and mean-spirited."

"So I have been told so many times since coming here. Mr. Blaylock seemed like a good person. Evasive, but good."

"He is one of few, I have no doubt."

"I am not convinced they're all bad. It is merely an excuse to keep me away."

Mrs. McKenna's brows arched. "On your uncle's part? Surely not. He only wishes to protect you, Charlotte. You can understand that, can't you?"

A tear slid down Charlotte's cheek. Mrs. McKenna went to her and picked up her hand. It gave Charlotte some comfort to know she was not alone in her worries.

"Think about it. There are no women there. Even though many are sick with the fever, there are those who are not. There is no telling what they might try with a woman in their midst."

"I would be with the sick, and not around anyone else. I'm not afraid. I can take care of myself. No one would bother me, knowing I'm nursing, seeing I am with my uncle and the reverend."

Mrs. McKenna scooted closer to Charlotte. "What is done is done. You are here, and here you must stay."

Blaylock's words kept coming back. *"Men have died."* Anguish drove Charlotte to weeping. She laid her head in her arms.

Mrs. McKenna lifted Charlotte's face. "Joy will come out of our sorrow. God will hear from heaven and safeguard Blaine."

Charlotte looked past the rippled window glass, past the rain and the sway of the trees. Her mind locked onto a place a day's journey away, along the canal and a mule-trodden towpath, to rich green woodlands, onto wetlands that bordered brooks and streams—and then to still, standing water, bottomed with mud inches deep.

Chapter 8

A mockingbird in the tree outside the window woke Charlotte the next morning. She threw back the quilt and looked outside. Illuminated clouds piled high over the horizon, signaling afternoon thunderstorms would cross over Goshen. She had slept restlessly—sleeping for brief moments and then waking. Her conscience plagued her. What kind of love was this, if she hadn't the boldness to go to Blaine? She dreamed of soothing his fevered brow, spooning broth into his mouth, comforting him.

The mockingbird stopped singing and flew off. The blacksmith's hammer clanged from his shop. She looked up and asked what was right to do. Would it be wrong to disobey her uncle? Could she remain in Goshen pacing the floors, wringing her hands? Then the urge to go to the blacksmith and speak to him compelled her.

She tiptoed past Mrs. McKenna's bedroom, down the staircase to the front door. Careful to close it without a sound, she turned and looked to see if anyone watched her. With no one in sight she hurried down the street, past the houses where smoke rose from the chimneys for the day's cookery. When she reached home, Robin raced up to her and curled around her legs.

"Hungry?"

He mewed and blinked his green eyes.

She headed inside and gave him a dish of cream. She stroked Robin's ears as he lapped it up and splashed bits of it over his whiskers. She stood and set the empty jug on the table. A wooden box with brass hinges, and a letter sealed with a scarlet wax stamp caught her eye. Taking the letter in hand, she broke the seal and unfolded the page.

Dearest Charlotte,

You will find in the box enough money to keep you while I'm away. I do not know how long I will be gone. There is always the risk I may not return for a long time. Try not to worry. Instead pray that all will go well and that I send home good news.

Charlotte lifted the lid to the box and found several coins inside. "An answer to prayer," she whispered. Tucking the silver inside the pocket of her dress, she headed to her room and packed a change of clothes in her valise, along with the small red leather Bible that had belonged to her mother. She shooed Robin outside and headed down the street. Abel the blacksmith stood in front of his forge hammering down a horseshoe. She paused in front of him.

"Morning, Miss Charlotte. Did you sleep well enough from all the worry you have?" His hammer fell over the iron and made a loud clang.

"I've had a struggle all night, Abel. When I woke, I had the thought to come to you."

He stilled his hammer. "Whatever it is, bring it to me and I'll fix it. Just finished Mrs. Vance's broken kettle. Looks good as new."

Charlotte kept her eyes fixed on the man. "I need something."

"Well, what is it?" He continued in his work, hammering the horseshoe and then dipping it into water. Steam rose.

"I need a horse, a mule, some transportation."

Abel set the horseshoe down and then his hammer. "What's in your mind, Miss Charlotte? Didn't Dr. Verger tell you to stay put?"

"He did, but things have changed. Things are more desperate than we know. I have nursing skills, and the men need me. I must join my uncle, even if I have to walk to the canal and board a packet boat on my own. I'll have to walk the rest of the way. I need a horse."

"I see, and you were hoping I could supply one?"

"You're the one I thought of."

"I suppose you're going to tell me this divinely came to you."

"Whether I do or not, I have no other way to convince you." She stepped closer. "You must help. If not you, I will go to every person in Goshen and ask for a horse."

"You shouldn't be thinking of going to Montezuma, miss. Ask one of the men to go."

"My uncle needs a nurse. He cannot possibly take care of all the sick there. Please, Abel."

Abel scratched his beard. "I've got a good horse. What are you willing to pay?"

"You won't loan him to me?"

Abel pursed his lips. "I don't want money, Miss Charlotte."

"Then what do you want?"

"A pie."

"Pie?"

"Yes, pie. I want an apple pie big enough for two men."

"You shall have it, and if you like my baking, I'll make you another. Just let me have your horse. I promise to bring him back."

He made a motion with his head for her to follow him. Indeed, his horse proved to be a sturdy one with a shiny coat and broad neck. A white streak went from between his ears down to his nose. "You take care of Danny," Abel said. "And you put him in a good packet boat, not one that'll overcharge you. Bet you didn't think you'd need money for that." He dug into his pocket beneath his apron. "Here, this should do it."

Charlotte ran her hand down the horse's nose and it made a low grunt in his throat. She turned to Abel with the urge to throw her arms around him. She hesitated, but did so, and he laughed. "Thank you, Abel. God bless you."

He saddled the gentle steed then helped her into the saddle. "Godspeed, Miss Charlotte. If you're lucky, you might catch up with the doctor and reverend. The rain may have slowed them down."

She gathered up the reins and brought the horse out into the road. Mrs. McKenna came out of her house and called out in a frantic voice, "Charlotte, where are you going?"

"To Montezuma, Mrs. McKenna. To the swamp and Blaine."

She kicked the sides of the horse and it moved into a gallop, under a wind that pushed away the storm clouds and opened up an azure sky.

⫘————⫘

Charlotte had little to eat during her long ride from Goshen Creek to Rome into the early afternoon. She drew rein alongside a lush meadow and rested Danny. Sitting beneath a willow, she staved off much of her hunger with the bits of hardtack she had brought but knew it wouldn't last. She carried on, moving the horse into a canter. Her body ached as the hours stretched on. She hoped to make it to Utica before the sun skimmed along the ridges in the distance.

When Charlotte reached the canal towpath, she reined in her horse and looked up and down the canal. Several packet boats were moored and there were people mingling about, with animals, goods, and crates. A young boy brushed down the coat of a mule hitched to another. An orphan, no doubt, who had traveled a long way to find work. Charlotte clicked her tongue and walked her horse over to him.

"Excuse me, but can you tell me which of these boats has room for me and this horse?"

"There's that big one over there, miss. She's a seventy-footer. I heard the captain say he had room."

"You have my thanks." She handed him a few pennies and moved on.

Her horse insisted on eating grass, and she shook the reins. "Come on." She clicked her tongue and punched his ribs with her heels. Danny shook his shaggy mane and then lumbered on toward the large packet boat. Charlotte dismounted alongside the vessel. A man, she assumed to be its captain, leaned against a barrel. Smoking a long pipe, he drew it from his mouth and looked at her.

"Are you the captain?" Charlotte asked.

"I'm he. You need passage?"

"Yes, sir, for me and my horse."

"To where?"

"As far as you can take me, then I will ride to Montezuma."

He frowned. "What you want to do that for? We hear there's swamp fever in that camp. You ain't one of those women that. . ."

She thrust out her chin. "No, I am not. I'm going there to assist my uncle, a physician."

"Oh, I see. Didn't mean to offend."

"I'm sure you didn't. Is your packet swift?"

"It's more comfortable and faster than traveling overland. This ole girl will cut your travel in half, especially with the rain we've had. We go as far as Utica."

"Do you know of anyone who escorts people west from there?"

He shook his head. "Can't say as I do."

"How much is the fare, sir?"

"Show me what you can spare."

She reached into her bag and showed him all the coins she had. "It's everything."

"Hmm. You say you're going to the swamp to help the sick?"

"It is my intention."

"Well, tell you what. I got plenty of passengers to keep me well enough. I'll take you on for nothing. I'll just have you pay for any oats or hay your horse gobbles up."

A smile burst across Charlotte's face. "You are too kind, sir. Still, I cannot take charity. . . ."

"I got a rule, young woman. No one argues with the captain of this boat."

"All right, but if there is some work I can do to repay you. . ."

He gave her a shake of his head and a grin. "You can board now. I'll have one of my crewmen take care of your horse."

"Thank you, sir." Charlotte glanced over at the boat.

"I got a cow in there, but I don't think she'll mind the company."

"He will be safe, I mean, he won't be bothered by the movement of the boat, will he?"

"I've never had a problem before. Oh, and you should go see up top on my boat. We got a rail all along the sides, and there are chairs for passengers. It's very pleasant to ride up there. You can see everything. It's your choice."

Charlotte gripped her horse's bridle. "When do we sail, if that is the proper word?"

The captain pulled out his watch. "I expect we'll be under way in about fifteen minutes. So, choose your place."

He pushed away from the barrel and called his men over. Charlotte thanked the captain and stepped up the gangplank and into the boat. "Up or down, miss?" a crewman asked.

"Oh, down, please. I'm nervous about the roof. I could tip the chair and fall into the canal."

The crewman chuckled. "Never has happened before. The inside is safer though."

He showed her the way in. Pleasantly surprised by the beauty of the wood interior, she took a seat in the rear. Several passengers sat along the benches beneath the windows, some reading newspapers. Tired from the long ride, Charlotte rested her head against the wall and hugged her bag. She hadn't brought much with her except for a bar of lye soap, her brush and comb, and a change of clothes.

A woman near her noticed Charlotte's discomfort. She reached inside her bag and handed her a biscuit. "I have plenty," she said. "Go ahead and take it."

"You are so kind." Charlotte bit into it and her eyes widened. "I must say, your recipe is the best I've ever tasted. I'm so grateful."

"Oh, it's nothing more than butter and flour. You've been traveling a long time?"

"Since this morning from Goshen Creek."

"And where are you headed?"

"To the Montezuma Swamp."

The woman cringed. "Oh, you shouldn't. That's not a good place for a woman, and there is fever there. Our doctor went there to help but returned."

"Why?" Charlotte was appalled a physician would leave the sick, unless he was urgently called home on a desperate family matter.

"He said there was nothing he could do, that the fever had to run its course." The woman leaned in. "I find it cowardly."

"My uncle is a doctor and he's gone too, along with our village's minister. I'm going there to help. I'm trained at nursing and will do a lot of good."

"Dear me, you'll have to travel the rest of the way on foot."

"I have a horse."

"That is better than walking, but still, so dangerous for you to go alone."

Charlotte bit into the biscuit. "I'm not afraid. God is with me."

The woman reached over and patted Charlotte's hand. "Only the daring take such risks. You must take great care of yourself as well."

"I plan to. Thank you for talking to me. I'm feeling a little lost right now."

"I'm going to Utica to visit my sister. You are welcome to come with me and stay the night before you make your journey."

"I am obliged to you. But I must continue on my way."

"But it will be nighttime."

"We are to have a full moon."

"And you depend on that?"

The woman's question caused Charlotte to think. Indeed, traveling on horseback along unfamiliar pathways presented a serious risk. If she took up the offer, it could delay her by hours, maybe even a day. She rallied her courage and graciously answered, "It is a matter of life or death, ma'am."

Other passengers came in and took their seats. The packet boat filled up quickly. Charlotte's eyes widened. She gripped the handle of her valise and sucked in a breath. Coming through the passageway were Uncle Henry and Reverend McKenna.

"Is something wrong, dear?" the woman asked.

Charlotte did not know what to say. "It is very crowded," she said quietly.

"The rain kept us from traveling up the canal last night. The roads were flooded. Wagons and carriages were stuck, and people on horseback had to delay their journeys. I myself came in a stagecoach with three others and had to stay overnight. Was the weather bad for you too?"

Charlotte did not answer. She watched the two men make their way toward her. The reverend, ahead of her uncle, paused and shook a man's hand when the gentleman addressed him. The packet boat jerked, and Charlotte turned and looked out the window.

"Ah," said the woman, "we've drifted away from the bank to the center of the canal."

She looked down at Charlotte's hem. "Not a lick of mud on you. I'm sure you're glad for that. Hems are so difficult to clean. New York mud is mostly red clay, and it stains, believe you me. I cannot tell you how many hems I have ruined from mud. Had to throw them all into the rag bin. I try to take care, but it is so difficult with the streets in Rome. When it rains, there is mud and mire everywhere. Even on the steps into houses. . ."

Charlotte wished the woman would stop talking. Her uncle and Reverend McKenna were headed right for her. Her pulse throbbed with the fear of discovery. What would she say to her devoted guardian? He was going to be angry, embarrass her in front of everyone, put her off the boat and send her home. Shame washed over her and heat rose in her face. She had disobeyed him, but for good reason. She could not forsake the man she loved. How would she explain her defiance and convince her uncle to allow her to continue with him?

Uncle Henry reached a man of considerable girth, whose large feet jutted out into the aisle. "Excuse me, sir. Would you mind clearing the way, please?"

Her uncle's tone was anything other than civil. He was irritated and looked tired. He and the reverend must have been delayed by weather like the woman said, and spent the night.

With a smirk, the man drew in his boots, with no apology given. Uncle Henry and Reverend McKenna slipped past him. The light from the outside showed dimly on their faces. Uncle Henry's darkened the moment he met Charlotte's eyes.

Chapter 9

Charlotte drew herself up, ready to meet her uncle's ire. She would meet him stare for stare and not cower. At the end of the aisle, Uncle Henry halted abruptly. He glanced at Reverend McKenna then back at Charlotte. Shock tightened the muscles in his face, and he looked at her with disbelief.

"Hello, Uncle Henry."

His eyes widened and he drew in a deep breath. "My word, Charlotte!"

"I know I've shocked you. I'm sorry."

Reverend McKenna stepped beside Uncle Henry. "I cannot believe it, Henry. It's Charlotte."

"Certainly it's Charlotte. I should have had you under lock and key, my girl. What do you mean ignoring my wishes and traveling out here alone? What did you think you'd be doing?"

"Following you, Uncle, so to help the man I am to wed."

The woman beside her gasped. "Oh dear. The three of you must be mindful not to quarrel in front of the passengers. It would be exceedingly rude."

Uncle Henry removed his hat and gave the woman a nod. "Forgive me, madam. We will find seats where we will be out of your earshot."

The woman raised her brows. Had Charlotte's uncle offended her, insinuated she was a busybody, an eavesdropper? Charlotte gave her a sympathetic glance then stood with her valise in hand. Her uncle made an impatient gesture, and she headed to the other side of the packet boat.

The woman touched Charlotte's arm. "Godspeed, my dear." She then looked at Uncle Henry. "Do not be harsh with the poor girl, sir. She is on an honorable mission and should be praised for it."

When they were seated, Charlotte picked up her uncle's hand. "Please don't be angry with me," she said. "I had to come."

"This is beyond all comprehension, Charlotte. Don't you understand the danger you've taken? You could have met any manner of bad person on the way. If you had made it into the camp, you'd be exposed to a deadly illness, a young woman surrounded by surly men. This is not a game."

His stern tone, his tightened jaw and pinched brow, stung her to answer.

After a cool silence between them, she said, "I'm aware this is not a game, Uncle. I was very careful coming all this way. No one bothered me."

"Just how did you get here, child?" the reverend inquired.

"I borrowed a horse, sir. He is in the rear packet."

"Along with our own." Reverend McKenna leaned toward Uncle Henry. "What is done is done, Henry. The best thing to do is for us to watch over Charlotte by keeping her close to us. She will be a great help in nursing the sick, and her constitution is a strong one. You mustn't fear for her."

Uncle Henry crossed his arms. "What I should do is send her home the first chance I get."

"Please don't, Uncle. You'll see. I'll come in very handy."

He gave her a sidelong glare. "Perhaps. . .as long as you are willing to do as you are told. . .and listen to my instructions."

"I promise I will do whatever you ask of me. . .except return home."

"You're worried about my nephew, aren't you, Charlotte?" said Reverend McKenna.

"My heart is aching, Reverend. I love Blaine, and it pains me to think he is suffering with this outbreak."

"We shall seek him out. What better person would there be to tend to him if he is ill than the girl who has risked so much to be near him?"

Uncle Henry drew in a breath. "Reverend, you know I have a great deal of respect for you not only as my pastor but as my friend. Frankly, I haven't a clue how I could argue with anything you have said. But try to understand my disappointment in my niece."

Charlotte scooted forward. "Have you changed your mind?"

Uncle Henry looked at her. "Oh, I'll never say what you've done was wise. Nevertheless, the reverend is right. I cannot send you home. It would only add to the risk you've already taken. But here are the rules."

"I'm listening."

"You will not leave our sides."

"I won't."

"You will not wander or stray. You will stay where I tell you. There will be places in the camp you are not to go."

"Yes, Uncle Henry."

"You will do what I tell you to do, listen to my instructions on how to care for the sick, and carry them out exactly as I outline."

"I will do my utmost, I promise."

Reverend McKenna smiled. "No man knows the mind of the Lord. He works in ways we may not understand. As in this case, we do not know how many lives Charlotte will help to save, Henry. One of them may be my nephew's life."

Uncle Henry eased back on the bench. The tightness of his brows and jaw softened. "Who am I to question God's ways?"

"Who indeed." The reverend slapped his hands on his knees. "Now, let us enjoy the ride along this glorious canal. Do you suppose they have any food aboard for passengers? I've coin weighing down my pocket and a stomach for a beefsteak."

Chapter 10

Age-old trees bowed along the towpath of the canal and shadowed the packed earth into deep brown. The packet boat moved in a whisper through placid water. Long leisurely hours passed, and the occupants disembarked once they reached the town of Utica. It was midmorning and the sky above was clear of clouds. Waiting on the bank, Charlotte watched the crew unload the horses. The poor beasts, she thought. To be cramped in a small space all this time. At least the captain had provided water and oats—but not without a fee.

She held the bridle to the horse the smith had loaned her and ran her hand down his velvety nose. She held her palm under it, and the horse ravished the sugar cubes she offered.

Uncle Henry stroked the neck of his restless mare to calm her. Then he checked her over from her hooves up to her withers.

"She's in good shape. Help me with the saddling, Charlotte. The reverend would but doesn't know how." Uncle Henry smiled over at Reverend McKenna.

"Much to my shame, what your uncle has told you is true. I only know how to hitch a horse to a carriage or wagon."

She handed her horse's reins over to him. "Haven't you ridden before?"

"Oh, often, but with the help of another to saddle such magnificent beasts."

They readied the first two horses and fed them each an apple. Uncle Henry set the saddle for Charlotte's horse atop the saddle blanket. Charlotte positioned it and attached the girth to the girth billets and dropped the stirrups. She looked at her uncle with a plea before climbing up. She wanted to hurry on and not linger in the town.

"There's no reason to ride into town, is there?" she said. "We don't need anything, do we?"

"Not a thing, my girl. We will be on our way. No time to waste."

She set her foot into the stirrup, and he helped her up. "It would be faster if I rode like a boy," she said as she drew the reins through her hands. "But I know you'd disapprove."

◆━━━━◆

They had plenty of hardtack and jerky in their saddlebags, as well as apples and sugar. It proved enough to sustain them, and fresh water was gotten out of the streams. They traveled on through a halcyon calm, over ancient paths and narrow trails made so by generations of Iroquois hunters. On the first night, they slept beneath the stars. A fire blazed not for warmth but to deter any creatures that might find their way into their camp.

Unafraid, Charlotte lay awake staring up at the star-studded sky in awe of meteors that crossed the ebony expanse. She prayed silently for Blaine, for the others, and for the three that were desperate to reach them.

In the morning, they prayed with Reverend McKenna, ate their hardtack, and drank water from a spring running hard nearby. Uncle Henry extinguished the embers of the fire, and they continued on their journey.

After grueling hours of making their way through dense woods, then into meadows deep in withered wildflowers and grass, the camp appeared. Ragged tents were interspersed between wagons and unsaddled horses. Uncle Henry moved his mount down a slope onto level ground with Charlotte and the reverend in the rear. Charlotte's heart beat hard against her breast as she searched the camp for Blaine.

One man seated on a barrel whittling a piece of wood saw them and stood. Mud caked his boots, marred his breeches and shirt. He set his hands on his hips and looked at the newcomers. "The camp is closed," he said.

Uncle Henry reined in and dismounted. "I'm a doctor, and this young woman is my niece who will assist me. This gentleman is Reverend McKenna."

The reverend drew off his hat. "You may know of my nephew, Blaine McKenna."

"Aye, I do, Reverend. You'll find him over that way. We've moved the sick into those tents." He gave Uncle Henry a desperate look. "What do you know of this fever?"

"Enough to help save some. Not to worry, it is not spread from man to man."

"That is a relief. If you follow me, I'll take you there."

Charlotte started to climb down out of the saddle. The man stopped her. "Best you stay atop your horse, miss. This mud will ruin your dress. It's the type that'll never wash out."

She remembered the woman in the packet saying as much, and hiked her skirts above the heels of her boots. She urged her horse on with a nudge of her knee. She would have crawled to Blaine if she had to. Anxious to reach him, a cold chill passed over her as they went through the camp. Mud and mire made up the ground—not a blade of grass to be seen.

Men drew out of their tents. Their eyes wide and wondering. Finally, the man stopped in front of a large tent. From within, Charlotte could hear men moan. Were they too late? Had the fever so advanced upon the poor souls that with all efforts none could be saved?

The tent flap flung back and two men carried out a body wrapped in a shroud. A cold chill rushed over Charlotte and she hurried to slip off the saddle. "The name of this man?"

The bearers looked curiously at her. "John O'Toole, miss."

She breathed out and shut her eyes. "I am sad for the poor man. Tell us, do you know if Blaine McKenna is inside?"

"You'll have to look. Who are these gentlemen?"

"Dr. Verger and Reverend McKenna."

The bearer at the foot of the dead man sighed. "God bless you, sirs."

"Are there other doctors inside?" Uncle Henry asked.

"We had two, but they've given up and gone home. Said there was nothing they could do for the men. We're all a lost cause."

"No, sir. None is to be given up on, not while I am here." Uncle Henry unlatched his bag of medicines.

Reverend McKenna asked if there were ministers in the camp. "Christians, yes, but none ordained to speak a word over the dead," a bearer replied.

"Then I am obliged to do it." He walked on with the bearers down the muddy thoroughfare after removing his Bible from his saddlebag.

Uncle Henry grabbed Charlotte's hand. "Are you ready?"

She looked at him and nodded. "Yes, Uncle."

He opened the flap for her to enter. Stepping through, she waited for him. The inside air stifled her. The smell of sweat and unwashed men shocked her. The heavy canvas blocked all sunlight and made the interior dark and gloomy. Her uncle went to a table, and he set down his medical bag. He drew off his coat and rolled up his sleeves.

"We must first assess each patient and treat the ones that are able to be saved first."

Charlotte frowned.

"It is necessary, Charlotte."

"I understand." A sober sense of loss coursed through her. Could they not save them all? And Blaine. Where was he?

"You must check to see how much fresh water there is, if there are any clean clothes, and if there is any means to provide cleanliness."

Charlotte nodded and helped him line up his bottles of medicine as he spoke. "But first, I want you to look for Blaine. Come back to me when you find him. It will be a comfort for you and the reverend."

Chapter 11

Between the long rows of cots, Charlotte walked, searched, and longed to find Blaine. Beads of sweat covered men's faces and soaked their hair. The unbearable stench caused her to recoil, but she moved on. Hands reached out to her. Blurry eyes locked onto her face. The heat inside the tent grew insufferable.

"Uncle, can we not open the flaps and let fresh air in?" she said, turning and calling out to him.

"Yes, do it, Charlotte. Why are there not others in here to help? They've left these men alone to suffer. If you see any passing by, call to them and tell them I need them."

When she opened up the tent, the breeze came through, calming the heat and bitter air. Charlotte looked down at a man close to her.

"That is better, is it not?" She leaned down when he moved his gaze to her. He whispered for water, and she found a tumbler and a jug. Such a small amount to be found, her heart ached and she wondered how these men had managed with so little help. A man in shabby brown work clothes tucked his head through the opening and drew up beside her.

"The word has gotten out a party has arrived with help. You are among them?"

"Yes," Charlotte said. "I'm here to nurse the sick. My uncle is the doctor."

The man looked down. "May I help?"

"Indeed you may. The jugs need to be filled with fresh water. Can you do that?"

He nodded enthusiastically. "Meant to this morning, but we're overwhelmed."

"When you go out, please try to find others to help."

"I know it looks bleak, miss, that we haven't been caring for our friends. There are those of us that have, and we are worn down to the bone. I'll fetch that water now."

Charlotte thanked him. Her eyes caught the sunlight. She raised her hand to cover them and saw the workers roused by the news of their arrival. In the cot beside where she stood came a whisper. Then a hand touched her, and she turned. She dropped to her knees and touched his face with tears in her eyes.

At first, Blaine's words were wandering, but then, as if a mist lifted from his mind, he knew her. He gripped her hands. "Charlotte." He moved to look closer at her. "Tell me this is a dream, is it really you? The fever. . . I am. . ."

"Shh."

"You should not have come. The fever, Charlotte."

"I have done what I was told, Blaine McKenna. Now, lie quiet. I will take care of you."

She wetted a cloth with the little water she found and dabbed his feverish face. He opened his eyes to see her bending over him.

"Uncle Henry is here with medicine. And your uncle has come as well." She wrung out the cloth and touched his cheeks and neck with it.

A smile quivered over his lips. "I am to die? Am I at home?"

"I do not believe it is the Lord's will. He has brought us here to you."

"I am not afraid if He has called me."

"There is no need, my love." She stroked his hair with a sob upon her lips. She leaned in and kissed him. He shut his eyes and fell back into a stupor.

Charlotte hurried to her uncle. "Uncle Henry, I have found him. His fever is strong and. . ."

"The bark, Charlotte." He hurried forward and handed her a flask. Then he followed her to Blaine's bedside. He set his fingers on Blaine's pulse and felt the heat upon his head. "Give the medicine to him every hour. Give it to all the men. They are not yet at death's door."

A group of canal workers walked into the tent and stood together with Reverend McKenna, who was overjoyed to see his nephew. Charlotte poured fresh water into a basin and looked at the group. One man spoke up. "As God would have us, we are to do as this angel asks."

"Not just I, sirs. Do as my uncle says. He is the doctor here."

"And so we shall, miss," said another. "But as you have need, you have but to ask."

Reverend McKenna called Charlotte over. She went to him and he took up her hand. "Can I not give you some praise, Charlotte?"

She smiled at him. "For what, sir? If it be my appearance, I look a fright."

He returned the smile. "Not your appearance but for your bravery. You traveled alone for miles out of love for my nephew and you have found him."

◆——•——◆

Charlotte sat at the head of Blaine's cot with him cradled in her arms. She stayed there throughout the nights, spooned water and medicine into his mouth. In the mornings, she fed him weak tea and broth until the fever finally broke.

She thanked God for her beloved's recovery and the recovery of others, but not without sorrow that many had gone on to their eternal rest. Exhaustion claimed Uncle Henry. He dozed in a chair, the pocket watch he used to take the men's pulses in his hand. Charlotte set a blanket over him every night and then sat under candlelight beside Blaine.

On the fourth day, a heavy frost covered sparse blades of grass and bracken. Hair-thin ice covered puddles and streams of murky water. An early winter had its blessings. Cold temperatures fell at the descent of the sun and extinguished the threat that had besieged the camp.

Blaine dressed and pulled on his boots. Charlotte brought him a bowl of water and handed him the lye soap she had brought. She watched him wash his face and hands and then turn to her with the tips of his hair dripping. She handed him a towel.

"I wonder about the flush of your cheeks. Are you feeling all right?"

She smiled. "Can't you tell it is a blush?"

"I've made you blush? But I've spoken nothing tender."

"You do not have to. Standing near you, seeing you have returned to the world, is enough to cause it."

Blaine glanced around the room. "I'm sure you've been given many compliments since coming here."

"A few."

"And it is good to see empty cots, knowing their occupants are upright once again."

"It is."

Blaine set the towel aside and drew her to him. "Remember the day I asked you to be my wife?"

"You made my heart pound."

"And you said yes."

She nodded. "I did."

"You still mean it?"

Her smile lifted and she set her hand on his cheek. "Of course I do."

"Even though I don't deserve you?"

"Blaine. . ."

"Ah, here comes my uncle." Blaine motioned the reverend to come closer. "Will you wed us, Uncle?"

"Here, nephew? In this tent of suffering?"

"If Charlotte agrees, what better place for us to take our vows than here? Here is where she nursed me back to health. Make me her husband, and I promise she'll have a wedding feast the likes of which has not been seen in Goshen Creek."

Charlotte looked down at her dress. "I am hardly the vision of a bride," she said. "But. . .yes, I will marry you now. Let this be the place."

"Since it is agreed," said Reverend McKenna, "you must tell your uncle. There is a tree outside with grass around it and the sun shining through the branches."

Within the half hour, Charlotte stood under the tree beside Blaine. The fingertips she resigned to him were warm in his grip. Hand in hand, they stood in front of the reverend, Uncle Henry next them, along with a gathering of canal workers.

The man who had first greeted her drew off his cap. "I never thought I'd see a wedding performed in this mudhole."

"Nor I," said another man who was looking on.

"Makes me want to return to my wife," said another.

And so, they were wedded. Blaine kissed both her hands and then kissed her mouth long and soft. She embraced him and laughed. "Oh, what stories we shall have to tell our children."

Chapter 12

Along the trails leading from Montezuma to Utica, Charlotte contemplated the events that she had lived through since the time when she first saw the saltbox house in Goshen Creek to the day she stood with Blaine before his clergyman uncle. Sighing deeply atop her horse, she relished the idea that long journeys were at an end. Now they had a home to make, children that would come to fill it, and a long life ahead.

Trees stretched bare branches across the road that led into the village. After a long journey home, Charlotte slid off the saddle, her hands on Blaine's shoulders as he helped her down.

He held the horse's reins and Charlotte walked alongside. In the rear, her uncle and Reverend McKenna, still in the saddle, talked. The reverend raised his voice periodically in recitation of the Psalms. Charlotte smiled. Indeed the Lord was worthy of praise for bringing them home, especially Blaine, who had suffered through a most desperate illness.

Overhead a bough of evergreen stretched from one side of the road to the other. People gathered, waved their hands and hats, and cheered. Charlotte's uncle and Reverend McKenna dismounted. They shook hands, patted the men on the backs, and welcomed them home. The women embraced Charlotte.

Mrs. McKenna stepped forward out of the crowd and threw her arms around Blaine. "Dear boy. You've come home safe and sound." She moved back and looked him over. "A bit leaner, but here you be. Did the fever come upon you?"

"It did, Aunt. But as you see, I'm recovered." He looked at his bride. "If it were not for Charlotte, I do not know what would have happened. She's been my angel."

" 'Tis true," said Uncle Henry. "Charlotte was the best of nurses. Not only did she minister to Blaine day and night but to the other sick fellows."

Reverend McKenna put his arm around his wife. "And tell everyone the rest. Tell them the good news, Blaine."

Blaine swept off his hat and drew Charlotte into his arms. "We are married," he shouted.

Cheers burst from the crowd. Hats were thrown into the air. An elderly man did a jig, and Mrs. McKenna's eyes filled with happy tears.

Mrs. McKenna threw open her arms. "How did this come about? Was it you, my love, that wed them?" Reverend McKenna nodded. Mrs. McKenna looked at her friends. "Mrs. Vance. Mrs. Schmidt. We must plan a great reception in the hall for this couple. What say you?"

Mrs. Schmidt set her hands on her hips. "I say we give Charlotte everything she wishes. A wedding cake should be first."

Mrs. Vance chattered on as the crowd drew away with the reverend and good doctor. Blaine held Charlotte close and walked on toward the little saltbox house with the swept porch and steps. They smiled at each other and listened to the women's excited chatter, making out a list of dishes and treats to set upon the wedding table.

They paused at the gate. "I blush to ask, but where shall we go?" Charlotte asked.

"Go inside and pack your belongings." Blaine nudged her on the chin.

Charlotte blinked. "And go where?"

"You remember the day I asked you to marry me, don't you?"

"Of course I do, but..."

"Do you think I would wed you without having a threshold to carry you over?"

She lowered her eyes. "I had not thought on it."

Blaine squashed on his hat. "Do you need me to help you pack?" His question came with a hint of humor and a little insistence.

Charlotte raised her hem. She turned and hurried up the steps and breathlessly made her way to her old room. There she threw her clothes into her trunk and shut it tight. She went to the window and pushed open the shutters. "My chest is ready."

She watched him rush in, and soon she was following him back down the staircase as he carried the cedar trunk on his shoulders. "What's in this, Charlotte?" he said with a grunt.

"A lavender silk gown that I shall wear tonight."

Side by side, they headed down the dusty thoroughfare, past the McKenna house, and then to a corner. Several yards from where they stood, Charlotte got her first glimpse of a house with cedar shakes. Blaine picked up his pace and set the trunk down by the door.

"Come here." He held out his hand.

"This is ours?"

"It is. Tell me you like it." He reached for her.

She picked up her skirts and ran to him. "Our house! Our home!"

Blaine lifted her in his arms, pushed open the door with his shoulder, and carried her over the threshold. Airy muslin curtains hung over the windows but could not block out the sun. It spread across the floor, over the furnishings, and fireplace. Charlotte looked at Blaine with love-lit eyes and kissed him. She rested her head against his shoulder, and the sound of his breathing caused her heart to leap.

"Will you go back to the camp, my love?" She struggled to keep the tears from forming in her eyes.

"My work is done," he said. "I'm to stay here."

"Always? You won't go away again?"

He smiled. "The Bible speaks of vines and olive branches around a man's table, my love. That is what I wish for, for you and me, right here in Goshen Creek."

She placed the tip of her finger against his chin. "That is exactly what I longed to hear."

That night, as the candlewicks burned low and Charlotte lay in her beloved's arms, she pictured the canal stretching on to the west toward Lake Erie, mirroring the sun and clouds by day, the moon and the silver stars by night. She thanked God for bringing her to Goshen Creek. No frills, no airs, the love of friends and family. As she drifted off to sleep, her last thoughts were of Blaine teaching their sons *and daughters* the joy of climbing trees.

Rita Gerlach lives in central Maryland with her husband and two sons. She is a bestselling author of eight inspirational historical novels including the Daughters of the Potomac series of which *Romantic Times* Book Review Magazine said, "Creating characters with intense realism and compassion is one of Gerlach's gifts."

Digging for Love

by Ramona Cecil

Dedication

To my beautiful granddaughter, Emily
May you grow to be a strong Proverbs 31 woman.

Commit thy works unto the LORD, *and thy thoughts shall be established.*
PROVERBS 16:3

Acknowledgments

Local History and Genealogy Division of Rochester Public Library,
Rochester, New York—Special thanks to Jay Osborne,
Amy Pepe, and Brandon Fess
Nancy M. Greco, Lavery Library, St. John Fisher College,
Rochester, New York
Ashley Maready, Erie Canal Museum,
Syracuse, New York

Chapter 1

Rochester, New York, August 1822

P a's gonna tan our hides for sure."

Emily Nichols frowned at her little brother scuffing beside her along the dirt path that led down to the Genesee River. "Don't be such a worrier, Jasper. Papa Ed just said I was not to go near the river alone because of the Irish ruffians working on the aqueduct. And I'm *not* alone. I have you and Patches with me." She glanced at the little white and brown dog trotting near the hem of her blue linen skirt and smiled. "Besides, I'm eighteen—too old to spank—and Papa Ed has never once struck me." It was true. In the dozen years since Pa died and Mama married Papa Ed, her stepfather had never laid a hand on her in anger.

As they neared the rocky berm that sloped down a hundred feet or so to the river's edge, the sound of pickaxes striking rock, the bray of mules, and harsh, unintelligible voices wafting up from the riverbed assailed Emily's ears. The acrid smell of gunpowder tinged the air, tickling her nose.

Jasper's brown eyes grew wide in his freckled face making him look even younger than his ten years. His voice lowered to a near whisper. "Pa says the Irish are wild and wicked, even worse than the convicts that worked on the canal last year. A man stayin' at the inn told me the Irish eat children."

Emily suppressed a laugh. "You can't believe everything you hear, Jasper. I expect the man was trying to scare you, and you know Papa Ed hates the Irish because an Irishman robbed and killed his father when he was young. Besides, we won't get anywhere near the workers. I just want to make a sketch."

She settled herself on a limestone outcropping and flipped open the new sketchbook she'd purchased earlier at Smith's Store. "Mama says when the aqueduct is finished and carries the canal across the river, it will change Rochester forever. I want to have pictures of how it looks during the building." A tinge of sadness crept into her voice as she pulled a pencil from her apron pocket. As much as she welcomed the Erie Canal's arrival at Rochester and the prosperity it was sure to bring, her artist eye couldn't help being offended by how the coffer dams, wagons full of stone, and gouged-out banks marred the river's previous beauty.

Jasper emitted a bored sigh. He dropped the bag of spices and sewing thread they'd purchased for Mama at Smith's Store—the reason for their afternoon outing—and plunked down cross-legged beside Emily in the grass.

"It's ugly now, but they say it will be pretty when it's done." As she sketched Emily imagined the canal boat trip to New York City that Papa Ed had promised them. Her pulse quickened with thoughts of visiting that city's art museums and showing the curators her own sketches and pastels that she dreamed of exhibiting there one day.

Yip, yip!

The dog's barks yanked Emily's attention from her sketchbook to her pet nosing around an elderberry bush. "Get away from there, Patches."

Patches's ears perked. She cocked her furry head and emitted a whimper. The next moment Emily heard a faint, shrill whistle.

Jasper jumped up, his face lit with excitement. "They're gonna blast stone!"

Alarm sparked in Emily's chest. She'd heard horrific stories of people injured and killed by jagged bits of stone flung by the black powder blasts. "Go on home, Jasper." She looked a few feet along the berm where Patches had wandered to another bush. "I'll get Patches and catch up with you."

Jasper frowned. "Aw, I want to see 'em blast the rock."

She glared at him. "If you don't mind me, Papa Ed won't have to tan your hide, because I will. Now shoo!"

To her relief Jasper sighed but headed back up the path. Emily started in the direction she last saw Patches.

◆—◆ ·—◆

"O'Grady!"

Seamus O'Grady cringed at the supervisor's gravelly voice. From the moment Seamus arrived at the Rochester worksite the supervisor seemed to take an immediate disliking to him. The man's attitude wasn't unique, as many of the locals here held the Irish in disdain, but Seamus didn't have to please the other locals. He *did* need to please Art Mercer.

"Boss?" Forcing as pleasant a smile as he could manage, Seamus turned from helping Taffy Jenkins lift a slab of stone onto a cart.

Mercer's eyes narrowed to angry slits and a blue vein throbbed at his left temple—never a good sign. "Why ain't ya over there borin' blast holes like I told ya to?" He huffed a frustrated breath that stank of rancid pork fat.

"Beggin' your pardon, boss." Seamus took a step back and tried not to meet Mercer's glower. "I was doin' that just a bit ago, boss, but me boyo here needed a wee bit o' help with this rock, so I—"

"I swear!" Mercer snatched his black felt hat off his thinning pate, unleashing a wave of malodorous scent to Seamus's nose. "I thought the convicts were hard to deal with last year, but you Irish have 'em beat fer contrariness!" He smacked the hat against his knee. "At least the convicts' iron balls and chains kept 'em tethered to a job."

Seamus looked at the thin Welshman struggling beneath the weight of the overloaded cart and his insides gnarled in sympathy. "Jenkins has been feelin' poorly and I wasn't sure he could—"

"Look." Mercer heaved another rancid sigh, and a rare flash of compassion crossed his eyes. "Every man here has to pull his own weight. I can't have Jenkins or any other man slowin' down the work." His look hardened again and he poked the air in front of Seamus's chest with his grimy forefinger. "From now on you do what I tell ya to do. Disobey me again and I'll dock your pay a full week, understood?"

Seamus nodded. "Yes, boss."

Relief sluiced through him, replacing the tension seeping from his body as he watched Mercer's retreating figure. In the future he must do his best not to anger Art Mercer. Ma, Liam, and Cullen back in Ireland depended on Seamus earning enough money to bring them to America. He couldn't afford to have even a penny docked from his pay.

The thought of his family caused a knot of longing to ball in his gut. Worry over how they were managing alone gripped him. Images of Ma darning clothes late into the night by lamplight, Liam and Cullen working long hours at the stables, and the three of them sharing a meager bit of broth and bread brought tears to Seamus's eyes. At the same time it solidified his resolve to earn their passage price to America. In Ireland their condition would never improve. At least here he could look after them and their hard work could earn them a better life.

Three sharp bursts of the warning whistle indicating a fuse was about to be lit yanked Seamus from his reverie. He started to head for cover behind a slab wagon when the sound of a dog barking drew his attention to the spot where he'd helped to bore blast holes in bedrock earlier. A little brown and white dog bounced around the lit fuse, yipping and pawing at the sparking line of string.

Fear for the hapless animal gripped Seamus's chest. In another moment the blast would disintegrate the poor little beastie. Reason detached and Seamus found himself barreling toward the pup.

Chapter 2

At the last instant, Seamus scooped up the dog and stamped out the sparking fuse before the black powder blew them both to smithereens.

A cheer went up from his fellow workmen emerging from their hiding places. Art Mercer strode toward Seamus, an angry scowl pruning up his purple face and his fists clenched at his side.

"O'Grady, what are you doin'?"

Seamus turned to Mercer and his heart dropped to his stomach like a stone. He wondered if the ball of white and brown fur squirming in his arms was worth his last six days of hard labor. Ma's parting words before he left for America flashed in his mind. *"If ya should find yourself in a hard spot, son, jist use that sharp wit o' yours and a bit of the O'Grady charm."*

Seamus met Mercer's scowl with the innocent look he used to give Ma when she caught him stealing a scone before dinner. "The way wasn't clear, boss. I listened well when ya told us all that a blast can't be stopped unless a life be at risk." He held out the little dog that gave a yip and licked the back of his hand. "I know what a kind and decent man ya are, boss. I knew you wouldn't want ta see this little beastie blown ta pieces. I couldn't bear ta see ya carry that kind o' burden." He shook his head. "No, sir, I'd put m'self in harm's way b'fore I'd see your soul burdened—"

"All right, all right!" Mercer batted the air with his hand. "That's enough of your blather. Get that dog outta here and put in another fuse."

Seamus blew out a relieved sigh as he watched Mercer walk away. He looked down at the dog. "Well, wee bit o' trouble, your hide's intact, but ya near cost me a week's wages. Where have you come from anyway?"

"Patches!"

Seamus looked up to see a young woman scrambling down the embankment. A look of relief bloomed on her angelic face. Strands of her dark brown hair had pulled free from their moorings atop her head and fell appealingly about her shoulders.

The little dog in his arms began to bark and squirm. He should let it go to scamper off to its obvious mistress. But, like iron to a magnet, he found himself drawn to the girl and made his way toward her.

"Patches." Her heart pounding, Emily somehow managed to make it down the embankment without tumbling into the shallow river water. The little dog's yips had led her to where she spotted Patches barking at something that looked like a sparking serpent. The same moment she'd realized the danger they were both in she also realized she could never reach Patches before the rocky embankment exploded. She'd closed her eyes and waited for the blast. When the explosion never happened, she'd opened her eyes to see a man holding Patches and another man yelling at him.

"Does this wee bit o' trouble belong to you then?" The man with Patches in the crook of one arm strode toward her. He reached out his free hand and grasped hers to help her down onto a slab of dry limestone.

"Yes. I'm sorry if Patches caused you problems." Emily liked the feel of his strong, calloused hand in hers and felt bereft when he relinquished it. She reached out and took Patches from him. For the first time she focused on the man's face. Tanned from the August sun and framed by a shock of thick, dark, curly hair, it was as handsome a face as she'd ever seen and, living at an inn, she'd seen a lot of faces. Blue eyes—blue as an October sky—twinkled with fun. Tiny lines at the outside corners of his eyes suggested he was quick to laugh.

He grinned and those intense blue eyes looked into hers as if he might see all the way to her soul. "No harm done, miss. None indeed."

"Thank you for saving her. You are the one who saved her, aren't you?" Emily cringed. *Why am I babbling?*

"Excuse me poor manners." He put his left arm behind him and his right across his chest and dipped a deep bow. "Seamus O'Grady, late of Dublin, Ireland, at your service, ma'am."

Emily secured Patches in her left arm and held out her right hand. "Emily Nichols. My stepfather, Edward Tompkins, is proprietor of the Riverside Inn on Carroll Street."

Seamus took her hand, wrapping it in the same warm strength she'd experienced earlier, and held it a bit longer than necessary. "A pleasure it is to meet ya, Miss Nichols. Your inn's the big brown brick buildin' with green shutters then?" He looked upward in the direction of Carroll Street.

Emily nodded.

His grin turned wry. "I fear me pockets are not deep enough for your establishment." He glanced eastward over his shoulder. "I'm stayin' across the river in the part they call Dublin with me friend Terrence Maguire and his missus."

Emily decided it might be best not to tell him it was just as well that he couldn't afford to stay at the Riverside Inn since Papa Ed didn't like Irishmen.

Patches whimpered and wriggled in Emily's arms. As much as she enjoyed staring into Seamus O'Grady's blue eyes, she needed to get home. Mama and Papa Ed were doubtless wondering why she hadn't returned.

"O'Grady!"

Emily glanced past Seamus and saw the man who had yelled at him earlier advancing toward them.

"Well, thank you again, Mr. O'Grady." She turned to head back up the embankment with Patches.

"Will I see ya again then, Miss Nichols?"

She turned back at his voice. Her pulse quickened at the hope in his eyes.

"Perhaps."

All the way home her conscience assailed her. She shouldn't have said that. Jasper was right. She *shouldn't* have ventured so close to the construction site in the first place. While any notion of returning felt both disobedient and reckless, the thought of not seeing Seamus O'Grady again left a hollow sensation in her chest.

Still holding Patches, Emily slipped into the inn's side door hoping to avoid Mama and Papa Ed.

"Well it's about time, young lady." Papa Ed, wiping his hands on the stained apron covering his rotund girth, appeared in the hallway, sending Emily's heart vaulting to her throat. "Thought I was goin' to have to go searchin' for you." Despite his gruff tone, the concern in her stepfather's eyes smote Emily with regret.

"I'm sorry, Papa Ed." She rubbed the dog's soft fur—more to soothe herself than Patches. "Patches got away and I had to go find her."

Papa Ed frowned, deepening the wrinkles across his broad forehead. "That pup is more trouble than she's worth."

His use of the word "trouble" reminded Emily of Seamus O'Grady calling Patches a "wee bit o' trouble." As cross as Papa Ed was about her tardiness, he would doubtless be furious if he knew she'd gone down to the river and talked with one of the Irish canal workers. She'd never once lied to Papa Ed, and she sent up a quick prayer that he wouldn't inquire into the details of her afternoon adventure.

He expelled an impatient huff. "Well, put the dog outside and clean yourself up. Your mother will need your help in the kitchen. We have three new boarders, and one is an engineer on the canal project—a well-connected gentleman from New York City." He crossed his arms over his broad chest and fixed her with a stern look. "As I've told you many times, Emily, we must impress upon our guests that we run a first-rate establishment if we want to attract a better class of clientele when the canal connects us to New York City."

"Yes, Papa Ed." Eager to cut short any further interrogation, Emily nodded and hurried to do as her stepfather asked.

That night as she lay awake in bed she couldn't get the handsome Irishman with the merry blue eyes and strong, calloused hands from her mind. As she grappled for an excuse to again venture near the construction site, she realized that she'd left her new sketchbook on the rock where she'd sat and sketched the scene below.

The next morning she hurried through her chores, hoping to find time to steal away and retrieve the sketchbook and, perchance, catch a glimpse of Seamus O'Grady.

"Emily." In the kitchen Mama turned from the pantry. "I heard our new guest, Mr. VanderMeer—the canal engineer—tell Edward that he is especially partial to Marlborough cakes. I thought I'd make some for dinner tonight, but the recipe calls for eight eggs and we are down to our last two dozen." Her expression turned apologetic. "With the inn full, I know we all have extra work, but I need you to run down to old Mrs. Hannock's and purchase an extra three dozen of those good brown eggs her chickens lay."

"Yes, of course, Mama." Emily paused in drying a meat platter and tried to keep the excitement from her voice. Hannock's egg and poultry shop was located across from the spot where she had left her sketchbook.

Fifteen minutes later, with her egg basket on her arm, Emily left the dusty road that divided the village of Rochester from the Genesee River and made her way toward the worn path that led to the spot where she and Jasper had stopped yesterday.

She lifted her skirt hems from the damp grass, still sparkling in the sun with morning dew. A quick search brought her to the stone outcropping where her sketchbook lay just as she'd left it. The temptation to sit and begin another sketch grew too strong to resist.

Closing her eyes, she luxuriated in a moment of serenity away from the inn. She lifted her face to the warmth of the sun's rays and listened. The tranquil sound of the river's current, the bright chirping of chickadees, and the soulful call of the mourning doves mixed discordantly with the construction sounds below.

At a touch on her shoulder she jerked and gasped, and her eyes flew open.

"Sorry. I didn't mean to startle ya." Seamus O'Grady stood before her, his black, shapeless hat in his hands. "I saw ya up here and feared your little dog might wander down into trouble again."

Emily's heart jumped to her throat and began to race. Heat leaped to her face, and she hoped he would attribute any heightened color in her cheeks to the sun's warmth. She stood up, though she wasn't sure why. "Patches didn't come with me today." She held up her sketchbook. "I forgot this yesterday, so I stopped to look for it on my way to an errand." She showed him the sketch she'd made the day before.

"You're an artist." A look of interest and appreciation bloomed on his face as he gazed at her drawing.

"I suppose I am." She wished her heart would stop doing somersaults. Perhaps more talk would make it behave. "I hope to one day exhibit and sell my drawings in New York City." She hadn't shared that with anyone, not even Mama. What was it about this man that compelled her to spill the contents of her heart to him as easily as opening a sack of flour?

"I think you could." His kind smile seeped into a deep, sweet place in her heart.

"Mama says I can have whatever I want if I believe I can. Like it says in the Bible, 'And all things, whatsoever ye shall ask in prayer—'"

"'Believing, ye shall receive,'" he said, finishing Matthew 21:22. "Me ma is always remindin' me 'n' me brothers o' that verse too."

"Oh, does your family live in Rochester?"

He shook his head. The merry light in his eyes dimmed, causing her to regret the question. "No, they're back in Dublin, Ireland." His countenance brightened and the beguiling lilt returned to his voice. "But I'm goin' ta bring them here when I've earned enough money for their passage."

"How many brothers do you have?" She should go. She still needed to get the eggs. If she didn't return soon, Mama would likely send Jasper looking for her.

"Two. Liam is sixteen and Cullen is fourteen. They work at the stable in front o' the house where they and me ma lives."

"So your family owns a stable?" How she loved listening to his beautiful Irish brogue. The temptation to keep him talking overruled her better judgment.

He shook his head. "No, me da and us boys worked at the stable till me da died. When he died. . .well, it was just us boys then." The light returned to his features with his smile. "And do you have brothers 'n' sisters then?"

"One brother. Jasper." Emily smiled as she always did when she spoke of her little brother. "He's ten and he's actually my half brother." She laughed, thinking of Jasper's expression whenever she called him by that term. "But he hates for me to call him that." Another giggle escaped her lips. "He says he's a whole boy, so how could he be only half a brother?"

Seamus laughed. Their gazes locked and held for a long moment. Something important seemed to pass between them that scared up a bevy of butterflies in Emily's stomach. To her embarrassment, he was the first to break the silence.

"Do you come here often then?" He gazed around the grassy berm dotted with limestone outcroppings and elderberry, honeysuckle, and chokeberry shrubs. "It's lovely here."

"Before the construction began I came most days except in the winter when the snow gets too deep." Emily couldn't stop a note of sadness from creeping into her voice. "I used to love making sketches and pastels of the river view from here, but now, with all the construction. . ."

"I would love to have a picture of it—the way it was before." His expression reminded her of Jasper's when her brother begged for a sweet from the kitchen. "I would pay," he hurried to add. "We get paid on Saturday."

Emily shook her head. Seamus needed his money to bring his family from Ireland, yet she didn't want to hurt his pride. "I've never sold a picture, but I will draw you one from memory if you'd take it as a gift for saving Patches." She sat down on the stone, pulled the ever-present pencil from her pocket, and began sketching.

One long whistle blast pierced the air.

Seamus puffed out a sigh. "I have to go, but I'll come back this time tomorrow and claim my gift."

Before Emily could tell him she didn't expect to be back tomorrow, he had gone.

Chapter 3

"A h, Ma." Seamus expelled a wistful sigh. "I wish ya were here ta tell me what ya think I should do."

A knock sounded at the cabin door, yanking him from the dear words scrawled on the pages of Ma's latest letter. His heart squeezed, wondering how many long hours of washing, ironing, and mending it must have cost her to purchase this precious bit of writing paper.

At the persistent knocking he folded the pages and left them on the oak table to answer the door.

"Terrence. Iona. Are ye to home then?"

At Father Patrick Gallagher's bright voice from the other side of the door, Seamus's heart lifted. He'd met the young priest his first evening at the Maguire home and they'd quickly become friends. He hurried to open the heavy log door.

"Ah, Seamus, me boy." Father Patrick's grin split his shaven face beneath his wide-brimmed, black felt hat. His six-foot frame, clad in his long dark robe, filled the doorway, blotting out the waning daylight behind him.

"Terrence and Iona are not here at the moment, Father. They've gone ta visit the McDonalds." Seamus glanced over the priest's left shoulder in the direction of that homestead.

"That would be me next stop." His smile still in place, the priest looked past Seamus to the interior of the cabin. "But it's a long trek from me sister's home across the river on Washington Street. Could do with a short rest and cup o' water, if you don't mind."

"Of course, Father, come in." Seamus stepped aside to allow the priest's entrance. "Sit yourself down." Seamus indicated the oak table and four chairs that centered the cabin's main room. In truth, Father Patrick's appearance couldn't be more welcome.

Emily Nichols had released a cyclone of emotions inside Seamus. He couldn't get the brown-haired, hazel-eyed beauty out of his mind. All day he'd wrestled with the question of whether or not he should see her again.

From the moment he'd caught sight of her scrambling down the riverbank, her beauty and spunk had beguiled him. Her linen apron and common cloth frock had suggested that she held a station equal to his. But when she told him that her stepfather owned the Riverside Inn, he'd considered her above his station and beyond his reach. Indeed, he doubted he'd ever see her again. So this morning when he'd spied her on the grassy area above the river, good sense told him to ignore her presence and put her out of his mind. The devil on his shoulder urged him to do otherwise and the temptation to climb up and renew their acquaintance grew too strong to resist. All the while they'd talked she'd burrowed deeper under his skin. He knew the moment the words left his mouth that he shouldn't have promised to return tomorrow for his gift, but he had.

Feeling the need for guidance, he'd pulled out Ma's last letter, hoping to glean a bit of wisdom that might help him sort out the roiling emotions in his chest.

"So how is our newest Dubliner farin'?" Father Patrick pulled out a chair and sat at the table while Seamus dipped a cup into the bucket of water by the hearth.

"I'm doin' well, Father." Seamus set the cup of water on the table in front of the priest and ignored the pang of guilt that accompanied his less than honest answer.

"Ah, that is good to hear, me boy." Father Patrick took off his hat, revealing his short-cropped fiery-red hair. He set the hat on the table and took a long drink of the water.

Seamus joined him at the table. "I just pulled the bucket from the well a bit ago, so it should still be some'at cool."

Father Patrick ran the back of his hand across his mouth, his grin widening. "I thank you and bless you, dear boy. It's refreshin' as a summer rain on a parched field." He drained the cup and set it down. "I've come to spread the word that the Female Charitable Society, of which me sister is a member, is plannin' a fish dinner for all the canal workers Friday next. It seems to have become a concern of the ladies that the men building the canal aren't gettin' proper nutrition."

Seamus returned Father Patrick's grin. "I'm eatin' a sight better'n I was in Ireland, and Iona keeps a bountiful table."

Father Patrick shrugged. "Even so, me sister says her group is hopin' for a good-sized crowd. Besides, a wee bit o' socialization can't hurt," he added with a wink.

Seamus gave a soft, wry snort. "Company too grand can make for trouble as well, Father."

Father Patrick gave Seamus a knowing smile. "Is there somethin' you'd like to share with me, son?"

Seamus heaved a sigh and met the priest's attentive gaze. "I've met a young woman."

"Ah, so ya feel the need for spiritual guidance in a romantic matter?" Smiling, he leaned back in his chair and crossed his arms over his chest.

"More a compassionate ear." Seamus grinned. "But I'm knowin' it'll come with a healthy helpin' o' scripture as well."

"That it will, sure enough." Father Patrick cocked his head. "And what are your concerns about the young lady?"

Seamus glanced down at a patch on his shirtsleeve Iona had mended then lifted his gaze back to the priest's face. "She's a good, God-fearin' girl, I could tell that straightaway," he said, wanting to dispel any concerns the clergyman might have about Emily's moral character. He shook his head at the memory of her beauty. "Pretty as an angel with a heart as pure as an angel's too."

Father Patrick's smile turned indulgent. "Then what is the problem, son?"

Seamus dropped his gaze again. "I fear she is above me station, Father. I might as well try to fish for the North Star."

"Has the young lady shown any interest in you then?"

"I believe she has." Seamus met Father Patrick's questioning look and, as he'd done countless times since his last encounter with Emily, wondered if he'd misinterpreted her kindness for interest. Remembering her blush and lingering looks as well as her eagerness to offer him one of her pictures, a renewed confidence surged back. "Yes, I'm sure of it. I saw it in her face."

The priest gazed up at the cabin's rough-hewn ceiling beams and his expression turned pensive. "Acts 10:34 and 35 tells us, 'Then Peter opened his mouth, and said, Of a truth I perceive that God is no respecter of persons: But in every nation he that feareth him, and worketh righteousness, is accepted with him.' And again in Romans 2:11 we read, 'For there is no respect of persons with God.'" He lowered his gaze back to Seamus's face. "Why did ya leave the old country and come across the sea to America, son?"

Seamus blinked, bewildered by the priest's question. "For the chance ta earn a better life for me, Ma, Liam, and Cullen. To be free ta make our own way."

Father Patrick nodded. "Ah, yes, freedom." His brow furrowed, and the look in his eyes turned intense. "America is not like the old country, Seamus. Here you can rise as far as your will and your wits will take you." His smile turned kind. "Me boy, God sees no different stations between you and the young lady who has caught your eye, and here in America, your ambition can make that so."

"Then you're sayin' it wouldn't be wrong of me to pursue a friendship with the lady?" Seamus perked up and a new wellspring of hope rose in his chest.

The priest reached over and slapped Seamus's knee, his grin splitting his face. "The American Declaration of Independence agrees with God that all men are created equal. As long as your lady fair is unwed and a good Christian lass, I say pursue her and see where God takes your friendship." He rose from the stool.

"Who knows, perhaps the young lady is part of God's plan for you—part of the reason He planted in your heart to come to America. Remember the Lord's words in Jeremiah. 'For I know the thoughts that I think toward you, saith the Lord, thoughts of peace, and not of evil, to give you an expected end.'" He patted Seamus's shoulder. "Just remember to keep listenin' for God's will, son. He'll never steer you wrong."

"Thank ya, Father." Joy flooded Seamus's chest. He pumped the priest's hand, his face aching with the wide smile he couldn't restrain. The morrow he had dreaded a few moments ago could not come soon enough.

◆━━━━━◆

"You must be good today, Patches." Clutching her box of pastels and her sketchbook to her chest, Emily glanced down at her pet trotting alongside her as they crossed Main Street to Mill Street. Her heartbeat matched her quick-paced steps. She'd awakened early and finished her morning chores to allow time to steal away from the inn and give Seamus his drawing. "If Papa Ed finds out we've come down to the river, we'll both be in trouble."

With every step, her willful disobedience of Papa Ed's instructions to stay away from the construction site rasped against her conscience like a wool carder. Mama's voice quoting Colossians 3:20 rang in her ears, convicting her. *Children, obey your parents in all things: for this is well pleasing unto the Lord.*

She glanced about to assure herself that none of the Rochester residents stirring along Mill Street noticed her step from the street and head toward the berm above the river. Guilt curled in her belly threatening to reject her hasty breakfast of milk and buttered day-old bread. At the same time, knowing Papa Ed's order had sprung from his dislike and distrust of the Irish, a flash of righteous indignation sparked inside her, assuaging a measure of her guilt. That Papa Ed would undoubtedly forbid her friendship with Seamus simply because he was Irish seemed both unreasonable and uncharitable.

Still, she wouldn't prolong her disobedience. She'd brought her pastels with the thought of capturing the pink and blue hues of the dawn sky, but instead she'd give Seamus his promised picture and head back to the inn.

"I'd begun to wonder if ya were comin' after all."

At Seamus's voice, Emily gasped and spun around.

"Sorry. I didn't mean ta scare ya again. Truly." His blue eyes sparked with fun, making her wonder at the sincerity of his words. He grinned down at Patches then bent and scratched behind the dog's ears. "Well there, wee bit o' trouble. It's good to see you again too."

He rose and met Emily's gaze, sending her settling heart bounding again. "If I knew I was that frightenin' I'd have used it more often with me brothers."

"You're not. You just startled me, that's all." Her racing heart stoked the heat rising in her face. To hide her flaming cheeks and calm her emotions, she looked down at the sketchbook and box of pastels in her arms. "I brought you a picture I drew of the river before the work began." She set the pastels down on a limestone outcropping, slipped the sketch from the book, and held it out to him. "I sketched this in the springtime when the river was much higher than it is now."

As Seamus took the picture from her hands his fingers grazed hers, sending pleasant tingles up her arm.

"I first did it as a pencil sketch," she said to cover her disconcertion at his touch. "Later I went over it with my pastels to add color."

Admiration and wonder lit Seamus's face as he perused the drawing. "This is lovely." He looked at her, all levity gone from his features. "Thank you, Emily. I will treasure this all my days." His gaze swung back to the picture and his voice thickened. "It reminds me some'at o' the River Anna Liffey that flows through Dublin town back in Ireland."

The sadness in his voice pinched Emily's heart. A desire to ease his homesickness gripped her. "I could try to draw you a picture of that river if you'd describe it to me." She moved her box of pastels to the grass and sat on the rock with her open sketchbook on her lap.

Seamus sat in the dewy grass at her feet. Patches turned from sniffing at the box of chalky crayons to jump into his lap. As Seamus stroked the dog's fur, a distant look came into his eyes and he seemed to gaze at a vision he alone could see. "Ah, 'tis grand. On a fine summer day the water's as blue as. . ." He seemed to falter in search of an apt metaphor.

"As blue as your eyes?" Emily couldn't help suggesting as she reached into her box of pastels for a corresponding color.

He rubbed the dog's fur and smiled up at her, sending her heart galloping. "Aye, I suppose so." He turned his gaze back to the river below them, but his distant look suggested he wasn't seeing the shallow waters of the Genesee. "The Anna Liffey's gentle curves caress the grass along its banks, grass so green it hurts your eyes to look at it."

As Emily worked, trying to create on paper the picture he painted with his words, she realized he was as much a poet as she was an artist. With quick strokes she let his words guide her as she attempted to replicate the light gray stone that made up the arch of Sarah's Bridge, the buildings he described at one end of the bridge, and three skiffs with brightly colored sails bobbing along the wide stream. When she finally handed him what she'd drawn, an odd look came into his eyes.

Neglected, Patches jumped from his lap to nose around the base of a nearby sumac bush.

Emily's heart sank as Seamus gazed in silence at the picture. She'd clearly missed the mark. "I'm sure I got a lot wrong—"

"No. This is it. This *is* the River Anna Liffey. You drew it exactly as I remember it." His face, full of wonder, swung up to meet her gaze.

For a long moment their gazes held and Emily felt as if she were drowning in the blue depths of his eyes—the blue depths of the Anna Liffey. She had to break the spell.

"Tell me about Dublin, Ireland. What is it like there?"

A shrill whistle from below intruded.

Seamus hopped to his feet, rolled up the two pictures, and tucked them inside his linen shirt.

The whistle blew again.

Seamus gave an exasperated huff, glanced down toward the worksite, then looked at Emily, his eyes full of hope. "Come back tomorrow mornin' and I'll tell you." He grasped both her hands in his and kissed them then scurried down the embankment.

For a long moment Emily sat stunned, looking at the backs of her hands still warm from Seamus's kisses. Her heart writhed. She'd disobeyed her parents by coming here, risking punishment and, perhaps the worst punishment, disappointing them and losing their trust. The thought of having to choose between disappointing Mama and Papa Ed or sweet Seamus felt excruciating. Yet sometime before tomorrow she must make that choice.

Chapter 4

Daft thing to do! Ya've gone bloomin' daft Seamus, me boy." Seamus mumbled the self-incriminations as he knelt in the canvas tent that housed sundry tools and the workers' lunch pails. A quick search revealed his lunch pail. He silently thanked Iona Maguire for painting his initials in red on the pail's tin lid. He lifted the lid and tucked in Emily's drawings. After he'd given in to the impulse to kiss her hands—the hands that had drawn an image of home better than any he could have conjured in his own mind—he'd skedaddled like a coward, afraid to see the reaction on her face.

"O'Grady!"

Art Mercer's angry voice brought Seamus scrambling to his feet and whisked away all thoughts of Emily.

Mercer poked his ugly face into the tent. His voice took on a faux politeness that dripped with scorn. "Do you think you could do us the honor of joining us at work this morning, Mr. O'Grady?" His scruffy-bearded face twisted in anger and his bloodshot eyes bulged. His voice rose to a near shout, all civility gone. "Or are you waitin' for a royal engraved invitation?"

"Sorry, boss. I had somethin' to put away. I was headed out this very instant." Seamus scurried out, backing up the other man.

Mercer expelled an exasperated huff. "If I didn't need every strong back I can get, I'd have given you the boot by now, O'Grady. But soon you'll be somebody else's problem. Mr. Drake wants a dozen men sent over to the town of Greece to cut and load sandstone. Get your lunch tin, 'cause you'll be headin'—"

"Boss." Terrence Maguire ran up, his breathless voice full of urgency.

Mercer turned from Seamus. "What is it, Maguire?"

"Sorry for the intrusion, boss, but a big chunk of stone fell on a wagon tongue and snapped it right in two. We fixed the wood tongue, but we can't straighten the iron tongue supports."

Mercer groaned. "We can't afford to lose a wagon." He heaved a sigh. "Take the supports up to Bray's blacksmith shop on Main Street and get 'em fixed."

Terrance shook his head. "I done been up there. Shop's closed. Missus says Bray's down sick."

Mercer groaned, and cursed beneath his breath.

"I can fix 'em, boss." Still attempting to process the news that he'd be leaving Rochester and Emily, Seamus piped up. "I been smithin' for four years. If Mr. Bray will let me use his shop, I could have those supports fixed in two shakes of a sheep's tail."

"Splendid idea!" Wearing his usual congenial smile, Amasa Drake strode up to the men. He clapped Seamus on the shoulder but looked at Mercer. "I know Bray. If I vouch for Mr. O'Grady, I'm sure Bray will agree to it."

Mercer gave a grudging shrug. "I'll leave the problem to you then. . .Mr. Drake." Frowning, he stalked off.

Seamus had to suppress a grin as he watched his surly boss stomp away. Being outranked by the much younger Amasa Drake clearly chafed Art Mercer. Raised on a nearby farm and not yet in his thirties, Amasa Drake stood as a living example of Father Patrick's assertion that, here in America, a man could rise above his station at birth. Now if Seamus could somehow convince Amasa not to send him to the town of Greece to cut sandstone, perhaps Seamus's own American dream could still include Emily Nichols.

◆•——•◆

"I know how much you enjoy your drawing, Emily." Mama's long-suffering tone as she hung the breadboard warned Emily of a coming "but." "But you can't let your drawing take away time from your chores."

Emily turned from the step-top cookstove where she'd gone to take meat pies from the oven. She opened her mouth, not sure how to respond.

Mama fisted her hands on either side of her waist. "Do not tell me an untruth, Emily. I saw you return to the inn this morning with your pastel box and sketchbook."

Emily bent and grasped the iron handle of the oven door with a folded towel. She welcomed the rush of heat to her face as she opened the door and pulled out the pan of pork and vegetable pies. Mama would attribute any telltale color in her cheeks to the oven's heat. "I got up early and finished my morning chores before I went out, Mama." She strove to keep her voice nonchalant as she carried the pan of pasties to the worktable. "The dawn sky is so pretty, I like to get it on paper." None of what she said was a lie.

Mama crooked her head to one side and her fond smile spoke of patience. "You know Papa Ed and I are proud of your artwork, but we do have an inn to run and we need everyone doing their part to make it a success. Mr. Vander-Meer says when the canal is finished Rochester could double in size. When people begin arriving on the canal from New York City, we want to attract the best patrons." Grinning, she walked to Emily and chucked her under the chin. "Remember, Emily, a better class of patrons will greatly improve your chances of snagging a wealthy husband."

Emily transferred the meat pies to a stoneware platter and managed a weak smile. Since Emily turned eighteen Mama seemed set on finding her a wealthy husband. For Emily, thoughts of marriage ranked far below her aspirations of achieving recognition as a serious artist. What would Mama say if she knew that the one man who'd captured Emily's interest was a penniless Irish immigrant? She shuddered to imagine Papa Ed's reaction.

Mama exchanged her stained apron for a clean starched one, and her tone turned teasing. "Speaking of eligible gentlemen, I believe Mr. VanderMeer is unattached." Mama helped Emily off with her stained work apron and on with a clean, snowy-white one. "He's only a few years older than you, and I've not met a more handsome young man."

You haven't met Seamus O'Grady. Emily swallowed down the words perched on the tip of her tongue.

Mama tied the apron strings behind Emily's waist, fiddling with them as if to make a more perfect bow. "He's waiting in the dining room for his luncheon of pasties this very minute." She cocked her head and grinned. "I've noticed him looking at you. With but a little effort, I do think you could catch his eye."

Emily had taken to using humor as a way to sidestep Mama's talk of marriage. "Well, I won't drop the pasties in his lap," she said then giggled at the image her words conjured in her mind.

Mama gasped and a horrified look came over her face. "Do not even say such a thing, Emily. Gilbert VanderMeer's family goes back to the founding of New Amsterdam. They're rich as Croesus, and Mr. VanderMeer told Edward that he has political aspirations."

Emily picked up the platter of pasties and smiled. "Don't worry, Mama. You know I'm always courteous to all our guests." She declined the temptation to say that a man of Gilbert VanderMeer's station, who could doubtless choose a wife from any number of New York City's socialites, wouldn't give her a second look. Instead she left Mama's fantasies intact and headed out of the kitchen.

"Well, it wouldn't hurt to be a little extra courteous to Mr. VanderMeer." Mama's whispered voice as she followed Emily out of the kitchen toward the dining room sounded more like a command than a suggestion.

In the dining room, Gilbert VanderMeer sat at one end of the long table perusing the latest edition of the *Rochester Telegraph*. Emily couldn't deny that the young engineer cut a dashing figure in his emerald-green double-breasted tailcoat that nipped into his trim waist, snowy waistcoat, high-collar shirt and cravat, and buff pantaloons. She suspected that his sandy-brown hair combed in the latest fashion to appear haphazard and windblown across his forehead had required painstaking effort to achieve. His handsome profile suggested an absorbed aloofness. Emily had found the young engineer's demeanor, while polite, somewhat stiff and off-putting.

"Your pasties, Mr. VanderMeer," Emily muttered.

"Oh, thank you, Miss Tompkins." Hurrying to fold and set aside the newspaper, he smiled up at her. "They smell wonderful."

Emily decided against correcting him on her surname. "They are pork."

"Emily made them herself," Mama said as she poured him a glass of cold milk.

Mr. VanderMeer's smile widened as it bounced between Mama and Emily. "Then I'm sure they will taste as wonderful as they smell." His brown-eyed gaze slid back to Emily's face and lingered there. "You must be a lady of many accomplishments, Miss Tompkins. Your mother mentioned to me at breakfast that you are something of an artist."

"I do like to draw." Emily cringed, wishing Mama would exercise more subtlety in her pursuit of a son-in-law.

Mama, who'd moved a step behind Mr. VanderMeer's chair, widened her eyes and made a rolling hand movement as if to encourage Emily to expound on her statement. When she didn't, Mama stepped back into Mr. VanderMeer's view. "You should see Emily's beautiful skyscapes, Mr. VanderMeer."

His countenance lit with interest. "I would love to see them, Miss Tompkins." He spread his linen napkin over his lap. "As it happens, my mother is a great patron of the arts. Perhaps when I return to New York City you'll allow me to take her an example of your work."

Mama's eyes widened again and her mouth formed an *O* of happy surprise before she delicately cleared her throat. When she spoke, her voice held a note of careful contrition. "Emily's surname is actually Nichols, Mr. VanderMeer. Her father was my late husband, Emmett Nichols." She swung a hopeful look between Emily and Mr. VanderMeer before leaving to attend to a family of guests who'd entered the room.

Mr. VanderMeer's handsome face pinked and took on a pained, apologetic expression. "Please forgive my faux pas, Miss Nichols." He raised himself enough in his chair to execute a quick bow. "I hope you'll accept my apology as well as my condolences." His brown eyes turned kind, warming Emily's heart.

"No apology necessary, Mr. VanderMeer. Of course you would assume Papa Ed—Mr. Tompkins—is my natural father."

"And a fine man he is." Mr. VanderMeer's smiling gaze latched on to Emily's and held for a long moment, turning her cheeks warm.

"Yes, he is," she finally managed. "Well, Mr. VanderMeer. . ." Emily wished her voice didn't sound so breathless. "I'll leave you to enjoy your meal." She turned to leave.

He stood up and took her hand, halting her. "Please, call me Gilbert. May I call you Emily?"

Emily's heart throbbed in her throat. Could Mama be right? The notion that a man of Mr. VanderMeer's standing could find her interesting sent her mind reeling.

"Well, may I?" His hand still held hers and she couldn't help comparing its softness to the calloused palm of Seamus O'Grady. At the memory of Seamus her heart did an unexpected hop.

"Yes, of course. . .Gilbert." Emily slipped her hand from his, quirked a wobbly smile, and hurried to join Mama in tending to the other guests.

She pushed down the irrational hope bubbling up inside her. While she still rejected Mama's notion that Gilbert VanderMeer would ever consider her for a wife, the thought of getting her sketches and pastels into the hands of a New York City art patron felt heady.

Later that afternoon as she swept the foyer, Emily contemplated which picture she should choose for Gilbert to take to his mother. Perhaps she should make a new one, specifically drawn with Mrs. VanderMeer's tastes in mind. The thought reminded her of the picture she'd made for Seamus of Dublin's River Anna Liffey. Her pulse quickened at the memory of his blue eyes glistening with moisture as he gazed at her drawing. If she could manage to evoke the same depth of emotion in Gilbert VanderMeer's mother that she'd elicited from Seamus, perhaps her dream of exhibiting and selling her art in New York City could become a reality. Thoughts of Seamus also reminded her that she had left him with the assumption that she would meet him again tomorrow morning on the grassy berm above the river.

Emily groaned. Mama had all but forbidden her to leave the inn again to sketch. She would need to invent another errand that would take her out at dawn.

"Surely sweeping is not that hard, Emily." Papa Ed chuckled as he sidestepped the little pile of dirt she'd gathered near the front door. "I've never heard you groan over such an easy chore."

Emily pasted on a smile and tried to think of a truthful response. "It just seems the more I sweep the more dirt gets tracked in." At least it was an honest answer.

"Then perhaps you'll be happy to learn that you'll be spending less time cleaning and more time baking." Papa Ed crossed his arms over his broad chest and gave her a fond smile. "It seems your pasties have made quite an impression on Mr. VanderMeer. He suggested we sell them to the men working on the aqueduct. Said he heard several of the workers grumbling about their lunch victuals." He nodded. "After some thought, I do believe it's a capital idea. While it wouldn't bring in a lot of money, every extra penny we make helps pay the mortgage."

At the word "mortgage" an uncomfortable knot twisted in Emily's midsection. Ever since Papa Ed borrowed money to renovate the inn and purchase nicer furniture in hopes of attracting patrons, money had been tight.

Papa Ed nodded again. "You could make them and Jasper could sell them. It would be good business experience for the lad. And if the word gets about that we have good food here, it could bring us more customers." He wagged his finger at her. "So, young lady, there will be no more gallivanting off in the mornings to draw sunrises. That time will be better spent making pasties."

Chapter 5

Emily's mind whirled with the emotions roiling in her chest. Her spirit crumpled at the thought of spending her mornings in the kitchen baking. Between the baking and her regular chores, there would be no time for her sketching let alone seeing Seamus. Papa Ed might as well lock her in the root cellar.

Please, Lord, help me find a way to change Papa Ed's mind.

"The bread oven in the kitchen fireplace should bake a dozen pies in a couple of batches. I think I still have that little pushcart in the shed. Haven't used it in several years." Papa Ed's thoughts seemed to be gathering momentum as he fashioned his plans. "It's a bit rickety, but I could take it down to Gil Watson's cooper shop and have him fix it up and make it safe for Jasper to push."

At his last comment, inspiration struck and Emily grasped it like the heaven-sent gift it seemed. "I don't know, Papa Ed. Do you think it wise to allow Jasper to go alone to sell the pasties? He is only ten after all. I'm not sure he is responsible enough to handle the pasties, the money, and the cart all by himself."

"Hmm." Papa Ed grasped his chin and his brow scrunched in deliberation. "Rochester is not the small, innocent village it was a few years ago. And the lad would be dealing with Irish ruffians."

The temptation to tell him that all the Irish were not unscrupulous ruffians tugged hard. She knew at least one Irishman who was sweet, kind, and God-fearing.

Papa Ed heaved a sigh and his expression turned sorrowful. "I'm afraid you're right, lass. I know it will be an extra burden on you, but I agree. You'll need to go with Jasper, if you don't mind."

Thank You, Lord. Thank You!

Emily strove to contain her joy. No need in inviting suspicion by showing her jubilance. She schooled her features to a dutiful smile. "Of course I will go, Papa Ed."

"Good lass." Smiling, Papa Ed patted her cheek. "I'll get that pushcart down to Watson's shop straightaway. He headed out the door, striding with a purpose.

◆—•———•—◆

Two days later Emily couldn't help smiling to herself as she pushed the little refurbished cart down Carroll Street with Jasper and Patches tagging alongside. Rising before sunup, she'd managed to produce fifteen pork and vegetable pasties before breakfast.

A nip in the morning breeze reminded her of the waning summer. Autumn—Emily's favorite season to capture in her sketchbook—would soon cloak the Irondequoit Valley in its vivid hues of red and gold. Already some leaves were showing tinges of yellow. Before leaving the inn, she'd tucked her sketchbook in the cart alongside the pasties.

Papa Ed suggested that a spot near the Main Street Bridge would catch most of the workers on their way down to the construction site and be public enough for safety. Emily settled the cart in a sunny spot near an elm tree. When the sun became too warm, she could move the cart to the shade of the tree.

"Pa says if we sell all our pies, I can keep a penny for myself." Jasper picked up a stick and began to play with Patches.

Emily grinned as she resituated baskets of pies in the cart. "Then you'll need to actually sell the pasties instead of playing with Patches."

The sound of distant voices drew her attention to the Main Street Bridge where several scruffy-looking men in rough clothing had started across.

Emily found herself searching the group for Seamus. Over the past couple days she'd often wondered what he thought when she failed to meet him again at the spot where she sketched him the picture of his Irish river.

"Pasties! Get your pork pasties! Just a penny!" Jasper jumped out in front of the cart and began waving his arms as the men neared the west side of the river.

Emily cringed at Jasper's childlike enthusiasm, but couldn't deny its effectiveness. The next moment several of the men had gathered in front of the cart.

"I'll have one of your pasties, lad. Gettin' weary of beans and stale bread. Pork pasty sounds mighty good for a change." A scraggly bearded man at the front of the group reached into his pocket and brought out a penny, which he handed to Jasper.

Jasper took the coin from the man's grimy hand and then sold three more pies in quick succession.

Emily hurried to distribute the sold pasties then focused on securing the coins in a little drawstring bag in her pocket.

"Are ya the money changer then?"

At the teasing tone in the man's familiar Irish lilt, Emily's heart jumped to her throat. Heat leaped to her face as she looked up into Seamus O'Grady's blue eyes that twinkled with fun.

"I'll buy one of your pasties if you'll let me eat it here with you at lunchtime."

"The way they're goin', we'll be out of pasties by then." Jasper glanced down at the half-empty basket.

"You must be Jasper."

"How do you know my name?" Jasper's eyes grew wide, and Emily prayed Seamus wouldn't divulge their previous acquaintance.

Seamus's glance bounced between Jasper and Emily and his expression turned serious. "Why, I know many things, me lad."

Jasper's mouth gaped. "Are you Irish?" His voice turned breathless.

"That I am."

"You—you don't eat children, do you?" Jasper moved closer to Emily, and she had to stifle a giggle.

Seamus's brows lowered as if in contemplation. "Not if I can have a good pasty instead."

This time Emily's giggle broke free.

Seamus held out a penny, but Jasper leaned back as if reluctant to take it.

Emily took the coin and pocketed it then handed Seamus one of the plumper pies.

"It smells divine." For a long moment his blue gaze attached itself to hers. He opened his lunch tin and slipped the pie inside then replaced the lid. "So, will ya still be here if I come back at lunchtime?"

Emily's pulse quickened beneath his lingering gaze. She should tell him no. As Jasper said, the pasties would likely all be sold long before noon. Before she could open her mouth, Patches scampered over to Seamus's feet and began barking, her stubby tail swishing like a crazed metronome.

Seamus laughed then knelt and petted the pup's furry head. "Hey, wee bit o' trouble. How ya been keepin'? Stayin' out o' trouble, are ya?"

"You know Patches?" Jasper's curiosity seemed to overtake his fear of Seamus.

Seamus stood and grinned at Jasper. "I met your sister and Patches a few days ago."

A shrill whistle sounded.

Seamus's smile faded and he looked at Emily. "I have to go, but I'll be back at noon. It's hopin' I am, that you'll be here too."

Emily started to open her mouth to say she couldn't promise when the apothecary from Mill Street strode up, forcing her to turn her attention to him. By the time he'd bought four pasties for himself and his shopkeepers, Seamus had gone.

By noon they'd sold all but two pies. Still, Emily lingered beside the pushcart. She glanced southward toward the construction site hoping to see Seamus appear over the berm. When he didn't, the words from Proverbs 16:9 that Mama often quoted rang in her ears. *A man's heart deviseth his way: but the* LORD *directeth his steps."*

She sighed and folded the linen towels she'd used to cover the pasties. Perhaps it was just as well. Papa Ed would never allow her to be friends with Seamus. Perhaps this was God's way of guiding her away from him.

"Hey, Jasper, wanna go fishin' with me down by my pa's mill?" Freddie Atkinson, one of Jasper's best friends, raced up to her brother, who'd abandoned the cart to play with Patches. The barefoot boy held out his reed fishing pole, his freckled face eager beneath his tattered straw hat.

Jasper turned pleading eyes to Emily. "May I go? Pleeease? I'll do your evening chores."

Emily smiled. "You've worked hard all morning selling the pasties. I think you've earned some fishing time." She handed him one of the two remaining pies and wrapped the other in a towel and nestled it in a basket. "We might as well have these for our lunches." She schooled her expression to a stern look and wagged her finger at him. "Don't go any farther than Mr. Atkinson's mill pond, and be home by midafternoon."

"Thanks, sis." Jasper grinned and patted the side of his leg. "C'mon, Patches."

"Oh no." Emily hurried to scoop the little dog up in her arms. "The last time she went fishing with you she came back covered in mud and smelling of fish."

As Jasper and Freddie scampered off, Emily struggled to keep hold of the squirming, barking dog. She gave an exasperated huff. "I think I'll have to start putting you on a lead."

"Causin' ya trouble again, is she?"

Emily looked up into Seamus's smiling face and her heart made its usual hop at the sight of him. "She wants to go fishing with Jasper and his friend Freddie, but the last time she returned from a fishing trip with them she came home looking like a ball of mud and stinking of fish." Emily wished her giggle didn't sound so silly.

"Did ya sell all your pasties then?" Seamus looked at the cart.

"All but two. I gave Jasper one and I thought I'd have the other for lunch while I sketched."

With one arm across his chest and the other behind his back, Seamus dipped a bow. "Then may I have the pleasure of dining with you, m'lady?"

She should tell him no. Instead she smiled and said what she felt. "I would like that." She unwrapped the remaining pie and retrieved her sketchbook from the cart, wishing Seamus's nearness didn't make her pulse quicken so. "I'm sorry I wasn't able to meet you two days ago at the place where I made your sketch." With the pasty in one hand and her sketchbook in the other, Emily settled herself in the grass.

Seamus joined her and shrugged. "I wasn't there meself. I've spent me last two mornin's smithin' at Bray's Blacksmith Shop."

Emily paused to give thanks for the food and Seamus bowed his head. During their shared prayer she felt their connection tighten.

"You're a blacksmith?" The question popped out on the heels of her "Amen." She'd assumed the canal workers lacked any skills beyond digging ditches and hefting stone.

He reached into his lunch tin and pulled out the pasty he'd bought from her and Jasper earlier and a glass bottle of water with a cork stopper. He took a big bite of the pie and nodded. "Learned it from me da when I was but a wee lad younger than Jasper," he said when he'd cleared his mouth. He gazed toward the river, a distant look in his eyes. "Someday I'll have me own shop—O'Grady Brothers—with Liam and Cullen."

"Here in Rochester?" Emily couldn't help the hope blooming in her chest that Seamus planned to settle here. As she munched on her pasty, she propped her sketchbook against her drawn-up knees and began a sketch she hadn't expected to do.

He shrugged again, and she experienced a tinge of disappointment. "Perhaps, if the Maguires' landlord, Mr. James Dowlin', is willin' to help me and me brothers establish a shop."

Emily knew of the Irishman James Dowling who'd bought land some years ago on the river's east side and named the place Dublin. "I'm sure Mr. Dowling's place is not at all like the Dublin you're from," she said around a bite of pasty.

Smiling, he shook his head. "Not much, except for the Irish families like the Maguires who took me in." His smile quirked into a grin. "This pasty tastes divine. Did ya make it yourself then?"

Emily nodded. "I made them all this morning before breakfast."

He lowered his voice to a near whisper. "Don't go tellin' Iona Maguire, but this is the best thing I've tasted since I left Ireland. Better even, me thinks, than the pasties me own ma makes."

"Thank you." Emily's heart soared at his words, wondering why his praises of her pasties made her happier than the compliments she'd received from Gilbert VanderMeer. "Mama taught me to make them, but she says my crust is lighter than hers." She added some shading details to her sketch and frowned, not entirely pleased with her success in capturing the likeness of her subject.

His smile widened. "Your mother is right. The crust is like air."

"So what *is* Dublin, Ireland, like?" To better capture his likeness on paper she needed him more animated.

His expression turned distant. The wistful look in his eyes became pained. "Ah, 'tis a lovely place, but a hard place—hard as the cobbles that pave the streets."

Yes, this was the look she needed. As he talked, she added the pencil strokes that brought the image to life on the paper. She sketched with quick, sure strokes, her heart breaking for him as he told of the overcrowded city that led to fevers like the one that took his father, the lack of food, and the discriminatory laws that made it impossible for his family to flourish. These dark images he juxtaposed incongruently with ones of achingly beautiful landscapes populated by a big-hearted people who found strength in their faith in God, joy in their songs, and poetry in the world around them.

"Lovely but hard," he reiterated. "Too hard." He shook his head. "Me heart will always carry a bit of the old sod, but it's here in America where I can make a better life for me, me brothers, and me mother. Me friend Father Patrick says that here in America whatever a man can dream, he can become." His blue gaze latched on to hers. "So your dream is to become a great artist in the city of New York?" A tightness came into his voice, thickening the musical lilt of his brogue.

She nodded. "Yes, that is my dream." For the first time her heart failed to dance at the thought of leaving Rochester and realizing her dream in New York City.

"So are ya goin' to show me what you've drawn?" He craned his neck as if to get a peek at her sketchbook.

Emily's heart thudded with trepidation as she turned the page toward him, unsure how he would respond to his portrait.

His eyes widened and his jaw went slack as a shrill whistle sounded in the distance. Without a word he corked his bottle of water, dropped it into his lunch tin with a clang, and strode south toward the construction site.

Chapter 6

Y ou drew this? Why this is very good, Emily." Surprised admiration filled Gilbert VanderMeer's voice as he gazed at the framed picture on the lobby wall. "I've noticed and admired this landscape of the Genesee River's Great Falls since my first day here at your inn." He leaned in and peered at the picture with a more scrutinizing gaze, his smile evaporating. "Of course, on closer examination I can see that it bears the marks of an amateur talent."

At the caveat to his earlier compliment, Emily's pride in one of her favorite works deflated. Earlier today Seamus had left her confidence in her artistic ability bruised when he walked away without comment after seeing the portrait she'd drawn of him. She didn't need another blow from Gilbert VanderMeer.

"Mama insisted on hanging it in the lobby." Emily hated the quaver in her voice. "I'm sure it doesn't deserve such a prominent spot—"

"No, no, my dear." Gilbert turned from the picture and grasped her hand, his expression apologetic. "Your landscape is delightful. You've drawn such a wonderful rendition of the site, I can almost hear the roar of the water as it cascades over the falls. I certainly did not mean to sound critical." His smile turned kind. "Too many hours spent picking apart the works of the great masters with my mother, I suppose." He glanced back at the picture. "The shading could be more subtle, but your talent is undeniable and, to my eye, quite considerable. I believe that with some direction from professors at one of the better artistic academies in France or England you could produce paintings to rival that of the best landscape artists. I'd venture to say that, with training, your work could bring top dollar at the best art auctions." He arched a brow. "Have you done any work with paint and canvas?"

"No." Emily's spirit sagged. He might as well have suggested that she sprout wings and fly to the moon. She slipped her hand from his and turned away so he wouldn't see the tears welling in her eyes. She picked up her feather duster from the sideboard and resumed the work she'd been doing when Gilbert entered the lobby and inquired about the picture. "I'm afraid artistic academies in Europe are beyond my family's means." She paused to swallow a wad of tears. "I would love to work with paint and canvas, but I can scarcely afford sketchbooks. I only have pastels because two years ago when Mr. Stowell and Mr. Bishop brought their traveling art exhibition to Rochester one of the artists stayed here at our inn. When he learned of my interest in drawing he gave me a box of pastels, which he said were falling out of favor and he didn't much use anymore."

Gilbert crossed the room to her, took the duster from her hand and set it on the table, then took her hands in his. "Emily, your pastels are lovely, but they don't last like oil paint. With a talent like yours, your time is wasted dusting and making pasties." He grinned. "As delicious as your pasties are. You should have a paintbrush in your hand, not a feather duster or a wad of dough. As I said before, my mother is a patron of the arts. When she sees your work, I'm sure she'll be happy to sponsor such a budding talent."

At the thought of studying art abroad, Emily's heart skipped a beat and her breath caught in her throat. Then reality slammed her back to earth. "I could never accept such an extravagant gift from a total stranger. Your mother doesn't even know me."

"She could know you." Enthusiasm infused his voice as he gazed into her eyes. "I must confess I find you quite beguiling, Emily. I would like for us to become better acquainted. In the interim, if you will allow me, I would be more than happy to provide you with canvas and paint so you could have a more lasting medium with which to work."

Joy exploded in Emily's chest like fireworks. Reason doused it. While Gilbert's offer of patronage might be honorable and genuine, the notion of accepting gifts from a gentleman she scarcely knew bothered her.

Somehow she managed a feeble smile. "Thank you for your kind offer, Mr. Vand—"

He raised a brow, his smile admonishing.

"Gilbert," she corrected herself. "But I couldn't accept any gifts without my parents' approval." With that, she fled the room.

Later that afternoon as she headed to the kitchen to help Mama and their maid Sophie prepare supper, Emily's emotions still churned from her conversation with Gilbert. Her heart writhed. He'd made clear his intentions of pursuing a relationship with her. As much as she longed to accept his offer, any gifts would doubtless come attached with expectations that she would reciprocate his feelings, something Emily wasn't sure she could do. Deep inside, she knew that Gilbert VanderMeer didn't cause her heart to skip the way Seamus O'Grady did.

"Emily." Papa Ed's voice beckoned from the chest-high partition that divided the lobby from the inn's office.

Emily pushed open the little hinged gate that led to the office area.

Papa Ed's mustache bristled with his broad smile. "Come, lass, I have something for you."

Emily smiled. Papa Ed must have figured her share of the pasty sales. "The pasty sales went well. Jasper and I sold all but two, which we had for lunch."

Papa Ed nodded and ducked behind the partition. "Aye, lass. I'm that pleased with the pasty sales. So much so, I'd like for you and Jasper to continue selling them every day—except for Sundays and when the weather is inclement, of course." He grunted as he bent and pulled a box from the shelves inside the partition and set it on the smooth surface above. "Mr. VanderMeer very much admires your pictures. He suggested that while you're out sellin' the pasties you should use the time to practice your artwork as well. Said God has given you a great talent and you should use it. Your mother and I agree." He dove back down and came up with a stack of rectangular canvas pieces about ten inches by twelve inches and plopped them on the partition top as well, then he pulled out a wooden easel, which he unfolded and set in front of her.

Emily gasped and stared, unbelieving, at the articles before her. When she could move she walked to the desk and lifted the box's lid. Inside she found jars of powdered pigment in varying colors, an array of brushes, a jar of linseed oil, and a palette on which to mix the colors.

She gaped at her stepfather. "But Papa Ed, can we afford these?"

His countenance sagged with a sorrowful look. "I wish we could, lass, but you know we struggle to keep the roof over our heads. These are gifts from Mr. VanderMeer." Papa Ed brightened and winked at Emily. "Looks to me like our girl has an admirer." His eyes grew watery. "For years your mother and I have worked ourselves into the ground to make this inn a success. He pulled Emily into a hug. "I'm that pleased, lass. With a connection like Gilbert VanderMeer, our days of skimpin' and penny-pinchin' will be over. No more worrying each month about bringing in enough money to pay the mortgage. When the canal is finished VanderMeer will see to it that the cream of New York society flocks to the Riverside Inn like bees to a hive. The mortgage will be paid, and we'll own this place free and clear and have the most prosperous establishment in Rochester."

❖——❖

Dear Lord, what am I to do? The prayer Emily had prayed since yesterday afternoon continued to roll unanswered through her mind and heart as she pushed the cart of pasties toward the Main Street Bridge. Jasper, with Patches on a lead, ran ahead, oblivious to the tumult inside her.

When Papa Ed gave her the art supplies, he'd all but danced with her in the lobby, sure that a marriage proposal from Gilbert VanderMeer was soon to come. Mama had already begun planning the wedding, wondering if the Riverside Inn could accommodate a reception worthy of the New York VanderMeers. When Emily attempted to restrain her parents' exuberance by reminding them that

Gilbert had not yet presented her with a proposal of marriage or had even asked Papa Ed's permission to court her, they'd refused to hear it. "When God opens a door, you walk through it," Mama had said.

Emily sighed as she settled the cart beneath the branches of the elm tree where they'd set up shop yesterday. Any notion of returning Gilbert's gifts was out of the question. Despite her warnings to Mama and Papa Ed not to get ahead of themselves concerning Gilbert's intentions toward her, she couldn't deny that she'd seen interest in his eyes. Gilbert VanderMeer could give her and her family everything they'd ever dreamed of. As Mama always said, "You can love a rich man as well as a poor man." But as much as Emily tried, she couldn't make her heart smile at the thought of Gilbert. When he took her hand, his touch didn't quicken her pulse. The only man who'd made her heart dance was Seamus O'Grady.

Her heart pricked at the memory of Seamus's expression when she showed him the sketch she'd drawn of him. She rearranged the baskets of still-warm chicken pasties on the cart's top shelf. With each pie she made this morning she'd wondered if it would be the one Seamus would buy.

A soft sigh puffed from her lips. Seamus O'Grady would likely not be buying any of her pies today. She'd drawn his portrait without his permission in order to have his likeness at hand whenever she wanted to look at it. Obviously her poor rendering had offended him. *Now he will likely avoid me—*

"Emily!" Jasper tugged on her sleeve, his voice an urgent whisper. "Here comes that Irishman again."

Emily looked up to see Seamus striding toward them. Her heart vaulted to her throat, settled for an instant, then raced like a frightened rabbit. She hoped the tree's shade obscured the heightened color in her burning cheeks.

No smile graced his well-shaped lips, and the twinkle had gone from his blue eyes. "I'm sorry for walkin' away from you yesterday."

Emily waved her hand and forced a weak smile she couldn't sustain. "I'm the one who should apologize. I certainly didn't mean to offend you with my drawing. I just wanted—"

He shook his head. "No, it was amazin'. It was as if you'd reached into me chest, snatched me soul, and put it on the paper." His blue eyes turned watery. "I'd never seen me likeness on paper. It shook me like an earth tremor." He glanced down for an instant before meeting her eyes again. "That you'd want to draw me likeness touched me so deep it struck me dumb. Me mind wouldn't work. Me tongue wouldn't work. So when the whistle blew, I just walked away."

"So are ya gonna buy a pasty or not, mate?"

At the impatient voice from someone in the growing line behind Seamus, he dug into his pocket and pulled out a penny, which he handed to Jasper with a wink. "There, me lad. Give me the biggest one you have."

Jasper handed him a pie. "I think she made 'em all the same size."

Seamus gave Emily a lingering look. "I'll be back at lunchtime."

Emily gazed at Seamus's broad back as he walked toward the construction site, joy effervescing inside her like bubbles in soda water. *Seamus doesn't hate me.*

Emily put two pasties aside for her and Jasper's lunches along with the two jars of water she'd brought to wash them down. However quickly the remaining pies sold, she was determined to stay and visit with Seamus. At least now she could stay with a clear—or at least a somewhat clear—conscience. This morning, with Mama and Papa Ed's blessings, she'd stowed her new artist supplies on the cart's bottom shelf. She could hardly wait to mix colors on her palette and brush them onto a canvas.

Like yesterday, the pasties all sold by noontime. Emily unwrapped the two she'd saved and handed one to her brother along with a jar of water and the two of them settled down in the grass beneath the tree.

Jasper sniffed his pie. "The pork ones were good, but these chicken ones smell even better."

"That they do, me lad." Seamus came striding up wearing the grin that always caused Emily's pulse to race. "I can't wait to dig into me own." Clutching his lunch pail in front of him, he dipped a deep bow. "Miss Nichols, may I join you and young Master Tompkins for lunch?"

Emily couldn't suppress a giggle. "Why, Mr. O'Grady, we would be honored."

Seamus settled down beside Emily. "Would it be all right with ya if I said grace for the meal?"

Emily nodded, touched that he would want to lead them in prayer. Mama always said you can tell a lot about a man by the way he prays.

"Dear Lord, we thank Ya for this food and the precious hands that prepared it."

Emily's pulse quickened. Did he consider her precious?

"I thank Ya that I wasn't sent to the other town to cut stone and can be here to share this meal with Emily and Jasper."

Caught up in his beautiful Irish lilt, Emily found herself struggling to focus on his words as he went on to pray for his family in Ireland, Emily and Jasper's family, the Maguires, his friend Father Patrick, and his fellow workers.

"Whew, and I thought Pa's prayers were long," Jasper said following Seamus's "Amen."

Emily and Seamus shared a laugh, his gaze holding hers for a long moment.

"So will ya be sketchin' somethin' today, Emily?" Seamus asked between bites of his pasty.

"Better than that." She set her pie aside on her linen napkin and stood to retrieve her art supplies from the bottom of the cart.

Jasper gave a bored groan. "May I take Patches down to Freddie's pa's mill and watch them grind flour?"

Emily nodded. "If you're finished eating." She couldn't help feeling relieved that Jasper would rather do something other than be with her and Seamus. While she'd warned Jasper about mentioning Seamus to Mama and Papa Ed, the more time her brother spent with Seamus, the more apt he was to let something slip out about Emily's friendship with the Irishman.

"I am," Jasper said as he fed the last bit of crust to Patches, jumped to his feet, and started toward the street.

"Stay out of trouble, keep Patches on the lead, and be home for afternoon chores," Emily called after him.

"I will," Jasper hollered back as he and Patches ran toward the Main Street Bridge.

Seamus chuckled. "He's a good lad. Reminds me of me brother Cullen a few years ago." Sadness crept into his voice, something Emily had noticed whenever he mentioned his family.

She hurried to set up the easel, hoping the change of subject would brighten his mood.

As she situated a canvas on the easel, Seamus's eyes widened and he gave a low whistle. "Ah, now that is the stuff of a proper artist."

Emily smiled, deciding not to divulge how the new art supplies came into her possession. "Oil painting is new to me, so I think I'll begin with something easy like the bridge." She dipped a brush into the blob of gray paint on her palette and began tentative strokes to get a feel of the brush in her hand. Her confidence growing, she added more colors and the bridge began to take shape.

"Soon you will be able to paint a picture of the aqueduct. Mr. Drake hopes to have it finished by the end of the year." He gave a little laugh. "But I fear his hopes are higher than the canal itself. The way it's goin', I don't see it finished before the middle of next year." He sprang to his feet. "Ah, that reminds me. I have some'at for you." He dug into his pocket and pulled out a pink stone. "It's red medina sandstone. What we're usin' to build the aqueduct." He held it out to her. "The color matches the roses in your cheeks, I think."

Emily took the stone from his hand and the touch of his fingers against her palm sent pleasant tingles up her arm. She gazed at the rough pink stone and unexpected tears sprang to her eyes. She swallowed them down. "Thank you. It's beautiful."

"And strong. Strong and beautiful, like you." His voice turned husky.

"I will treasure it always." And she knew she would. She smiled up at him, her heart thudding in her chest. Seamus possessed a simple honesty that allowed her to feel free to show her emotions, so different from Gilbert's stiff and proper demeanor. Within the span of a day she had received two very different gifts from two very different men. While she knew Gilbert's gift had cost a good deal of money, Seamus's gift had cost nothing. Yet between the gifts, it was the pink stone in her hand she most treasured.

Seamus grinned. "Mayhap you can use it to choose just the right color when you paint a picture of the grand new aqueduct."

Emily dropped the stone into her apron pocket and turned her focus back to her work with the canvas. "So when the aqueduct is finished will you be moving with the construction crew to help dig another section of the canal?" Though she strove to keep her voice nonchalant, it sounded strained to her ears.

"I reckon that depends on if I've saved enough money by then to bring me family here and if Mr. Dowlin' will help me establish me blacksmith shop."

"I hope you can stay." The words popped unintended from Emily's mouth. Her cheeks grew warm, but she didn't care if he saw her blush. She wanted him to know how she felt.

"So do I." His tone turned so tender it made her heart ache, then it brightened. "I want to see all the grand pictures you paint of the aqueduct and the new stone canal."

The sound of a whistle wafted from the construction site. Emily and Seamus looked at each other. Neither spoke, but a volume of sentiments passed between them. He never touched her, but his gaze covered her face with tender caresses.

He broke the silence. "I'll see you tomorrow then?"

"Yes, I would like that very much." Her voice sounded foreign in her ears.

Emily watched him walk away. In one hand she held Gilbert's paintbrush. With the other she reached in and wrapped her fingers around Seamus's stone.

Dear Lord, what am I to do?

Chapter 7

Seamus sat on his cot in the corner of the Maguire's cabin, his mood as dreary as the rainy October morning. With the rain, Emily wouldn't be selling pasties at the Main Street Bridge this morning. Over the past two months his visits with her at lunchtime had become the one bright spot in the drudgery of his days. In truth, his heart hungered for her company far more than his belly hungered for her pasties. Each day, from the moment he woke, he looked forward to seeing her smiling face, laughing with her as he watched her create her beautiful paintings, and sharing his heart about everything but the one thing that burned in his chest like an unquenchable flame—his growing love for her.

"Me beans and pork may not be as tasty as the pasties you're used to lad, but at least they'll fill your belly on a cold, wet day." Iona Maguire's voice yanked Seamus from his bittersweet musings.

Seamus smiled and reached for his shoes tucked under his bed. "You know I like everythin' you cook, Iona."

At the hearth, Iona went back to dipping beans and chunks of pork into a jar. Glancing over her shoulder, she grinned and shot Seamus a knowing look. "But I'm thinkin' maybe it's the young lady's company ya crave more than her pasties."

"Mayhap." Seamus finished tying his shoes and tugged on his wool shirt and began buttoning it up. The autumn days had turned cool. Soon he'd need to wear a coat and scarf and gloves to work.

Iona put the jar of beans in his lunch tin then nestled a generous slice of corn bread beside it. The lines on her forehead deepened with her frown and she sighed. "I'm not your ma, not even kin. But the Lord has put ya on me heart, and I feel it's me place to give ya me mind as I'd do for me own boy."

Seamus stifled a groan. With her son at sea Iona had latched on to Seamus as an outlet for her maternal nurturing. While he appreciated her concern and often found her ministrations comforting, they could, at times, feel smothering.

She set the lunch pail on the table and cocked her head toward the nearest chair. "Come sit and let me tell ya what's on me heart." She fetched the Bible from the cupboard and, with a soft grunt, sat across the table from him.

In no mood for a sermon, Seamus shook his head and glanced at the door. "I really should be gettin' on."

Iona shook her head as she opened the Bible and thumbed through the pages. "It's plenty early and Terrence is still outside cuttin' wood. You can sit for a wee bit an' hear what I have to say. Ah, there it is." She focused on the page before her and proceeded to read the words from Proverbs 31. " 'Who can find a virtuous woman? For her price is far above rubies. The heart of her husband doth safely trust in her, so that he shall have no need of spoil.' "

As she read about the woman rising while it is yet night and giving meat to her household, Seamus couldn't help thinking of Emily rising early every morning to make pasties to sell. Her dreams of selling her paintings showed her willingness to work with her hands using the talent God had given her.

" 'Favour is deceitful and beauty is vain: but a woman that feareth the Lord, she shall be praised. Give her of the fruit of her hands; and let her own works praise her in the gates.' " Iona looked at Seamus. "Does this sound like the lass that has captured your heart?"

"It does. It sounds just like Emily." Seamus hated the defensive tone in his voice. He strove for patience. "I appreciate your concern and for remindin' me o' the scriptures, but I must go to work now." He started to stand up.

"Sit back down, lad." Her voice broached no resistance. Iona heaved another sigh as he obeyed. "You haven't been here that long, but 'tis gen'rally known that her stepfather, Edward Tompkins, bears a strong dislike for the Irish." She waved her hand. "Now I wouldn't blame the lass for not mentionin' it to ya, but it seems to me it's only fair that ya know what you're up against. I'm that fond o' ya lad, and I wouldn't want to see your heart broke."

Anger balled in Seamus's belly. He forced a stiff smile as he rose and strained to get a better grip on his temper. "I thank ya for the warnin', Iona, but I can fight me own battles, and Emily Nichols is worth fightin' for."

As he walked the half mile from Dublin to Rochester the words from Proverbs 31 kept running through his mind. *The heart of her husband doth safely trust in her.* He'd thought he could trust Emily and that their relationship had grown so close there was nothing they couldn't confide in each other. It hurt to think that she was too afraid or too embarrassed to confide in him about her stepfather's feelings toward the Irish.

Another thought planted itself in his mind and seeped down to sour in his gut. Or, unlike him, perhaps Emily didn't expect or even desire for their relationship to go any deeper or lead to anything more permanent. Despite what he told Iona, he couldn't help wondering what else Emily might not have shared with him.

◆—◆ · ◆◆

Emily gripped Patches's lead as she made her way down the street, skirting the many puddles the morning rain had deposited. The canopy of steel-gray clouds still lingering above mirrored her melancholy mood. She knew why. She missed Seamus. The rain had precluded her and Jasper from making their usual trek to the bridge this morning. Without a protective covering they'd have been soaked to the skin before they'd sold a single pasty.

She paused to tug Patches away from a mud puddle. "Get away from there you wee bit o' trouble." Realizing she'd used Seamus's description of the dog, she laughed. Seamus had become such a large part of her life, she couldn't imagine—didn't want to imagine—life without him. She reached her free hand into her apron pocket and fingered the rough piece of stone he'd given her weeks earlier, and smiled. Despite the chill wind that tugged at her wool cape and stung her cheeks, the thought of him warmed her. Her heart ached to show him the painting she'd finished of the Genesee River resplendent in the bright colors of autumn. Nothing she painted felt finished until Seamus had seen it. Her soul hungered for his thoughts. His company. Him.

Her smile widened remembering how, two days ago, he'd teased her as she struggled to replicate the vibrant colors of the leaves that adorned the trees along the river. He'd grinned at her from the shade of the elm tree. "Ah, perhaps it is that God has used colors they can't make into powders" he'd said, sending her a wink that set her heart prancing.

Her smile at the memory faded as another image muscled its way into her thoughts. Two weeks ago, before he left for New York City on business having to do with the construction of the Erie Canal, Gilbert had given her more colored powders. Since his initial gift he'd continued to lavish her with art supplies, and with each gift, she'd felt more beholden to him. At the same time his gifts had failed to purchase a scintilla more of her affection. Indeed, while one day of not seeing Seamus's smiling face relegated her to doldrums, she hadn't missed Gilbert an instant in the fortnight since he left Rochester. But while Papa Ed would never consider Seamus as a suitor for Emily's hand, he prayed daily for just such a petition from Gilbert VanderMeer.

Dear Lord, what am I to do?

Emily's tortured heart sagged like the sodden flag hanging from the pole outside the post office. All she could feel about Gilbert's absence was gladness for a reprieve from his romantic overtures, which had grown more ardent over the past month. The day before he left they'd passed in the inn's main hallway. He'd caught her arm and leaned toward her and she was sure he'd tried to kiss her. Stunned and frightened, she'd pulled away from his grasp. He'd apologized, saying he'd thought she'd tripped and he was attempting to save her from a fall. She hadn't entirely believed him, but she wasn't certain enough of his intentions to mention the incident to Mama or Papa Ed. Even if she had told them, they'd become so enamored with the notion of Gilbert becoming their son-in-law that they'd likely have dismissed her concerns out of hand.

She sighed again, wishing she had someone in whom to confide about her conflicted heart. Mama would be no help, partial as she was toward Gilbert and, of course, Emily had never mentioned Seamus and her friendship with him because of Papa Ed's bias against Irish people. Emily might have confided in the housemaids, Sophie or Beth, who were near her age, but she didn't entirely trust them not to divulge any such conversation to Mama or worse, Papa Ed.

"Come, Patches, we need to get the mail." She yanked the pup away from barking at a squirrel and headed up the post office steps.

Inside a half-dozen people stood in line in front of the counter behind which postal clerk George Draper presided.

"Is there anythin' for a Terrance and Iona Maguire, or for Seamus O'Grady?" The plump woman at the front of the line asked in a thick Irish accent.

Emily's heart quickened. This had to be the Iona Maguire at whose home Seamus resided. If she couldn't see Seamus today, at least she could have the Maguire woman give him her regards and let him know that if the weather cleared she'd be back at the bridge selling pasties tomorrow morning.

"Ah, Seamus will be that thrilled." Smiling, the woman dropped the letter George handed her into the basket on her arm and headed toward the door.

Emily approached the woman. "You know Seamus O'Grady?"

The woman's eyebrows arched as she looked at Emily then down at Patches. She smiled and a look of recognition replaced her bemused expression. "Ah, you must be Miss Nichols. Glancing down, she grinned. "And this must be Patches." She held out her hand. "I'm Iona Maguire. Seamus is stayin' with me and me husband, Terrance, over in Dublin."

That Seamus had mentioned her and Patches to Iona warmed Emily's heart. She shook the woman's hand. "Would you let Seamus know that I should be back selling pasties at the bridge tomorrow morning?"

"That I will." A pensive expression pinched her brows together. "I think me body needs to rest a wee bit 'fore I head back home." She glanced at the bench along the post office wall. "Would ya sit and visit with me a bit, lass?"

"Yes, I'd like that." Perhaps Iona was God's answer to Emily's prayer for a confidant. Seamus had spoken of Iona as a woman of deep faith. Though Emily didn't feel comfortable mentioning Gilbert VanderMeer to Iona, a talk with her might help Emily untangle her snarled emotions.

When they'd both sat, Iona smiled and reached down and petted Patches. "Seamus calls this one—"

"A wee bit o' trouble," they both said in unison, and Emily laughed.

Iona's smile faded. "Seamus speaks admirin' o' ya, lass. More than admirin'."

"And I admire Seamus very much. He's become. . .a very special friend." Emily had kept her feelings about Seamus bottled up for so long, it felt good to let them out.

Iona glanced down at Patches before returning her gaze to Emily. "I've kinda adopted the boy as me own while he's away from his own mam. I wouldn't want to see 'im hurt."

"Neither would I." Emily's heart thudded. Had Seamus shared with Iona that he held a special affection for Emily?

Iona's smile returned. "Seamus has shown me some o' your lovely pictures. 'Tis a true gift from God, ya have."

"Thank you." Emily's smile wobbled. "I wish, like Solomon, God had given me the gift of wisdom instead."

Iona cocked her head and her expression turned sympathetic. "Is it your stepda's hard feelin's toward the Irish that's troublin' ya, lass?"

Heat leaped to Emily's face. She nodded and looked at her hands folded in her lap. "Yes, that's part of it." Of course Edward Tompkin's aversion to the Irish would be common knowledge in Dublin. "I haven't told my parents about my friendship with Seamus. Every day I like him more and more. I'm afraid if I tell them, they will forbid me to see him. I don't know what to do."

Iona took her hands. "O' course you've got to be respectful to your parents, lass, but if God is leadin' you toward the man He has chosen for you, you can't let yer stepda bar the way on account o' his own hard feelin's." She sighed. "Me own mam and da didn't like me Terrance at first, him bein' a fardowner from Dublin and us from County Tipperary. But by and by, the Lord softened me folks' hearts to Terrance, and they blessed our union."

"But how will I know what man, if any, God has chosen for me?" Emily ignored the tears springing in her eyes.

Iona patted Emily's hands. " 'Trust in the Lord with all thine heart; and lean not unto thine own understanding. In all thy ways acknowledge him, and he shall direct thy paths.' "

At the familiar verses from Proverbs Emily managed a weak smile. "Mama reminds me of that all the time, but what if I meet more than one man along that path? How will I know which one to choose?"

Iona's expression turned thoughtful. "Well, o' course the first thing is he has to be a Christian man. Like it says in Second Corinthians, 'Be ye not unequally yoked together with unbelievers.' Next, ya need to decide whether or not the man you're considerin' is a good man. Our Lord tells us in the Gospel of Matthew, 'A good man out of the good treasure of the heart bringeth forth good things: and an evil man out of the evil treasure bringeth forth evil things.' " She nodded. "Watch what he says. How he acts. If he's good, you'll see it. If he's bad, you'll see that too. And like the scripture says in Galatians, ya want to look for the fruits o' the Spirit. Love, joy, peace, long-sufferin', gentleness, goodness, faith, meekness, and temperance." She let go of Emily's hand and crossed her arms over her chest. "If he has all the fruits o' the Spirit, he's got the Holy Spirit in 'im and he's a good man. To know if he's the man for you, ya gotta pray and wait for God to tell you, 'cause He will."

Emily smiled. Over the past weeks she had seen in Seamus many of the fruits of the Spirit Iona had mentioned. "Thank you, Iona. I will continue to pray and ask God to guide me. I do hope we can talk again sometime." She dropped her gaze to her hands, uncertain if such an occasion would come again.

"So do I, lass." Iona rose with a groan and patted Emily on the shoulder. She winked. "I'll tell Seamus to look for ya and your pasty cart tomorrow," she said and walked out of the post office.

Though still conflicted, Emily's heart felt lighter as she headed home. Iona's voice reciting the fruits of the Spirit played through her mind. *Love, joy, peace, long-suffering, gentleness, goodness, faith, meekness, temperance.* She could attribute every one of those to Seamus. On the other hand, aside from a measure of generosity by gifting her with the art supplies, she couldn't say if Gilbert possessed any of those qualities.

When she reached the inn she picked up Patches and carried her inside. "I'll need to wash your paws before I can let you run loose inside."

In the lobby her heart jolted then sank to her stomach at the sight of Gilbert sitting in a wing chair and reading a newspaper.

He looked up, smiled, and rose as he set the paper aside. "How is my favorite artist?"

"I'm well, thank you." Her words belied the queasy feeling in her stomach. She pasted on a stiff smile. "I do hope your trip from New York City was a pleasant one."

He shrugged. "Tolerable, but not nearly as pleasant or as quick as the trip will be when one can travel the entire distance by canal. Speaking of the canal, I was about to head to the aqueduct construction site. Would you do me the honor of accompanying me on the stroll?" His confident demeanor showed no hint of uncertainty. Gilbert VanderMeer didn't expect rejection. "I have much to share with you concerning my discussions with my mother about your art."

Emily's heart quickened at the prospect that Mrs. VanderMeer had decided to sponsor her artwork. "What—what did she say?"

"Patience, my dear. All in good time." His gentle chide accompanied a patronizing smile. He looked at Patches squirming in Emily's arms and his smile faded to a frown. "I'm afraid you will need to leave your pet at home though. I couldn't guarantee the dog's safety should she slip her lead, you understand."

"Yes of course. I'll take her to the backyard." Emily doubted that fear for Patches's safety was the reason Gilbert preferred leaving the dog behind. She'd gotten the distinct impression that he didn't care for dogs, or at least small yippy dogs like Patches. More than once she'd noticed him ignoring Patches's attempts to make friends with him when he couldn't manage to avoid the pup entirely.

A few minutes later, her arm linked with Gilbert's, Emily descended the wood steps that led to the construction site. She found herself searching the area for Seamus but couldn't spot him.

"When finished, the length of the aqueduct will exceed 802 feet and will be supported by nine arches across the Genesee and two additional arches, which will span the mill race canals on either side of the river." Gilbert waved his arm in an arc as he gazed at the three completed arches. "The arches and bed of the canal are being constructed with red medina sandstone quarried at a site over in the town of Greece and floated here down a canal dug for that purpose. I can promise you that these piers engineered by Alfred Hovey and Nate Roberts won't be swept away by the first spring freshet like the ones Britton put in last year."

Continuing to search for Seamus, Emily fingered the piece of red medina sandstone in her pocket and smiled. What would Gilbert say if he knew she possessed a piece of the aqueduct's building material?

"But I see I'm boring you with all my talk of engineering."

"Not at all." Emily lifted her smile to him. "I'm eager to make a painting of the completed aqueduct."

Gilbert gazed at the project under construction. "Hopefully you can begin that painting before next year." His tone turned derogatory. "That is, if Amasa Drake and his foremen can prod these lazy Irish to make better progress."

Anger sparked in Emily's chest. How dare Gilbert disparage Seamus and his fellow workers who labored long, difficult, and dangerous hours in all kinds of inclement weather? She strove to keep the anger from her voice. "I'm sure the workers are doing their best, and I hear the work is very dangerous."

Gilbert snorted and shrugged as he guided her toward the steps leading up to the berm above the river. "They are adequate when pushed and only marginally better than the convicts from the prison over in Auburn that Britton employed last year."

Though seething inside, Emily managed to hold her tongue while they made their way up the steps.

Back up on the street, Gilbert turned to her and smiled. "But enough talk of the aqueduct. I have wonderful news for you. Mother loves your artwork and would like to sponsor you."

Emily's breath caught in her throat. She clasped her hand to her chest where her heart felt as if it might beat through. "You are not jesting? Your mother wants to sponsor me?" Tears sprang to her eyes as her misty dream seemed to take shape before her.

"Of course I am not jesting, my dear." His grin turned sheepish as he patted her hand on his arm. "I must confess that finding your talent has put me back in good graces with Mother. For some time she has accused me of abandoning interest in her art patronage while I've pursued engineering and fostering a future run for the state senate." A self-satisfied look accompanied his widening grin. "Because of you, I am once again Mother's favorite offspring."

◆━━━━◆

Seamus trudged toward the Main Street Bridge on his way home from work, his tortured heart sagging with his shoulders. A cyclone of anger, pain, and confusion swirled in his chest. The image of Emily walking arm in arm with one of the canal engineers still chewed at his heart. Of course, she'd never pledged any measure of devotion to him. Still, he'd felt they had a special bond, a budding relationship ready to burst into something far deeper and sweeter.

He kicked at a stone in his way, sending it flying a good rod in front of him. The action did nothing to relieve the ache in his chest.

"Hey Seamus, look out. Ya almost hit me with that rock." Jasper, with his reed fishing pole propped against his shoulder, walked toward Seamus from the east side of the bridge.

Remorse smote Seamus. The scripture about envy rotting the bones sprang to his mind. The condition of his bones he couldn't tell, but his innards sure felt rotten. "Sorry I am, lad. I didn't see ya. Are ya all right then?"

Jasper shrugged. "Yeah, the rock missed me." He sighed and hung his head. "Just down in the dumps, I guess. I fished all afternoon and didn't get one bite."

Seamus gave him a sad smile. "Yeah, reckon I'm a wee bit down in the dumps meself." His curiosity about Emily's companion got the better of him. "I saw Emily walkin' with a gentleman this afternoon. Would ya know who he might be?"

Jasper shifted the pole on his shoulder and nodded. "Mr. VanderMeer. I saw her leave the inn with him before I went fishin'. He's an engineer on the canal. Pa says he's rich as Croesus and when he marries Emily we'll be rich too."

Chapter 8

Dawn streaked the morning sky with ribbons of pink. The sight reminded Seamus of one of Emily's sky pictures. The thought fueled the turmoil still raging in his chest. When Father Patrick had encouraged Seamus to pursue a friendship with Emily he hadn't promised that friendship would grow to anything more lasting. As it turned out, it hadn't—wouldn't. It was hard enough to accept that his growing dream of one day making Emily his wife would never come true, but learning that she didn't trust the strength of their friendship enough to share with him that she was promised to another twisted in his heart like a dull dagger.

The shock he'd experienced at Jasper's revelation yesterday afternoon had left him blessedly numb for the rest of his walk home. The pain set in when Iona Maguire mentioned that she'd made Emily's acquaintance at the post office earlier in the day then commenced to spend the evening singing Emily's praises. "You were right, me lad," she'd said. "The lass has a face like an angel and a sweet and true heart for the Lord. Ya could do a whole lot worse choosin' a wife, I'm thinkin', despite her hard-hearted stepda." She'd given his shoulder a maternal pat. "From the way she spoke I could tell she has great affection for you, but her heart is troubled—conflicted. You'll need to be patient with her, lad." Iona had gone on to recount in excruciating detail how her own parents had been against her marrying Terrance and how he'd eventually won them over.

Struggling to come to terms with what he'd learned from Jasper, Seamus couldn't bring himself to share the news that Emily was already promised to another man—a wealthy man.

He inhaled a deep breath as he neared the Main Street Bridge. This morning when he crossed the Genesee he'd also be crossing the Rubicon. For Emily's sake as well as his own, they could no longer meet at lunchtime.

Last night he'd lain awake, robbed of sleep by his aching heart. Yesterday he'd told Iona that Emily was worth fighting for, and he still believed that. But to what end? Even if he could, by some miracle, win her away from VanderMeer, what could he offer her? Nothing beyond an unsure future filled with hard work that would leave her no time to paint, allowing her God-given gift to wither and her dreams to go unrealized. In a few years their love would lay in tatters, soiled with bitterness, resentment, and regret.

The reality of what he needed to do curdled in his belly like a nasty tonic. He steeled his resolve as he crossed the bridge. Gilbert VanderMeer could make Emily's dreams come true. Iona said she'd sensed that Emily's heart was conflicted about Seamus, and now Seamus knew why. The best thing he could do for Emily was to step out of her life and allow VanderMeer to give her the future she dreamed of.

As he neared Emily's pasty cart her greeting smile flayed his heart. *You can do it, boyo. You got to do it.*

"It's chicken pasties today, Seamus. Your favorite." Her lovely hazel eyes seemed to sparkle especially bright.

"It's sorry I am, Emily. But I won't be buyin' any pasties today or any other day." He lifted his lunch tin that held the jar of leftover beans and pork. "I've decided I need to save all me money to pay for me family's passage to America."

At the hurt look in her eyes he almost caved. *Be strong, me lad. For Emily's sake, be strong.*

"But you can still come by at lunchtime and visit." The hope in her eyes continued to slash at his heart. "I have wonderful news to share and a new painting I want to show you—"

Seamus forced his head to shake. "No. I wish ya well, Emily, and I'll be thinkin' o' ya and prayin' for ya." The smile came easier to his lips than he would have thought. "Someday when you're a great artist in New York City, mayhap you'll remember your old friend Seamus." Willing his feet to move, he turned and headed toward the worksite before she could see the tears welling in his eyes.

All morning the image of Emily's face full of pain and disbelief haunted Seamus. She'd said she had wonderful news. She doubtless wanted to inform him about her engagement to Gilbert VanderMeer. His heart wouldn't be at ease until he'd left her with a happier memory of him than the way they'd parted this morning. He could at least congratulate her on her engagement and ask to see her new painting.

When the whistle announcing lunch break blew, Seamus headed up to the bridge with no small amount of trepidation. Finding the spot beneath the elm tree vacant, disappointment vied with relief in his conflicted heart. He gazed at the place as if gazing long enough might make her appear. When she didn't he turned and started to go, then something near the base of the tree caught his eye. Before he picked it up he realized it was Emily's sketchbook. He would return it to her and say a proper goodbye.

As he neared the amber two-story building on Carroll Street with its sign hanging from a wrought-iron bracket over the front door that read RIVERSIDE INN, Seamus paused. At the thought of facing Emily's stepfather his mouth dried and his throat constricted. Whispering a prayer for God's guidance, he inhaled a breath of courage and headed into the building.

Inside, he gazed about. A well-worn blue and claret carpet covered the floor. The lobby, furnished with sturdy pieces of furniture, looked grand but not pretentious. Next to the stone fireplace that took up the majority of one wall hung a picture of the Genesee River that Seamus recognized as one of Emily's pastel drawings.

Finding no one at the front desk, his trepidation turned to uncertainty. The thought occurred to simply leave the sketchbook at the front desk, but knowing how much Emily valued the book, he'd rather make sure she got it back. He started down the hallway in search of anyone who might be able to help him and met a well-dressed gentleman coming from the other direction. The man looked like the one he'd seen walking with Emily yesterday. Jealousy flashed in Seamus's chest, but he forced his lips into a smile. "Is the inn keeper, Mr. Tompkins about?"

The man, whom Seamus assumed was Mr. Gilbert VanderMeer, regarded Seamus with an unsmiling, critical gaze. "I'm afraid I couldn't say. I just came from my room. If you're here to do work I suggest you check at the kitchen door around back."

Seamus shook his head. "I'm not here to do work. I'm returning Miss Nichols's sketchbook. Found it over by the bridge where she sells her pasties." He held up the book.

The man took it from his hand and began perusing the pages. When he came to the page on which Emily had sketched Seamus's features his brows lifted. His gaze bounced a couple of times between the sketch and Seamus's face. "You know Emily?"

Seamus couldn't help smiling. "Yes, we are friends. I visit her at lunchtime most days as she sketches. She wasn't there today, but I found this and I've come to return it."

"I see." VanderMeer frowned as his gaze went to the lunch tin Seamus still clutched in his hand. His tone turned imperious. "Gilbert VanderMeer, Esquire. Engineer on the Erie Canal aqueduct being built across the Genesee." He didn't offer Seamus his hand. "I'm a close friend of Miss Nichols as well." He straightened his back and looked down his nose at Seamus, not an easy feat considering his inch or so deficit in stature. "And you are?"

"Seamus O'Grady. I'm one of the lads buildin' the aqueduct." That VanderMeer had introduced himself as a friend of Emily's and not her intended, surprised Seamus. "Do you know if Emily is about?"

"I don't believe so." His derisive tone suggested he didn't consider Seamus worthy of a more elaborate answer. "Thank you for returning the book. I will see that Emily gets it." VanderMeer's comment felt like a dismissal.

Seamus nodded and headed out of the inn. Later, as he worked inside a coffer dam digging out soil and rocks to prepare the riverbed for another pier, he couldn't shake the melancholy gripping him. That he hadn't gotten to see Emily, apologize for his brusque parting comments this morning, and personally hand her the sketchbook left him feeling empty inside. Besides that, his exchange with Gilbert VanderMeer still chafed. His gut twisted at the thought of Emily marrying the arrogant engineer. *What a pompous—*

"O'Grady!" Art Mercer's voice penetrated Seamus's thoughts.

"Boss?" Seamus looked up from his work and into Mercer's scowling face.

"Good. I was afraid you'd gone deaf." His permanent scowl deepened. "We're gonna need a half-dozen more clamps for tomorrow's work. I need you to go up to Bray's shop and get them made and be back here before quittin' time."

Seamus nodded and sank his shovel into the dark muck of the riverbed, glad for an opportunity to be alone with his thoughts. "I'll get 'em."

The rest of the afternoon, as he worked at the forge fashioning the clamps, he tried to shake the vision of Emily clinging to Gilbert VanderMeer's arm and smiling up into his haughty face. Every time he smashed the hammer down on the red-hot metal he couldn't help imagining it was VanderMeer's face. The instant the image formed in his mind, regret filled him. *"Wrath is cruel, and anger is outrageous; but who is able to stand before envy?"* The words from Proverbs convicted him. *Lord, take the hate and envy from me heart, and help me to be happy for Emily.*

By the time he had made the clamps and headed back to the worksite, his heart felt at peace. *"A man's heart deviseth his way: but the LORD directeth his steps."* Despite his love for Emily, marrying her wasn't part of the Lord's plans for him. As Solomon advised in Proverbs, Seamus would trust his future to the Lord and allow Him to direct his paths.

As he neared the river the sound of a dog barking and the distressed tone of a child's voice calling out yanked him from his musings. Looking down the gorge, he saw what looked like a small boy in the swollen, fast-moving stream. Leaving the sack of iron clamps on the berm, he hurried down to the river's edge, and his heart shot to his throat. In the middle of the river, Jasper clung to a half-submerged tree that had fallen across the stream while Patches stood barking from the river's edge.

"Help! H–help!" Jasper's eyes looked wild with fear as he clung to his precarious perch, his head going under the water then bobbing back up.

"Hold on, lad! I'm comin'!" Seamus ripped off his shirt and shoes and dove into the rushing stream. The icy water snatched the breath from his lungs and he couldn't imagine how little Jasper managed to keep holding on. If the river tore the boy loose, he'd go hurtling to his death down the Great Falls less than a mile away.

"S–Seamus! H–help!" Already Jasper's voice sounded weaker, his words garbled from his shivering.

"I'm comin', lad, hold on!" Seamus pushed with all his strength against the relentless force of the moving water that tried its hardest to carry him down the river and away from Jasper. Seamus had always considered himself a strong swimmer, but he'd never matched his strength against anything as powerful as the watery force he now battled.

"H–help! I—I can't hold on."

Jasper's frantic calls sent a surge of energy through Seamus's arms, now burning with exertion. With it, renewed resolve flowed through his body with a might equal to the waters of the Genesee pushing against him. He would save Emily's little brother or die trying. *Dear Lord, get me to him before he lets go. Just get me to him.*

The distance between him and the boy shortened two arm lengths as Seamus found strength he didn't know he possessed. *Please, Lord, help me. A wee bit farther. Just a wee bit more.*

To Seamus's horror, an instant before he reached Jasper the boy let go of the branch. Seamus lunged and managed to snag the collar of the boy's shirt and pull him back to the fallen tree. He wrapped one arm around a sturdy limb while managing to hang on to Jasper with the other. He allowed himself a few seconds of rest, but he needed to get Jasper out of the water as quickly as he could.

"If ya can get him around the tree, we'll pull 'im out."

Seamus glanced up to see a small crowd of people who'd gathered on the east side of the river. A feeling of relief as powerful as the raging river washed over him. Many of the people he recognized from the Dublin area. Digging deep inside himself, he found one more surge of strength and managed to move himself and Jasper around the tree limbs and to the eastern bank.

Many hands reached down and lifted Jasper from Seamus's arms, now drained of strength. The next moment he felt himself pulled onto dry ground. Someone had wrapped Jasper in a big wool coat. Another coat wrapped around Seamus's bare torso, bringing blessed warmth to his freezing skin.

A man Seamus didn't recognize emerged from the crowd and strode toward him. Unsmiling, he looked down where Seamus sat shivering on the riverbank beneath the wool coat. "Are you Seamus O'Grady?"

Seamus nodded, unable to speak through his chattering teeth.

"I'm Sheriff John Patterson, and I'm putting you under arrest for the theft of fifty dollars from the Riverside Inn."

Chapter 9

S eamus didn't do it, Papa Ed. I don't know who took the money, but I know Seamus O'Grady, and he's not a thief!" Emily jumped up from her seat beside her brother's bed to confront her stepfather. She pointed to her brother lying in the bed and tucked beneath heavy quilts. "Seamus saved Jasper."

A moment earlier when Papa Ed came into the room and declared that the sheriff had caught the man responsible for taking the money bag that had gone missing from the office and that the thief was an Irish blackguard by the name of Seamus O'Grady, his words had struck Emily dumb. Now, as the shock dissipated, her voice returned. Anger and fear for Seamus gripped her.

Mama, seated on the other side of the bed, pressed her hand to her chest. "And we're thankful for that, Emily. But that doesn't excuse the man from taking the mortgage money Papa Ed left in the office." She shook her finger at Emily. "It was wrong of you not to tell us you knew the man. I could hardly believe it when Jasper told us that you'd been acquainted with him for months. But how—"

Papa Ed shook his head. "It's my fault. I should never have sent them out to sell pasties to those ruffians." He glared at Emily, his angry frown deepening. "Jasper is a child, but you should know better, Emily. I'm that disappointed in you, girl. You never once mentioned the man to us, and Jasper says you've been consorting with him for months. Worse, you told your little brother to keep it from us as well."

Emily crossed her arms over her chest to stop her body from shaking with anger. "Because I knew you would forbid me to see Seamus for no other reason than that he is Irish."

Papa Ed's voice lowered to a near growl. "And now you see what's come of it. You befriend the blackguards and they steal from you. They're all no-account thieves, just like the man that robbed and killed my own dad thirty years ago in England."

Emily stomped her foot. "They are not!" Tears flowed down her face. "Seamus is a good, sweet, God-fearing man. He loves the Lord. He would never hurt anyone, and he would never steal."

Papa Ed heaved a frustrated sigh. "I know you want to believe that, Emily, but the man has you beguiled and bamboozled. Mr. VanderMeer said the O'Grady fellow was in the inn and that he saw him near the office. I left the mortgage money in the green canvas money bag behind the front desk when Mrs. Richards came complaining about a stuck lock on her door. When I returned from fixing the lock, the money was gone." He crossed his arms over his chest and glared at her. "Best I can tell, Mr. VanderMeer and O'Grady were the only people near the office while I was gone." His brows shot up. "And I can't believe Mr. VanderMeer, with his fortune, would have need of my fifty dollars."

Emily refused to believe Seamus would steal from them. There had to be another explanation. "Maybe you misplaced the money. Maybe you'd planned to put it under the desk and forgot."

Papa Ed emitted a frustrated huff and his voice rose. "I did not forget where I put the money, Emily. I've looked the place over and the money is simply not here!" Worry lines dragged down his features and his voice sounded weary. "Now we will miss a mortgage payment. I just pray the banker will be understanding."

A knock sounded at the door. At Papa Ed's gruff request the door opened and the maid Beth stuck her blond head into the room. "Mr. Tompkins, Sheriff Patterson is in the lobby and would like to speak with you."

Papa Ed headed out, and Emily followed.

Sheriff Patterson met them in the lobby, a wide smile straightening the mustache above his lip. "Found your money bag. Still has the fifty dollars inside." He held up the familiar green canvas bag.

Papa Ed took the bag with an unsteady hand then sank to the nearest overstuffed chair. "Thank you, Sheriff. Where did you find it?"

"After we searched the Maguire cabin and didn't find it, Mr. VanderMeer suggested we search the O'Grady fellow's lunch tin in the tool tent down at the construction site." The sheriff grinned. "We did, and that's exactly where we found it."

Seamus sat on the straw tick cot in the jail's tiny cell, his open Bible on his lap. *"Fear thou not; for I am with thee: be not dismayed; for I am thy God: I will strengthen thee; yea, I will help thee; yea, I will uphold thee with the right hand of my righteousness."*

The words from Isaiah 41:10 blurred before his eyes.

He closed the book. He hadn't felt lower in the two days since his arrest. Despite his adamant insistence that he didn't steal the money from the Riverside Inn, no one but Iona and Terrance Maguire seemed to believe him. Then when the sheriff found the stolen money bag in his lunch tin—something Seamus couldn't explain—his fate appeared sealed.

Except for daily visits from Iona and Terrance, who'd brought him the Bible, clothes, and food, Seamus was left alone to contemplate his bleak future. Even Father Patrick, who'd left for the town of Greece the day Seamus was arrested, had not yet returned to minister to him.

Despite the encouraging words from the book of Isaiah, Seamus's spirit sagged. He'd lost his freedom, he might never see Ma, Liam, and Cullen again, and, the most painful thought of all, Emily must now think him a thief.

"I'd like to see Seamus O'Grady."

At the sound of Emily's voice Seamus's heart thudded. He put the Bible on the cot and stood, wishing he could see around the partial wall dividing his cell from the jail's front area where the sheriff's desk sat.

"Hmm. I have to check this." Sheriff Patterson's voice. "All right."

The next moment Emily appeared around the partition, a basket in her hand and tears in her eyes. "I brought you chicken pasties for your lunch."

Seamus swallowed down the lump of tears gathering in his throat and gripped the iron bars in front of him. In spite of his dire situation, he couldn't help smiling. Of course Emily would come. With her sweet heart full of Christian charity—despite the crime she might think he committed—he shouldn't be surprised that she would obey the Lord's direction to visit those in prison. He had to at least try to convince her of his innocence. "I thank ya for that kindness Emily, but you need to know that I didn't do it. I tell you true, I never took that money from your inn. I came to return your sketchbook. That's all. I never saw any money bag and I don't know how it got into me lunch tin."

"I believe you." Tears flooded down her cheeks. "I know you would never do that."

A weight as heavy as the sandstone slabs they used in building the aqueduct lifted from his heart. *Thank You, Lord. Thank You.* He had to swallow hard again. "Why? Why do you believe me?"

She set the basket on the floor and covered his hands with hers as she gazed into his eyes. "Because I know you, Seamus. And I love you."

Seamus's heart seemed to stop in his chest. When it began beating again, it galloped like a wild pony across the moor. He shook his head as if the motion might clear the confusion from his mind. "But I thought you're promised to Mr. VanderMeer. Jasper said when you marry him your family will be rich."

Emily's smile turned wry. "Mama and Papa Ed would like that to happen, but Mr. VanderMeer has not asked me, and even if he did, I would refuse his offer." She leaned closer to the bars. "I could never marry Gilbert when I love you."

Seamus's heart pounded like a triple-time drumbeat. "And I love you, Emily Nichols. I love ya more than life." As he gazed into her lovely eyes glistening with tears, the urge to kiss her grew too strong to resist. Bending his head, he leaned his face into the space between two bars and pressed his lips to hers.

The world stood still as she returned the pressure of his caresses. All his troubles and worries fell away as he and the woman he loved floated in a beautiful sphere where they alone existed.

"I've come to see Seamus O'Grady."

At Father Patrick's voice Seamus's beautiful bubble burst, slamming him back to earth. He and Emily sprang apart.

"Seamus, me boy." Father Patrick appeared from behind the partition, his expression both solemn and apologetic. "I'm that sorry I couldn't come sooner, lad. I only returned to Rochester this day and learned o' your situation."

Seamus bounced his smile between Emily and Father Patrick. "As ya see, the Lord's own angel has been ministerin' to me."

"You must be Emily." Father Patrick shifted his smile to Emily. "It's a fine thing you've done, lass, especially considerin' it was your family that was robbed. The Lord will bless your charity—"

"Seamus didn't do it, Father. I know he didn't." Emily's determined look and stalwart defense made Seamus's heart sing.

Father Patrick turned a serious face to Seamus. "So tell me what happened, lad."

Seamus recounted the events of two days ago with Emily chiming in to add details Seamus forgot to mention.

"Papa Ed always puts the monthly mortgage payment in a green canvas bag to take to the bank." Emily held out her hands, palms up. "We just can't figure out how it got into Seamus's lunch tin."

Seamus shook his head. "I know it wasn't in there when I left the inn and returned to the worksite, because I ate before going back to work."

Father Patrick's rusty brows shot up as he turned to Emily. "A green bag, ya say?"

Emily nodded.

Father Patrick's brows knit in contemplation as he turned to Seamus. "And where did ya put your empty lunch tin?"

"In the tool tent where we all put our lunch tins." Seamus couldn't imagine how that bit of information could help his case.

"Is the tool tent that little canvas tent on the east bank of the river?"

Seamus nodded. "Yes, it's the only tent near the construction site."

Father Patrick frowned and looked down at the floor. "I was there that afternoon. Was called to comfort poor Joe Doyle, whose leg got crushed by a sandstone slab."

Seamus nodded. Terrance had told him of the accident that happened while Seamus was working at the blacksmith shop.

Father Patrick lifted a grim face to Seamus. "When I was leavin' the river I spied a gentleman—well dressed, mind ya—duckin' into the tent." His gaze turned intense. "He had a wee green bag in his hand."

Emily gasped.

"Did anyone else see what you saw?" Seamus's hope withered as quickly as it had blossomed. Would Father Patrick be believed, since he was such close friends with Seamus?

Father Patrick nodded. "The foreman, Mercer, did. He called to the man—I'm thinkin' he said 'Mr. VanderMeer.'"

Seamus and Emily exchanged a wide-eyed look, and Emily emitted another gasp.

Father Patrick looked at Seamus and Emily. "Mercer asked if the man needed help findin' somethin', but the VanderMeer fellow said no and hurried away."

Emily turned a frantic face to Father Patrick. "We must tell the sheriff what you saw and get Mr. Mercer to confirm it."

"I couldn't help but hear your conversation." Sheriff Patterson walked into the cell area. "If what you say is true, Father, we have the wrong man in custody." He turned to Emily. "Do you know if VanderMeer is at your inn at the moment?"

Emily nodded. "He always has his lunch in the dining room at this hour of the day."

The sheriff unlocked and opened the cell door. "Father, I release this man to your custody." He cocked his head, indicating that Seamus should leave the cell. "You all head down to the Riverside Inn. I'll go fetch Mercer, but don't alert VanderMeer until I get there." His gaze took in the three of them. "Hopefully we can get this sorted out without a trial."

Outside, Seamus inhaled a lungful of crisp autumn air, allowing himself a moment to luxuriate in his freedom. Still, he kept a tight rein on his hopes. If Mercer didn't confirm what Father Patrick witnessed, Seamus could be right back in jail awaiting the circuit judge. His gut clenched. Mercer had never made his dislike of Seamus a secret. He could very well disavow the incident.

Minutes later, flanked by Emily and Father Patrick, Seamus stood in the lobby of the Riverside Inn for the second time. He met Edward Tompkins's withering glare with an unflinching gaze as they waited for Sheriff Patterson to return with Art Mercer. "I didn't steal your money, sir."

Edward Tompkins scoffed. "Not likely."

The front door opened and Sheriff Patterson and Art Mercer entered the lobby. Seamus's heart sank at Mercer's glower.

The sheriff looked at Emily's stepfather. "Mr. Tompkins, would you please fetch Mr. VanderMeer from the dining room?"

Tompkins hesitated, but nodded and headed out of the lobby. A couple minutes later he returned with VanderMeer

At the sight of the group, Gilbert VanderMeer stopped short. The color drained from his face, and for a moment, he glanced about like a cornered animal. At length he appeared to remember his status. He squared his shoulders and lifted his arrogant chin as he addressed the sheriff. "If you've brought this man for me to identify, I can confirm this is the man I saw in the lobby the afternoon of the theft."

Sheriff Patterson didn't reply. Instead he turned to Father Patrick. "Is this the man you saw enter the tool tent carrying a green bag?"

Father Patrick nodded. "Yes, Sheriff, of that, I am certain."

The sheriff looked at Art Mercer. "Mr. Mercer, can you confirm Father Gallagher's testimony?"

Seamus looked at his boss's sour expression and his heart shuddered. Sheriff Patterson had handed Mercer the perfect opportunity to get rid of Seamus for good.

Art Mercer seemed to study Gilbert VanderMeer for a long moment while Seamus held his breath. At last he nodded, and Seamus feared his knees might buckle from the flood of relief sluicing through him.

Mercer crossed his arms over his chest. "I keep a sharp eye on who goes in and comes out o' the tool tent. Saw him go in with a green bag and come out without it. Figured it was somethin' Mr. Drake had instructed him to put in the tent, so I never thought any more about it." He looked straight at Seamus. "I won't deny that you've been a pain in my neck, O'Grady, but I've never borne false witness against any man and I don't mean to start now."

Sheriff Patterson looked at Gilbert VanderMeer. "What say you, Mr. VanderMeer?"

VanderMeer licked his lips, and Seamus saw surrender in his eyes. His gaze hardened as he looked at Emily, who had taken Seamus's hand in hers. "For the past several seasons I've enjoyed the attention of the most desirable debutantes New York City has to offer." His glance dropped to Emily's and Seamus's clasped hands and he scoffed. "I refused to stand by and allow an ignorant ditch digger to best me in pursuit of a lady's affection." He turned to Tompkins, his voice derisive. "I made sure you got your money back, Tompkins. There was no theft."

The sheriff looked at Tompkins. "I'd say that is for you to decide, Mr. Tompkins. Do you wish to press charges against Mr. VanderMeer or not?"

For a moment Tompkins looked conflicted then shook his head. "No, like Mr. VanderMeer said, he didn't intend to keep my money, and I did get it back." He glared at VanderMeer. "But I want you out of my inn today, and I forbid you to ever see my daughter again."

VanderMeer looked at Emily and snorted. "And you can forget about my mother sponsoring your art, Miss Nichols." He gave her a leering stare that made Seamus want to pound him into the ground. VanderMeer's nose wrinkled as if he smelled something bad. "I'd have tired of you in a few months anyway."

Emily's grip on Seamus's hand tightened. "I don't want a sponsorship from you or your mother." The love in her eyes as she gazed up at Seamus sent his heart galloping. "I have everything I want right here."

VanderMeer gave another snort and strode out of the lobby.

The men exchanged handshakes.

"Thank you, Sheriff." Seamus's throat tightened with emotion. "Thank you for believin' me."

Sheriff Patterson smiled. "Just doing my job, son. Glad it worked out this way."

Seamus shook Art Mercer's proffered hand. "Thank you for your honesty, boss."

For the first time he saw Mercer grin. "We need your strong back and black-smithin' skills to finish this aqueduct." Then the grin faded to his natural scowl and his voice turned gruff. "So be at work on time tomorrow morning." With that, he left the inn with the sheriff.

Grinning, Father Patrick patted Seamus's shoulder. " 'And we know that all things work together for good to them that love God, to them who are the called according to his purpose.' " His smile slid between Seamus and Emily. "I'm thinkin' God's just got started with His blessin's." With a wink, he headed out the door.

When the others had gone Edward Tompkins walked to Seamus, a look of remorse in his eyes. "I owe you an apology, son. I—all of us—owe you a great debt for what you did to save Jasper." His eyes turned watery. "I'd have lost my boy over the Great Falls if you hadn't risked your life to pull him out." He looked down and cleared his throat as if to get a better grip on his emotions. "I ask your forgiveness for being too eager to blame you for somethin' you didn't do."

Emily squeezed Seamus's hand, sending joy flooding through him. He reached out his free hand and shook her stepfather's. "Glad I am that I was there to pull your lad from the river, sir. I don't blame you for thinkin' I took the money, but, as the Lord instructs us to do, I do forgive you."

The taut lines in Edward Tompkins's features relaxed to an easy smile. He cocked his head. "You know, I've been thinking of adding a blacksmith shop to the inn. Emily tells me you have that skill, and I'd like to offer you a job when the aqueduct is finished."

Seamus's heart felt full to bursting. "Thank you, sir. I'd like that. I would indeed." Da's often repeated advice at the anvil to strike while the iron is hot flitted into his mind. Sending up a silent prayer for courage and God's blessing, Seamus cleared his throat and straightened. "Mr. Tompkins, I care for Emily very much and I believe she cares for me as well. I humbly ask your permission to keep company with your daughter."

"Please, Papa Ed." Emily's voice sounded breathless as she gripped his hand harder.

An array of emotions seemed to cross Edward Tompkins's face. In the end his expression settled on a smile. "You have my blessing, and I'm sure Emily's mother will agree." He grinned and touched Emily's nose. "But be warned, the girl can be headstrong. I'll go tell your mother and Jasper the good news."

When Tompkins left the lobby, Seamus took both of Emily's hands in his, a niggling regret tarnishing his joy. "Sorry I am, me love, that ya lost your sponsor for your paintin'." Sorrow dragged his head down. "I can't make you and your family rich."

Emily took his face in her hands, her touch sending delicious shivers through his body. Her gaze seemed to reach to his very soul. "As I told Gilbert, I have everything I want right here. God gave me the gift and the desire to paint, and He will show me what He wants me to do with it."

Unable to resist the temptation, Seamus pulled her into a kiss and let her sweet lips transport him to the blissful sphere he'd experienced with her in the jail. When he finally released her lips he still held her in his arms, unwilling to let her go. "Will ya be me bride then, Miss Nichols? Me Erie Canal bride?"

Her pretty brow furrowed. "Hmm, I must think about that." Her pensive look melted into a grin and a musical giggle bubbled from her lips. "Why, yes, Mr. O'Grady, I do believe I will."

He had to kiss her again.

Epilogue

One year later. . .

Emily's eyes misted, blurring the large oil painting Seamus situated on the easel.

"A man's heart deviseth his way: but the LORD directeth his steps." Once again the words from Proverbs filled her heart and mind as she marveled at how God had answered her and Seamus's prayers, but in a much different way than they had ever imagined.

Since that fateful day a year ago in the Riverside Inn's lobby, the Lord had showered them with so many blessings. Then, two weeks ago when the traveling art exhibitor Mr. Stowell arrived in Rochester and approached her about exhibiting some of her work in his and Mr. Bishop's coming exhibit, she'd wept with happiness. Her dream of seeing her artwork in a public exhibit was coming true.

"Ah, a grand thing it is, me love." He stepped back from the painting to slip his arm around her waist and hug her against him. "The grandest piece in all of Mr. Stowell's and Mr. Bishop's exhibit."

"You have to say that. You're my husband." *Her husband.* Six months after their wedding, she still loved the sound of it. She smiled up at his handsome face then glanced across the room where Jasper, Liam, and Cullen stood spellbound before the exhibitors' grand mechanical panorama. "I doubt our brothers would agree."

His smiling gaze followed hers and his throat moved with a hard swallow. "Such a blessin' it is to have 'em here—and Ma too."

Emily hugged his waist tighter. Good to his word, Papa Ed, with Seamus's help, built a blacksmith shop onto the inn where Seamus and his brothers now stayed busy. The flood of visitors the Erie Canal had brought to Rochester had more than paid for the addition as well as paying off the mortgage and bringing Seamus's family to America.

Her gaze turned back to the oil painting she'd made of the new aqueduct that Seamus had helped to build and now spanned the Genesee River. Her hand went to her throat to finger the chip of medina sandstone Seamus had given her all those months ago. At their engagement he'd had it made into a pendant and attached to a silver chain for her to wear as a necklace.

"I'm that proud of me wife." Seamus bent and kissed her cheek.

"As you should be." Matthew Brown, the village president, strode up to them, his face beaming above his high shirt collar and ivory silk cravat. "I've been admiring your magnificent painting of our grand new aqueduct, Mrs. O'Grady. Which"—he held his hand out to Seamus—"I understand you had a hand in building."

"That I did, sir." Seamus shook the man's hand.

Mr. Brown's gaze slid back to the painting. "The Erie Canal and our aqueduct are making Rochester a boomtown. They're calling us the Young Lion of the West." He turned to Emily. "If you are in a mind to sell this magnificent piece of art, I would like to purchase it to hang in the courthouse."

Dumbstruck, Emily exchanged a stunned look with Seamus.

"I understand if you don't want to sell it, but I'd be willing to compensate you very handsomely." President Brown seemed to interpret her silence as hesitancy.

Emily blinked back the tears welling in her eyes and held out her hand to him. "I would be honored to have my work hang in the Rochester Court House, President Brown."

"Excellent." He took and patted her proffered hand. "After the exhibit, I will send someone to your stepfather's establishment to negotiate a price." His brow lifted. "You have an extraordinary talent, my dear. I predict you will become quite famous."

He turned to Seamus. "And Mr. O'Grady, we owe you and all the men who built the canal a great debt. You may have thought you were digging a canal, but what you were digging was a more prosperous future for all of New York State."

As he walked away Seamus shook his head. "He's wrong, ya know. It wasn't for the money I was diggin'. I was diggin' for the love of me family—Ma, Liam, Cullen, and. . ." He pulled Emily into an embrace. "You. I was diggin' for you."

He bent and kissed her and she didn't care if the whole room stared. When he released her lips she whispered, "I know, my darling. You were digging for love."

Ramona Cecil is a wife, mother, grandmother, freelance poet, and award-winning inspirational romance writer. Now empty nesters, she and her husband make their home in Indiana. A member of American Christian Fiction Writers and American Christian Fiction Writers Indiana Chapter, her work has won awards in a number of inspirational writing contests. Over eighty of her inspirational verses have been published on a wide array of items for the Christian gift market. She enjoys a speaking ministry, sharing her journey to publication while encouraging aspiring writers. When not writing, her hobbies include reading, gardening, and visiting places of historical interest.

Return to Sweetwater Cove

by Christina Miller

Acknowledgments

It takes a team to write a book, and Jesus has given me the best. Many thanks to. . .

My ACFW Scribes 202 critique group: Julie Arduini, Bunny (BJ) Bassett, Marie Bast, Kathleen Friesen, Laura Hilton, Linda Hoover, and Heidi Kortman

My brainstorming crew: Susan Holloway, Lisa Jordan, and Dana Lynn

My longtime friend Rose McCauley, for her great idea of romance along the Erie Canal

My editors: Rebecca Germany and Ellen Tarver

My ever-amazing agent: Steve Laube

My mother, Linda Fill, who reads each scene and encourages me until I write "The End"

My husband, Jan, who seeks first the Lord and His kingdom

Jesus, who makes all things new

Therefore, if any man be in Christ, he is a new creature:
old things are passed away; behold, all things are become new.
2 CORINTHIANS 5:17

Chapter 1

Sweetwater Cove, New York
June, 1825

Doing the right thing shouldn't feel this bad.

As his coach-and-six hit an uneven cobblestone in the narrow street, still muddy in morning's first light after the storm, Josiah slid a protective hand onto the tapestry-wrapped marble statue beside him. Sweetwater Cove—where the Erie Canal crossed their little bend in the creek. Where the people prided themselves on their kindness and hospitality. Where everyone was one big family.

Everyone except Josiah Wells—the son of the town drunk.

He could never shed the title, and he hadn't fooled himself into thinking he could gain any of the town's respect, let alone his self-respect, by coming home. Repaying his debt, if that were possible, wouldn't do it either.

No, Sweetwater Cove would either accept his restitution and service, as the elderly Mrs. Patience Bennett had assured him they would, or those sweet waters would turn sour as September persimmons. And since Josiah had no choice but to find out which it would be, he might as well get it over with quickly.

As he crossed the old river bridge next to the new aqueduct, he twisted in the padded leather seat to catch his first glimpse of Lafayette Park. But instead of serene landscaping beside still waters, he caught sight of uprooted oaks and sycamores, benches broken under the weight of their limbs, flower beds littered with branches and leaves. Even the old white gazebo—the one place he wished he wouldn't have to see—lay crushed under the weight of a fallen sycamore.

Unfortunately, the terrible memories there would remain.

When he came to the church, its doors already stood open, spilling out voices, laughter, a baby giggling. . .a congregation preparing for worship. Who knew—perhaps those happy sounds would continue once he went inside for this morning's Sunday service.

And perhaps not.

In the midst of the joyful noises, a woman's voice rang out and grated against his ear. "Stop! I implore you. . . ."

A woman in trouble?

He twisted in his seat, half standing, readying himself to render aid, when he saw Mrs. Patience Bennett blustering toward him, her graying auburn hair tumbling down around her shoulders and ample arms. She waved and "yoo-hooed" her way up the street from her inn, still as theatrical as the last time Josiah had seen her, and still as peppy.

As his carriage eased to a halt in front of Sweetwater Church, Josiah unfastened the door, fearing she might otherwise wrangle it open herself. He caught the distress in her bright green eyes just as leather-faced Constable Robbins, who'd sent Josiah packing to New Rochelle all those years ago, rushed toward his conveyance.

"Stop! Don't make a move!"

Did Robbins mean to send him away again, or even arrest him, in his first minutes here? Without giving him opportunity to make things right in Sweetwater Cove?

If so, he'd take it like a man, not as his father had. Josiah snatched his Bible and *Book of Common Prayer* from the seat beside him and bounded from the carriage to face them.

But instead of apprehending him, the constable strode past him and behind the coach, where he snatched the wrist of a towheaded boy crouched there and yanked him to his feet. "Hand over the peashooter, Little Gilly."

Little. . .Gilly?

Josiah hastened to the child. Surely the blue-eyed, lanky boy wasn't the son of Gilly Bennett—the man to whom Josiah owed his first apology in Sweetwater Cove. The man who haunted Josiah's thoughts to this day. The man he could never repay. But this Gilly looked nothing like the dark-haired, stocky boy who'd been Josiah's friend in their youth.

"I didn't do nothin'. I was just lookin'." The boy's pitiful wail, the look of fear in his eyes, were Gilly Bennett's.

Josiah gritted his teeth against the dark memories that wail brought back.

"I saw you take aim at the horses." Robbins turned to Josiah, his beefy hand still encircling the boy's wrist. This man apparently still kept Sweetwater Cove citizens on a short leash. "I won't let him bother you again, sir."

With effort, Josiah relaxed his jaw and ruffled Little Gilly's fine hair. Those blue eyes reminded him of someone. . . . "He wasn't bothering—"

"We've had a terrible turn of events. You must give us time to repair the park before your inspection." Mrs. Bennett seized Josiah's arm and turned him toward herself as a scrappy little rat terrier barked and nipped at the horses' hooves. She turned to the dog and shook her finger at him. "General Washington! Stop worrying the horses."

General. . .who?

The matron turned her attention back to Josiah. "Oh dear. I hope you're alone. You haven't brought the marquis today, have you?"

"Mrs. Bennett, I fear you're confused," Josiah said, tipping his hat to her then patting General Washington's white fur when he trotted up and barked. "Brought whom?"

"Why, the Marquis de Lafayette. Who else would have a coach as fine as this? You're his secretary, are you not?"

The marquis?

He glanced up the street at Sweetwater Cove's modest homes, the towns-folk walking or traveling to church in farm wagons or humble carriages. Mrs. Bennett was right. Josiah's coach-and-six—or rather, his late adoptive father's coach—was the only fine conveyance in sight.

The boy broke free from the constable's grip and dashed toward the inn's summer kitchen. Robbins caught up with him at the well and pointed him back toward the church.

As they approached, a willowy woman hastened from the manse. About Josiah's age and with the same light hair as Little Gilly, she stopped on the brick sidewalk and called the boy's name. He trudged toward her, the dog following and the constable heading up the street.

Mrs. Bennett peered into the empty carriage. "I say, sir, is the marquis in there?"

It was past time to clear up the confusion. "No, I'm—"

"Josiah Brown." The blond woman spoke the birth name Josiah hadn't heard since he'd left Sweetwater Cove fifteen years ago. She covered her mouth with her hand, her fair face paling in the morning sun. "Oh no. . .why did you come back?"

Her words slashed into his chest, left him breathless. Betsy Tanner. The girl who'd stolen his long-ago boyish heart. The girl with eyes as blue as the ocean waters of New Rochelle. The girl who'd defended him, prayed for him, believed in him.

Now the woman who clearly didn't want him in Sweetwater Cove.

No, doing the right thing shouldn't feel this bad. But soon it might feel a lot worse.

The last thing Betsy wanted was to be trapped in conversation with both Josiah Brown and matchmaking Mother Bennett. Especially since he'd grown from a nice-looking boy into an impossibly handsome man, his dark hair fashionably short, his gray eyes expressive enough to stop a girl's heart. After all these years, Betsy had thought she was safe from anyone discovering her secret: her late hus-band, Gilly Bennett, hadn't been her first love.

Nor had her first kiss been his.

Now that Josiah was back in town, would he tell—or would someone guess—that she'd given him a sweet, almost holy kiss the night he left, along with her delphinium-scented hanky to remember her by?

And thereby add yet another layer of guilt to her already-brutal load?

"Josiah Brown?" Mother Bennett stepped closer and squinted into his face, still refusing to wear her spectacles in public, even in the weak morning light. Then she patted his cheek as if he were Little Gilly's age. "Of course. I'm ashamed I didn't recognize our new parson."

Parson? Josiah Brown? "That's not possible."

Mother Bennett pulled her lacy Sunday hanky from her sleeve and fanned her reddening face.

His gray eyes darkened in the grayer morning half-light, as solemn as ever.

"You told us the new parson's name is Reverend Wells." Betsy's gaze landed on the black Bible in his hand, his prayer book, his sober black preacher's suit. Mother Bennett seemed right, but. . .

"I took my adoptive father's last name."

And apparently had followed the elder Reverend Wells into the ministry. But wait. . .

If he was the new parson, then that meant she'd once kissed the man who had just come here to be—

Her pastor.

Heat blazed into her face and neck. How could this have happened? Why hadn't she been told?

Drawing a deep breath, she stilled her racing mind. That kiss had happened fifteen years ago. He wouldn't remember it, and she'd not remind him.

But when she chanced a glance at him, his intense gaze told her otherwise.

A puffing sound reminded her that Little Gilly was still present, and she looked down to see him aiming a dried pea at their elderly neighbor. She forcefully set her disquieting thoughts aside and instead reached for her son's peashooter and hustled him into church before he could cause more trouble. Betsy had enough of that already. With Little Gilly inside, General Washington wagged his little white tail and lay down next to Josiah, clearly declaring him worthy of friendship.

Well, the dog didn't have all the facts.

Josiah—Reverend Wells—touched his palm to his forehead, as if deep in thought, then he turned those gray eyes on Betsy again. "You didn't know I was the one called to this church?"

No, and the enormity of yet another truth struck her hard in her middle. "No one in this town knows."

"But how—" He looked as confused as Betsy felt. "Mrs. Bennett, can you explain? Did this church call me here without knowing who I am?"

"We didn't exactly. . ." The older lady fanned herself even faster. "I've known for months that you were the man for the job."

Josiah shook his head as Betsy sometimes did when she couldn't stop Little Gilly's mischievousness. "First you thought I was the Marquis de Lafayette's employee, and now I learn the town thinks I'm a stranger, come to pastor their church." He looked at Betsy, and for the first time, she saw a hint of a twinkle in his eye. "Does anyone else in this town have a new identity? Are you still Betsy Tanner, or are you someone else too?"

His new lightheartedness took her aback. When had he developed a sense of humor? She couldn't help smiling. "I'm Betsy Bennett now. I was Gilly's wife."

The shine left his gaze, and instantly she missed its glow. He bowed his head a moment. "I didn't know he was—gone."

"Seven years ago Saturday next," Mother Bennett said. "I want to honor him on the date of his passing. That's why I'm relieved it was you in that carriage and not the marquis's man."

He looked at Betsy, the breeze blowing his short hair into the slightest disarray, his lips barely parted, looking for all the world like the confused boy he'd once been.

And no wonder, with Mother Bennett rambling as always when she was excited.

"She's referring to Lafayette's grand tour of the United States. The date of Gilly's death is also the date Lafayette will pass through Sweetwater Cove."

"Indeed," Mother Bennet said. "Even now, General Lafayette is riding the finished portions of the canal, and next Saturday he will stop at our inn for refreshments. We'd hoped he would stay for the dedication of the newly renovated Lafayette Park, since my late father-in-law served under him at Battle Forge." Mother Bennett's gaze shifted toward the park on the other side of the aqueduct. "But with the damage the park sustained during last night's storm, we're not ready for him."

Damage? Betsy turned toward the park, shielding her eyes from the morning sun. "What happened?"

"Trees down, flower beds destroyed. . ." Mother Bennett's eyes welled up with tears, and no wonder, after her weeks of hard work at the park.

Betsy felt like crying too, but perhaps her mother-in-law was merely exaggerating as she was wont to do. "Surely it's not as bad as that."

"It's worse," Josiah said. "One of the uprooted trees landed on the gazebo. I passed it when I came into town."

Mother Bennett turned back toward the towpath, where Constable Robbins and all three aldermen gathered with Papa Bennett. "It's demolished. And with the marquis due in less than a week."

Betsy's favorite spot in Sweetwater Cove, gone.

◆—◆———◆◆

A chilly wind blew up from the north as if it circled around to make sure it had done all the damage it could. Betsy rubbed her arms, where goose bumps prickled them. With trees uprooted, landscaping destroyed, and the precious gazebo smashed under a tree, the aldermen would cancel the marquis's visit to Sweetwater Cove. Which meant Betsy would miss her one chance to give him a reception he'd always remember. And that meant she'd also miss her one chance to honor Gilly's memory in the only way she knew would have made him proud.

The only way she knew to ease even a little of her guilt over his death.

"But first things first. Reverend, we need to get you settled in the manse before the service." Mother Bennett drew a deep breath and glanced at Little Gilly as he sneaked out of the church and pulled a slingshot from the back of his waistband. "I'd ask my grandson to help with your trunks, but I'm not sure he wouldn't shoot out the windows with that weapon of his."

Josiah gestured toward the carriage driver then took out his pocket watch and glanced at it. "My driver will take in a few items of value, and we'll unload the rest later. That way, he can join us for church."

With the exuberance of youth, the driver leaped down from the conveyance's high seat. He looked no older than Josiah had been when they'd sent him away. . . .

"The manse has been relocated," Mother Bennett said, her voice quivering a little, as if they'd moved the house only last week. "Mr. Bennett is the mayor now, and he got permission to build the new manse on the other side of the church, on the empty lot you boys used to play in. Before the fire."

At the mention of the fire, Josiah hesitated, as if letting Mother Bennett's words settle into his heart.

"Oh Reverend, I shouldn't have mentioned the fire. . . ." A rare remorse softened the poor dear's face as she leaned closer, peering into Josiah's eyes with her nearsighted gaze.

Then those gray eyes softened, took on a sense of peace that shouldn't be there, considering the circumstances of that fire.

"Mrs. Bennett, before I took this church, I planned to make restitution for the fire. You needn't distress yourself about opening the topic."

The clouds had broken, brightening the sky to full light, and the trees lining the street glowed with the strange cheery sunshine that often followed a stormy night. Betsy checked the timepiece pinned to her bodice. Ten minutes of nine, and Mother Bennett had yet to inform Josiah of the church's opinion of him—the boy who had once burned down the church, as well as half the town.

A familiar tune drifted up the towpath, interrupting her thoughts. She glanced around to see Papa Bennett striding up the dirt path toward them, whistling.

"Oh no." Mother Bennett pulled out her hanky again and waved it before her face. "He's whistling the 'Doxology.' You know what that means."

She surely did. It meant bad news.

The whistling stopped as Papa Bennett drew near. He hesitated before extending his hand. "The constable suspected you were the new preacher, Josiah—ah—Reverend."

Josiah hastened to accept the gesture. "Shall I call you Mr. Bennett or Mayor Bennett?"

"Mr., Deacon, or Mayor Bennett—I'm one and the same. We have quite the mess, I'd say."

Breaking the handshake, Papa Bennett eased his hands to his hips and surveyed the church, the river, the aqueduct, the town. His gaze seemed to take in all the nuances of the little burg he governed, served. Loved. "I'm not going to sugarcoat this. The church, in fact, the whole town, isn't going to like this arrangement. How did such a misunderstanding come about?"

Josiah opened his mouth as if to speak, but then he closed it again.

"The church will see what a fine man he's become, and they'll love him before the benediction is over." Mother Bennett whipped her hanky about, creating her own little storm that blew tendrils of hair around her face, her gaze firing from one man to the other and back.

She may be right, but. . .

Oh my word.

As the truth hit her, Betsy swiveled her gaze to Josiah, who tightened his mouth. Apparently, he'd figured out Mother Bennett's plot too.

Papa Bennett straightened, stretching his lean, six-foot frame to the limit as he always used to when disciplining his son. "Patience Bennett, what have you done?"

At the sound of her husband's voice, she dropped her hanky to the grass and let a tear run down her cheek. "He's the man for this church. I know it!"

"But, dearest, you intentionally withheld his former name from the deaconate. From the whole church. You can't force the hand of the Lord like that."

"I didn't force it. I merely nudged it a bit."

"Very well. As head deacon, I assign you the task of revealing his identity to the church."

She shook her head, making her curls bounce. "No, Cyrus. The Bible says a woman is to be silent in the church." The feigned sweetness in her voice would have made Betsy laugh under other circumstances.

"You've not been silent all these months you've corresponded with the reverend. We're not going to be hypocrites now."

"I have a better idea, as long as you're in favor of women speaking in the church," Mother Bennett said. "Let's allow Betsy to introduce him."

Betsy pointed to herself. "Me? I had nothing to do with this."

Papa Bennett hesitated. "You might be right, Patience. Betsy, if you express confidence in the reverend, the newcomers will respond, because they don't know about. . .about the fire. And you've made friends of them all. That will give you a base of support, Reverend."

Betsy did have confidence that he'd make a great minister, if the people let him. If only they didn't have that long-ago kiss between them.

Then again, they'd been children at the time. Perhaps she made too much of it.

Josiah shook his head, his dark curls gleaming in the morning sunlight, his gray eyes darkening. "If the church isn't in agreement, I'll not stay."

"It's a deacon board decision. And two of the three deacons are on your side: Constable Robbins and me."

"Robbins? Why would he believe in a man with my past?"

"He's a Christian lawman who believes people can change."

Josiah wouldn't be able to argue with that.

"Besides," Papa Bennett said, "it will be a mutual favor. There's another issue stirring up Sweetwater Cove. I went to the park with the aldermen early this morning, and it's a disaster. They want to cancel the marquis's visit and sell the park to avoid the cost of fixing it up again."

"Sell it?" Betsy drew in a quick breath. "All of them are in favor?"

"The constable and I will vote to keep it. The three aldermen will vote to sell. Maynard Swift is one of them, his crony Ebenezer Crouch is another, and Horace Stryker, his banker, is third. Since the park is next to the docks, Swift wants to buy it and build a drinking house and another dry-goods store."

"But Sweetwater Cove isn't big enough for two stores, even including canal traffic trade. One or the other would go out of business. Mine, no doubt," Betsy said. "And a drinking house—we're not that kind of town. It would ruin us."

"Swift can afford to take a loss at his store until yours goes under. Then he'll have all the business. No doubt he'd also call for a vote to repeal our law against alcohol sales in Sweetwater Cove. He's the sort of man who'd do that."

She ached with the frustration, the anxiety of the situation. "I never thought this would happen in Sweetwater Cove."

"Well, I saw the drinking house coming. Since it's the Sabbath, we can't officially vote today, so we'll do it in the morning. The way I see it, there's only one way to keep the park: get the parson to help restore it."

His words made Mother Bennett beam with joy while Josiah winced. "How will that help?" he asked.

"There's no kind way to say this, son." Her father-in-law laid his slender hand on Josiah's shoulder. "The aldermen know that many of our citizens will want to keep the park. A lot of them also remember the past, and they'll think you can't get the job done. So, in order to keep peace in the community, I can convince them to give you a week to try and, as they'll think, to fail."

"That's a terrible plan," Mother Bennett said, and Betsy had to agree.

"No other way will work. Neither you nor Betsy can accomplish either job on your own." Papa Bennett's voice rang with confidence, as always. "Betsy, you'll do all you can to help the church believe in Josiah. And I don't just mean today. Josiah, you'll work alongside Betsy at the park. I'm willing to risk my reputation and office by recommending this plan, because I want to keep that drinking house out of our town, and because I agree that Josiah is God's man for the job. But I won't do it unless you two work together on both ventures."

Mother Bennett's eyes gleamed in a way Betsy hadn't seen since the last wedding performed in Sweetwater Cove. A match her mother-in-law had spent considerable time and effort to make.

Betsy drew a deep breath. "Mother Bennett, is this scheme your idea?"

Before the dear lady could respond, Papa Bennett shook his head. "This is entirely my plan. And no, I'm not matchmaking. I leave that up to Patience. The important issue now is your willingness to work together."

In the ensuing silence, he said, "Decide now."

If only Papa Bennett wouldn't make her choose in front of Josiah. Despite his reputation in Sweetwater Cove, he looked strong, capable—reliable. But could she trust her heart with him? After all, she'd once loved him. *Heavenly Father, please show me what to do. . . .*

Of a sudden, Little Gilly's face appeared in her mind's eye. She couldn't fail him. Even if she could somehow provide for him with another store in town, she couldn't let Maynard Swift build that drinking house. Couldn't let that tavern influence Gilly, which it would, especially since he passed his after-school hours at the store and docks.

She had to do it for Little Gilly, even if it meant spending time with Josiah. Lots of time.

"I will." Josiah's voice didn't waver, and neither would his conviction, she was sure.

She hastened to make her promise, before she could change her mind. "I will as well."

Betsy had been wrong to think the worst thing that could happen today was to spend a little time with Josiah in Mother Bennett's presence. No, working this closely with him would be much, much worse.

Chapter 2

Mrs. Bennett had been wrong. The benediction was over, and the whole church didn't love him, despite Betsy's introduction and encouragement to welcome him.

With the exception of the Bennetts and Constable Robbins, he'd received a chilly reception from the members who still recalled the day Josiah burned down Sweetwater Cove Church.

Now, with everyone gone except the Bennetts, Josiah chose to forgive each man who'd ignored his outstretched hand and every woman who'd pretended not to see his friendly nod as they filed out of church. If he were to bear good fruit as the pastor of this church, he'd need to change his reputation. Somehow.

"The Sweetwater Cove minister always takes his meals at our inn, at our expense," Deacon Bennett said as they shut the doors behind them and took the four stone steps to the churchyard.

"Very generous, Deacon. My thanks. I wasn't looking forward to eating alone."

"Several of our older widowers have moved into our inn, for companionship and hot meals. As they get to know you at the table, they'll warm up to you."

He felt the deacon's bony hand land on his shoulder as they strode up the inn's brick walk. Comforting, and yet strange. Comforting to have a fatherly touch. Strange to have compassion from Gilly's father. From Betsy's father-in-law.

Because while using mealtimes to build relationships with church members was a great idea, Josiah wasn't so sure he wanted to sit with Betsy three times a day for the foreseeable future. Not that she wasn't pretty and sweet, but because she was. And he could never allow himself to fall in love with the widow of the man he'd maimed for life. Experience told him that if he spent too much time with her, that was exactly what would happen.

If he hoped to make this work, he'd have to guard his heart, closely. Diligently. Intensely.

Inside, Deacon Bennett waved him toward an empty chair near the end of the table, next to one of the church's widowers, who sat by the open window. Ebenezer Crouch, if Josiah remembered right. He greeted the elderly man and had no more than sat down when Crouch shouted a gravelly "Bah!" and shoved his chair back from the table. He stomped from the room in an odd, stuttering, lumbago-induced gait, muttering something about preachers and deacons.

Josiah chanced a glance at Betsy, across the table. The fingers she held over her mouth couldn't hide the smile in her eyes.

"Don't worry about him," Betsy said. "My father used to say Mr. Crouch was born a grouchy old man. After Gilly passed away and I took over the store, I asked Mr. Crouch to stay on as my clerk, but I try to keep him in the storeroom or outside sweeping the docks and away from my customers."

A wise decision.

She reached for the empty bowl in front of him and ladled it full of some savory-smelling concoction then set it before him. "It's your favorite."

Chicken and dumplings.

Oh, the joy. A big bowl of hot chicken and dumplings could make the worst day bearable.

And when Betsy passed him a plate of salt-rising bread, fresh butter, and a bowl of oak-leaf lettuce with vinegar dressing, the combination of foods made him feel as if he'd come home. He picked up his pewter spoon and took his first bite of the savory dinner. Seasoned just right and thickened naturally by the dumplings, the dish brought back soothing memories of his frequent visits here with Gilly.

He took a long drink of his honey-sweetened chamomile tea and treasured the moment while he could, tucked it away in his memory against the hard times he knew would come.

"Our plan didn't work so well this morning," Betsy said as she sipped her own tea.

Although the room had nearly cleared out, he leaned in close to murmur in her ear, catching a whiff of a sweet flower fragrance. Something about it was familiar. . . . Ah. Delphiniums.

"No, but maybe this afternoon could be better. After dinner, let's take Little Gilly to the park and find out exactly what we need to do to it." He glanced around the room. "Where is he?"

"He wanted to have his meal in the kitchen with the cook. He likes to eat quickly on Sundays so he can get outside—"

The banging of the front door, followed by pounding footsteps and the sound of barking, cut her off. Little Gilly came racing through the dining room, slingshot in hand and General Washington barking at his heels. He slid around the staircase, then Josiah thought he heard the sound of a door scraping open and shut again. This time, General Washington's bark sounded muffled, as if he was in the cellar.

Or the storage room under the stairs.

Before they could react, the front door opened and slammed shut yet again. This time, Constable Robbins strode in, whipped off his straw top hat, and pitched it onto a nearby chair. "Where's Little Gilly?"

Josiah stood and approached the man whose face was stiffening into a frown. "What's wrong?"

"I warned him about his slingshot, but he hit one of your horses with a rock, right in the flank. I'm going to throw that pint-sized weapon of his in the canal." Robbins craned his neck, peering around the room. "Might throw Little Gilly in there too."

The man's voice held enough humor to let Josiah know the boy was in no danger of getting tossed in the drink. Still, Little Gilly needed to learn to behave. "Is the horse injured?"

"He's fine. But Little Gilly isn't. He gets in some kind of trouble nearly every day. Think you could have a talk with him, Parson?" Robbins retrieved his hat. "Since you were his father's best friend, the boy might listen to you."

Have a talk with Little Gilly? Easy enough, but the child needed more than that. A lot more. He needed to learn to be a man.

He needed a father.

The truth struck him like a breaking wave in a New Rochelle hurricane. He could never make restitution to Gilly now, could never repay his friend for the childish impulsiveness and anger that had caused his friend's lifelong limp.

Therefore, it was Josiah's job to take care of Gilly's son and widow.

He owed it to the child's father.

Lord, I never expected a dilemma like this when I came back to Sweetwater Cove. How exactly did one go about taking care of a family not his own? The idea seemed so overwhelming, he feared choking on his dumplings if he ate another bite.

Could Josiah do it? Little Gilly was eight, but Josiah had been fourteen when Papa, his adoptive father, took him in. As a younger boy, would Little Gilly be easier to teach, or more difficult? *Please show me what to do, Lord.*

General Washington let out a yelp from the storage room. Easy or not, it seemed the Lord was asking Josiah to step in and do the job.

"I'll take care of it." Josiah reached for the constable's hand and silently made the handshake his pledge to help bring up Little Gilly right. The way his friend Gilly would have.

Never mind that he had no idea where to begin.

◆—————◆

Josiah would have felt more comfortable dealing with a hundred deacon boards than with one eight-year-old boy. Nevertheless, after consulting Betsy, he got up from the now-empty table, and they strode across the pegged floor to the stairs. She opened the door to the closet, where Little Gilly sat cross-legged, his face buried in General Washington's white, furry coat.

He looked up with big, tear-filled eyes.

"Little Gilly, come up to your room with us," Betsy said, her voice gentle. "Reverend Wells wants to talk to you."

The boy sniffed and wiped his nose on his sleeve. "Don't want to."

Now what?

After a moment of prayer for wisdom, he listened for the still, small voice of God in his heart. A word from heaven, some wise instruction, a Bible passage, perhaps. Instead, a memory flashed through his mind.

He knew instantly what to do.

With the threat of withholding her son's blackberry cobbler at supper tonight, Betsy persuaded him to leave the closet and climb the stairs to his room.

Gilly's room. The same warm, third-story bedroom where Josiah had spent many a pleasant weekend during his years in Sweetwater Cove.

Now Little Gilly plopped on the small rope bed, its quilt spotless and its pillow fluffy. Betsy sat beside him, and Josiah took the Windsor armchair next to the bed. "Did you know I lived in Sweetwater Cove when I was your age?"

The boy shook his head, his gaze fastened on the braided rug under his feet.

"My parents were killed when I was fourteen, when their wagon ran off the Wilsonville Bridge. I was so angry, I got in a lot of trouble, and Constable Robbins sent me to live with a preacher and his wife in New Rochelle."

Little Gilly squirmed a bit at the mention of trouble, head still down.

"I remember a hot day in New Rochelle, the first Saturday after school let out for summer. I kept thinking about Sweetwater Cove, how the wild flags bloomed on the banks of Sweetwater River. The tadpoles would have turned to tiny frogs by then, and bluegill would be jumping clean out of the water."

"Like today," Betsy said, slipping her arm around the boy.

"But I was stuck inside my new father's big church that day. He'd told me to empty the ashes from the stoves and polish them for summer. So I was trapped in New Rochelle, with no fishing pole, no frogs, no wild flags—just my strange new parents."

Josiah could still feel that surge of anger, of fear, that had made him misbehave that day. "I was so scared and angry, I grabbed the bellows from the mantel and pumped them hard, until I'd blown ashes on the tables, chairs, the floor—all over the church's parlor."

Little Gilly sat up, his red, watery eyes big. "What'd your new father do?"

"He heard the sound of the bellows and came in to find the room covered in ashes."

"Were you sorry?"

"Not yet. But my fear left me then; because my anger had grown so big, I didn't have room for the fear anymore. I didn't know why my parents had to die. My mother was a good woman, but even though my father wasn't devout and kind, like the New Rochelle couple who took me in, he was my father. And I didn't know why I had to leave everything dear to me, everything familiar, and come to New Rochelle."

General Washington's toenails clicked on the stairs, and soon he burst into the room and jumped onto the bed. Little Gilly pulled him into his lap and buried his face in the dog's fur. "Did you find out why?" he said, his voice muffled in General Washington's coat.

"Why they had to die? No." Why he'd been sent away? Of course—his own bad behavior.

"What did your new father say to you?"

"He said, 'Son, I've kept you cooped up inside too long, just as you've kept your anger cooped up inside you. The best remedy I know for both is to go fishing.'"

"Did you go?" Little Gilly kept his face firmly planted in the dog's fur until Betsy coaxed him to sit up.

"That afternoon, even though I thought I'd never again spend a day on a riverbank, Papa and I fished the Hudson River. After that, everything changed."

Could Josiah be like a father to Little Gilly, as Papa Wells had been to him? He'd certainly had a good example to follow.

"Little Gilly," he said, fighting to speak through the lump that suddenly developed in his throat, "I'm going to do all I can to make sure I'll always be here in Sweetwater Cove. And I will look after you like a father."

The boy looked up at him, his blue eyes shimmering, melting. Holding his gaze. Trusting. "Like a real father? Because mine went to heaven, you know."

Josiah swallowed hard. He owed it to Gilly, and besides, the child had already fit himself right into Josiah's heart. "I'll be like a father to you, Little Gilly." He held out his hand to the boy. "I think we've all been cooped up in here too long. Let's go fishing."

Chapter 3

Whoever heard of a preacher who did kitchen work—and did it well? Even more, whoever heard of a preacher who could convince her eight-year-old son that it was manly to help the women with the dishes? Without complaining. Without asking, "Are we almost done?" more than two or three times.

Betsy breathed a silent prayer of thanks. Apparently, Josiah's influence was working.

The cook and her assistant stepped out the back door of the kitchen dependency and into the yard to hang up the wet towels and dishrags. Betsy untied her apron and hung it on the hook by the door. She glanced at Josiah as he lifted Little Gilly high enough to set the bread plate on the top shelf.

"All done. Ready to go fishing." Little Gilly's enthusiasm hurt a little. Between working at her store and helping at the inn, Betsy had neglected an important aspect of his upbringing: a man's influence. Papa Bennett loved him, it was true. But his work took most of his time, both now and when Gilly was a boy.

She closed her eyes for a moment and offered another silent prayer, thanking God for Josiah's return to Sweetwater Cove.

She had no more than whispered, "Amen," when Little Gilly tugged on her sleeve, looking up at her with pleading eyes. "When can we go?"

"The sooner we leave, the better," she said. "Don't forget we also have to look at the damage in the park." And find out if they could possibly restore it before the marquis's visit.

She sighed. So much depended on that park, on stopping Mr. Swift from building his store and drinking house. If they couldn't, Sweetwater Cove would never be the same.

And Betsy would never be able to change. Honoring Gilly at the marquis's reception, letting Little Gilly shake Lafayette's hand—these were the only things that could help her to shed even a portion of her guilt, let alone her failure as a wife, even for a few moments.

Mother Bennett's quick footsteps sounded on the brick walk between the inn and its kitchen.

"Cyrus found my Gilly's fishing tackle, just as you asked. It's been in the stable attic since the last day Gilly fished the river," she called as she burst through the doorway. "Betsy, come with me. I want to show you something."

The older woman grabbed Betsy's hand and all but dragged her to the inn, Josiah and Little Gilly following at a distance. "The tackle's in the front hallway, Reverend. And keep an eye on Little Gilly. Swanhilde Hansen saw a wolf drinking from the canal this morning."

Inside her bedroom Mother Bennett rummaged in the top shelf of her walnut wardrobe and finally pulled out a hatbox. "Here it is." She held it as if it contained the finest china, and her smile was that of an excited girl. "I thought you might like to borrow this today."

Betsy took the box and opened it. Removing the paper, she discovered a new bonnet in the latest fashion, the exact color of her eyes. Not the hue of Mother Bennett's striking green ones. She raised her gaze. "This is yours?"

"Yes, yes, try it on. Quickly." Her voice raised in pitch and volume as she adjusted the cheval mirror in the corner. "Don't make him wait."

"Little Gilly? He's too excited about fishing to take off without us."

Her mother-in-law pursed her lips in mock exasperation. "Not Little Gilly. The reverend."

Very well. Looking in the mirror, she put on the hat—the perfect hat for her eye color, hair color, and the shape of her face. How had the older lady done it?

Betsy slowly removed it, set it back in the box. "Mother Bennett, you didn't buy that hat for yourself."

"Well, who do you think I bought it for? Cyrus?" She reached in the box and took out the bonnet again. Set it on Betsy's head at a jaunty angle.

"You never wear blue. You always say it clashes with your eyes and your skin color." Betsy took Mother Bennett's soft hands. "Are you playing matchmaker?"

"I don't stoop to manipulation," she said with mirth in her eyes, clearly knowing she told an outright lie.

Betsy gave the dear woman a hug. "I'll bet you ordered this bonnet as soon as Josiah accepted the call to Sweetwater Cove."

"Not quite that soon."

Betsy couldn't stop her laugh from bursting out. "I know you have good intentions, but I don't want to marry again. I intend to be faithful to Gilly's memory."

Mother Bennett just smiled at Betsy's reflection in the mirror—that familiar, maddening smile she always used when she thought she knew what was best for someone else. And to Betsy's dismay, she was usually right. "Your son needs a father. And Cyrus and I agree that the reverend is just the man to take care of you and Little Gilly."

"I see right through your matchmaking scheme." Betsy smiled to soften her words. "I'm sorry to break your perfect record; however, I fear I will be the first person you fail to find a mate for. But it's true that Josiah has promised to take care of Little Gilly, to be like a father to him."

"Good. Tie the ribbon in a big, fluffy bow under your left ear, dear."

The woman just wasn't listening. "He said he'd take care of Little Gilly, not marry me. I'm wearing my third-best, light blue bonnet today. I'm not dressing to impress the new preacher."

Regardless of his kindness and soft gray eyes, his care for her son. Under no circumstances could she let anyone in Sweetwater Cove think she was.

And guess that she'd once loved him. Or, worse, think she loved him now.

Especially considering the circumstances of her late husband's death. She took off the hat and placed it in Mother Bennett's hands. "I love you like a mother, but I'm not wearing your bonnet."

She kissed her mother-in-law's cheek on the way to her room for her third-best hat.

"You will!" Mother Bennett called down the hall.

❖━━━━❖

What a comfort to know God does not necessarily give us what we deserve. Especially today. Betsy deserved to raise her son alone, with no kind childhood friend or parents-in-law to help. But instead, in His mercy, He had given her friends, family, and a town and church to fight for.

Walking between her and Josiah and carrying his father's worm jar in one arm, Little Gilly reached for Josiah's hand. Josiah took it and swung it in rhythm with their gait as they ambled down the inn's brick walk to the street.

The simple gesture did something unexplainable to her heart, and somehow she knew she'd always remember it.

"Which would you rather do," Josiah said to Little Gilly, "fish for an hour and then assess the park's damage, or go to the park first and then fish until dark?"

"Fish until dark," Little Gilly said at once, falling perfectly in line with the plan she and Josiah had discussed before coming outside.

If nothing else, the parson was quickly becoming adept at handling Little Gilly.

"Then that's what we'll do." He shifted his load of two fishing rods, one long and one shorter, both with brass reels, while Betsy carried the net. General Washington trotted in front of them as if he thought they needed his help to find the way. "Want to walk or take the carriage?"

"Walk!" Little Gilly shouted. "Can we fish in the canal? Then we can watch the boats go by. And when we're done there, we can fish the river, off the aqueduct.

My friend Ichabod saw Constable Robbins doing that."

"You'd have to drop your line straight down into the river," Betsy said.

"I think it'll reach, don't you, Little Gilly?"

At the wild nodding of his head, Betsy placed her finger under his chin. "It would be easy to fall off the aqueduct and into the river. Or the canal."

"I'll watch him." The fatherly look Josiah gave him mirrored the way Gilly used to look at their son. At once it both shattered and began to heal something in her heart.

At the park, Little Gilly dashed to the riverbank, General Washington at his heels, and climbed atop the giant cottonwood that had crushed the gazebo under its weight. After calling him to come down from there, Betsy reached into the pink silk drawstring bag dangling from her wrist and produced the little treasure she'd held on to for fifteen years. Held it out to Josiah.

He set the fishing gear on the ground and put out his hand.

"A ring?" He turned it over.

She waited.

"It's my marquis ring. My grandfather's ring." His quick, shy smile made him look like the boy she once knew. "How did you find this? I've mourned its loss all these years."

"I found it in the gazebo the day after you left."

Of course. "I always wondered if I'd lost it there."

"I should have found a way to get it back to you. I was only a girl, and I should have known better. But as young as I was, I still knew it was quite valuable, and I was afraid my father would make me give it to the church or the people with the burned-out houses. It was wrong of me." She watched him examine the ring, turn it over in his hand.

He looked up at her, his eyes full. "This was my maternal grandfather's. He was a captain in the marquis's army. I'll always be grateful you returned it to me."

"By the time I was old enough to know I should have told my father about it, everyone had lost track of you. We knew you'd lost your adoptive parents and had left New Rochelle, but we didn't know where you were."

He pushed the ring onto his finger.

"Does it fit?" she asked, watching.

"A little tight, but tight is better than loose. I don't want to lose it again."

Josiah moved more slowly after that, whether from fatigue or emotions, she couldn't tell. She let him set the pace, taking in the tree trunks and limbs strewn about the property, the exposed tree roots, the crushed little monument.

"Every bench destroyed, plants broken or smashed under fallen trees. Even with volunteers, this will take you and me weeks to clean up, repair, and replant." Josiah stashed the fishing poles behind the nearest fallen tree and called to Little

Gilly to put the worm jar there too.

"True, but the damage isn't so extensive that we can't eventually do it. So why do the aldermen think it's beyond restoration?"

"Good question." Josiah kicked a rock from the base of the monument. He bent and ran his fingers over the words in the toppled, broken limestone slab then plucked a blue delphinium that had grown beside the stone and had somehow been spared when the tree came down. He handed it to her. "What's this stone?"

"A monument to the marquis and General Washington. The man, not the dog." Betsy held the blossom to her face and breathed deeply of its scent, aware of the flower's brush with death as well as its survival. "We placed it here after—after you left."

He stood and faced her, and she had the impression that he understood her hesitation. "Go ahead and say it. You had this one made after I smashed the old one, when I found out the preacher and Constable Robbins were sending me away. The gazebo was the only place I could think of to hide from them afterward, until they found me and put me on a coach for the coast. Betsy, we're going to have to address your family's reluctance to mention my past sins. I realize you're trying to spare my feelings, but I don't want you to feel awkward. Just say what you need to say, and don't worry about offending me."

How refreshing. They should have done so when he'd arrived. "We merely want you to know we're on your side, especially with the church acting the way it did this morning."

"Not everyone was rude." His roguish smile almost made her believe Sweetwater Cove's sour attitude didn't affect him. "General Washington grinned at me and licked my hand after the preaching."

She wanted to smile but felt only sadness at his joke. "The dog is not your only friend in this town. All the Bennetts respect and care about you, and so does Constable Robbins. If only I could tell you how much my mother-in-law thinks of you. Then you'd understand." She touched the brim of her third-best bonnet, ran her finger over the big, puffy bow she'd tied under her left ear. At least she'd obeyed that much of her mother-in-law's orders.

Josiah laid his hand on her arm. "She's special to you, isn't she?"

Funny how the warmth of his hand somehow brought a measure of comfort. "I lost my parents and Gilly in the same week, in an epidemic of yellow fever. Gilly's parents had it too, but somehow my son and I didn't get it. I took care of all of them, and Little Gilly was only eleven months old. The minute Mother Bennett could raise her head off the pillow, she took over with Papa Bennett and Gilly's care, and she helped with Little Gilly too. All so I could stay with my parents, who were far sicker." A sting of tears blurred her vision, and she swiped them away. "I'm thankful I have this much of my family left."

Then she felt guilty for saying that, since Josiah didn't have a single living relative.

"But the worst part was my baby's first birthday," she went on while she still had the courage to tell the story. "Before the fever hit, Gilly and I had planned a party for him. We'd invited our parents and a dozen friends to share a big meal with us in the inn's dining room."

She hesitated. How could any woman describe the worst moment of her life? "I baked the cake, roasted the beef, mashed the potatoes as if I thought we'd actually have a party. I don't know what I was thinking. Maybe I was so exhausted and overcome with grief that I didn't think at all, just kept working as I had for the past month. But when I brought the roast out of the kitchen, nearly every dining room chair was empty. It was just me, my son, my in-laws, and my two best girlfriends from my school days. I had brought out the fishing rod Gilly made for Little Gilly, hoping his son would love to fish too. I looked at that pole, sitting among a tiny pile of presents. My only thought was, 'Papa Bennett doesn't fish. Who's going to teach Little Gilly how to fish?'"

Her voice broke as she admitted, for the first time, the fears that had gripped her that day, had formed her thinking from that time until now. If she'd taken better care of Gilly, then he'd be the one in the park with her and her son today. Her parents would be here too. If only she had watched them closer, fed them better, worked harder—something.

As always, her mind drifted to those days, what she could remember of them. Feeding and bathing Gilly and his parents. Running as fast as she could from the inn to her parents' home, back again to take care of the Bennetts. Feeding her baby. Starting the routine all over again. Then the day of her ultimate failure...

And as always, the questions: What should she have done differently? Why hadn't she paid more attention to Gilly's early complaints of headache and pain in his knees? If she'd realized he was sick, she'd have insisted he rest and possibly ward off the disease. How could she have failed to nurse her husband back to health?

How could she have slept late at her parents' house instead of coming home to Gilly on his last day on earth?

She glanced at the fallen tree Little Gilly was climbing on again. "We'd better get over there before he breaks a leg."

Josiah stood with her, leaving a cool spot on her arm where his hand had been. "I know we haven't seen each other in many years," he said, "but you're the same girl you were before I left Sweetwater Cove. If anybody could have saved Gilly, it would have been you. I don't think you have anything to feel guilty for."

Easy for him to say.

Josiah nodded toward the towpath. "Who's that?"

The lone figure approached along the dirt path, picking his way around mud puddles and mule droppings as if his shoes were made of spun silk. Which they may well have been.

Maynard Swift, her enemy. Their enemy.

She and Josiah apparently weren't the only ones formulating their plans for the park today. She bit her lip to hold back the words that wanted to shoot from her angry heart. Maybe God would give Maynard what he deserved, and maybe He wouldn't, but she had no intention of letting Maynard Swift take this park.

Chapter 4

As the figure drew nearer, something about his posture, his strutting gait, looked disturbingly familiar to Josiah.

The beefy man approached like a crown prince and looked like a dandy with his silk knee breeches and purple velvet tailcoat, his beaver-felt top hat set at an arrogant angle. But when Josiah saw the man's self-assured, toothy smile, he recognized him. Maynard Swift. The man who had supplied Josiah's father with the whiskey that ruined their family all those years ago. Even though Sweetwater Cove was a dry community, with liquor sales illegal inside its wide boundaries.

Of course the nefarious businessman would come here today, of all days. Never had he shown up anywhere but for to steal, and to kill, and to destroy.

He passed the aqueduct and stopped in front of Josiah and Betsy, jabbing his silver-handled cane at the rain-soaked sod. Raised his brows at Josiah's plain black suit. "Is that you, Brown?"

He said it as if the past fifteen years had melted away, and Josiah had just been caught after burning down half the town.

"I'm the Reverend Josiah Wells." It took all Josiah's self-control to maintain a gentle tone.

"You look a lot like an impertinent boy I used to know."

Yes, impertinence had come easily during Swift's routine visits years ago, and Josiah had taken many licks for it in the woodshed. Back then, he'd been a mere boy under his father's rule, powerless against Maynard Swift. Now Josiah would cautiously give him the benefit of the doubt, knowing some men changed as a result of hearing the Gospel of Jesus, but he'd keep an eye on him. He wasn't about to let the man touch any of his people again.

Josiah hesitated. His people? He cast a quick glance at Betsy. At Little Gilly, still climbing on the tree. Yes, in this long day, they had become his people. And yes, Josiah would make sure Maynard Swift didn't touch them, literally or figuratively.

Josiah took a long look at Swift—stopping just short of staring him down. Might he have changed from renegade whiskey runner to upstanding family man? Perhaps some circumstance, some tragedy in his life had softened his heart and allowed the good seed of the Gospel to sink into good soil. Josiah was bound to find out. "I'm not that boy anymore. How have you been, Mr. Swift? Have you a wife and children?"

"I'm married to my business, as always."

Ah. "The same business you used to conduct with my father?"

Although Maynard might have been trying to smile, it looked more like a sneer. And it proved to Josiah that he still preyed upon the weak of this town.

Men like Josiah's father. Men who couldn't resist the pull of strong drink. Men Josiah now vowed to protect from Maynard Swift—no matter what.

"Pleasant day for a stroll in the park, isn't it?" Maynard said, his gaze taking in the fluttering hem of Betsy's yellow dress.

"It was until now." A good thirty-five years Maynard's junior, Josiah could easily have taken him down if he initiated a physical altercation, but that wasn't Swift's style. Nor Josiah's. However, if this degenerate man continued to look at Betsy as though she were a slice of cherry pie, they would all find out just how quickly their styles could change.

"Yes, I agree. It was much more pleasant before I encountered the man who once set Sweetwater Cove on fire."

He always knew just what to say to provoke a man. But Josiah was not going to give him the satisfaction.

Before he could open his mouth to politely suggest that Maynard had somewhere else to go, Betsy pointed her slim finger at the renegade. "You know that was an accident. Josiah had just buried his parents, and he was only fourteen. He went in the church to grieve, and it was cold outside—"

"I know the whole sad story. The church ladies had arranged greenery around the candles, and he was fool enough to light them and go to sleep."

"He was fourteen. We all did foolish things at that age."

Swift's mud-colored eyes turned downright ugly. "Yes, we do. Foolish things in churches, and foolish things in gazebos in the park."

What? Had this rascal seen their kiss, the night before the constable sent Josiah away? If so, whom had he told? Mr. and Mrs. Bennett? *Gilly?* Could he somehow have twisted their sweet, gentle kiss into something sordid, and gained satisfaction from it? Josiah clenched his fists, held them steady, to keep from throwing the man into the canal.

"Simmer down, Brown." Swift smiled, showing huge gold teeth. "I love a clever rhyme like that."

"The name's Wells. And your idea of clever is different than mine."

"I should have suspected as much." He lifted his cane, pointed its odd, flower-shaped tip at Josiah like a gun. "I've seen all I need to see. This park has sustained too much damage for repair. On the morrow, I will make an offer on it."

When he had headed back up the towpath and out of earshot, Josiah clasped Betsy's elbow and turned her in the opposite direction. "Come on, Little Gilly."

The boy stood from digging his worms, grabbed his worm jar, and trotted up to Josiah.

"We're walking your mother home, and then we'll come back and fish," Josiah said.

"Why? Did you see a wolf?" the boy asked, looking around.

Josiah glanced behind him, making sure Swift was on his way. "Indeed I did. The biggest, ugliest wolf in New York."

<hr>

This must be a taste of what fatherhood felt like.

After seeing Betsy home, Josiah and Little Gilly had raced back to the park for their fishing tackle, and as they reached the fallen tree where they'd stashed their gear, the boy had flung himself into Josiah's arms.

Could this have been the first time a man had ever run with the boy? Even if Gilly had lived, he couldn't have run, since Josiah had shoved him from the old Wilsonville Bridge the day before he left town, and had broken his leg. According to Mrs. Bennett's letters to Josiah, Gilly had a profound limp the rest of his life.

Ironic that Josiah was the one to run with Gilly's son.

"Canal first, or river?" he asked the boy.

"I'll fish the canal while you fish the river, and then we'll switch."

"Think we can do both at the same time?"

Little Gilly's head bobbed until his little brown cap slid sideways.

When they reached the canal, arms full of fishing gear, a bright blue packet boat crept up beside them on the canal's tranquil waters. Its passengers reclined atop the boat and waved to him and Little Gilly. When they had passed, the boy scrambled to follow the mules as they towed the packet along the aqueduct and over the river. Josiah trailed behind him, set down his gear, and baited hooks. "You were right. This is a great place to fish. I admit I've never tried to fish from an aqueduct. In fact, I've never been on one before."

He handed the small pole with baited hook to Little Gilly, who edged close to the canal. Josiah showed him how to cast with the wide brass reel and wait for the tug on the line. Watching him, he couldn't help but wonder if this was the rod Gilly had made for the boy. Under the layers of dust and dirt lay a polished, shiny stick with some sort of sealer on it, as he could tell from the areas he'd rubbed clean while baiting the hook.

Without an immediate nibble, Little Gilly soon sat down on the grass between the towpath and the water. "Mama says you knew my papa."

Josiah swallowed. "We were best friends."

"They say I don't look like him."

"You look like your mother."

"Why'd you leave here?"

He should have anticipated that question. He thought, prayed a moment before answering. "My parents had died, and a couple from New Rochelle took me in to finish raising me."

"I know, but you said you didn't want to leave. Couldn't anybody here raise you?"

How could he answer that? "I guess not."

Little Gilly's long silence unnerved him a bit. It was hard telling what the boy was thinking.

After a few nibbles and finally a catch, Josiah strung the bluegill on a thin length of rope he found in the tackle basket. The other end was fastened to a spike, so he threw the fish into the canal and pushed the spike into the dirt. Then he baited his hook and tossed it over the stone railing. It dropped about ten feet into the river below.

Leaning against the waist-high stone ledge, he took in the docks, the stores. Especially the one with the sign that read, DRY GOODS. GILLY BENNETT, PROPRIETOR. Betsy certainly had the prime location in Sweetwater Cove, with a short dock on the front of the store that connected to the river, and another, much longer dock that stretched from the store's side entrance to the canal. Little wonder that Maynard Swift wanted to close her down. He probably hoped she'd sell cheap, having gone out of business, and he could pick up the best commercial spot in many miles.

He gazed farther down the canal. Swift Warehouse sat only a few hundred feet from Bennett's Dry Goods. Yes, if Maynard could pick up her store, he would have a sweet setup.

Another boat, this one a line boat carrying goods, drifted down the canal toward them. Little Gilly jerked his hook out of the water and handed the pole to Josiah so he could walk alongside the mules, one hand on the back of the animal nearest him. The still waters of the canal, the methodic plodding steps of the mules, the droning insects around him, all gave Josiah a sense of peace, of contentment. The docks were quiet today, with all the businesses closed, and the canal traffic slow.

By the time Little Gilly returned, having seen the mules a quarter mile or so down the towpath, Josiah could have taken a nap. However, the boy grabbed his pole. "Want to switch places?"

Sitting by the canal sounded better than standing at the rail on the river side, so he reeled in his line, cast his hook into the canal, and sat in the grass beside the water. But instead of moving to the rail and casting into the river, Little Gilly sat beside him, pole and hook in the grass.

"You like being a preacher?"

"I do when people behave." He smiled, only half joking.

"What about when they don't?"

He chuckled. "Then you make the best of it. Try to show them the right way."

The boy lay in the grass, his arms folded under his head, and gazed into the sky. "I don't know why people don't behave."

"No one behaves all the time."

"What if you get tired of making the best of it, and they won't listen to the right way?" Little Gilly lifted his head and looked at him with his broken heart in his big eyes.

Josiah pulled in his line, set it aside. Turned to the child. "Does somebody mistreat you, Little Gilly?"

He could see the muscles working in the boy's jaw. "Everybody here except my mama calls you 'Reverend' or 'Parson.' Do your friends call you that?"

"My friends call me Josiah."

Silence.

"Little Gilly?"

He turned his face away.

Josiah laid his hand on the child's shoulder. "What's wrong?"

"I hate that name!" He sat up and folded his arms over his bent knees, laid down his head.

What? "When you get older, they won't call you 'Little' anymore."

"I don't like 'Gilly' either."

"But it's a fine name. It was your father's name."

"Don't care. It's sissy."

"Did someone tell you it was sissy?"

He raised his head. Met Josiah's gaze. "At school, they call me Little Silly Gilly. I'm not that little, and I'm not silly."

Josiah paused. The boy was right. He seemed average size for his age, and he certainly wasn't silly. Mischievous, like all boys, but not silly. His mother and grandmother had no doubt seen to that. "Some children are silly—are foolish. They say hurtful things without knowing what they're talking about. What if we think of a different name for you?"

"I like Robert."

Josiah couldn't hold in his laugh. "We probably can't change it completely. But what if we started calling you Gil? Or Gilbert? That was your father's full name."

"It's my full name too. Do you think people would call me Gilbert?"

The spark of hope in his voice, his eyes, warmed Josiah's heart. "Here's what we'll do. I'll tell your mother you want to be called Gilbert. And I'll call you Gilbert. And anytime someone calls you Little Gilly, just ask them politely to call you Gilbert. It might take awhile, but it'll catch on."

"Gilbert. My name is Gilbert Bennett." He stood and hurled himself at Josiah, wrapped his arms around his waist.

And drew out a sense of protectiveness Josiah hadn't known he had.

After a moment, Gilbert picked up his fishing pole and cast the line far down the canal. "I'm Gilbert Bennett!"

Chapter 5

His stomach full, his work schedule full—but his heart?

Alone in the manse's parlor that evening, Josiah lowered himself to the worn leather wing chair by the hearth. He propped his feet on his trunk, which he hadn't yet unloaded and taken to the attic. With his few possessions unpacked, other than this trunk, he felt no more or less settled than he ever had.

He blinked back the trace of moisture in his eyes as he recalled Little Gilly's transformation into Gilbert. In some ways, it was as if the boy had nearly become a man, set free from childish ways. Of course, Gilbert had a long way to go before he'd truly be a man. But today had been a start. For both him and Josiah.

Now, if he could only decide what to do with the trunk's contents.

How did you make restitution to a whole town? Tonight Deacon Bennett gave him the names of the families who'd lost their homes in the fire. Over the years, they'd all moved away. The church had been rebuilt.

He lifted his feet from the trunk. Opened the lid, revealed the gold coins inside. How could he fulfill his dream of giving half of his inheritance from Papa Wells to Sweetwater Cove if he had no one to give it to?

Of course, his marble statue of the marquis would help spruce up the park. And he'd need to use his money to replace the plants, benches, and gazebo, since the town's park fund was depleted. He could also replenish the town's funds to ensure the park's future care.

However, Deacon Bennett's afternoon plea for volunteers to help restore the park had gone nearly unheeded, with only Constable Robbins and Mrs. Bennett offering to help. It seemed the citizens of Sweetwater Cove were afraid to cross Maynard Swift.

If Swift was that powerful, could Josiah and Betsy hope to hold on to the park, saving her store from ruin and saving the town from the influence of strong drink?

Did Josiah have what it would take to protect both Betsy and Sweetwater Cove?

On impulse, he opened the secret compartment in the trunk's lid. Took out his marquis ring. The ring itself was in the shape of an oblong octagon, its gold unmarred by time. He ran his finger over the top of the ring—over the portrait of the marquis as a young man, his hair powdered and fashioned in a queue and tied with a bow.

No doubt the ring had value beyond measure. But to Josiah, its value lay in the hope it once gave him.

"This was my father's ring, Josiah. A soldier during the Revolution. A man the marquis trusted, a man to be proud of." His mother's melodic voice wafted through his mind, his memory of it still sharp. *"This ring will save you one day. Hold on to it. . . ."*

He'd known she meant he shouldn't let his father have it.

"Remember, you're a Brown, but you're also a Sullivan, because I'm a Sullivan. Your grandfather was a patriot, an officer in the Continental Army. He was a hero. Someday you'll be someone's hero too."

Even as a child, Josiah had understood his mother meant him to use the ring to escape Sweetwater Cove, escape the poverty his father's drunkenness had forced upon them. Escape the shame. And yet, here he was, back in his hometown and reunited with his ring, with his mother's legacy.

What could it mean?

The one thing he knew for sure was that God had called him to return to Sweetwater Cove. Could he be a hero here?

What could be more heroic than preventing Maynard Swift from ruining other families as he had Josiah's?

Perhaps, once the marquis's visit was over, Josiah could even find a way to catch Swift violating the town's dry liquor status. No alcohol sales were permitted within the town's boundaries, from Gray's Knob to the north, to Wilsonville to the south.

At once he knew what to do with the ring, at least for now. Tomorrow, when the bank opened, he would deposit his gold specie. But not his ring. It would stay hidden in the trunk.

Lifting the lid again, he stopped. Why hide it? Pa was no longer here to take it from him.

He slid the ring back onto his finger, vowing never to take it off. Never to forget that Betsy had found it and kept it for him.

This was his home again. As he'd pledged himself to Gilbert, he now pledged himself to Sweetwater Cove, the town the Lord had given him to shepherd.

His heart was still empty in many ways, might always be empty, alone. But after fifteen years of wrestling with his heart, his past, he could finally stop.

He'd come home.

———◆———

Monday, Josiah's favorite day of the week. Monday mornings were full of possibilities and potential, a fresh start. Today he washed and dressed by lamplight in the gray dawn and hastened to the livery for his carriage.

There he realized his folly in keeping Papa Wells's coach-and-six in Sweetwater Cove. Using the conveyance Papa had left behind instead of buying another had seemed prudent at the time, but now? His hired driver long gone, he'd need to sit aloft the carriage on the high driver's seat and bump around town with no one, nothing inside, save his trunk of gold specie. With six horses pulling it. Although comfortable for his long trip from New Rochelle, this conveyance was not only conspicuous but also ridiculous here.

Nonetheless, a half hour later, he drove to the bank and deposited his gold. Returned the coach-and-six to the livery and asked the owner to put a FOR SALE sign on it.

From there he strode to the park. Sure enough, Deacon Bennett had delivered a shovel, hoe, and ax as he'd promised. But standing here alone, facing a mess like this. . .

Could he do it? Could he get the job done?

Certainly not by standing here and looking.

He rolled up the sleeves of his white work shirt and grabbed the ax, headed toward the farthest fallen tree, the one lying on the gazebo. Within minutes, he heard footsteps behind him.

"There's your boss, gentlemen."

Josiah turned at the sound of Betsy's voice. He looked up to see her and a dozen or so men, all dressed in rough laborers' clothing and caps, striding toward him and the pile of freshly painted lumber that had once been the gazebo. As they drew nearer, he noticed her faded brown dress and worn boots, the thick gloves in her hand. His heart warmed at the sight of her here to work. He also saw that these workers weren't men, but youths. What could she have to do with a gang of young men who looked as if they'd just finished plowing and planting a hundred-acre field?

But these men carried saws, axes, and hatchets. Not plows, harrows, and hoes.

"Come and meet your cleanup crew," Betsy called in a lilting voice.

What—only an hour into the workday, she'd found enough men to clear out this mess? He approached the crowd and offered his hand.

"This is the Reverend Josiah Wells," she said.

Although he'd been Josiah Wells longer than he'd been Josiah Brown, the name still sounded strange on her lips.

With the breeze blowing wispy curls across her forehead, she laid her hand on the shoulder of the stockiest young man. "This is August Schmidt, the foreman. I recruited him and his men at the docks."

Josiah scanned the crew. "Men" was an exaggeration. Other than August, none of them looked more than fifteen years old. "Don't you already have jobs?"

"We did until today," August said in a thick German accent. "Our boss owns six liners, but today he said he can't pay us."

"He left you here with no pay?" Josiah glanced around at the motley gang, but no one responded.

"My boys don't speak English," August said, "but they're hard workers."

Josiah knew one sure way to discover the truth of that statement. He walked the length of the line of men, examining their hands. If a laborer claimed to be a hard worker, his hands would prove it. Sure enough, they boasted callouses, dirt beneath their nails, and a blister or two. "I'm sure you'll want to get jobs on another liner as soon as you can, but I'm happy you're here today."

"You don't understand." Betsy's grin widened to bring out her dimples.

Oh, he had forgotten those dimples. He averted his gaze.

"They're not here for just a day. They're here to get the job done."

He'd always known Betsy was a motivator, understood how to cast her vision and encourage others to pick it up. But he didn't know just how well she could do it until now. He stepped a few yards away, motioning for Betsy to join him. When they were out of August's earshot, he leaned in to whisper. "How did you do this?"

"This morning, I heard singing out on the canal dock," she said, keeping her voice low as well. "I didn't know the words, but the tune was the 'Doxology.' Of course, my first thought was of Papa Bennett and his habit of whistling that tune to encourage himself during trouble." She smiled, all the way to her eyes. Then a ray of sun pushed through the morning fog and turned those blue eyes to crystal.

Could this ragtag crew be the answer to their prayers?

"These men were doing the same thing, only singing instead of whistling. In German," she said, clearly believing God had sent them. "So I told August the truth. How we could lose the park to a man who wants to build a drinking house. How whiskey had destroyed your early life, but you'd come back anyway to show this town that Jesus was more than enough to help us through any struggle. As I suspected, all these young men come from bad home lives, so they immediately agreed to help us keep our park, especially when I told them Sweetwater Cove is a dry community and doesn't allow liquor sales."

Those dimples popped out again. "With your approval, they'll work in exchange for room and board."

No pay?

Josiah's mind raced as he considered alternatives. God had answered their prayers by sending these men. Josiah was now confident of that. But he also knew his part in this. "I approve of them as workers, but a worker is worthy of his hire. I'll make sure they receive their usual pay plus twenty percent."

Footsteps clattered on the slate walk then. With her customary yoo-hoo-ing and wild waving, Mrs. Bennett hastened toward them, also wearing outdoor-work attire. "The aldermen have voted. We have until Friday to fix the park."

Good. "Over there is the new crew that's going to make that happen. Have you room to house them, and plenty to feed them?" he asked as she drew near. He stepped closer and lowered his voice. "I can assure you of payment."

Her sweet face blossomed with her smile. "They'll need to double up in their rooms, and I might need to hire another cook, but yes! Where did you find them?"

"I didn't. Your brilliant daughter-in-law made all the arrangements."

"She's more like my own daughter." She patted Betsy's cheek, her words bringing a tender smile to Betsy's lips before the two hastened to their work.

At last, Josiah could begin his restitution to Sweetwater Cove. He cast his gaze over the men already at work with their saws, the women clearing away the smaller branches and leaves.

Yes, Monday was definitely the best day of the week.

Chapter 6

Something about this felt a little too much like courting.

Late the next morning, Betsy glanced again at the note Mother Bennett had pressed into her hand. Exactly why did Josiah feel the need to accompany Betsy from her store to the park? And why had he bothered to write a note to tell her so and then asked her mother-in-law to deliver it? Surely he knew she'd read it on the way. He could have merely told Mother Bennett and thereby saved a sheet of paper.

"The reverend said he would escort you to the park at exactly twelve noon." Mother Bennett quoted the note word for word while maneuvering around three barrels of flour Betsy's dockworkers had just brought in from the canal dock. "He also told me to remind you not to go alone, because there are wolves about. What do you suppose he meant by that?"

"Maynard Swift. He calls him a wolf," Betsy whispered.

Her mother-in-law's green eyes grew wide. "Yes, he is. Fortunately, you have the reverend to fend off the wolf."

"Mother Bennett, I don't 'have' the reverend in any sense of the word."

"Perhaps not yet." She peered out the window then put her finger to her lips. "Here he comes. You know where my blue bonnet is, if you need it."

The store now empty for the first time that day, Betsy folded the note and slipped it into her money box. All morning, she'd wanted nothing more than to dash to the park and see what Josiah had accomplished.

With the doors open to both the canal dock and the river dock, the musical tones of packet boat horns and the salty voices of burly line boat captains floated into the store. Betsy glanced at the timepiece pinned to her dress. A quarter to twelve. She smoothed her hair, brushing back a few curls that refused to stay in her chignon.

Her dockworkers rolled in the last barrels of flour and carried in the final baskets of fresh vegetables and sacks of oats and sugar. By the time she'd logged the last of the supplies and settled up with the captain, Josiah strode into the store, stepped around the barrels.

She took in his stylish brown trousers and white shirt, a gentleman's work

223

attire with a dusting of garden soil. To her dismay, Josiah looked as handsome in them as he had in his black suit two days ago. Maybe more so, since she knew he'd gotten dirty for her sake, for her town's sake. Funny how a man's good heart made him more attractive.

"I counted four liners at the canal docks," Josiah said, waving toward the door. "Do you usually have that many on a Tuesday morning?"

"Sometimes more. The packets often stop too, so the passengers can buy a meal." She pointed to a table full of sandwiches, boiled eggs, and little cakes. "Mother Bennett, come with us, so you can see the progress at the park too."

"No, no. I'll stay here in case Little Gilly comes for a bite of lunch."

Betsy had to admit, it was a nice try. "I sent his lunch with him to school, so you can come with us. And don't forget, he wants us to call him Gilbert."

"Of course. Gilbert." Mother Bennett shot her gaze about the store until it landed on a ten-pound bag of salt on the counter. She hastened toward it. "I'll put away some of the stock first. Take your time. Maybe even walk out to the woods and see if you can find some wild ferns to transplant. Don't worry, I'll be along directly to see the park."

Mother Bennett picked up the salt and lugged it to the storage room, peeking at them over her shoulder.

Honestly, this was getting embarrassing.

"Looked like most of the goods landed in Maynard Swift's warehouse," Josiah said as he held the door. If he'd picked up on Mother Bennett's plot to make them take a romantic walk alone, he didn't let on.

"Mr. Swift keeps a large stock," she said. "He has a draying service and ships goods to the Wilsonville area every week."

"Well, I heard this morning he added another vehicle to his fleet. My coach-and-six."

She frowned. "He already has a landau and a runabout. Why would he want your coach as well? Because it's so fine? Or just because it was yours?"

"I don't know, but if I'd known Maynard Swift was going to buy my carriage, I wouldn't have put it up for sale."

As they stepped outside to the canal dock, Josiah offered his arm. She hesitated, still needing to keep an emotional and physical distance from this handsome man. By no means could she form an attachment to him. "About those wolves, Josiah..."

Now he wiggled his elbow, a hint of a grin on his face. "That wolf, Maynard Swift, might bite, but I won't. Allow me to escort you, Betsy."

Against her good judgment, she slipped her hand in the crook of his arm as they started down the towpath and then took Concord Street toward the park. His genuine concern touched her heart. To have a man offer a strong arm and his protection—well, other than Papa Bennett, she hadn't had that in a long time. Certainly not from a man as kind and handsome as Josiah.

"Morning, Mrs. Bennett," Swanhilde Hanson's distinctive voice rang out from behind her.

Betsy turned to see Mother Bennett slipping behind an oak as if she thought she could hide from Betsy's eyes. Swanhilde, by her side, gaped at the sight of the mayor's wife ducking behind a tree.

Josiah turned too, and smiled at the sight of the older woman's pink dress bulging out on either side of the oak. "Catch up with us, Mother Bennett," he called, a laugh in his voice.

He'd called her Mother Bennett? This was something new. She rather liked it.

"Let's go back and get her. I hear that Swanhilde is a widow. If we don't get there soon, your mother-in-law will have her married." Josiah spun and grabbed Betsy's hand as they jogged toward the older woman.

As they approached, Mother Bennett poked her head around the tree trunk. Swanhilde made a hasty retreat.

Josiah offered an arm to Mother Bennett, and Betsy smiled as her mother-in-law succumbed to his courtly bow and took his arm.

"I do love a stroll in the spring," she said. "Cyrus never has time—"

At the sudden noise of nearby high-pitched yelling, Mother Bennett gasped as if she'd been caught with her spectacles on. "Little Gilly!"

Betsy turned toward the sounds of war as a neighbor boy, Ichabod Beedle, and Little Gilly—Gilbert—rolled over each other, punching and kicking, all the way down Ichabod's porch steps. She broke away from Josiah and raced to separate the two hooligans, but Josiah beat her to it. He held on to Ichabod while she clasped her son's wrist and turned him toward herself. He tried to yank his arm away, but she pulled him even closer.

Dear Father in heaven, I don't know what to do with him. He gets in trouble, no matter what I do. . . .

"We were going to the park to see the work Josiah did this morning. But I believe I'll need to take you home to your room for discipline instead," she said, her disappointment deep, both in her son's behavior and in the fact she would now need to forgo her outing. Her face flushed a little. Her outing to see the park, of course. Not Josiah.

She glanced down at the ripped knee of Gilbert's trousers, at his shirt, which was as dirty as Josiah's work clothes. "What happened?"

Her son stopped his struggle against her and looked at Josiah. "I told him politely to call me Gilbert, like you said."

Josiah looked at his small captive. "Didn't you want to call him Gilbert?"

"Sure," Ichabod yelled. "I called him Gilbert four times!"

Josiah glanced at Betsy and at Mother Bennett, who by this time had climbed the porch steps and stood a safe distance away. "Then what was the problem, Gilbert?"

"He wanted to change his name too. The boys call him Ick. But we couldn't think of a good way to change Ichabod. No matter what you do, it sounds awful."

Betsy had to give him that. She pushed away a strand of hair that had come down during the altercation. "I still don't know why you were fighting."

"He wanted to use his middle name." Gilbert struggled against Betsy again, trying to get away.

Josiah grabbed Gilbert's arm, still holding Ichabod with the other hand. "Why was that wrong?"

"His middle name is Robert. If I can't be Robert, he can't either." He reached for Ichabod, or Robert, but Josiah intervened, pulling the other boy farther away.

At a safe distance from Gilbert, he turned him loose. "Robert, please go inside."

"I said he can't be Robert!" Gilbert screamed.

Betsy walked her son down the steps. "I don't want to hear you yell like that again. You're Gilly Bennett's son, and we don't act that way in this family."

When "Robert" had gone inside and slammed the door, Josiah and Mother Bennett joined them in the yard.

"Please allow me a moment with Gilbert," Josiah said.

At her nod, he knelt on one knee in the grass, his eyes now level with her son's. She and Mother Bennett stepped away, giving them privacy. As the minister spoke in low tones, Gilbert inched closer and sat on Josiah's bent knee. When he pulled a shiny object from his coat pocket, the boy broke out in his biggest grin since Christmas.

Josiah was bribing him with a coin for good conduct? That seemed akin to rewarding him for terrible behavior.

Betsy moved toward them, but her mother-in-law stopped her. "I know what you're thinking, but this might not be as bad as it looks. May I give an opinion?"

Mother Bennett, getting involved in Gilbert's discipline? What other surprise might this day bring?

"I think my grandson needs a better influence in his life than Ichabod Beetle—or Robert, or whoever he is—can give. Little Gilly, make that Gilbert, would benefit from the company of a minister of the Gospel."

Betsy sighed. Another matchmaking scheme.

Mother Bennett blinked her green eyes as if holding back tears. "I know what you're thinking, but this time, I'm not talking about a match between you and the reverend. I know Cyrus doesn't have enough time to spend with Gilbert. I'm asking you to give our minister a chance to make the boy into a man. To disciple him, so to speak. I think you can trust the reverend."

Oh. That was different.

If her mother-in-law had been in the habit of interfering with Little Gilly's—Gilbert's—upbringing, Betsy might have balked at her advice. But since Mother Bennett had always held her tongue before this, Betsy felt bound to let the sweet woman have her way.

And to have Mother Bennett agree to allow another man into her grandson's life—almost to take Gilly's place as a father to the boy—was more than Betsy could have hoped for. She silently blessed her mother-in-law for her selflessness and common sense.

Now she stepped closer to listen and learn how Josiah would deal with boys.

"I need some good men to help me get the park cleaned up and then plant some flowers and rebuild the benches and gazebo," he said. "How about you and Robert?"

"For a half eagle?"

"It's yours when the job's done. But we have to have the park ready before the marquis's visit on Friday."

"Can I go tell Ichabod?"

Josiah closed his hand on the coin. "It's not a deal unless you call him Robert."

Betsy drew in a breath. *Oh, bless the man.*

Gilbert's lip pooched out in a pout. "That's not fair."

"Maybe not, but if we call you by a man's name, you have to act like a man. That means you sometimes have to give in to someone else. If you can do that, I'll hire you to help me at the park. But I need a man's help. Not a boy's."

Gilbert didn't hesitate a moment. "I'll call him Robert."

"Good man."

As Gilbert scampered off, Betsy gave thanks to God for Josiah's wisdom, his ability to reach her son's heart.

Yes, Mother Bennett's plan would work, as long as Betsy could continue to think of Josiah as no more than Gilly's handsome friend, Gilbert's friend and mentor.

Although she might have a little more trouble keeping her own rule than she'd like to admit.

◆———・——◆

If drinking what seemed like gallons of tea in one evening could make an angry congregation forget their grievances against the pastor, then Josiah had no more worries.

Late the next evening, as he and Betsy left the last home on their visitation list, dusk had begun to fall, but the full moon lit the street as they started toward the inn.

"Deacon Bennett was right," he said. "The church members love you, and you know exactly what to say to get them to lower their guard with me."

"You did most of the guard-lowering yourself. Once they got to know you a little, they started to love you too." She rubbed her stomach. "I've never had so much tea. Or so many sweets. But at least they served a different dessert at each house, almost as if they'd planned it. I loved the blueberry pie at the last house."

The night music of cicadas and bullfrogs seeped into Josiah's soul and soothed something there that had remained rough all these years, despite his happy home with Mama and Papa Wells. He'd needed to come home, and he hadn't known it until this moment.

Yes, Sweetwater Cove felt like home, perhaps for the first time.

Not just at the inn, where he'd spent happy days with Gilly and his family. Even in his lonely bachelor manse, he felt at home.

Had that feeling started when he slipped his grandfather's ring onto his finger? Or had the first nuances come when he saw Betsy for the first time in all those years?

Regardless, he now gave thanks for his home. The place he wanted to live for the rest of his life.

Their steps had slowed, perhaps because of his calming ruminations, but now as they passed the park, it seemed natural to pause. "Would you like to stop here for a moment? It's still light enough, and we could look at the moon's reflection in the river."

After her reluctance to take his arm yesterday, he hadn't offered it again. But tonight, in the moonlit park, he took her hand and placed it at his elbow. "I don't want you to trip over a stick or branch."

"Even in the dim moonlight, I can see great progress. Most of the fallen trees are gone. Are Gilbert and Robert doing a good job cleaning up the park's debris?" She giggled, a sweet, tinkling sound. "I can't get used to calling them that."

"They start each sentence with each other's names. 'Gilbert, hand me a saw.' 'Robert, help me carry this limb.'"

She smiled, her eyes shining in the dusk. "You're doing a wonderful job with the boys. Gilbert is different since you came to town. He's happier. Even when you correct him, he adores you."

"Trust me, it's mutual."

Reaching the river, they stopped. Took in the sight of the huge, yellow full moon reflecting in the water. A beautiful spot.

A beautiful girl.

He realized then where they were: at the setting of the old gazebo, the splintered wood now gone and the site ready for rebuilding. The spot of their first kiss where he'd realized, too late, that he didn't want to leave Sweetwater Cove. Didn't want to leave his home.

Didn't want to leave Betsy.

Now he took both her hands, bent down, and kissed her—slowly, softly, as if the years hadn't come and gone and left them both alone. As if they were young again, hopeful for love, hopeful for a future together.

And when she kissed him back, she tasted of blueberries and tea and smelled of blue delphiniums, her hands freeing themselves from his and her arms curling around his waist as if they'd never been apart since that night. As if they'd always been together.

Except they hadn't.

His spine stiffened in her embrace. He was kissing his best friend's widow. The friend who'd walked with a limp Josiah gave him.

Kissing a member of the congregation the Lord had charged him with tending. Not with kissing.

No. He pulled away, turned from her. "I'm sorry. I shouldn't have done that. I don't know what I was thinking. . . ."

For much too long, she said nothing, didn't move. Finally, she touched his arm. "It's all right. We'll just call it a mistake."

Her voice cracked as she declared their kiss a lapse of judgment, breaking his heart a little more than he'd like to admit—even if he knew as well as she did that kissing her was wrong. She looked away then returned her gaze to his, a mixture of guilt and wistfulness turning those beautiful blue eyes an even softer hue, like frost-touched delphiniums. "We'll blame it on the moon."

"Right. The moon."

And with those few words, she saved him. Saved his pride and tried to rescue his feelings as well. Which made him want, more than anything, to kiss her again.

A kiss from Betsy tonight was more than he could ever have hoped for. With a past like his, a man had to be grateful for every little bit of comfort he got.

Even if he never got it again.

Chapter 7

Could anything possibly feel worse than sharing a spectacular kiss with a sweet, strong, handsome man, and then realizing he regretted the kiss, even before it was over?

In the kitchen dependency before full daylight the next morning, pouring boiling water over a blueberry stain in yesterday's white dress, Betsy once more let those moments wash over her, change her. Just a little.

If only she could forget that kiss. Forget the way he'd made her feel—as if her past sins didn't disqualify her for future love. As if Josiah's kiss could erase her inadequacies. As if his love could somehow put to rest her conviction, her guilt.

Then again, perhaps she'd rather recall every detail for the rest of her life, painful as that would be. Because today she could no longer deny her feelings for Josiah, her one-sided love for him.

Or the fact she could never marry him, even if he felt the same about her—which he clearly didn't.

She wrung out her dress and folded it over a few times so it wouldn't drag on the ground on her way to the backyard. What could she do with those emotions? She couldn't rinse them from her heart the way she'd rinsed the berry stain from her dress.

Carrying the garment outside, she braced herself for her day. Today was Thursday, and they had to have the park ready by noon tomorrow, both to keep the park and for the marquis's visit. This day, she didn't have the luxury of soaking in her sentiments or sinking in her sorrows.

Shivering a little in the morning air, she reached the boxwood hedge and spread her dress on the bushes to dry. Since Papa Bennett's and Constable Robbins's muffled-sounding voices drifted through the partially open window of Papa Bennett's office, Betsy hurried to leave them to their privacy. But as she turned back toward the inn, she caught sight of Gilbert's slingshot near the far corner of the hedge.

She hastened to pick it up.

Between the hedge and the office, Ebenezer Crouch kneeled under the window.

Eavesdropping on the mayor and the constable's morning meeting?

Facing the other way, Mr. Crouch hadn't seen her. Betsy froze for a moment then crept backward, toward the inn.

She eased open the screen door, slipped inside. Drew a deep breath.

As soon as Papa Bennett came in for breakfast, she'd have a talk with him and Constable Robbins.

About twenty minutes later, the front door opened and slammed hard. The sound of feet running on the pegged floors announced Robert's arrival. He raced into the dining room and slid into Mr. Crouch's chair by the window.

"Got any bacon this morning?" Robert eyed the platter in Betsy's hand as she carried out the sausage.

"Gilbert's grandmother was putting it on a platter when I left the kitchen." Betsy set the sausage in front of Papa Bennett's plate, where he liked it. Mother Bennett rang the dinner bell, so Betsy took her seat.

"Preacher works us so hard at the park, I'm starving all the time," Robert said. "But the park looks great. Some of the women in town have dug up some of their flowers and plants, and have donated them to the park. The preacher says lots of families are coming to help. And we built new benches yesterday."

Gilbert scampered in with General Washington trotting along behind, then Mother Bennett brought the bacon and handed Robert a slice. "Betsy, I'll bring in your dress for you at about three o'clock, so it'll have time to bleach in the sun. The almanac says it's supposed to be dry today."

After prayer, Gilbert grabbed the sausage platter. "What's supposed to be dry, Grandmother?"

"Sweetwater Cove. What did you think?"

"This town's been dry for years," the boy said, "so what's so special about today?"

His grandmother squinted at him. "Gilbert, it is not. We have rain or snow nearly every week of the year."

"All I know is, that's what Mr. Crouch said."

The front door banged again, and this time they heard Ebenezer Crouch's waddling, lumbago-driven footsteps.

Papa Bennett and Constable Robbins came in the back door as Mr. Crouch appeared from the front. He stopped for an instant, his face reddening and his mouth pinched. "Ichabod Beedle, what are you doing in my chair?"

"Eatin' bacon," the boy said around a mouthful. "Please call me Robert."

"Robert? Your father named you Ichabod eight years ago, and that's what I'm going to call you. Get out of my chair."

"That's not what the preacher said—"

"Robert, please give Mr. Crouch his chair." Betsy stood, unable to eat anyway.

"You may sit in mine."

"The window's closed!" Mr. Crouch stomped over and shoved the window all the way open, even in the cool morning air. Glaring at both boys, he slumped into his chair.

Mother Bennett passed him a covered pot. "Porridge, Mr. Crouch?"

"Porridge? Bah!" He slammed back his chair and stomped upstairs.

Something was wrong here.

"Perhaps Mr. Crouch simply needs a wife."

Papa Bennett's gaze shot to his wife, his eyes wide. "Patience, I forbid it. You may not abuse any woman in Sweetwater Cove by making her a match with Crouch the grouch."

Mother Bennett merely lifted one shoulder in response.

As soon as Betsy heard Mr. Crouch's footsteps in the second-story hallway above them, she knelt beside the chair Papa Bennett had taken while Crouch had been blustering about the window. "I saw Mr. Crouch eavesdropping on your meeting with Constable Robbins this morning."

Papa Bennett stopped with his porridge spoon halfway to his mouth. "Crouch?" He frowned at the constable next to him.

"I always thought there was more wrong with him than grouchiness," Robbins said, setting down his forkful of sausage. "Why would he care what we talk about in our morning meetings?"

"He was there about half an hour before Mother Bennett rang the bell. What were you discussing then?"

"Our schedules, as we do first thing every morning." Constable Robbins took a swig of his tea. "I told the mayor I planned to patrol the north end of the Gray's Knob road all morning."

Could Mr. Crouch have a reason for wanting that information?

"Robert, please go to the stairs, and if Mr. Crouch starts to come back down, run back here and tell us," Papa Bennett said.

As Robert dashed to the stairs, bacon in hand, Betsy turned again to her son. "Keep your voice quiet, but tell us exactly what Mr. Crouch said about Sweetwater Cove being dry," she said in low tones.

Gilbert frowned the way he always did when he was thinking hard. "He said Sweetwater Cove has been dry for years, but it's overdue for a change. That was all. Does that mean he wants it to rain?"

"No, son," Papa Bennett said. "When we say a town is dry, that means it's against the law to sell alcohol within its boundaries. Sweetwater Cove is a dry town."

"Who was he talking to when he said it?" Betsy asked.

"Mr. Swift. The man with the gold teeth."

And the black heart.

◆———‧———◆

I'm a fool. Josiah took in the park's fresh landscaping, the new benches and flower beds, the morning's first bright rays resting on them as if declaring their delight. If only he could make a fresh start with Betsy. Could somehow erase last night's kiss from their history. Could make her forget the kiss. Go back to being nothing more than friends.

But he couldn't turn back time, couldn't take back that kiss. Couldn't forget. No, he would never again look at her and not remember.

Nor could he deny that he still loved her—had never stopped.

He kicked at a stick in the grass, sent it flying toward the river. After making such a fool of himself here last night, he dreaded seeing her, seeing her confusion and that brave smile that reached no higher than her lips.

He knew better than to hope she cared for him. In fact, he didn't want her to, because he could never marry her. This park had changed, and he'd changed, but one thing would never change: because of his past, he wasn't worthy of love. Especially hers.

But these thoughts were fruitless, and he'd already wrestled them most of the night. To make things worse, Maynard Swift came rumbling by in Josiah's old coach-and-six, the Wells family crest now covered over with some slap-dash paint job—was that a caricature of a wolf? As the conveyance drew nearer, the picture looked clearer. Sure enough, a childish painting of a wolf now defaced the carriage door. Had Swift painted the eyesore himself?

Josiah shook his head. There truly was no accounting for taste.

With more important issues demanding his attention, he put the carriage and the two wolves from his mind. As usual since last night, his thoughts turned to Betsy and that kiss.

But with no new revelation and no solution after another ten minutes of ruminating, he gave his attention to the park instead, walking its perimeter, assessing their work. The donated flowers were planted, the gazebo rebuilt. Of a sudden, he realized what was missing. The shade garden.

He remembered it from his youth—a section of ground beneath the densest trees.

Did they have any more flower donations, something that would grow in the shade? He checked the spot under the biggest oak, where the ladies had dropped off their plants. Nothing left.

He searched under the trees nearer the street. None there either.

Then came the moment he'd dreaded. Betsy strode up the street toward the park, Gilbert and Robert at her side.

In the early light, she looked even more beautiful in her brown work dress than she had last night in the moonlight. Today she wore her hair in a long blond braid over her shoulder and tied with a strip of brown cloth.

Everything about her spoke of gentleness, kindness, sweetness—from her wholesome, modest dress and hair to the way she interacted with the boys. Sharing her life with them, she showed them how a godly woman acted, trained them to speak as young Christian men, taught them to worship God in their everyday lives by giving their best to their work.

He'd been right. He was far from worthy of this woman's love.

Stepping from the street to the park's thick grass, she graced him with a smile he didn't deserve. "Tomorrow's the day, and the park looks wonderful. You've done a marvelous job."

Her tone, the faint circles under her eyes, revealed her heart, made him wonder if she'd slept any more than he had last night. Perhaps pretending the kiss hadn't happened was the better way, at least for today. Since the boys were with her, they couldn't talk about it, even if they wanted to. So for now he'd go along with it. "We need to plant something in that bare spot under those trees. Do you remember what we used to have there?"

"In the shade garden? Wild ferns."

Of course. "Can we get some?"

"They grow under the Wilsonville Bridge." She hesitated. "But if you don't want to go there. . ."

No, he'd go. If Sweetwater Cove was to be his home, he'd have to face the bridge sooner or later.

The bridge he'd shoved Gilly off and maimed him. The bridge his father had driven off and killed himself and Ma.

He'd go.

Right then, a bank of clouds moved in, dimming the bright rays of light. "We'd better go now, in case it rains later. Let's see if a boat is going that way."

They took the towpath to the canal docks, and within minutes, he had their passage secured. When they'd fetched spades and some boxes from her store, they boarded a barn-red packet, the boys choosing a front seat on the boat's roof. Within moments, the mule team pulled them toward the Wilsonville docks, the still waters calming him and soothing his mind.

"Is Mr. Crouch minding the store for you today?" Josiah asked as they left Sweetwater Cove behind, now passing cornfields and cows.

"He's there, but so is Papa Bennett." She glanced around at the other passengers and lowered her voice. "Sheriff Robbins is looking for Maynard Swift today. He thinks Swift and Mr. Crouch are working together to sell whiskey in Sweetwater Cove."

When she described Ebenezer Crouch's bizarre behavior of this morning, along with Gilbert's report of his overheard conversation between Crouch and

Maynard Swift, Josiah sat back in the packet and stared at the canal town they now approached. Wilsonville. What had he recently heard about Wilsonville...?

"Maynard Swift's uncle has a drinking house on the Wilsonville docks," he said, remembering. But Wilsonville was a wet town, its limits starting on the other side of the old bridge, so how could that affect Sweetwater Cove?

Within a half hour, they docked and carried the spades and boxes along the weedy path to the old Wilsonville Bridge. Five minutes in, the breeze turned to a brisker wind, so they picked up their pace.

"It's going to rain, so as soon as we get to the bridge, you boys start digging ferns." As Gilbert and Robert nodded their assent and argued over who could dig the most ferns, Josiah dodged a clump of wild daisies. "As overgrown as this path is, they must not use the bridge much."

"They built a wider one in town. Some say Mr. Swift's uncle influenced the town to build it, since the old bridge is too narrow for big wagons. To avoid canal fees and transport fees, he drives those wagons to Wilsonville and across the new bridge, then he takes his goods to the outlying towns."

Upon reaching the bridge, Josiah caught his breath. Looked down at the water below. Crossed the bridge, Betsy following, to the spot where an abandoned shed of some kind stood. "The two most tragic events of my life happened right here." One he'd caused; the other had formed him.

Betsy drew nearer and laid her hand on his arm. "I know how much it hurts to lose both parents at the same time."

He could feel the deep frown forming on his forehead, but he couldn't stop it. "I always think of my parents' deaths as one event. Gilly is the other."

Her eyes widened, their blue hue intensifying with her apparent confusion. "Gilly?"

What? Had she somehow forgotten?

The boys clambered down to the river below and started digging ferns while Josiah tried to figure out who had the faulty memory, him or Betsy. "I'm talking about the day of my parents' funerals. When I wanted to come here and see the spot where they'd—passed. You and Gilly came with me."

"Of course." A misty rain had begun to fall, and she brushed her cheeks dry.

"We were standing on the bridge, and Gilly said I was an orphan now." Either the mist or his own angst had turned his skin clammy. "I pushed him. I never meant him to go over the bridge, and I certainly never meant him to land on a rock."

"I remember." The tenderness in her eyes could have made him weep, had he not been working so hard to figure out why she couldn't remember that day. "You yelled, 'Don't ever call me an orphan again!'"

"Orphans get sent away."

She let that statement hang in the air.

"I pushed him off the bridge, Betsy." His voice came out low, gravelly. "Don't you remember?"

"Yes, it was one of his many childhood accidents." She moved a step closer, studied his eyes as if trying to figure out what was wrong with him, instead of the other way around. "What was so tragic about this one?"

He had to push down his irritation. Why couldn't she understand? "I think a lifelong limp qualifies as a tragedy."

She gaped at him a second. "Lifelong? He was running again three months later."

Running? Three months?

"Gilly's limp was caused by a different accident."

That couldn't be. Betsy was mistaken. "But a year after I pushed him, the minister wrote to Papa Wells and told him Gilly couldn't walk properly since his accident. And during my correspondence with Mrs. Bennett about the pastorate, I asked her about his leg. She wrote back and said he'd walked with a limp ever since he was a boy. I pushed him from the bridge. He landed on a rock."

"You think that caused his limp?"

What else would he have thought?

"Trust me, his leg was fine after that fall. You didn't hurt him that badly."

He hadn't?

That meant all this time, he'd carried the guilt of laming Gilly—and he hadn't?

But wait. . . "Mrs. Bennett clearly said he limped his entire life."

"On his left leg. Not the one he hurt in the fall."

Then what?

"He broke his leg while trying to train a feisty colt. They both went down, and the colt fell on him. The colt caused his limp. You didn't."

He looked away, scrubbed his face with his hand. He hadn't caused Gilly's limp. *Jesus, thank You. . . .*

"We got our boxes full," Gilbert yelled from below.

Before Josiah could reply, the rumbling of a conveyance sounded from down the path. Through the trees, Josiah recognized his old coach-and-six.

The one the livery man had sold to Maynard Swift.

If he was delivering goods to the Wilsonville area, why wasn't he in a draying wagon instead?

Something didn't seem right here. Not the fine carriage in this remote place, and not bringing it to the decaying, abandoned bridge. Especially since Wilsonville had a nice, new one.

"Boys, hide under the bridge," he called. "I don't want the man in the carriage to see us."

"Josiah, what—" Betsy shielded her eyes with her hand, looked in the direction of the carriage.

"It's Swift. I don't know what's going on, but I have a bad feeling."

The sound of a horse's hooves pounding the dry road pulled his attention in the opposite direction. Within moments, an old mare and rickety wagon approached from the bushes on the Wilsonville side of the bridge.

Josiah glanced around. "No time to get under the bridge." Touching her shoulder and guiding her through the underbrush, he hurried her to the old shed, and they hunkered down behind it. Josiah sneaked to the corner and peeked around.

Maynard Swift had stopped the carriage in front of the shed, and now he climbed down from the driver's seat, cane in hand, and peered up the weedy path toward Wilsonville. Shouted across the bridge.

Ebenezer Crouch somehow flung himself down from the driver's seat and wobbled the rest of the way to the bridge. But when he crossed it, he stepped out of Josiah's line of vision. Josiah heard the jangle of keys and the scraping of a door, old hinges squeaking.

"Ten gallons enough for today?"

Josiah recognized Swift's voice. Stole to the other corner for a good view. If nothing else, he'd witness the exchange of money so he could testify against them.

"For now, but I'll need another fifteen tomorrow," Crouch said, "since the men will want to celebrate the old French fellow coming to Sweetwater Cove."

"Trust me, he's not coming to the cove. I took care of that earlier today."

At that, Betsy's eyes flew open wide.

Not coming? They had to get home, fast.

Chapter 8

As Papa Bennett, Constable Robbins, Josiah, and Betsy gathered in the office behind the inn, Betsy admitted to herself how gullible she'd been. How many years had she known that Ebenezer Crouch was the strangest man in town? Ever since she was born?

No matter now. With Gilbert, Robert, and Mother Bennett as lookouts in the yard, it was time to let their two town authorities know that two of their aldermen and one of Papa Bennett's tenants were breaking Sweetwater Cove law. Remembering Mr. Crouch's penchant for eavesdropping through open windows, she moved to the east window and closed it then did the same with the west.

"Josiah, Betsy, I did all I could do." Papa Bennett's voice was low, husky. "Maynard Swift accused me of a conflict of interest in our vote on Monday. Said I voted to let you try to save the park because I didn't want him to build a dry-goods store to compete with yours. He has called for a vote, this time to sell him the park immediately. All three aldermen will vote to sell."

"Is that legal?" Josiah said.

"According to the town ordinance, yes."

"But I saw him take money from Ebenezer Crouch in exchange for whiskey."

Constable Robbins drew a deep breath, let it out in a huff. "Did you hear him say it was alcohol?"

"No, but—"

"Did you smell or taste it?"

"Of course not."

"Then you don't have evidence. For all we know, he could have been selling sweet cider."

Betsy gazed out the window where Mr. Crouch had eavesdropped. "I saw him under your office window, listening to your private conversation."

"I can't even get him on trespassing, because he lives here. Unless you have a signed agreement that he, as a tenant, can't come within a certain distance of your office."

There had to be something, some way, to prevent that new vote. . . .

Gilbert and his dog ran up the walk and inside the office. "Guess what General Washington found?"

Betsy turned him around at the door. "Play with your dog outside for a while, Gilbert."

"But he found cane prints outside the dining room window." He tugged at Betsy's sleeve. "They're Mr. Swift's. Come and see them."

Betsy pulled her sleeve out of her son's hand. "What's a cane print?"

"Like a footprint, but made with a walking cane. Remember Sunday when we saw him at the park, before we went fishing? When he left, he pointed his cane at the reverend, and the end of it was shaped like a flower."

"I remember it had some kind of funny tip," Betsy said.

"There's a cane print outside the window Mr. Crouch opened at breakfast. Come on, you need to see it." Gilbert and General Washington raced out of the office, toward the house.

To avoid hurting her son's feelings, Betsy followed him to the window, and sure enough, between a tall cedar and the house she found a dozen or so prints the same size and shape as Mr. Swift's cane.

Constable Robbins came out and examined the prints as well. "I've seen that cane tip before. It's the only one in town. We need to look at this from inside."

Minutes later, in the dining room, the constable sat at his customary spot at the table. "Everybody take your usual seats. We're going to figure out why Maynard Swift spent time loitering outside your window. Let's talk about the events of this morning, in order."

It still didn't make sense, even seemed like a waste of time, but Betsy made herself cooperate anyway. "I'm first. I saw Mr. Crouch eavesdropping on you and Papa Bennett in Papa's office."

"He heard me telling the mayor I would be north of town all morning," the constable said.

Mother Bennett pointed to the front dining room entrance. "He must have gone around the house, because he came in the front door. He didn't want us to know he'd been in the backyard at that hour. I had just rung the bell."

After a few moments, Papa Bennett pushed back his chair and crossed one ankle over the other knee—his thinking pose. "Then Robbins and I came in the same time Crouch did. That's all that happened."

"No, I was in his chair, and he made me move," Robert said. "Even though a chair was empty on the other side of the table."

"And he opened this window," Betsy said.

Gilbert jumped up. "And then he yelled, 'Bah!' the way he always does when he doesn't like the food."

"I remember his parents having bad table manners as well." Mother Bennett frowned her disapproval.

"What if it wasn't bad manners?" Josiah said from the corner, next to the sideboard. "He might have been giving information to Swift—a message."

"What kind of message?" Gilbert's face wrinkled into a frown. "That he didn't like porridge?"

Josiah stepped over and mussed the boy's hair, drawing a grin from him. "That the constable would be out of the way this morning. I think they use it as a code. Crouch listens at the office window to discover Constable Robbins's plans for the morning, and he probably listens any other time you meet as well. Then Swift hides behind the cedar at mealtimes. If it's safe to take the liquor to the old bridge, Crouch hollers. If not, he's quiet and eats. Or does he bellow like that at every meal?"

Even Papa Bennett looked impressed with Josiah's deduction. "You never know when you're going to hear that billy-goat yell of his."

"He sometimes does it at noon too. He did it at Sunday dinner," Josiah said.

Constable Robbins eyed him as if considering the theory. "That means he eavesdrops on us every time we're both here. I often come in before dinner and let the mayor know where I'll be in the afternoons."

Papa Bennett stood and pushed in his chair. "Come on, Robbins. Let's make him think you'll be back at Gray's Knob this afternoon. Then we'll both get to the Wilsonville Bridge before they do and catch them with the liquor."

When Papa Bennett and Constable Robbins had left for the office and Josiah had headed back to the park, Mother Bennett crooked her finger at Betsy. "Come upstairs with me, just for a moment."

When they reached Mother Bennet's room, they sat in the two rockers before the window. "We need to talk, but you're not going to like what I have to say to you."

Not again. "Please, no more matchmaking. I know you've put many happy couples together, and I also know how much you enjoy that. But please don't—"

"You don't understand. I'm not matchmaking today. Once the two parties are in love, the matchmaking is over. Then it's time to plan the wedding." Her round face took on a glow that never would have been there if she'd known how things really stood. "The reverend is in love with you, Betsy."

In love with her? Oh no. She took her mother-in-law's hand, held it to her own cheek. "You're mistaken. I know he isn't."

"Betsy, you know the reverend better than I do, and I can plainly see he loves you. Are you sure you aren't merely refusing to face the fact that he's in love with you? I admit I don't understand why, because you're as much in love with him as he is with you."

"But I couldn't hurt you and Papa Bennett by marrying again, not after your kindness to me all these years."

The older woman pulled her hand away. "That's not the way it works. And it's not complete truth. I remember the days, back when you children were growing up, when everyone said you and Josiah were a perfect match. Even I believed it."

"No, Mother Bennett—"

"I know that if Gilly could come back, you'd be a faithful wife to him. But it's time for you to marry again, and it's time for Gilbert to have a father." Her eyes turned soft. "Don't be ashamed of the feelings the two of you had when you were young. Truth be told, Cyrus wasn't my first love either."

What? Dared she ask who?

At her mother-in-law's raised brow, she feared the truth would be a secret forever.

"My mother's favorite Bible verse was this: 'Therefore if any man be in Christ, he is a new creature: old things are passed away; behold, all things are become new,'" Mother Bennet said. "Jesus can remake any part of us, even the things we're ashamed of."

If Mother Bennett didn't regret her first love, maybe Betsy didn't have to regret hers either.

"But what of Gilbert? If I marry Josiah, we'll move to a different home with him. To the manse, if there's enough room. Gilbert would miss being close to you and Papa Bennett every day."

"Must you?" Mother Bennett spread out her hands. "Could you not all live here with us?"

"A man living with his wife's in-laws from her first marriage? Whoever heard of such a thing?"

"Nobody. That's because it's a new thing."

A new thing. What would Josiah say? But in a flash, she knew. He'd always loved spending time here in this old inn with the Bennetts—sometimes stayed here for weeks at a time. He loved feeling like one of the family, fitting in, feeling safe. Yes, Josiah would agree to live here.

And what better way to celebrate this new thing than with a new bonnet? Betsy crossed the room to Mother Bennett's walnut wardrobe, pulled out the hatbox, and opened it. The blue bonnet, never worn, seemed almost to speak to her lonely heart.

She took it from the box. Settled it on her head and made a puffy bow under her left ear.

A fresh start, a fresh life, a fresh love.

Old things passed away, all things new. . .and better.

Chapter 9

Josiah should have insisted on going to the Wilsonville Bridge with the constable and Deacon Bennett. As it was, he alternated between making a nuisance of himself in Betsy's store and pacing the canal dock, watching for the packet that would, he hoped, soon carry the two lawbreakers back to Sweetwater Cove.

Betsy had locked up the store and joined him on the dock when the packet came around the bend. As it drew nearer, all he wanted to do was race down the dock to meet it. Had he been right? Had Swift sold alcohol to Crouch within Sweetwater Cove's boundary? Because if Josiah had been wrong about that. . .

"I can tell what you're thinking," Betsy said, stepping nearer. "Even if the worst happens, 'all things are become new.' God can give us a second chance, whether we keep the park or not."

He hadn't thought about it that way, but she was right. "Maybe we can have a second chance with a lot of things."

Nonetheless, as soon as passengers started to disembark, he watched for Constable Robbins and the deacon. They got out last along with Swift and Crouch, whose hands were tied behind their backs, with Deacon Bennett whistling the *Doxology*. In that moment, Josiah knew that "all things" had already become new for him, in every sense.

He stepped back, out of the way. His questions could wait until supper. Now that he knew the church, Sweetwater Cove, and Betsy were going to be fine, he'd soon have a different kind of question to ask.

"You were right about the whiskey, Josiah," Deacon Bennett said later, as the family and tenants gathered for supper. "Maynard Swift started transporting and selling it when Ebenezer Crouch moved into the inn last fall. The shed where they exchanged money is inside Sweetwater Cove's boundary. They're in the jail, waiting for the circuit judge. Robbins raided Swift's warehouse this afternoon and found a big stash of liquor there as well."

"What about the vote?" Betsy asked as she set a platter of roast beef on the table.

"Now that Swift and Crouch are in jail, we have only two voters, Horace

Stryker and me," Constable Robbins said. "Since we no longer have a buyer for the park, Horace said he won't pursue the vote. So the park is safe."

The next morning, Josiah planted the last of the ferns in the shade garden, just hours before the biggest event Sweetwater Cove had ever seen. In the midst of the ferns stood his statue of the Marquis de Lafayette, covered with a white blanket and ready for the unveiling.

Thirty minutes before General Lafayette's scheduled arrival, muted notes from a faraway band floated through the air from the canal. Josiah wandered over to the new gazebo to catch a glimpse of the flotilla—and its band—off in the distance.

As the boats floated nearer and the music grew louder, Josiah joined Mayor Bennett at the docks to welcome Sweetwater Cove's favorite war hero. Rather than mules, six horses pulled each flag- and banner-covered boat, and the town's girls tossed bouquets to the marquis, his son, his secretary and valet, and the local dignitaries who had joined him on his way down the canal.

Lafayette had barely come ashore when Mayor Bennett began his speech. "Sweetwater Cove welcomes Monsieur Marie Joseph Paul Yves Roch Gilbert du Motier, also known as the Marquis de Lafayette—a general in the Continental Army, without whose assistance we all would still be British subjects. General, we wish to rededicate this park in your honor."

When the time for the statue unveiling came, Lafayette shook Josiah's hand then Gilbert's.

"And who are you?" he said to Gilbert with his aristocratic French accent.

"My name is Gilbert too, sir. Gilbert Bennett, son of Mr. Gilbert Bennett." He tugged on the cord, and the blanket fell from the statue.

Hours later, after the reception at the Bennetts' inn, dusk fell as the marquis's flotilla pulled away from the dock, its path lit by hundreds of torches along both sides of the canal. Josiah watched from the new gazebo, his sense of relief at the day's end mingling with his anticipation of speaking to Betsy tonight.

Soon, hearing soft footsteps ambling toward him, he turned to find her approaching the gazebo, a bouquet of fresh delphiniums in her gloved hand. The blue of her bonnet turned her eyes a hue of blue he'd never seen there before, and those eyes somehow pulled something clear and sweet and precious from the hidden places of his heart, dropping it forever before his own eyes. Always to stay in the front of his mind. Always to be the center of his life. Always to remind him of the day he surrendered his heart to her.

"The marquis received dozens of flowers tonight, but these are for us." She held out the bouquet to him.

He took it, laid it on the gazebo's wide rail. "Remember the verse you quoted about all things being made new?" he said before he could even think. "Do you suppose we could have a second chance?"

She lowered her gaze then looked out at the distant boats, the last Sweetwater Cove citizens trickling out of the park. Finally her eyes found his once more. "And have our first kiss all over again, here in the gazebo?"

That would do, for a start.

Josiah stepped closer, brushed a wisp of golden hair from her face. And this time, when he kissed her, she again smelled of delphiniums, but this time she tasted of summer and sweet chamomile tea and promise. Especially promise.

She felt perfect in his arms as she brought her gloved fingers to his face, cupped his cheek with her hand.

Finally she broke the kiss, pulled away a fraction, and met his gaze with those so-blue eyes. "Can we call this a second-chance first kiss? Because it's really our third kiss. . . ."

Josiah slid his arm around her waist. "More than that, I want another chance at a life together. You and me, husband and wife—and Gilbert too. Marry me, Betsy? Start a new life, right away?"

Her tinkling laugh made him laugh too. "Yes, I'll marry you. My first love and my last."

He leaned over and kissed her again on her pretty lips. The old had truly passed away, and the new had come.

Betsy Wells's Chicken and Dumplings

Ingredients:

(*For cooking chicken*)
1 whole chicken
1 diced onion, optional
1 teaspoon poultry seasoning
Salt and pepper to taste

(*For making dumplings*)
2 cups water
½ cup butter
4 cups white flour, plus extra for rolling out dumplings
1 tablespoon salt

Directions:

Boil the chicken, onion, and poultry seasoning for at least an hour and a half. If you like your meat and onion "falling apart," boil up to 3 hours. (This is Betsy's preference.) Remove meat to a platter and cover with an old towel to keep the meat moist. Reserve the broth.

In a medium saucepan, heat the water and butter. In a large bowl, stir together the flour and salt. When water/butter has boiled, pour it into the flour and stir very quickly to make dough. When dough has cooled enough for handling, dust a wooden board with flour and use a floured rolling pin to roll ¼ of the dough thin. Cut dumplings with a sharp knife. (Betsy would have used a pizza cutter if she'd had one.) Repeat with remaining dough.

Debone the chicken and add chicken to the broth. Season the broth with salt and pepper. If you want a soupier dish to serve in a bowl, use all the broth. If you want to put the chicken and dumplings on your plate, or place them atop mashed potatoes, just use about ¾ of the broth. Bring it to a boil. Drop dumplings one by one into the broth as you get them rolled out. (If Betsy had had a freezer, she would have made her dumplings ahead of time and laid them in layers on cookie sheets, with waxed paper between each layer, and frozen them before using. She would not have thawed them before dropping. Betsy also knows from experience that waxed paper is flammable, so she now makes sure she keeps the paper away from the flame.)

When all the dumplings are in the broth, use a flat-ended spatula or turner to lift the dumplings from the bottom, but never stir them. Stirring will make them clump together. Simmer until the dumplings are tender, approximately 10 to 15 minutes. If serving on the plate or atop mashed potatoes, use a slotted spoon.

(This is the author's family recipe. She once made it and served it to a handsome young preacher who came calling. The preacher proposed marriage almost before his bowl was empty. Thirty years later, the author still serves chicken and dumplings to the handsome preacher.)

Christina Miller has always lived in the past. Her passion for history began with her grandmother's stories of 1920s rural southern Indiana. When Christina began to write fiction, she believed God was calling her to write what she knew: history. Bethany College of Missions graduate, pastor's wife, and worship leader, she lives on the family farm with her husband of thirty years and Sugar, their talking dog.

Journey of the Heart

by Johnnie Alexander

Dedication

In memory of my dad, John Alexander.
With a wide grin and twinkling eyes,
he often mispronounced "Chillicothe" on purpose.
(It rhymes with chilla-coffee.)

*Thou shalt not deliver unto his master the servant
which is escaped from his master unto thee.*
DEUTERONOMY 23:15

Chapter 1

Circleville, Ohio
June 1852

C harity Sinclair furrowed her brow as she read what she'd written for the umpteenth time. The facts—scratched in dark brown ink on wood pulp paper—were horrid and stark. But she needed something more to convince her fence-sitting neighbors to join the cause.

Perhaps her entire approach was wrong. She should be shouting the injustice on the Capitol steps instead of hiding behind a dilettante facade and masculine pseudonym. In these unsettled times, though, the deception provided safety. For the sake of her father and her aunt, Charity lived the exhausting pretense that pressed against her spirit.

She dipped the quill into the square bottle then blotted the excess ink. But the words she longed to write refused to take shape. The ink dried on her quill as she considered and discarded one idea after another.

The chime of the church bells startled her from her reverie. Noon already. The morning hours had slipped away, leaving no more time to shape impassioned words. The harsh facts needed to be enough.

For anyone with a heart, they *would* be enough.

With a flash of last-minute inspiration, she dipped her pen again and scribbled a last paragraph:

> *More brave runaways will face capture. More brave citizens will be jailed. Help us overturn the Fugitive Slave Act. Stand for freedom.*

"Charity," Aunt Stella called from the foot of the stairs. "Your papa needs you in the post office."

"I'll be down in a minute."

"Customers are waiting."

"Only a moment more. I promise." Charity scanned the page a final time. The spare words weren't what she envisioned when she took up her pen. But if the simplicity, the directness of her message, emboldened even one person to join their cause, her efforts wouldn't be in vain.

She prayed for that one anonymous person as she signed the name chosen for all her antislavery writings.

Moses Freed.

Underneath the pseudonym, she added a decorative flourish. After placing a blotting sheet over the page, she slipped it into a folder and checked the time on her desk clock. Seven minutes after twelve.

If she didn't hurry, she wouldn't be in the post office when Tavish Dunbar arrived for his mail. She pinched her cheeks, re-pinned a loose strand of hair, and shook out her skirt.

"Charity," Aunt Stella called again. "What's keeping you?"

"I'm coming." Charity grabbed the folder from her desk and scurried down the half-flight of stairs.

Aunt Stella, her hands folded primly at her waist, waited on the broad landing that divided two short stairways. One led to the family's residence; the other to the rooms assigned to the post office. A rectangle of sunlight, shining through the stained-glass window above the landing, reflected brilliant colors onto the beige carpeting.

"Poise and polish, Charity." Aunt Stella's tender gaze softened her stern admonition. "A lady mustn't appear flushed in public."

Charity pressed her palm against her abdomen and straightened her posture. "I'm sorry I'm late."

"Save your apologies for your papa. Did you finish?"

"It's not my best. The words. . .they escaped me."

"Those who eagerly await a message from Moses Freed will not be displeased. I am sure of it."

"I wish I had your confidence." Charity held out the folder. "Please be careful."

"You always say that. And I always am."

"I'm glad of it." Charity spontaneously kissed her aunt's soft cheek. "Papa and I need you."

The corners of Aunt Stella's thin lips lifted in a cheerful smile. "Go on now," she urged. Without waiting for a response, she descended the stairs to the family's living area.

Charity rushed down the opposite staircase then pushed open the door into the post office. Papa stood at the counter, his back to her, as he handed a parcel to a young woman balancing a toddler on one hip. Several other clients waited for assistance.

On her way to the counter, Charity glanced at the cubbyholes lining the back wall. An assorted stack of envelopes protruded from the box assigned to Tavish Dunbar. Despite her tardiness she wasn't too late. Her heart fluttered in nervous anticipation, though she also dreaded his coming. Even their briefest conversations sparked an unsettling combination of delight and frustration that tied her in knots. His intelligence and quiet demeanor appealed to all her romantic notions of the perfect hero. But in his eyes, she was far from the perfect heroine.

If only he knew the truth.

But the risk of letting him in on her secret was too great.

❖—·——·—❖

After a quick meal at his desk, Tavish Dunbar gripped the tube containing his latest plans for the building that housed both the post office and the postmaster's residence. He'd been ecstatic when the Circleville Squaring Company hired him to assist with changing the town's layout. The opportunity was as unique as the problem the Ohio General Assembly mandated the company to solve.

If he'd known how difficult the task would be, he might have refused.

No, not the task, he corrected himself.

The difficulty was with the postmaster. Grover Sinclair found fault with every renovation plan presented to him.

Not this time.

With the tube tucked under his arm, Tavish strolled from the architectural offices near the Ohio-Erie Canal to the post office. Along the way, he admired the work the company had accomplished before he'd joined them. The history behind the singular project had captivated his attention, and he probably knew more about the town than many longtime residents.

Settled over forty years before, in 1810, the seat of Pickaway County had been built in concentric circles on top of a Hopewell Indian Mound. But within twenty years, the residents tired of their rounded streets. Their complaints led to the formation of Tavish's employer.

After another twenty years of straightening curved streets and renovating curved buildings, the town's dream of a typical grid layout was close to completion.

Tavish's pulse quickened when he reached the three-story brick building with its unusual quarter-moon-shaped facade, but only because he planned to confront the postmaster. The roiling in his stomach had nothing to do with the lovely but vapid Charity Sinclair.

A bell clanged as Tavish pulled open one half of the heavy double door. Mr. Sinclair was deep in conversation with an older gentleman at one end of the long counter while his daughter tied string around a parcel at the other.

"Good afternoon, Miss Sinclair."

"How nice to see you, Mr. Dunbar." Charity's gaze shifted to the tube beneath his arm, and for a moment her expression froze. Then she smiled, though without warmth. "You've come for your mail."

"That's one reason—"

"I'll get it for you." She gathered the contents of his cubbyhole and handed them to him.

"Thank you." He hadn't planned to get distracted by his mail, but his cousin's fine handwriting graced the lilac envelope on top of the stack. Her frequent letters eased the loneliness that overwhelmed him more than he cared to admit.

Funny, the little things that turned his heart toward the home he'd been so eager to leave. A favorite hymn sung at church evoking the memory of his cousin's clear soprano. His landlady's delectable peach cobbler, almost as delicious as Cook's. A stranger's boisterous laugh, reminiscent of Uncle Ned and his fondness for practical jokes.

"You have a faithful correspondent," Charity said lightly. "I believe we receive one of those lovely envelopes at least once a week. Sometimes more."

"She wants me to come home."

"To Syracuse?" Charity's cheeks flushed. "I noticed the return address when I sorted the mail. But you needn't worry. Postal regulations are adamantly clear. We never comment on a person's personal correspondence, nor business correspondence, to anyone. Not even that person."

Tavish waved the envelope. "You commented on this to me."

"A momentary lapse in professionalism. On behalf of the postal service, I apologize."

She flashed her heart-thumping smile before he could brace himself. His insides quivered, but his features stayed composed in the polite smile he'd mastered for uncomfortable situations. At least something from his boyhood training in etiquette and fine manners served him well in this small town.

If only someone had trained him in the fine art of *not* being captivated by the wrong young woman.

"That must be an extremely difficult regulation to follow," he said. Especially for someone with a known propensity for flightiness.

"But rules must be followed, mustn't they?"

Her tone caught him by surprise and his gaze met hers. The engaging smile reappeared, but he steadied himself. What had she said? Nothing witty or brilliant. Something mundane about following rules. Yet something in her tone—it was as if the topic had shifted from postal regulations to something else. But to what?

"Rules should be followed, yes," he stammered. "That's how an organization—such as this post office—functions. How society functions."

"Do you believe *all* rules should be followed?"

"Off the top of my head, I can't think of any that should not."

"Then I suppose I'll never have the misfortune of visiting you in jail."

"I should hope not." He held her gaze, determined not to lose himself in the depths of her brown eyes. "I must say, Miss Sinclair, the purpose of this conversation eludes me."

"It's as simple as anything, Mr. Dunbar. If you don't break rules, you won't be arrested and spend the rest of your days behind bars."

"I certainly have no plans to do so."

"What an upstanding citizen you are. If only those already in jail had followed your example."

"I'm not that—"

"Is there anything else we can do for you today? A stamp, perhaps, for when you reply to your correspondent? Of whom I shall not speak."

Unsure how to respond, he gripped the blueprints tube and glanced in Mr. Sinclair's direction.

He wasn't there.

"Your father. Where did he go?"

"He isn't here."

"I can see that." Tavish tapped his fingers against the tube. "I brought the latest plans."

"You should have said something before he left. But you seemed so intent on talking about the merits of rules—I felt it impolite to interrupt."

"Me? You were the one. . ." It was no use. Not with a girl like Charity Sinclair. For a fraction of a second a glint appeared in her eyes he'd never noticed before. A hint of superiority?

"When will he return?" he asked.

"As I'm sure you know, the post office is closed from one to two every afternoon." Charity glanced at the clock. "It's now twelve thirty-eight. I doubt he'll return until we reopen."

"But he'll be here this afternoon?"

"Perhaps. I can't say for sure."

The bell clanged as a woman entered the door.

"Excuse me, please." Charity moved to the counter's opposite end to assist her customer.

Tavish chewed the inside of his lip. Surely Grover Sinclair hadn't snuck out of the post office to avoid talking to him. But why else had he left?

A knot formed at the base of his neck, and he exhaled a heavy sigh. Should he leave? Or wait for Charity?

The woman appeared to be in a hurry, but Charity peppered her with questions about the latest shipment of bonnets and ribbons at the dress shop in the next block.

So that was her game. To delay the woman until he grew impatient and left.

He could play that game too.

Sunday's newspaper, containing the latest installment of Charles Dickens's *Bleak House*, rested on the counter. Since he hadn't read it yesterday, he'd do so while he waited. Charity couldn't ignore him forever.

He scanned the headlines then flipped to the next page. The top editorial asked, "Who Is Moses Freed?"

"Good question," Tavish muttered.

No one appeared to know who wrote the pamphlets and letters in support of the abolitionist movement. The known leaders of the local group denied any role in writing or disseminating the correspondence.

Though would they admit it if they did?

Mr. Freed's primary goal seemed to be to overturn the Fugitive Slave Act of 1850. More commonly known as the Bloodhound Law, the Act forced those in the Free States to return escaped slaves to their masters and rewarded law enforcement officials who arrested abolitionists caught harboring slaves. Last autumn, a judge had indicted around forty people for treason under the Act.

"You're still here, Mr. Dunbar."

He shifted his gaze from the newspaper to Charity. Confidence exuded from her dark eyes, the confidence of a girl who accepted her attractiveness as a given.

Her charms might work on others, but she'd find him immune to her feminine wiles. The woman of his dreams cared more about literature and art then fabrics and notions.

"I was reading this article about Moses Freed. Quite the mystery man."

"Or a coward." Charity dismissed the topic with a flick of her wrist.

"Have you read what he writes?"

"Should I?"

"I'd think a young woman of your standing in the community would want to know what's happening around her."

"And I think a man should have the courage of his convictions. Why doesn't he reveal himself?"

"Maybe he doesn't want to go to jail."

"No one is jailed for their words."

"But they are for their actions. I imagine this Moses Freed, whoever he is, does much more than write about the slavery issue. His anecdotes are too vivid, too real. He must have firsthand knowledge of certain events."

"You admire him."

"I suppose I do."

"But you wouldn't help him."

"Why would you say that?"

"You'd be breaking the law."

The knot in his neck loosened into a dull ache. He hadn't been thinking about the Bloodhound Law or any other law when he talked about following rules.

Had she been testing him?

Impossible.

Charity stared at him, obviously expecting a response.

"Whoever this is," he said, tapping the paper with his fingers, "is doing fine on his own. I'm not sure what help I could be."

Disappointment flickered across her expression—at least, he believed it was disappointment. The moment happened so quickly he couldn't be sure. But now her expression was impassive, like one of the china dolls at the mercantile.

Beautiful and fragile. But only for display.

Chapter 2

He didn't know what help he could be?

Charity tamped down her temper. Playing this little charade was easy with most people, but she found the pretense almost impossible to maintain with Tavish Dunbar. His mere presence weakened her knees and hampered her breathing.

But now? She'd have to fight those feelings. Their work was too important to take any risks, and Mr. Dunbar couldn't know their secrets.

"Papa says the same." She forced a lightness she didn't feel into her tone. "And he's right, as usual. I suppose when Moses Freed's true identity is revealed, we'll all be shocked."

"Like in *Bleak House*. When we discover that the heroine is the daughter of... though perhaps I'd be spoiling the story for you. Are you reading it?"

"Would you be surprised if I said yes?"

"It's an exciting tale. I'd be pleased to have someone to discuss it with." His voice dropped, and she pretended not to notice his obvious regret. The arrogant cad. He didn't believe she could contribute to an intelligent discussion of the characters or themes of Dickens's novel.

If only he knew.

"Unfortunately, I have little time for reading. The post office keeps me quite busy." The lie slipped from her lips with an ease that pained her.

Tavish lifted his eyebrows and made a show of looking around the space, surprisingly empty for this time of day.

"I can see why," he said drily.

"I have social commitments as well." She grimaced at how defensive she sounded. And to what purpose? Even if he did like her. . .that would be even worse. Several young men in town enjoyed her company. But she couldn't respect anyone who admired the woman she pretended to be.

A sad state to be sure.

"I'm sure your calendar is filled with afternoon teas and fancy suppers," Tavish said.

"Also sewing circle, charity drives, and the rose garden club." The activities were Aunt Stella's more than hers, but he didn't need to know that.

"I suppose you attend all the local dances," he said.

"I love dancing." Finally—an honest statement. "Don't you? I don't recall seeing you at any."

"I attended two or three when I first arrived. But the mothers in this town are more interested in me than I am in their daughters." He spoke without pride or conceit, and his ears reddened as if the admission embarrassed him.

Touched by his endearing expression, Charity wanted to forget propriety and fall into his arms. She might have if not for the counter separating them. Did that zealous desire lump her in with those gossiping mothers? She loathed the thought, and yet. . .if she steered the conversation in the right direction, maybe she could learn more about the sender of the lilac notes.

"I remember hearing speculation about your family background. Some say you're the heir to a wealthy shipping magnate."

"I heard that one. It's not true."

"Others say you are seeking an heiress to make your fortune."

"In this town?"

"Even a small fortune is large to someone without any."

"I'm here for my job. Which I can't do without your father's cooperation."

"He does not mean to be difficult."

Tavish folded the newspaper and tapped his tube. "We need to review these plans. Will any time this afternoon be convenient?"

"I can't speak for Papa," Charity said, drawing out her words. "But it would be impossible for me to join you. My afternoon is completely booked."

"No offense, Miss Charity. But I'm sure your father's approval would be sufficient."

"No offense taken, Mr. Dunbar. However, these are plans for the renovation of my home. Both my aunt and I must be present."

"Another day this week then?"

"I couldn't say."

"Then I propose this plan. I will return at two with a chair, and I will sit in this lobby until an appointment can be made."

"That seems presumptuous."

"Perhaps. But I intend to be on these premises for the rest of the day. The rest of the night if need be."

Between them, Charity and Papa had delayed the inevitable for weeks, but God hadn't answered their prayer for a miracle. The resolve in Tavish's voice, in his eyes, made it clear that they'd run out of time.

"Mr. Dunbar. . ." She paused to swallow the nub in her throat. "Would you be so kind as to accept an invitation to dinner tomorrow?"

His lips tilted in a victorious smile. "Miss Sinclair, I would be delighted to accept such an invitation."

"You are too kind. We dine shortly after one. You may use the residential entrance."

"Thank you." He picked up his mail and the tube. "There's no danger of the invitation being postponed, rescinded, canceled, or rescheduled, is there? Because if any of those events occur, I'll spend tomorrow afternoon here in the post office and tomorrow evening at the residential door."

"Do not insult me, Mr. Dunbar. I am not such a hostess."

He'd won this battle but not the war. They—she, Papa, and Aunt Stella—would examine his blueprints, exclaim over his brilliance, then plot their tactics for postponing the work.

She'd done her best to stall. Now it was Papa's turn.

◆━━━━━◆

"I didn't have a choice," Charity said to Papa and Aunt Stella when she joined them at the dinner table. "This time tomorrow, he'll be sitting right there." She pointed to the empty chair opposite her own.

Grover Sinclair scratched the side of his neck with his forefinger, a habit that indicated his unease. "Don't blame yourself, daughter. It's not like the work will begin immediately. I still hope to convince the city council to leave this section of the street as it is."

"An homage to the original circle design," Aunt Stella said. "It's a brilliant idea."

"I think so," Papa said. "Future generations may appreciate a reminder of the town's original layout."

"If the early settlers hadn't been so creative, we wouldn't be in this situation now." Charity scooped mashed potatoes onto her plate.

"I suppose the circle design made sense back then," Aunt Stella said as she passed the gravy boat to Charity. "But now people are more interested in the future than in the past. The redesign, the construction, have created a boom for the town. We're living in a prosperous time."

"A boom that will end as soon as the renovations are completed," Papa said. "Will the laborers stay around when there is no more work to do? Most will probably pack up and move on."

Charity raked her potatoes with her fork so the gravy flowed over the tines. Without work, the laborers would leave. When the renovation of the post office was complete, would Tavish go too? Maybe he was counting the days till he could return home. Return to the woman with the perfect handwriting and expensive stationery.

Jealousy stabbed her heart. But something deeper pierced her spirit.

She hadn't allowed herself to think of a future with him—that was too improbable given her work—but to face a future without him? None of the characters in *Bleak House* could be any sadder than she at such a prospect.

"Is something wrong, Charity?" Aunt Stella asked. "You're not eating."

Startled from her reverie, Charity responded by returning to the topic she couldn't escape. "I'm not sure inviting Mr. Dunbar to dinner tomorrow was wise, Papa. But the words were out of my mouth before I knew I'd spoken them. Sometimes he just riles me all up."

"Charity!" Aunt Stella fluttered her napkin. "Your language, please. *Riles?*"

"There's no other way to say it, Aunt Stella. I'm perfectly calm and then something about him. . ."

"Riles you?" Papa teased.

"Yes, sir."

Charity ignored the glance exchanged by her aunt and father. They obviously suspected she cared for Mr. Dunbar. In a way, she did. But their earlier conversation had made it clear he'd do nothing for their cause. And she refused to give her heart, no matter how much she wanted to, to a man who held rules in higher regard than someone else's freedom.

"At least I don't have to meet with him today," Papa said. "Besides, I want all three of us to look at his plans, so we have to meet when the post office is closed. Our dinner hour and tomorrow evening were the only options. Frankly, I don't relish the thought of spending an entire evening with Mr. Dunbar. Dinner was the better choice."

"He seems like a nice gentleman to me," Aunt Stella said.

"I have nothing against him. But socializing with strangers is dangerous." Papa laid his hand on Charity's arm, and his eyes twinkled. "Even strangers as dashing as Mr. Dunbar."

"Oh Papa. Mr. Dunbar isn't at all dashing. He thinks I'm a ninny."

"Which shows he's a fool." Aunt Stella pushed away from the table. "And so am I. I forgot the blackberry jam."

"This time," Papa said while Aunt Stella went to the kitchen, "we'll give him our honest input. This is our home for now, but someday another postmaster will take over the post office and this residence. We want the place to be comfortable for them too."

"I plan to never leave." Charity's voice had a teasing lilt, but she wasn't joking. She envisioned herself living in the postmaster residence for the rest of her life. Women postmasters were rare, but no one was better equipped than she to take her father's place when he retired.

Her family hadn't lived here when she was born, but it was the only home she remembered. Aunt Stella's husband had been the former postmaster. Tragically, he and Mama died within days of each other from influenza when Charity was a toddler. Papa took his brother's place, and Aunt Stella stayed to care for her only niece.

"I hope you never will," Papa said. "But we can't know the future God has planned for you."

Aunt Stella returned to the table. "With all the excitement about Mr. Dunbar's visit, I almost forgot to tell you. Our friend was happy with the package you prepared for him."

Our friend.

He was the man who printed and distributed Charity's articles, though even she didn't know his true name. Aunt Stella always acted as their go-between.

"I'm glad to hear it," Charity said. "Though I'll have to write something brilliant next time to make up for the lackluster quality of this one."

"You underestimate yourself, child," Papa said. "Nothing you prepare for our friend is lackluster. You've got your mama's brains."

Charity's hands stilled. Papa seldom spoke of Mama, and Charity's heart always sped up when he did. If she didn't interrupt his thoughts, he might tell a story or two of their courtship or the early days of their marriage. Maybe even one about Charity as a baby. They'd been such a happy little family. Maybe she was foolish to mourn for someone she couldn't remember. Especially since she was quite content with her life, and she loved Aunt Stella as dearly as anyone could love a mother.

But the loss was real.

Mama's portrait hung in Papa's bedroom, and Charity had spent hours upon hours gazing into those lovely dark eyes when she was younger. She whispered secrets to the portrait, knowing the red lips wouldn't betray her.

She hadn't indulged in that kind of childish pastime for years. But perhaps it was time again to share a secret with Mama. A secret of the heart.

Chapter 3

Charity spent the afternoon working in the post office with Papa while Aunt Stella tended to her household duties. After supper that evening, the women tidied the kitchen then joined Papa in the parlor. When they entered, he placed the book he was reading on a side table.

"We don't want to interrupt your reading," Charity said as she took her usual seat and pulled her knitting from her workbasket.

"The words will still be there when I return to them," Papa said.

"You always say that."

"It's one of the few things in this world I can take for granted."

Aunt Stella sorted through her own workbasket and chose a partially finished doily to tat. As usual, she had several projects in various stages of completion—knitting, crocheting, embroidery. She did everything but quilt because that, in her view, took too much time. She completed a row of lace then rested her hands in her lap.

"I received a message from our friend shortly before supper. He asked if I'd go to Chillicothe tomorrow. Charity, you may come too, if you wish. We can visit Madame Garnier and select a new dress or two while we're there."

Charity's eyes brightened at the invitation. Abolitionists and free blacks worked together in the city, once the state capital and still a major economic center on the Scioto River, to operate the Underground Railroad. Fugitives who managed to cross the broad Ohio River found safety and shelter there while arrangements were made for their next destination.

The promise of new clothes was a bonus.

"Such short notice?" Papa said.

"Our friend received word of an important meeting, but he fears the authorities are suspicious of him. He saw the same man following him on three or four occasions during his last trip."

"Then perhaps I should go," Papa said. "It's too dangerous for you and Charity."

"I believe it's less dangerous," Aunt Stella replied. "Our enemies suspect Moses Freed is a man. They aren't looking for a woman."

"Maybe they are. You can't know that for sure."

"Only one or two of the abolitionists in Chillicothe know Charity is the author."

"I can't forbid you to go, Stella, but—"

"Papa, please. Aunt Stella and I always travel together. And we're always careful. Besides, it can't be any more dangerous than what we're already doing. Hiding fugitives here when we need to do so."

"At least here we are in our own home." He pulled out his pipe and tobacco but didn't fill the bowl. "I can keep an eye on you."

Charity knelt beside her father's chair and rested her hands upon his knee. "Don't you see why it's important I go, Papa? When I'm away from here, I can be myself."

The sigh she released came from deep inside her. "I get so tired of pretending to be someone I'm not. I'm afraid one day I'll wake up and that's who I'll truly be. A vain, silly girl who cares nothing for justice. For honor. For all the fine ideals you, my beloved papa, have instilled in my heart."

"You're not being fair, Charity. Using what I've taught you against me."

"Do not fear, Grover. No one ever suspects Charity of caring about anything other than shopping. The authorities don't believe us—an old woman and a young one—capable of being aligned with the abolitionists."

"See?" Charity tamped down the resentment building in her throat. "No one thinks me capable. Because I'm only a silly girl."

"I have never said that," Papa said. "I know how trying it is for you to show a false self to our friends and neighbors. It's not easy for me either."

"I know that, Papa."

Only a chosen few were privileged to know this side of Papa—the serious, thoughtful man who could brilliantly debate an issue, who was well acquainted with the works of the ancient philosophers and more modern ones too. Most only knew him as the amiable postmaster, quick with a kind word and an easy laugh. A man who enjoyed a good joke but steered clear of controversy. That wasn't a postmaster's place, he'd said to more than one political candidate.

"I imagine you'd like a break from your pretend self once in a while too," Charity said.

He stroked her hair. "I surely would, daughter. I surely would."

She flung her arms around his neck and kissed his cheek. "Oh, thank you, Papa. I knew you'd understand."

"Charity," he sputtered. "I have not said—"

"Did you hear that, Aunt Stella? Papa understands. I knew he would once he thought about it."

"Charity. . ."

She pleaded with her eyes, holding her breath as she waited for his next words.

He gave a resigned sigh. "Do not take any foolish chances."

"Never. Thank you, Papa." She dropped her knitting into her workbasket. "I need to pack."

"One blessing comes from this, Grover. You can cancel your plans with Mr. Dunbar," Aunt Stella said.

Another delay. Perhaps God was answering Charity's prayers after all.

◆━━━━━◆

Tavish spread out the blueprints on his desk to review them one more time before his dinner meeting with the Sinclairs. The front of the building curved inward, following the curve of the street. At least this building was being preserved. Many had been demolished to make room for the new straightened streets.

Because the Sinclair residence housed the post office, the federal government had added funds to its renovation. After the curving front wall was replaced with a straight one, the office layout could be rearranged to make use of the additional square footage. The upper rooms fronting the street would also be enlarged.

With all these modern improvements, Tavish couldn't comprehend why the Sinclairs were reluctant to look at his plans. He'd even heard that Grover Sinclair wanted the street to stay the way it was as some sort of historical monument to the past.

Much as he hated to admit it, Tavish wasn't opposed to the idea. But with the other side of the street in the process of rebuilding, Mr. Sinclair's proposal was a day late and a dollar short as Uncle Ned would say.

A knock sounded on his open door. "What are those?" his supervisor, Tom Manning, asked.

"Blueprints for the Sinclairs. I'm meeting them at one." He glanced at the wall clock. In less than half an hour, he'd be dining with the family. With Charity.

"It's about time. Those renovations need to be completed before winter sets in."

"With any luck, we can start tomorrow."

"Not that soon, I'm afraid." He placed a sheaf of documents on top of the blueprints. "I need you to go to Chillicothe."

"Another problem with a shipment?"

"I'd go myself, but I've got meetings of my own to attend."

"When do I leave?"

"The next packet boat comes through around two fifteen, two thirty."

"Six hours on the canal. Nothing else I'd rather do."

265

"Don't get smart, Dunbar." Manning folded his arms. "I need this issue resolved tomorrow."

"I haven't failed you yet, have I?"

"That's why I'm sending you." Manning's shoulders seemed to relax as he stopped in the doorframe on his way out of the office. "In fact, you may as well postpone the Sinclair meeting. A few more days won't make any difference."

"They're expecting me to dine with them. It's too late to cancel."

"Fine. As long as you're on that boat when it leaves."

"I will be," Travis said as Manning disappeared down the hall.

So much for an after-dinner stroll with Charity. Not that he wanted to spend time with her. But he'd heard the gardens behind the post office were well laid out and tended. He'd played with the idea of asking her if he could see for himself. His cousin would be interested, and he could describe them to her in his next letter.

Tavish pushed the envelope in his pocket then rolled up the plans. He had just enough time to pack his bag before going to the post office.

◆◆————◆◆

The canal boat stopped to replace the mule with a rested one before entering Thacker's Lock, named for the lockkeeper who lived in the sprawling brick house overlooking the canal. Charity and her aunt disembarked to stretch their legs and purchase lemonade and sandwiches from the lockkeeper's wife and children. They'd been traveling on the Ohio-Erie Canal since midmorning and should arrive in Chillicothe in a couple more hours.

Each mile marker they passed along the way had allowed Charity to shed more of her pretended persona. That always happened when she traveled away from home. She'd have been devastated if Papa had refused to allow her to accompany Aunt Stella on this trip.

The day was perfect. The weather was perfect. The lemonade was perfect.

A pleasant breeze skimmed across the still water, which brilliantly reflected the sun's cloud-softened glare. The brim of Charity's stylish hat shaded her eyes, so she didn't bother opening her parasol.

Sometimes, she had to admit, an alter ego was a good thing. The vain silly girl had excellent taste in clothes.

She smiled at the notion, her heart almost bursting with the freedom of being away from her hometown.

"You're happy," Aunt Stella said. "Mind sharing your thoughts?"

"It's nice to be away, that's all. And there's something festive about a last-minute trip on the canal."

"I'm glad you finagled your papa's permission to come with me. Though I'm not sure I should approve of your tactics."

"I only took advantage of an opportunity."

"By assuming permission not yet given."

Charity grabbed Aunt Stella's arm and pulled her into an awkward side-hug. "It worked, didn't it?"

"At least we put Mr. Dunbar off for a few more days."

Charity suppressed a sigh. *Tavish.* What would he think when he found only Papa at the post office?

"Talk about unfair finagling," she said. "I still think Papa should have sent a message to Mr. Dunbar to let him know we were leaving."

"I agree with you in principle. But it seemed a good joke to your father, and we had to let him win the second argument when he'd already lost the first one."

Aunt Stella had a point, but Charity's mood dampened as she pictured Tavish striding to the post office, that long silly tube tucked under his arm. She'd promised him this meeting wouldn't be postponed, rescinded, canceled, or rescheduled. Perhaps she should have stayed home with Papa.

The boat whistle sounded, and Charity joined her aunt in the queue to board the boat. Tavish might never forgive her, and she'd never be able to explain.

It was for the best.

If she repeated that lie often enough, maybe she'd believe it.

Chapter 4

Tavish arrived at the post office a few minutes before one. His pulse quickened, and he took a deep breath before opening the door. The postmaster, alone at the counter, opened his arms wide in a welcoming gesture. "Mr. Dunbar. Come in, come in."

"Thank you, Mr. Sinclair." Tavish's too-bright smile hid his disappointment that Charity wasn't with her father. He hadn't expected her to be, not really. After all, she'd only asked him to share their meal because he'd pushed her into a corner. Not a gentlemanly thing to do at all.

"I fear we must change our plans and dine elsewhere," Mr. Sinclair said. "The ladies have been called away. Quite at the last minute and most inconvenient. Still, it could not be helped."

"They aren't here?" The anticipation buoying Tavish's spirits clunked to his feet. "Where did they go?"

"My sister-in-law's personal affairs need her attention at times. I don't interfere or ask questions. My daughter frequently accompanies her aunt on these trips."

Another kind smile softened the rebuke, but it still stung. Stella Sinclair's personal affairs were none of his business, and Mr. Sinclair had no inclination to satisfy his curiosity.

"I hope this doesn't mean you plan to sit in my lobby for the rest of the day."

Tavish's ears warmed. "Miss Charity told you how I bullied her."

"She didn't present your conversation in such a way."

"Miss Charity is too kind. Still, I hoped to apologize, and I will. When I see her again."

Mr. Sinclair scratched the side of his neck. "Mr. Dunbar, any apologies are mine. I expect the ladies to be home in two or three days. Perhaps you'd join us for dinner after church."

Surprised by the invitation, Tavish didn't know what to say. A leisurely Sunday dinner—it had to be a trick.

"We can spend the afternoon examining your plans and suggesting all sorts of improvements, which you will deny as being unrealistic, impractical, and unaffordable." Mr. Sinclair chuckled, a hearty sound rising deep within his chest. "Sundays are for resting, but I promise we will not allow your fine presentation and our unimaginable schemes to seem like work. Not at all."

"I accept."

"Fine, fine. Now, shall we find somewhere to satisfy our stomachs?"

"I hope you will excuse me, Mr. Sinclair. My superior is sending me on a trip of my own this afternoon. I'm not quite ready—"

"Then go, Mr. Dunbar." The postmaster came from behind the counter and with sweeping gestures accompanied Tavish to the door. "I shall not detain you."

"Thank you. I will see you Sunday then."

"Sunday. Yes, yes. Sunday it is."

A moment later, Tavish was outside the post office, though he wasn't quite sure how he'd gotten there. On the other side of the glass, Mr. Sinclair waved, locked the double doors, then pulled the shades.

Guess he didn't want to have lunch with me any more than I wanted to have lunch with him.

Could anything have been more awkward than the two of them dining together? Tavish doubted they had anything in common. Mr. Sinclair probably would have droned on and on about Charity this and Charity that. Everyone in town knew how much he doted on his daughter.

Fortunately, Tavish had escaped that nonsense.

As he walked away from the post office, his stomach twisted with regret.

❖━━━❖

Excitement surged through Charity as she stepped onto the bustling dock when they arrived in Chillicothe. Danger surrounded any meeting with the abolitionists, but it was an energizing danger. These people risked their lives every day for the cause. Her own secret contribution paled in comparison. Sometimes she wished she could stay in this city, to revel in the intrigue and face peril head-on, instead of writing anonymous articles and tracts from the safe haven of her bedroom.

"There's something different about you, Charity, love," Aunt Stella whispered as they waited for their bags to be loaded onto their hotel's carriage.

"It's being here. I'm no longer the pampered daughter of the postmaster but someone different. Someone. . .people respect."

"I understand how you feel," Aunt Stella said. "It's like that for me too."

"It is?"

"People see what they want to see. Our neighbors at home view me as a childless widow dependent upon the kindness of relatives. But here? They listen to my opinions and ideas. There's something very good in that." She brushed a speck of dust from Charity's dress. "I fear at times I do this work more for my sake than those we help."

"God knows your heart, and so do I." A wave of emotion caught in Charity's throat. *Dependent upon the kindness. . .what nonsense.* "And you're like a mother to me. You know that."

Aunt Stella cupped Charity's cheek. "I couldn't love a child of my own more than I do you. But enough sentiment. Poise and polish, Charity. Poise and polish."

Charity followed her aunt to the open carriage, and they were soon on their way to the hotel. The streets bustled with chaotic activity, creating an energy that seemed alive. After the quiet serenity of the long canal ride, Charity thrilled at the comparative speed of the trotting horse and the commotion of people, so many people, scurrying along the sidewalks.

Her hometown paled in comparison.

But beneath Chillicothe's jovial facade existed a city of danger and intrigue as abolitionists and slave hunters warred with one another.

Experience had taught Charity that despite feeling adventurous right now, she'd soon be eager to return to the quieter pace of Circleville and the refuge of her home. To writing her articles and helping her aunt in the gardens. To assisting Papa in the post office.

To greeting Tavish Dunbar when he came for his mail, though definitely *not* to handing him lilac envelopes addressed with a feminine hand.

◆—◆

After freshening up at the hotel, Charity and Aunt Stella descended to the lobby. Aunt Stella carried a bundle of assorted tracts, including printed copies of Moses Freed's latest article, in a hatbox. The messenger sent by "our friend" had given her the materials so the abolitionists could forward them to newspapers and other groups throughout the region.

They walked to the edge of the warehouse district that lined the Scioto River. But when they turned the corner, Aunt Stella grabbed Charity's arm.

Several people stood outside the building where the abolitionists were to meet. Someone shouted, and a fight appeared to break out.

Without thinking, Charity started toward the crowd, but Aunt Stella tightened her grip. "Wait," she demanded. "It may not be safe."

"What if we can help?"

Aunt Stella frowned, the skin creasing between her eyes. "We'll walk along this side of the street. As curious passersby, no more. Understand?"

"I understand." Charity's pulse quickened as they neared the commotion. The slave hunters couldn't have discovered the abolitionists' secret meeting place. The location often changed—Charity hadn't been to the same place twice on her visits—and the abolitionists were especially careful.

"Perhaps it doesn't have anything to do with us." She tried to sound as hopeful as possible, uncertain whether she was trying to reassure Aunt Stella or herself.

That hope disappeared as a black teenager broke from the crowd. His eyes darted from side to side, and two uniformed men chased after him. He almost tripped but caught his balance and stumbled past Charity and Aunt Stella.

Charity reached for him, but Aunt Stella pulled her into a nearby doorway as the men slammed the teen onto the road.

"We have to help him," Charity insisted.

"We can't, love." Aunt Stella's voice was low. "Not this time."

Bile roiled in Charity's stomach, and she pressed her hand against her abdomen. How could this be happening?

Aunt Stella gasped, and Charity tore her gaze from the struggling young man. Her aunt stared across the street where more uniformed men were coming out of the meeting with three other men.

The abolitionists they planned to meet.

Charity's heart sank. "What do we do?" she whispered.

Aunt Stella hesitated then straightened her shoulders. "We walk away."

"How can we?"

"We have no choice."

Aunt Stella turned to leave when someone called her name. A tall man dressed in a three-piece suit and wearing a top hat emerged from the crowd and crossed the street.

"Stella Sinclair." His cultured voice modulated each syllable. "Is that you?"

"Gerald Marsh?" Aunt Stella gripped the string handle of the hatbox with both hands. "This is a surprise."

"A welcome one, I hope. It's been"—he tilted his head in thought—"more years than I wish. Why are you here?"

Aunt Stella avoided the question with a warm smile. She introduced the stranger to Charity then said, "Mr. Marsh and your uncle were boyhood friends."

"This can't be baby Charity," Mr. Marsh said. "Why, she's all grown up. And very lovely."

"I'm pleased to meet you, Mr. Marsh." Charity did her best to follow her aunt's example, but she found it hard to smile. Her gaze flickered to the uniformed men and their culprits—a free black man she'd met on her last trip and two white men she didn't recognize—then back again. Though she found it difficult to focus, she forced herself to make polite conversation. "Especially since you knew my uncle."

"He was a dear friend and a good man," Mr. Marsh said. "We all felt his loss. And that of your dear mother. You favor her, you know."

"You knew my mother?"

"We met once or twice." He switched his attention to Aunt Stella. "What brings you to Chillicothe?"

"We make the trip several times a year."

He gestured at the hatbox. "Shopping, I see."

Charity stiffened. Polite conversation. That's all this was. He couldn't know what was in the hatbox. Yet something dark, questioning, hovered behind his courteous manner.

"Yes," Aunt Stella said. "You must excuse us. We have an appointment with our dressmaker, and if we don't hurry, we'll be late."

"Is the new hat for you or for Miss Charity?" His tone was light, cheerful, but suspicion flickered in his eyes.

"An audacious question," Aunt Stella said, matching her tone to his.

He laughed, forcing humor where it didn't exist. "Pardon my boldness. I only wished to detain you a moment longer." He swept his arm toward the opposite side of the street. "Though I regret you were witness to such an outrage."

"What's happening?" Charity asked before Aunt Stella could respond.

He slid his eyes from Aunt Stella to Charity. A long moment passed while he seemed to appraise her, to consider his reply.

"Nothing to concern a genteel young woman such as yourself."

"I'd like to know."

"Laws were broken. Arrests have been made. Justice is being upheld."

Harsh words bubbled in Charity's throat, too many to say at once and none that would undo the travesty before her. She flinched as Aunt Stella gripped her elbow.

"Come along, Charity. Your papa will not thank me for exposing you to such a spectacle." Aunt Stella nodded to Mr. Marsh. "It was good to see you again, Gerald."

"Perhaps we could meet again. Under less dreadful circumstances."

"Perhaps."

"This evening for dinner?"

Aunt Stella startled, and her alarmed gaze sought Charity's assistance.

"The invitation is open to both of you," Mr. Marsh said. "We can reminisce about the days when we were young and foolish." He gave a lighthearted chuckle. "Ah, Miss Charity. The stories I can tell you about your uncle."

"It sounds delightful," Charity managed to say. "I fear we have another engagement."

"Tomorrow then?"

"You are most kind," Aunt Stella said, "but we are returning home tomorrow."

Charity hid her surprise, her expression frozen in a simpering smile. Aunt Stella rushed through a final goodbye, and Mr. Marsh tipped his hat. Charity resisted the urge to glance over her shoulder. She didn't need to see Mr. Marsh to know he stared after them.

Once they rounded the corner, Aunt Stella blew out a deep breath. "To think, I once fancied myself in love with that man."

"You did?"

"I might have married him. But he introduced me to your uncle, and my heart was no longer my own."

Charity wanted to know more of her aunt's love story, but she tucked her questions away for a more appropriate time. "What are we going to do?"

"Keep our appointment with Madame Garnier."

"What about the hatbox?"

"I don't know."

"Are we really going home tomorrow?"

They'd walked half a block more before Aunt Stella answered. "Gerald Marsh is an intelligent man. If he's involved—"

"Is he a slave hunter?"

"His family owned a small plantation northeast of Lexington. I suppose he inherited it."

"That boy—"

"Let's not talk about it." Aunt Stella's voice cracked. "Not now."

As they strolled past the downtown shops, Charity wanted to forget everything that had happened. But each nerve in her body tingled, and her senses were heightened. Every sound seemed magnified, from the cries of the newsboy to the squeak of the carriage wheels. The aroma of fresh-baked goods from a nearby bakery mingled with the less pleasant odors of horse manure and unwashed bodies. She wrinkled her nose as she took a deep breath and consciously relaxed her tense shoulders.

"What style dress will you ask Madame Garnier to make for you?"

Dear Aunt Stella. Somehow she'd managed to overcome her own anxiety. Her steady voice and calm presence were better than any tonic.

"I haven't decided on anything in particular." Despite her best efforts, Charity's voice quivered, and she cleared her throat. "I'm hoping she'll have new patterns to show us."

"I'm sure she will." Aunt Stella leaned close. "Don't fret, Charity. God is with us."

But was He with the runaway slave who had been so close to freedom?

She'd never forget the fear in his eyes. Or forgive herself for not intervening.

Chapter 5

Charity insisted they take a carriage from Madame Garnier's shop to the hotel. She hadn't been fooled by Aunt Stella's attempts to hide her weariness. She doubted her aunt, strong and vibrant in spite of her years, was troubled by physical exhaustion. Instead she seemed lost in burdensome memories.

When they entered the hotel lobby, Charity waited near the stairs while Aunt Stella retrieved the room key from the manager. They exchanged a few words, their voices too low for Charity to hear what was said.

But Aunt Stella seemed pleased. Her shoulders no longer slumped, and a cautious smile betrayed her improved mood.

"What did he say?" Charity whispered as they ascended the sweeping stairs.

"Wait and see."

Aunt Stella unlocked the door to their room and set the hatbox on a round table situated near the window. Both women removed the pins from their hats and tucked them away in the wardrobe. Charity started to sit at the table, expecting her aunt to join her, but Aunt Stella knocked three times on the connecting door.

"What are you doing?" Charity asked.

Aunt Stella held up her hand and bent her ear to the door. As three soft taps sounded, her smile broadened. "We have guests."

She unlocked the door and it opened from the other side.

Two men, strangers, crossed the threshold dividing the rooms. From their resemblance to each other, Charity guessed they were father and son. The younger man's hair was only a shade or two darker than the other man's, and they had the same hazel eyes.

The older man took both of Aunt Stella's hands. "When you weren't here by the time we arrived. . .I confess I worried for your safety."

"Were you there?"

"We saw it all through an upper window. What did Marsh say to you?"

"He asked about the hatbox. I'm sure he suspects our involvement." Aunt

Stella turned toward Charity. "My niece, Charity Sinclair."

Charity took a tentative step forward. Aunt Stella seemed to trust the men, but Charity had never seen them on any of her earlier visits. After what happened earlier, she wasn't inclined to be friendly.

"This is Elisha Lowe," Aunt Stella said, "and his son, Jesse."

"Why haven't we met before?" Charity asked.

"We're both attorneys from Portsmouth," Jesse said, sparking Charity's interest. That city flourished in the angle of land where the Scioto River flowed into the broad and mighty Ohio River. The Portsmouth abolitionists were only a river's-width away from the horrors and humiliations of slavery.

"We came to meet with the abolitionists here to discuss new strategies for outwitting those miserable slave hunters," Jesse continued. "They travel farther north into the Free States than they used to."

"Because of the blasted Bloodhound Law," Charity said.

"Charity! Your language, please. *Blasted*?"

"There's no other way to say it, Aunt Stella."

"I agree with your niece." Jesse's grin indicated his admiration, and Charity's cheeks flushed with warmth.

"Even a few months ago," Elisha said, "what happened this afternoon would not have happened. Not with such impunity."

"What will happen to the abolitionists?" Charity asked. She didn't need to ask about the fate of the young fugitive. He'd return to a life of misery. . .if he lived. An involuntary shudder shook her body.

"That depends on the judge." Elisha pressed his fingers against his temple. "The boy is Marsh's property, and he will insist on prison for those who hid him. At the least, they'll be charged a hefty fine. Hopefully, they won't be tried for treason."

"Are you representing them, Elisha?" Aunt Stella asked.

"Not at the initial hearing. It's best for now that I stay in the background."

"Is there nothing we can do?" Charity asked.

Jesse exchanged a look with his father, who hesitated then shook his head. Frustration hardened Jesse's tone. "We're out of options."

"It's too dangerous." Elisha clipped his words, and his expression sagged in defeat.

"What aren't you telling us?" Aunt Stella asked, her calm voice stilling the tension between the men.

Instead of answering, Elisha released a deep sigh and faced the empty hearth.

"We can't help the abolitionists." Jesse stared for a moment at his father's back then continued. "But Marsh's hunters only found one fugitive. The Underground needs to help the others."

Charity stifled a gasp, and the room was silent as the revelation settled around them. The Sinclairs had provided refuge in their secret room at the post office for dozens of runaways. Papa had escorted many from the post office to their next stop on the Underground. Aunt Stella had too, on the rare occasions when Papa couldn't. They'd never allowed Charity to be involved in that aspect of their work.

But neither of them had accompanied a runaway from one major city to another.

Charity's pulse quickened, and her stomach churned with excitement. "Do you have a plan?"

Jesse gave her a grateful look then glanced again at his father. "We do. That is, I mean, I do. But Father is right. It is dangerous. Even more so now."

Aunt Stella laid a comforting hand on Elisha's arm, and his hand covered hers. "I can't ask you to do this," he said.

"How many more fugitives are there?"

"Two. The young man's mother and his sister."

"What is your plan?"

Elisha nodded at Jesse, giving him the go-ahead.

"We put them in separate shipping crates. One will go our usual route on the Scioto River. The other will travel on the canal."

"We've never used the canal," Aunt Stella said.

A multitude of thoughts competed in Charity's head, but one burst through the rest. "You're splitting them up?"

"There's a good chance only one will make it to the safe house." Jesse's shoulders bowed. "But if we send them together, and choose the wrong route. . ."

He didn't need to finish the sentence.

"But Gerald won't suspect the canal," Aunt Stella insisted. "I can take them both."

"No, Stella, you can't," Elisha said. "Marsh knows we're looking at other routes. But not even he can be in two places at the same time. With God's hand upon us, one will reach safety. Hopefully, both."

Charity sank into a chair, her heart aching at the difficult decisions that had to be made. Only God knew what dangers and hardships this small family had experienced in their quest for freedom. Now the son had been captured.

His mother and sister must be sick with worry and frightened for their own welfare. Charity couldn't imagine experiencing such fear.

Jesse pulled a chair from the table and sat near her. His father and Aunt Stella conversed in quiet voices by the fireplace.

"What are their names?" she asked.

"Perhaps it's better you don't know. At least not yet."

"Secrecy." She sighed. "It's fun for a time. Exciting, even. But this time. . .I need to know."

"His name will probably be in the morning papers." Jesse stared at the floor, his shoulders bent as if they carried a great unseen weight. "David Webster. His sister is Sina Anne and his mother is Cordelia."

"Will they want their freedom? I mean since one of them has been captured. . ."

"We're strongly advising them not to go back. If David gets the chance, he'll run away again, and we'll do our best to reunite him with his family. But the chances of all three of them escaping again? They're not good."

They sat in silence, both lost in thoughts too deep to be shared with a new acquaintance.

Unbidden words and phrases formed themselves into sentences and paragraphs inside Charity's heart till her fingers itched to hold her quill pen. Moses Freed's next article, born of fear and sorrow, had written itself.

Tavish overslept at his hotel the next morning and, in his rush, nicked his chin shaving. He dabbed at the cut, and blood dotted the corner of his white handkerchief. Since he hadn't brought another, he folded the stain into the center of the handkerchief and stuck it in his pocket. Hopefully, this wasn't a harbinger of the rest of his day.

If he could get matters smoothed out at the shipping office this morning, he could be on his way home this afternoon.

He grabbed his hat and raced down the hotel's sweeping stairs. The mingling aromas of bacon and cinnamon rolls from the dining room tantalized his senses. His stomach responded with a soft grumble. Perhaps he could request a pastry to take with him. Though a hearty breakfast of eggs, hash browns, and bacon sure was tempting.

Still undecided, he stepped into the dining room and glanced around. Other hotel guests were seated at about half the tables. The soft hum of voices was punctuated by the sharp ring of metal cutlery against china.

A waiter handed Tavish a menu, and he scanned the offerings while guilt gnawed his insides. But he was already late, and a few more moments wouldn't make much difference. The task would get done. . .and done well. That's why Manning had sent him to do it.

He ordered coffee and a full breakfast then pulled a packet of papers from his briefcase. Though he'd reviewed the shipping information while floating down the canal the day before, it wouldn't hurt to go over it again.

More guests entered the dining room, passing his table on their way to one in an isolated corner.

Tavish leaned back, the papers forgotten, and stared at Charity Sinclair arm in arm with another man. Her aunt, with an escort of her own, preceded the younger couple to the table. The gnawing guilt gave way to pangs of jealousy.

Why hadn't Grover Sinclair told him Charity was in Chillicothe? Tavish replayed the conversation, best as he could remember it, in his mind.

The postmaster had made Tavish feel small for asking Charity's whereabouts, albeit in a polite and genteel manner. When Tavish mentioned his own trip, Grover had practically shoved him out the door.

He couldn't have known Tavish's destination nor did he have any reason to care. But why was Charity's trip such a big secret?

Unless. . .she had come to meet someone. And her father didn't want Tavish to know. Maybe she was secretly betrothed. Or maybe her father didn't know Charity was seeing— He dismissed that thought before it went any further. Charity wasn't the kind of girl to keep secrets from her father. Even if she were, it's doubtful she could persuade her aunt to do the same.

The waiter brought his meal, but he'd lost his appetite and the tantalizing aromas weren't as enticing as they'd been when he entered the dining room. He buried his nose in the paperwork, though none of the numbers made sense anymore, and he ate his breakfast without tasting it.

When he left, he paused at the entryway to take one last glance at the isolated table. Charity stared at him, and she seemed flustered when their eyes met. A small smile appeared and disappeared, and her posture looked unnaturally stiff. She turned toward her companion and touched his sleeve. He leaned toward her as she spoke, intent on her every word.

Tavish couldn't bear to see any more. He stopped by the desk to give the clerk his key.

"Will you be staying another night, sir?" he asked.

"It's too soon to know," Tavish said. *Though not if I can help it.* "I hope to conclude my business this morning. . . ." He shrugged and let the sentence hang.

"I understand, sir."

"Thank you." Tavish started to walk away but turned when an angel called his name.

Charity stood, hands clasped in front of her, a vision wrapped in pale blue and lace.

"Mr. Dunbar," she said again, her voice as soft as a rose petal and piercing as a thorn. Her eyes lowered, and thick lashes brushed her flushed cheek.

"Miss Sinclair." As if his legs had a mind of their own, he closed the distance between them. "This is a surprise."

"For me too."

An awkward silence filled the space between them, but how could he end it? Propriety forbid him from asking the question he most wanted to ask. *Who is that fellow, and why are you with him?*

He took a safer tack.

"Your father told me you had gone, but he didn't say where."

"This trip was most unexpected, I assure you. When I invited you to dinner, I didn't know—"

"Please. You needn't apologize. I didn't know I'd be traveling either until yesterday morning."

"You're here on business then."

"A mix-up with a shipping order. I'm on my way to the warehouses now."

"Then I mustn't keep you. I only wished to. . ." She hesitated, as if unsure what she wanted to say. "To give you my greetings."

"Will you be returning home soon?"

"Our plans are uncertain. And you?"

"Mine are uncertain as well. Perhaps our paths will cross on our way home."

"Perhaps." Her tone was pleasant enough, as was the smile that accompanied it. But something akin to dread dampened the warmth of her eyes.

She doesn't want to travel on the same boat as me.

Unexpected hurt burrowed into his heart, and he stopped its spread with indignation. It was better if they didn't. What would they talk about for five or six hours? Charity's latest hat? Her new gloves? He couldn't abide such nonsense.

"Will your gentleman friend be accompanying you?"

"My gentleman. . ." Her eyes narrowed then opened wide with understanding. "Oh no. He's not my b— No. He won't. No."

"Not my—" what? Not her beau?

His mind didn't care, but his heart prayed that's what she hadn't said.

✦•──•✦

Charity hated telling Tavish a lie—even when the lie wasn't a lie. Their plans had been made during a long evening of *what-ifs* and *what abouts*. Jesse and his father returned to the safe house where Cordelia Webster and her daughter were hidden to discuss the plans with them and their hosts. They'd taken the printed materials from the hatbox with them for the abolitionists to distribute.

After the men left, Aunt Stella locked the connecting door and ordered room service. She refused to leave the hotel since she had told Gerald Marsh earlier in the day that she and Charity had plans. She didn't want to run into him by accident or by his purpose.

Elisha Lowe had given them an update during breakfast. Sina Anne, in her midteens, had begged to travel with her mother. But with the slave hunters aggressively searching for the pair, none of the abolitionists considered it wise for her to do so. Her mother reluctantly agreed to the separation, and the plans were put in motion.

But nothing was "finalized" until they were actually *on* the boat.

The justification didn't absolve her guilt. At least what she said about Jesse Lowe was true. Strange, that Tavish assumed she and Jesse were a couple. Despite her stammering denial, he peered at her with disbelieving eyes. A change of subject was desperately needed.

"Did you and Papa dine together yesterday?"

"He invited me for Sunday dinner."

"I'm glad."

"Are you?" His tone, though flat, sounded like a challenge.

More than you know.

But she couldn't say those words to him.

It had been a mistake to seek him out. Their conversations never went the way she imagined in her dreams. But after seeing him in the dining area, she'd been compelled to follow him.

If only to exchange a hello.

However, the man who had stared at her across the room, with something akin to longing in his eyes, was not the man who stood before her now. In that short interval, he'd turned surly. Almost defiant.

A brush against her sleeve startled her.

"Excuse me for interrupting," Jesse said, darting a glance at Tavish. "My father and I must be on our way, but we'll see you again before you leave."

"I understand." She palmed her stomach to soothe the racing butterflies. This was truly happening. In a couple of hours, if all went as planned, she and Aunt Stella would be on the Ohio-Erie Canal with the most precious cargo the boat had ever transported. A teenaged stowaway packed in a storage crate as if she were someone's material possession instead of a human being. Charity despised treating Sina Anne that way, but under the circumstances, it was the only way to keep her hidden from prying eyes.

Aunt Stella and Elisha Lowe joined the group.

"What a pleasant surprise," Aunt Stella said to Tavish. She introduced the men to each other then touched Charity's elbow. A signal to go.

After the goodbyes were said. Charity walked with Aunt Stella to the hotel staircase. Aunt Stella ascended the stairs, but Charity paused at the bottom to glance over her shoulder. Jesse and his father were talking to the hotel manager, and Tavish stood near the doorway, his back to her. He seemed reluctant to leave.

She wanted to believe that, like her, he wished Jesse hadn't interrupted their conversation. That given another moment, she would have found the courage to say something, anything, to lighten his mood.

"Charity." Aunt Stella paused on a step. "Are you coming?"

Time slowed as Aunt Stella turned on the stair. The heel of her shoe caught in her hem, and she grabbed for the bannister but missed.

As Aunt Stella tumbled down the sweeping stairs, Charity screamed then fell to her knees beside her aunt's still body.

Chapter 6

Tavish was almost out the door when he heard the scream. He raced to Charity's side and knelt beside her. They were immediately joined by Mr. Lowe, his son, and the hotel manager. Elisha eased Mrs. Sinclair onto her back and carefully straightened her legs.

"She needs a doctor," he said to his son.

The manager gave directions, and Jesse raced out of the lobby.

"Is she all right?" Tavish asked.

Elisha ran his hand along one leg then the other. When he touched Mrs. Sinclair's calf, she moaned and her eyelids fluttered. "Forgive me," he said as he inched the heavy skirts past the injury.

Her stockings were torn, and deep bruises discolored her skin.

"I fear it's broken," Elisha said, his gaze directed at Charity. "We can't move her till the doctor arrives, but we can make her more comfortable."

The hotel manager ordered one of the staff hovering nearby to bring pillows and blankets. Mrs. Sinclair moaned again, and Charity bent over her.

"Aunt Stella?" Her voice cracked, and tears dampened her cheeks. "Can you hear me?"

Tavish's stomach felt empty despite the breakfast he'd eaten only a few minutes before. He should have gone for the doctor, searched for the bedding, anything except kneeling here doing nothing while Charity fretted over her aunt.

He started to place his arm around her shaking shoulders, but she bent forward until her face was next to her aunt's. He let his arm drop, even more frustrated by his helplessness. All he could do was stay beside her and hope his presence provided even a small bit of comfort.

Two maids arrived, their arms loaded with the pillows and blankets.

Finally. Something he could do.

He directed the placements of the pillows beneath Mrs. Sinclair's head and shoulders then covered her with both a sheet and a blanket. He placed another blanket, folded in half, around Charity.

"Thank you," she said.

The appreciation in her voice, tempered by worry, made him long to do more for her. But what?

The doctor bustled in, and Tavish stepped back to give him room. Charity and the doctor knelt on one side, and the Lowes knelt on the other. The hotel manager, the maids, and a few guests stood nearby.

Tavish was as much an outsider as any of these curious strangers.

Who didn't need to be gawking at the poor woman lying unconscious on the ground.

He unfolded a spare blanket and held it up as a type of screen. The manager must have noticed because he sent the staff on their way except for the tallest maid who was tasked with holding a second blanket.

Tavish's arms soon ached, but he refused to give in to the weariness. As long as the doctor tended to Mrs. Sinclair, he'd do his best to give her as much privacy as possible. On the other side of the blanket, voices murmured, but he only caught a few words now and again. One leg was definitely broken, but she hadn't yet regained consciousness. Or perhaps the doctor had given her something to keep her from waking up.

Several minutes passed, then the doctor stood to speak with the manager.

"Where is her room?" he asked.

"The second floor."

"It will be difficult getting her up the stairs."

"A room is available on this floor. It's small, with only one narrow bed."

"It'll do."

The doctor affixed a temporary splint to Mrs. Sinclair's leg. The blankets were folded together to make a type of sling, and Tavish helped Jesse Lowe and his father carry her to the end of a short corridor to the designated room. The manager hadn't exaggerated about the room's size. There was little room to move once they were all inside.

After she was placed on the bed, Tavish and the manager returned to the hallway to give the doctor his needed space.

"I suppose I should return to the front desk." The manager tugged at his jaw. "Nasty business, this, but Mrs. Sinclair is in good health. I'm sure she'll soon recover."

"Are you well acquainted with Mrs. Sinclair?" Tavish asked, his curiosity piqued by the manager's air of familiarity.

"She is a frequent guest."

"Her niece also?"

"Miss Charity almost always accompanies her aunt."

"And the Lowes?" Tavish should have bitten his tongue, but the question had escaped his lips before he could stop it.

The manager gave him an appraising look then gripped his hands behind his back. "You will excuse me. I have other matters to attend to."

Tavish merely nodded. The man must think him a rube to inquire about the Lowes that way. But all he'd wanted to know was how often Charity Sinclair and Jesse Lowe came here at the same time. Not that it was any of his business or he really cared.

He was merely curious.

Which was a lie he couldn't make himself believe no matter how often he told it to himself.

◆━━━━◆

Charity reluctantly allowed Jesse to lead her from the room. Aunt Stella had regained consciousness for only a moment, long enough to squeeze Charity's hand, but the doctor had quickly administered ether to put her out again.

Surprised to see Tavish in the corridor, Charity swiped at her damp cheeks. "Mr. Dunbar. How kind of you to stay."

He shifted from one foot to the other. "I didn't want to leave without knowing. . .how is she?"

"They're setting the break now." She maintained control of her voice though her legs quivered like jelly. At least Tavish's concern loosened the stones packing her stomach. For a moment, she thought he meant to reach for her. But seconds ticked, and the moment passed without a touch.

Just as well. Even his slightest gesture might compel her to seek comfort in his arms. Despite his kindness—the way he'd shielded Aunt Stella from the crowd, the care he took when moving her—she couldn't be sure he'd welcome such an embrace or wish to return it.

"I have business to see to." Jesse's intense gaze spoke more than his words. The plans they'd made late last night had to be canceled. "I'll return as soon as I can."

"Yes," Charity said. "We'll talk later."

He squeezed her hand, acknowledged Tavish with a nod, and hurried away.

"They're expecting me at the warehouse." Tavish pulled in his bottom lip as he avoided her gaze.

The stones in her stomach grew heavier. Though what had she expected? He wasn't here for pleasure.

He shifted his weight then stared at her. The tenderness in his eyes, gray as evening fog upon the water, caught her breath.

"I don't like to leave you."

"Will you. . ." She wanted to ask him to come back to the hotel, but she mustn't. For the sake of the cause he needed to return to Circleville, not linger here when new plans needed to be made.

"Will I what?"

Fresh tears threatened at the gentleness in his voice.

"Will you pray for my aunt's recovery?" She averted her eyes and blinked. After composing herself, she met his gaze again. "And when you return home, will you tell Papa what happened, and that you were with us?"

"I will do all of that and more. Whatever you need."

She didn't trust her voice so she said nothing. He clasped her elbow, no more than a second, then left. A chill filled the corridor as he walked away.

Only the lingering warmth of his touch remained.

At the rap on the door, Charity closed the book resting on her lap. She'd tried to pass the time by reading, but the words held no meaning as they flowed past her eyes. Too many thoughts demanded her focus instead, though even those were as flighty as a covey of startled quail. Prayers for Aunt Stella slid into reliving her conversation with Tavish then into worry over the frightened girl whose freedom depended on a plan that had gone horribly awry.

Charity opened the door for Jesse and his father. As they entered, their presence filled the tiny room.

"How is she?" Elisha gripped the wooden footboard and seemed to study Aunt Stella as she slept. He'd left a few minutes after Jesse and Tavish, leaving Charity alone with the doctor.

"We talked for a few moments when she regained consciousness. She's angry with herself for 'causing such a ruckus.' Her words, not mine."

Aunt Stella had complained about Charity treating her like an invalid, but the tightness around her eyes and mouth made it obvious she was in pain. Thankfully, the doctor had administered medication before he left that soon lulled her into a restful sleep.

"What did the doctor say about her recovery?"

"Nothing really. He promised to return in a couple of hours." Charity returned to the wooden chair tucked between the bed's headboard and a square table. Her muscles ached from leaning against the spindled back, but she didn't care. Being as close to Aunt Stella as possible was all that mattered.

Jesse hovered near his father. A restless tension seemed to energize his body. He didn't have enough room to pace, but neither could he stand still for more than a moment or two. "It will be days, maybe weeks before she can travel."

"Jesse!" Elisha admonished. "That topic is closed. We'll find another way."

"How?" The question was a croaked whisper, forced into the room by sheer will.

Everyone in the room stared at Aunt Stella. Her eyes fluttered, and her fingers clutched at the satin ribbon lining the blanket.

"How?" she asked again, her voice guttural but strong.

Elisha rounded the foot of the bed and clasped Aunt Stella's hands in his own. He murmured her name, and Charity feared for a moment he was going to cry. She exchanged glances with Jesse, who shrugged then turned away.

"Stella," Elisha said. "I'm sorry we woke you."

"Not sorry." She struggled to sit up, and Charity pressed her hand against her aunt's shoulder.

"You must rest," she said.

"Talk first." Aunt Stella blinked, widened her eyes as if to rid herself of the last traces of sleep, and settled her gaze on Elisha. "How?"

He shook his head then glanced at Jesse and tilted his head toward the door. Jesse opened it, apparently checking the corridor for eavesdroppers, then left the door slightly ajar while leaning against the frame. "It's safe to talk."

"We've sent a telegram to our friend," Elisha said. "He may have a plan. If not, we'll be forced to send the crate without an escort."

"You can't." Aunt Stella's voice still sounded hoarse. Charity poured water into a glass and helped her take a sip.

"The crate is already at the loading dock," Elisha said. "If Jesse or I try to remove it now, someone could get suspicious. After yesterday's arrests, everyone is on edge."

"Apparently Marsh is offering a larger reward than usual," Jesse said in disgust.

"She's already in the crate?" Startled by the revelation, Charity almost spilled the water. "She must be so frightened."

"It's not an ideal situation," Elisha admitted. "But it never is."

"We take a risk every time." Jesse turned his attention to the corridor.

Some of us more than others. The thought slipped into Charity's consciousness like a whisper from beyond herself.

I take risks. The responding thought, indignant and defensive, nauseated her.

She took risks writing articles, but her pseudonym protected her from opponents of the cause. The entire Sinclair family took risks hiding fugitives inside their residence. But Papa took most of the risk in those ventures, not Charity.

"I'll go," she said quietly.

The stunned silence of the others in the room pressed against her. Jesse responded first. "No. You can't."

"Why not?" she asked.

He seemed to flail for a reason he could put into words, then his gaze landed on Aunt Stella. "Your aunt needs you here."

Charity turned toward the bed. "I don't want to leave you. But we can't let her go alone."

Aunt Stella rested her palm on Charity's cheek. "My dear girl. I admire your courage, but this is not a game. It's too dangerous."

"It wasn't too dangerous before."

"That's because I was going too. If we were discovered, any punishment would have fallen on me."

"I have to do this." Charity stood and faced the men. "I will do this."

"No," Jesse muttered under his breath. "I'll go."

"You'd be followed for sure, and we'd all be caught." Elisha's shoulders slumped, and his gaze flickered to Aunt Stella.

"I can't allow this, Charity," she said. "Your papa would never forgive me—I'd never forgive myself—if anything happened to you."

Charity perched on the edge of the chair, as close to the bed as she could get. "Don't you see? I'll never forgive myself if that young girl doesn't make it. Her brother. . ." A knot lodged in Charity's throat, and she paused to compose herself. "I saw such fear in his eyes. And now, she's trapped inside a box all by herself without any idea of what's happening. No matter what might happen to me, I can't abandon her. I won't."

Aunt Stella closed her eyes and took several rhythmic breaths. Was she. . . yes, she was praying. Charity buried her face in the bedclothes and felt the calming weight of Aunt Stella's hand upon her hair. Her own prayer, a plea expressed with more feelings than words, flew from her heart.

"She can go." Aunt Stella's quiet voice floated into the silence.

Charity raised her eyes and met Elisha's gaze.

"I'll make the arrangements." He held up a cautionary finger. "Unless our friend sends word of a different plan. Then you will stay here with your aunt."

"He needs to know I volunteered."

"I'll send the message." Elisha retrieved his hat and ran his fingers around the brim. "Come, Jesse. The next canal boat heading north leaves in a little over an hour. We don't have much time."

Jesse held Charity's gaze, his eyes inscrutable, then he reluctantly followed his father from the room and shut the door behind him. Was he disappointed? Afraid for her? Charity wasn't sure, and she didn't have time to figure it out.

She clasped one of Aunt Stella's cold hands between both of hers. "I'll come back tomorrow on the early boat and stay with you until you can travel. I'll even sleep in this chair."

Aunt Stella chuckled. "None of your dramatics. While you're gone, I'll sweet-talk the manager into giving us more comfortable quarters."

Her smile disappeared, and she squeezed Charity's fingers. "Take no chances."

"None." Charity leaned over her aunt and kissed her forehead. "I need to pack a few things and talk to the manager. I don't want you left alone tonight."

"You are my dear girl." Aunt Stella rubbed her leg and groaned. "My dear brave girl."

If only Aunt Stella knew how much her insides quivered. Courage was a strange thing. She could be brave enough to take this trip only because she didn't have the courage to live with the consequences if she didn't.

If courage was one side of a coin, then cowardice was the other.

Chapter 7

Tavish read the telegram then read it again.

"Do you wish to send a reply, sir?" the messenger asked. He was young, probably no more than fourteen or fifteen, with a fine shadow of fuzz along his jawline.

"Respond 'confirmed.'" He dug in his pocket for change.

"Thank you, sir." The messenger accepted the tip then scurried from the warehouse offices.

Tavish dropped into a chair and read the telegram a third time. Tom Manning wanted him to return on the 1:15 canal boat to Circleville. That didn't give him much time.

But it wasn't the last-minute instruction that bothered him. Manning had sent him here to do a job. To stay here until that job was finished. Now he wanted him back at the office? He didn't even mention the shipping mix-up in his message.

What could have happened at home that required Tavish's immediate return?

He wouldn't know until he got there, and he didn't have time to speculate if he was going to be on board the 1:15. Especially since he had to return to the hotel for his bag.

And to check on Stella Sinclair.

He closed his eyes and saw Charity's face in the corridor outside the tiny room where he had helped to move Mrs. Sinclair. Every fiber of his being had longed to take her in his arms. To kiss her tear-dampened cheeks.

While reviewing shipping invoices earlier in the day, he had daydreamed of inviting Charity to dine with him that evening. Though knowing Charity, she wouldn't leave her aunt alone for more than a few minutes at a time. Which meant she wouldn't accept an invitation from Jesse Lowe either.

At least, Tavish hoped not.

He shoved a few papers in his briefcase then hailed a carriage to drive him to the hotel.

As soon as he arrived, he headed down the corridor to the tiny room and knocked on the door.

"Come in," Charity called.

"I hope I'm not intruding," he said as he entered.

He caught each nuance of her changing expression as she zipped from surprise to joy then settled on caution.

"Mr. Dunbar. You're making a habit of showing up when I least expect it."

"Which doesn't mean you aren't welcome." Stella Sinclair sat in the narrow bed, a mountain of pillows supporting her back and a knitted throw covering her legs. "Charity told me how you hid me from spectators after my nasty fall. How can I ever thank you for that kindness?"

"By getting well. Though you already appear much better."

"Nourishing soup and a long nap heals many ills. Never forget that, my young man."

"So your leg is mended?" he dared to tease. His smile faded as he noticed the hat and parasol on the square table. What possible invitation had Jesse Lowe used to tempt Charity away from her aunt?

Mrs. Sinclair's sharp eyes scrutinized his features, and he masked his sudden jealousy with another smile.

"The doctor says it may be weeks before I can travel. Though I have no intention of staying here any longer than necessary."

"You'll stay as long as you must," Charity said. "I'm afraid, Mr. Dunbar, that my aunt is a horrid patient."

"I can't blame her for wanting to be home."

"When do you return?" Mrs. Sinclair asked.

"I'm leaving on the next boat."

"So soon?"

"Mr. Manning, my superior, requested my immediate return." He turned to Charity. "Would you like me to take a message to your father? You could write it out while I retrieve my bag."

"Um. . ." Charity stared at her aunt.

"Providence is watching over us. Charity is taking the same boat."

"Aunt Stella!"

"You're leaving your aunt?"

Charity looked from one to the other, seemingly at a loss for words. Tavish did the same. Charity appeared confused, but Mrs. Sinclair's expression was almost furtive. As if she concealed a secret.

"Certain packages have been entrusted to our care that must be delivered as soon as possible. Charity is accompanying them."

Something didn't seem right, but he was at a loss to map out the underlying currents between the two women. The packages must be important for Charity to leave her aunt in such a state.

At least she wasn't going anywhere with Jesse Lowe.

He squashed the uncharitable thought. As much as he wanted to whisk Charity away, her aunt needed her here.

"If I may be so bold, I can supervise the delivery of the packages."

"That's very kind of you," Mrs. Sinclair said. "But Charity needs to return home. Perhaps you'd be kind enough to serve as her escort."

"I'd be honored. That is, if Miss Charity agrees."

Charity forced a smile. "Since my aunt deems it necessary, yes. I agree."

Not quite a rousing acceptance, but he wouldn't let it dampen his spirits. For the next five or six hours, he and Charity Sinclair would be traveling the Ohio-Erie Canal together. Even if she talked of nothing but hats and gloves and the latest fashions. . .he no longer cared.

They'd be together. Just the two of them.

It'd be a trip he'd never forget.

As soon as the door closed behind Tavish, Charity eased herself onto the side of the bed and faced her aunt. She lowered her voice to a forceful whisper. "How could you have done that? Asking him to be my escort?"

"Did I have a choice?" Aunt Stella tapped Charity's temple. "Think, child."

Charity straightened her posture then sagged as the answer became clear. "You thought it was better for him to know I'd be on the boat now than to find me there later."

"That's right. But I had another reason too."

"I knew it. You're playing matchmaker."

Aunt Stella gave her a quizzical look. "Is that what you thought?"

Charity averted her gaze, suddenly interested in the dust motes that danced in the sunbeam shining through the windowpanes.

"Is it?" Aunt Stella persisted.

"I don't know," Charity muttered.

Aunt Stella rubbed Charity's arm. "Oh my darling. If your heart is inclined to Mr. Dunbar and his to you, I'd dance a jig despite my broken leg. But today is not the day for shooting Cupid's arrows."

Charity flushed at the subtle rebuke. Unfortunately, the danger of her mission didn't stop her heart from yearning for Tavish's attentions.

"What is your other reason?" she asked to divert attention from her romantic foolishness.

When Aunt Stella didn't answer, Charity met her gaze. The soft light in Aunt Stella's eyes and her gentle smile quieted the turmoil swirling deep inside Charity.

"God answered my prayers for your safety," Aunt Stella whispered.

"With Mr. Dunbar?"

Aunt Stella nodded. "It's no coincidence he was summoned home."

Not a coinci—

"Elisha had a coded message from our friend," Aunt Stella continued. "He said you wouldn't be alone."

"You mean—"

"Say nothing to him. He may not know the role he is playing in our scheme."

"Is his boss our. . ."

Before she could finish the sentence, Aunt Stella placed her fingers against Charity's lips. "No more questions."

A knock sounded, then Tavish entered the room. "The hotel carriage is waiting for us. Do you have a bag?"

"It's there." Charity pointed to the valise near the table, and he gripped the handle. She kissed her aunt's soft cheek. "Listen to the doctor. And don't worry about us."

"You're in my prayers. Both of you."

"We'll be fine," Tavish said then grinned. "I promise to *deliver* Miss Charity safely to the post office."

Aunt Charity chuckled while Charity emitted an involuntary snort—most unladylike—at the lame joke.

She retrieved her hat and tied the broad ribbon beneath her chin. "I'll return tomorrow. As early as I can."

"Until then, my darling, poise and polish."

Charity blinked away sudden tears then took Tavish's arm. As they left, she looked back and, for the first time, didn't see her aunt as the vibrant woman who ran the Sinclair household and loved Charity as if she were her own, but as that woman's shadow. Her tousled gray hair, the weakness around her tired eyes and wrinkled mouth, seemed out of place. Charity would wish away the pain and weariness if she could and restore Aunt Stella's youthful vitality.

Tavish bent toward her, and his whisper tickled her ear. "Are you sure you want to leave her?"

She raised her eyes to his, and her heart skipped at the compassion—or was it something more?—his gaze bestowed upon her.

"I don't," she admitted.

"Then why not stay?"

Because I have a greater reason to go.

The thought pounded, loud and vivid, urging her to give it voice. But she couldn't. At least not in those words.

"Because I can't."

He almost said something else, but apparently changed his mind. He didn't like her answer—that much was obvious from the frown that tugged at his lips and the set of his jaw—but he accepted it.

Two days before Tavish said that Moses Freed should have the courage of his convictions and reveal himself. If only he knew Moses Freed walked beside him, and she'd have no courage at all if not for his presence.

＋・—・＋

During the carriage ride to the loading dock, Tavish tried to think of something, anything, to say to lift Charity's spirits. But nothing brilliant came to mind so he stayed silent. When they arrived, she graced him with a tiny smile as he lifted her from the carriage. Her waist within his hands, her hands upon his shoulders—their closeness felt right.

As if she belonged to him, and he belonged to her.

After a moment's hesitation, they separated. He carried both their bags to the dock, and Charity walked beside him.

This Charity was different than the Charity who presided over the post office with charm and nonsense. This Charity seemed an imperfect reflection of the Charity he knew.

Except it was the other way around.

The Charity he knew was an imperfect reflection of this Charity.

The girl, no, the woman beside him carried herself with depth and maturity while consumed with worry for her aunt.

In a flash of clarity, he realized he'd known this Charity existed all along. That buried knowledge, that sense of something false in her manner, had been the source of his frustration in their previous encounters.

But why the pretense?

Because the Sinclairs had secrets. How often had he sensed unspoken words passing between niece and aunt, between daughter and father?

Did their secret have anything to do with their reluctance to renovate their residence?

Somehow it all tied together.

They turned a corner and the canal glimmered ahead of them. At least the weather was perfect, and hopefully they'd have no delays between here and Circleville.

"The ticket office is over there," he said.

"I already have my ticket." She gazed toward the canal. "The water is so calm and serene. Why isn't life like that?"

"Would you want it to be? I mean day after day without any excitement?"

"Perhaps not."

The sad smile that barely lifted her lips zapped his heart. Something besides her aunt's health bothered her. Was it something to do with the family secret?

"What troubles you?"

The daring question surprised him as much as it did her. He'd never have believed Charity's transformation if he hadn't seen it with his own eyes.

She looked to the north, toward home, and her expression was hidden from him. Her shoulders squared, and her chin lifted then fell as a long breath shifted her posture. She faced him, tucked both her hands around his arm, and peered at him beneath long dark lashes.

"I'm scared stiff about Aunt Stella." She spoke, her voice warm and soft, in a different register. "But she's under the best of care, and I shouldn't be carrying on like a lamb that's been taken from her mama. Especially when the day is so beautiful."

Her gaze traveled again to the canal. "It is a beautiful day, isn't it?"

"Beautiful." His voice sounded calm, but his insides churned. This was the familiar Charity, but he no longer believed her to be false.

There weren't two Charitys. Only a chameleon—complex and intriguing—and he wanted more than anything to unravel her intricacies.

◆•——·——•◆

Charity waited on the platform while Tavish went inside the office to purchase his ticket. As if idly passing the time, she moved among the crates yet to be loaded into the boat's storage hold. Three crates were addressed to *General Delivery, Post Office, Circleville, Ohio.*

She had no idea what the two smaller ones contained. They were identical in shape and size, and each could easily hold a stack of folded blankets. The larger crate, though—she knew exactly what, *who*, it contained.

A near irresistible urge to linger near the crate, to reassure the girl safely hidden inside, swept over her. But she didn't dare. All she could do was pray that this particular crate remained unopened until it was inside the post office.

Her heart fluttered, beating against the wall of her chest. They should all be on board soon, and once they were, she could relax. This was the dangerous time.

Tavish came out of the ticket office and she hurried to join him, so he wouldn't notice her interest in any particular crate.

"There was a delay downriver," he said. "That's why they're still loading. But we can go ahead and board."

"I hope we can get seats beneath the awning. In the rush and bother of getting Aunt Stella settled, I completely went away without my parasol. Can you believe I'd do such a foolish thing?"

Tavish stared at her, his eyes boring into hers. She blinked then steadied her gaze.

"No. I don't believe Charity Sinclair would do such a thing. On the other hand, Charity Sinclair probably would."

"I don't understand."

"Neither do I." He held out his arm. "Shall we?"

She tucked her hand within the crook of his arm while puzzling over his words. Though what did they matter? He could say whatever he wanted as long as he didn't find out she was smuggling a stowaway.

Chapter 8

Tavish estimated about thirty to thirty-five passengers were on the boat when it finally left Chillicothe behind. A little more than half its capacity. He and Charity sat at a table beneath the awning with two older couples who apparently knew each other. They tried to draw Charity into their conversation, but she'd exhausted her playful banter as soon as they boarded. Since then, she'd hardly said a word. Instead she'd stared at the boarding passengers as they sauntered across the plank.

Once, when he tapped her arm to get her attention, she'd jumped then tried to deflect her reaction with a nervous giggle.

Now that they were on their way, she seemed less tense, as if she'd held her breath waiting for a giant balloon to pop that had instead deflated.

She greeted the others as they introduced themselves, hiding her distaste for their exuberant conversation beneath a polite veneer.

"Your aunt will be fine," he murmured.

Charity's eyes held a wistful expression as she stared past him to the surrounding countryside. "You are an extraordinarily kind man."

At that moment, he'd have traveled to the moon and back for her. What was it about this woman that did such strange things to him? Sometimes he wanted to never speak to her again, and other times, like now, he wanted to take her in his arms and never let go.

She faced him, a tentative smile teasing her lips. He wanted to trace their shape with his fingertips, but an unexpected insight stopped him. Despite all the time they'd spent together today, she'd not been *with* him.

Until now.

He held her gaze, lost in the deep brown of her eyes.

"Let's move," she whispered.

Caught by the spell she cast upon him, he could refuse her nothing. "Would you please excuse us?" he said to the others at the table. He stood and Charity, beaming her society smile, rose with him.

"I can't blame you for wanting her all to yourself," one gentleman said. "At your age, I'd do the same." The others in his party laughed with him, their merriment following Tavish and Charity as they strolled arm in arm to the rail.

The June sun beat upon them, and the cool breeze unloosened tendrils of Charity's hair from beneath her bonnet. She didn't seem to care. Instead she lifted her face to the breeze and closed her eyes. The tension in her cheeks and jaw slowly faded.

Tavish mimicked Charity, closing his eyes and letting the breeze flow about him. The scent of honeysuckle teased his nostrils. The rise and fall of conversation faded as he focused on the slap of the waves hitting the boat and the notes whistled by the boy driving the mule on the towpath. His thoughts stilled as his mind drifted into daydream.

"What are you thinking?" Charity asked.

Her voice startled him, and heat warmed his neck. "Nothing you'd be interested in."

"Allow me to decide."

"Look at that young boy. He spends every day outdoors with no cares or worries. He walks along the canal, tending the mule, whistling his songs."

"You envy him?"

"There are days when I wouldn't mind trading places with him."

"Given the opportunity, he'd probably be glad to make that trade."

"To sit at a desk surrounded by four walls and stacks of papers?" Tavish humphed. "I wouldn't be so sure."

"Perhaps not on a day like today. But when winter comes and he's walking the path without a sturdy pair of boots and a warm coat, would you trade places with him then?"

"Why wouldn't he have boots and a coat?"

"Some of the captains have a stone where a heart should be." Charity pushed a wispy strand of hair behind her ear. "They withhold the pay. Most of these boys are orphans and have no one to stand up for them."

"I didn't know."

"Too many people don't."

"You did."

"If a church is the soul of a community, the post office is its heart. My father and I hear about things that others don't." She leaned closer, the rhythm of her voice lulling him into intimacy. "We hear secrets, and we never share them. Bad news. Good news. Weeping and rejoicing."

Her words seeped into Tavish's spirit. How had he missed the deep inner beauty of this woman for so long?

Because she hides it.

But why? Did she think he was beneath her? What did she see when she looked at him?

His gaze veered to the boy. "I idealized what he does. How he lives. I never thought of his hardships."

"But you're thinking of them now."

"Yes."

Her eyes sparkled with amusement. "On a day like this, when the sun is shining and the honeysuckle is in bloom, I'd trade places with him too."

"Then you forgive my thoughtlessness?"

"You're not thoughtless." Her fingers brushed his jacket, as if removing non-existent dust. "I forgive your ignorance."

He wrapped his hand around hers and released his held breath when she didn't pull away.

"Why?"

Her eyes told him she understood the unspoken part of his question. Then their light dimmed, pressing a leaden weight against his chest, and she didn't answer.

Charity slid her hand from Tavish's grasp and sat on an empty bench near the front of the boat.

He'd asked her *why* and she'd instinctively known the intent of that tiny three-letter word. Not "Why do you forgive my ignorance?" but "Why are you different?"

She didn't have the words to answer that question.

Perhaps she shouldn't have confronted him with the plight of the young orphans who lived their lives according to the whims of the weather, the canal, and their captains. She could have played along with his "idealizing."

But she'd wanted to open his eyes to a deeper truth.

He'd seen the boy strolling along the path, whistling his tunes, and named it bliss. No thought was given to the boy's welfare, his dreams, or aspirations. By looking beyond the idyllic scene, he'd better understand the harsh realities these orphans faced.

But his eyes had been opened to another truth too. Never again could she fool him with her dilettante facade. He'd seen beneath her pretense, but she still had secrets to keep.

And an identity to protect.

Tavish didn't dare move. Charity's head rested against his shoulder, and her soft breathing added to the other rhythms of the moment. It was as if God Himself had lulled her to sleep with a lullaby.

He grunted at the fanciful notion.

Yet he couldn't shake the image.

Funny, how she made him see things as he'd never seen them before. What she didn't know was his idealized vision of the tow boy's life was nothing new. When he was younger, the future seemed to hold nothing but adventure for a wanderer who gave little thought to food and shelter.

Except that vagabond dream had been built on a falsehood. He'd never known hunger or lacked protection from winter's blistering chill. He'd never worried about the quality of his boots.

His dream of traveling west to the Mississippi River and south to the tip of Florida had been possible because he had the means—back then—to stay in hotels. He could hire a coach when he tired of walking.

But the dream ended when his father gambled away the last of the family's fortune then disappeared rather than face the consequences.

When Uncle Ned dictated he find a profession, Tavish didn't have the courage to hold on to his dream.

A world of lines, angles, and circles seemed the perfect antidote to vague visions of exploration. Though truth be told, he probably would have become an architect even if his father had held on to the money.

The dream of travel, the planning of routes and trails—that had been the fun of the venture.

The commotion began at the back of the boat, a slight murmur that barely entered his consciousness. But like a wave, it swept forward and grew. The passengers behind him stood, straining to see what all the fuss was about. Tavish tried to look over his shoulder without disturbing Charity's sleep, but he could see nothing except the backs of the other passengers.

Another sound, growing stronger each second, entered his awareness—the galloping of horses along the towpath.

"Charity," he whispered, slightly moving his shoulder while supporting her head. "Charity. Something is happening."

Her eyes batted open, and her cheeks turned pink. "Was I sleeping? I didn't mean to." She straightened then looked around as if getting her bearings.

"Just napping." Tavish stood on the bench for a better view of the path behind the boat.

The galloping came closer, punctuated by shouts from the riders. The tow boy halted his mule, and the tripper extended his pole to keep the boat centered as it drifted to a serene stop.

"What's going on?" shouted one of the passengers.

The captain walked along the rail, his focus on the riders.

Charity grabbed Tavish's arm and climbed onto the bench beside him.

"Who are they?" Her voice quivered.

"I don't know."

Were they about to be robbed? He'd heard stories of stagecoach robberies out beyond the Mississippi but never a canal boat holdup. But thieves could probably get rich from the passengers. The women wore jewels; the men had money. Hard to tell what was in the storage hold.

"We have to do something," Charity said.

"About what?"

She averted her gaze and drew in her bottom lip.

The storage hold.

"What's in your crates?"

"I don't. . . I can't. . ." She lowered her eyes.

He stared at her and tried to imagine what could be so valuable. "Do those riders want your crates?"

"I pray not."

Her voice was barely above a whisper, as if she spoke more to herself than to him. Perhaps he hadn't heard her correctly. Yet he knew he had.

"The best thing to do is to let them take whatever they want. Perhaps then they'll be on their way without harming anyone on board."

"You think they're robbers?" A nearby passenger stepped onto the bench beside them. "This will make an interesting tale for the campfire."

"We're about to find out," Tavish replied.

Beside him, Charity stood deathly still, the tension obvious in her shoulders. She seemed unable to take her eyes from the riders. The horses neared the edge of the canal, and the lead rider focused his gaze on the captain.

"Put out the plank," he shouted.

The captain turned toward the passengers. "Calm down, everyone. That's Sheriff Lem Hodges."

"What could he want?" Tavish asked.

Charity didn't answer, but all color had left her face and she nearly lost her balance. Tavish steadied her, but she didn't seem to notice his presence.

"What business you got stopping this boat?" the captain shouted.

"There's property on board that shouldn't be there."

"What are you talking about, Lem?"

"Put out the plank so I can come aboard."

"You can't search my boat."

Sheriff Hodges slid his revolver from its holster. "This here says I can."

Charity stepped from the bench and collapsed on the seat. Tavish jumped down and took her hands in his. "Please tell me, Charity. What's in those crates?"

"Pray with me?"

"Pray what?"

She hesitated a moment. "For blinded eyes." It was more of a question than a statement. He sat beside her, still holding her hands. Propriety said to let go, but he couldn't. And from her grip, she didn't want him to.

◆–•––•◆

I shouldn't hold his hand. What would Aunt Stella say?

But Charity couldn't let go.

Fear pulsated against her spine, within her stomach, and around her knees. Somehow, she had to conquer it.

Give me strength, Lord. For whatever happens next, give me courage.

Sina Anne's bravery had given her the strength to leave the only home she'd ever known for a promised land she could only imagine. Charity couldn't fail her.

Suddenly she thought of Jochebed, whose courage gave her the strength to entrust her precious child to the Nile River. Moses' mother had faced her fears for her son's safety, and God rewarded her bravery in His own miraculous way.

I have a secret too, Father. Not a baby, but a teenage girl who needs to be hidden from the slave hunters just as Moses needed to be hidden from the Egyptians who would have taken his life. Blind these men's eyes, Father, I beg You.

Her prayer was interrupted by Sheriff Hodges boarding the boat. He quietly exchanged a few words with the captain, but Charity couldn't make out what they were saying. From the captain's posture and demeanor, Charity guessed he wasn't happy with whatever the sheriff was saying to him. The whispered argument continued for a few moments, then Hodges, a big man who had the look of someone who never met a fight he didn't like, turned to the passengers.

The captain stepped in front of him.

"Ladies and gentlemen, these here men want to search the cargo hold. They promise to be quick, so we can be on our way as soon as they're done."

"What are you looking for, Sheriff?" someone asked.

"Never you mind that." Hodges motioned to his deputies then followed them to the hold.

Blind their eyes.

Charity stared after them until they disappeared. She turned around and involuntarily gasped as Gerald Marsh approached her.

"Miss Sinclair," he said smoothly as he gazed around the boat. "Where is your aunt?"

"She's not with me."

"Surely you're not traveling alone."

"She's traveling with me." Tavish extended his hand. "Tavish Dunbar."

Gerald ignored Tavish. "I'm disappointed Mrs. Sinclair isn't with you."

"She had an accident." Charity put as much sweetness and confidence in her voice as she could manage. "It was impossible for her to travel."

"I hope the injury isn't too grave."

"Thank you for your concern."

"I'm surprised you would leave her."

"I have business at home." Charity tucked her hand in the crook of Tavish's elbow. "Mr. Dunbar was kind enough to be my companion."

Gerald's gaze traveled over Tavish as if to take his measure. "How kind of Mr. Dunbar."

Charity glanced toward the entrance to the hold. If only she could have followed the men down the stairs. Perhaps it wasn't too late. Though that might have made the situation worse.

"What does the sheriff expect to find?" Tavish asked.

"You don't know?"

"How would I?"

Gerald scrutinized Charity, but she refused to let him intimidate her. His eyes grew cold, and a shiver raced up her spine.

"My dear Miss Charity. Did you not tell your beau the true purpose of your trip?"

Her first inclination, to deny Tavish was her beau, would give Gerald a victory—a small one, but a victory nonetheless. But neither would she give him the satisfaction of responding to his question.

"I didn't know Mr. Dunbar was in town until this morning."

"Your innocent act may fool others, but it doesn't fool me. Now if you'll excuse me, I must join the sheriff."

Several moments ticked by, each one seeming like a lifetime. Charity could hardly breathe, and fear muddled her thoughts.

Finally Marsh emerged from the hold, a smug smile marring his features. Charity's heart sank as the sheriff followed him, dragging Sina Anne by her arm. Straw stuck out from her hair and clung to her clothes. Her eyes held the same fear as her brother's the day before.

"We got what we came for, Captain." Sheriff Hodges motioned one of the deputies to remove Sina Anne from the boat.

Marsh brushed dirt from his hands and pointed at Charity. "This lady is her benefactor, Sheriff. Arrest her."

The sheriff took in Charity's appearance and frowned. "You can't expect me to arrest the likes of her."

"I absolutely expect you to do your job. Or you might find you don't have it much longer."

"Wait a minute." Tavish stepped between the two men. "What proof do you have of Miss Sinclair's involvement?"

"Where did you find my property?" Marsh asked the sheriff.

"Inside a crate."

"The address on the crate?"

Sheriff Hodges shifted uncomfortably. "The post office in Circleville."

Marsh gave a superior smile. "Sheriff, it's my pleasure to introduce you to Miss Charity Sinclair. Her father is the postmaster in Circleville."

"That's hardly proof," Tavish cut in.

"It's enough to make her suspect." Marsh glared at Tavish then at the sheriff. "Do your job."

"You have your slave—," Sheriff Hodges said, but Marsh cut him off before he could say any more.

"And you have your culprit. Arrest her."

"You can't," Tavish insisted.

"I don't have a choice." Sheriff Hodges glowered and his eyes narrowed to dark slits. "I'll arrest you too, if you interfere."

Tavish turned to Charity. "I'll come with you—"

"No." The sheriff glanced at the other passengers. "No one leaves this boat."

"I won't let you take her without me."

The captain stepped close to Tavish. "This isn't the time, son."

Charity clasped his hands before he could respond. She couldn't let him be arrested too. "I'll be fine." She paused to steady her quavering voice.

"Charity. . ."

She blinked away tears. "Whatever my fate, hers will be worse."

"I can assure you of that," Marsh said.

His words, his demeanor, galvanized Charity's fear. She didn't know if she had the courage to trade places with Sina Anne even if that were possible. But guilt added to her fear—guilt because what she said was true. Imprisonment would be awful, but no one would dare lay a hand on her. No one would beat her. The same couldn't be said for Sina Anne.

The pressure of Tavish's fingers brought her attention back to him.

"What can I do?" he asked softly.

For a tiny sliver of time, the world around her disappeared. The boat. Gerald Marsh. The captain.

Only she and Tavish existed, two people apart from everything else around them.

"Get word to my father. And pray."

He nodded, as if he could think of nothing else to say.

Sheriff Hodges gestured toward the plank. "Let's go."

A knot lodged in Charity's throat making it impossible for her to speak.

She preceded the sheriff across the plank. When they reached the towpath, she turned as the plank was withdrawn and the tripper pushed against the bank with his pole.

Tavish disappeared among the throng of passengers then reappeared at the back rail. She held his gaze until the sheriff put her on his horse and they galloped away.

Chapter 9

Tavish clenched the back rail of the boat, unable to take his eyes off the horses as they galloped south. He should never have let them take Charity. The horses veered slightly to the west, following a path through a stand of trees to the main road. When he couldn't see Charity any longer, Tavish threaded his way through the other passengers, ignoring their questions and comments until he found the captain.

"I have to get off this boat," Tavish said.

"You heard Hodges."

"Stop the boat."

"So you can what? Swim to shore? Then walk back to Chillicothe?"

"I can't... She needs me." *I need her.*

The captain pressed his lips together then seemed to make a decision. "We're almost to Thacker Locks. Maybe you can beg, borrow, or buy a horse there."

"I'll never catch up to them."

"Best if you don't."

"No, I've got to—"

"Use your head, boy. You know where they're going. From what Marsh said, your lady friend is going to jail. Least till her hearing."

Tavish lowered his head. Even the thought of Charity in a cell made him nauseous.

"It's the other girl you should be worried about."

Tavish absorbed the criticism. The captain was right. Charity might be fined, but he doubted any judge would imprison her. The girl, now that Marsh had her again—he couldn't stomach what might happen to her.

Charity's last request was for him to pray. He hadn't done much of that in his life. Growing up, he'd had everything he needed. After his father's bankruptcy, well, it had seemed unsporting to call on God then. Besides, he'd managed fine with his Uncle Ned's help. He learned to read blueprints, to understand the language of construction, and found he had a talent for architecture.

But now? He couldn't protect Charity or the girl from Marsh's vengeance. No one could.

They were alone. He was alone.

Yes, he would do as Charity asked. He would pray.

◆•————•◆

Charity sat on the bunk in the Chillicothe jail cell, her feet tucked beneath her skirts. Moments after the door clanged shut behind her, a mouse had skittered from one corner to another. She stifled the squeal rising from her throat, but her feet weren't touching that floor.

Though the bunk wasn't much better. The thin straw mattress provided little comfort, and she didn't want to know about any bugs scurrying in the straw beneath the threadbare ticking.

Her body ached from the ride. The saddle horn had pressed against her knee while she jostled against the sheriff's chest. She shuddered at the memory of his sweat soaking the back of her dress. When her hat flew off, he refused to stop for it, and now her hair hung in untidy strands around her face.

Gerald Marsh, riding with Sina Anne in front of him, had set the pace. Charity didn't know why he'd been in such a hurry. Thanks to the Bloodhound Law, no one could take the girl from him.

Sina Anne had no rights, even though she was on free soil. Before the Fugitive Law passed, a jury would have decided her fate. And the sheriff wouldn't have been forced to help Marsh with her recapture.

That law had changed everything.

Charity leaned against the wooden wall and silently prayed. Prayed the sheriff had delivered her message to Aunt Stella. Prayed Aunt Stella had informed Jesse or Elisha Lowe of her plight. Prayed for Sina Anne and a plan to rescue her from Gerald Marsh.

Time passed, marked by the lengthening beam of sunlight entering through a high window. The low hum of voices filtered through the closed door leading to the office. One voice rose above the others.

Tavish.

Elation bubbled inside her, and a silent prayer of thanks ascended to the heavens.

A moment later, Sheriff Hodges opened the door. "Someone's here to see you. Should I send him in?"

"Please." She rose from the bed, no longer concerned about the mouse, and shook out her skirts.

"Stay there." He unlocked the cell door, returned to the outer door, and gestured.

Tavish bounded into the cell and grasped her hands. "Are you all right?" he asked.

"I can't believe it." Only her deep-rooted sense of propriety prevented her from throwing her arms around his neck. "How did you get here?"

"Bought a horse at Thacker Lock and here I am." His warm smile chased away her lingering fear. "It's a long story, but it ends with you leaving this place."

"Now?"

"Soon. Marsh is insisting on a hefty fine."

She wanted to ask how hefty. Papa and Aunt Stella had savings, but would it be enough? The law called for fines of $1000. She doubted they could pay half that. Had Tavish...?

"As soon as you're released, we have to leave town."

"Can't I see Aunt Stella?"

"Hodges wants us gone so there's no more trouble with Marsh."

"But—"

"I talked to your aunt. She wants you to go with me." He pulled her into an embrace. Surprised, she involuntarily stiffened then let herself rest against him. "We're going home."

Home.

Such a lovely word. But her bliss lasted only a heartbeat or two.

Sina Anne was going home too. But the word meant something vastly different for her.

"I can't," Charity whispered.

"We don't have a choice."

"They haven't had time to reach the river. Not yet."

"Marsh hasn't left town. Apparently, he wants to be at your hearing."

"Then we still have time."

Tavish tilted her chin till their eyes met. "If we're caught trying to free her, we'll go to jail."

"For a while." The law said six months. She didn't know how well she could handle confinement, but what was a few months compared to a lifetime? "I can endure imprisonment as long as Sina Anne is free."

"We could fail."

"At least we'd have tried."

"We need a plan."

Another man might have argued with her. Or flat out told her no. But Charity sensed Tavish understood the consequences of regret. It was a burden neither of them wanted to carry.

Sheriff Hodges appeared in the doorway and gestured for them to join him. Charity preceded Tavish from the cell, and he rested his palm on the small of her back. Elisha Lowe waited for her in the office. He scrutinized her appearance.

"Were you ill-treated?"

Embarrassment burned her cheeks as she fussed with her loosened strands.

What a sight she must be! And Tavish hadn't said a word.

"She was taken against her will and forced to ride with him." Tavish pointed at the sheriff. "Of course she was ill-treated."

Elisha glared at Sheriff Hodges. "You gave her no water? No soap?"

"This isn't a hotel," the sheriff grumbled.

"Miss Sinclair must be allowed a few moments to herself before she sees the judge."

"There's a washstand and mirror back there." Sheriff Hodges tilted his head toward a small anteroom. "She's welcome to it."

As Charity walked past the sheriff's desk, a bound booklet with the name Moses Freed emblazoned across the cover caught her attention. She flipped through the pages then cast a glance at Elisha Lowe. He deliberately averted his gaze.

"Where did you get this?" she asked the sheriff.

"From Marsh."

"Where did he get it?"

"One of those crates addressed to the post office. Found these under a blanket."

"They're still on the boat?"

"Naw. Marsh emptied them overboard then stuck hay meant for the mules inside. Said it'd be a fine surprise for whoever opened it."

Charity couldn't help smiling as she turned toward Tavish. "Our prayers have been answered."

"How?" he asked.

"I've got a plan."

◆— —◆

Charity stood before Judge William Langford, hands clasped in front of her, as Gerald Marsh presented his evidence. He accused her of interfering with his efforts to reclaim his personal property and of treason for breaking the provisions of the Fugitive Slave Act.

Tavish and Elisha sat at the defense table. Jesse Lowe and the sheriff were the only spectators.

"Your only recourse, Your Honor," Marsh said, "is to find Miss Sinclair guilty and demand the strictest penalties for her action. Nothing else will stop these abolitionists from their misguided tactics and preserve law and order between the states."

Judge Langford cast his somber gaze on Charity. "Have you prepared a response, Miss Sinclair?"

"I have, Your Honor."

"Proceed."

Charity glanced at Tavish for support then took a calming breath. "Mr.

Marsh broke federal postal regulations when he opened a crate addressed to the Circleville post office."

Marsh's face reddened. "To retrieve stolen property."

"I'm not talking about the crate where Sina Anne Webster was hidden." Charity retrieved the Moses Freed booklet from the defense table. "He unlawfully opened the crate containing these booklets and destroyed most of them."

"That's abolitionist literature." Marsh's voice practically screeched with barely controlled rage.

"Which is free speech and still protected by the Bill of Rights, is it not, Your Honor?"

"It is, Miss Sinclair."

"I wish to file formal charges against Gerald Marsh for tampering with mail while it was under the purview of the United States Postal Service."

"You can't do that." Marsh faced the bench, palms spread out. "Judge Langford, she doesn't have the authority."

Charity returned to the defense table, and Elisha handed her a piece of paper.

"Your Honor, my father, Grover Sinclair, is the duly authorized postmaster of the Circleville Post Office. The crate in question was addressed to General Delivery at that specific post office. This telegram is from my father. In it he advises his attorney and mine, Elisha Lowe, Esquire, that I am acting on his behalf in this case."

The judge gestured with his fingers, and Charity handed him the telegram. He read it then stared at Marsh. "This is a serious charge. Did you do as the young lady claims?"

"It's no more serious than what she did."

"I'll ask you one more time. Mr. Marsh, did you destroy the contents of that crate?"

"I prefer not to answer that question."

Elisha stood and cleared his throat. "Your Honor, on behalf of my clients and with your permission, may I propose an agreement that could resolve these matters and keep both Miss Sinclair and Mr. Marsh from prison?"

"Please."

"Postmaster Sinclair will not file charges if Mr. Marsh agrees to release Sina Anne Webster and her brother David Webster into his daughter's custody, to no longer pursue them, and to no longer consider these two individuals as his property."

"What of their mother?" Marsh's voice dripped with contempt.

"Neither Miss Sinclair nor I have any knowledge of their mother's whereabouts."

"That's convenient."

"And true." Elisha graced Marsh with a confident smile.

"Anything else?" the judge asked.

"Against my advice," Elisha continued, "Miss Sinclair will accept whatever punishment Your Honor deems just as long as Sina Anne and her brother are freed."

Judge Langford fastened his gaze on Charity. With Aunt Stella's oft-repeated reminder flowing through her—*"poise and polish, my dear girl"*—she didn't waver under the judge's strict scrutiny.

After a long pause, his voice cracked the tense silence. "The fine is one thousand dollars. No jail time."

"We accept, Your Honor," Elisha said quickly.

"Shall I order your arrest, Mr. Marsh? Or do you accept Postmaster Sinclair's terms?"

"This is theft, Your Honor."

"Destroying the contents of that crate was theft."

Marsh's eyes narrowed as his gaze traveled from Charity to Elisha and back to Charity. His dour expression turned smug. "I accept. On one condition."

"Which is?" Judge Langford asked.

Marsh stretched out his arm and pointed his long finger at Charity. "She knows Moses Freed's true identity."

Elisha took a step forward. "What makes you think so?"

"If she doesn't," Marsh reasoned, "either the sender or recipient of the crate does. I want that man's name."

Charity spoke before Elisha or the judge could intervene. "Sina Anne and David will go free if I tell you?"

"They will."

"I'll give you the name. But not until we're all on the morning canal boat to Circleville."

"Congratulations, Miss Charity," Marsh said smugly. "You've saved yourself and my slaves. But 'Moses Freed' will be exposed."

Charity pressed her fingers against the sudden knot in her throat then relaxed as an indescribable calm eased the loss. The articles written under her pseudonym hadn't overturned the Fugitive Law, but the words she'd penned had given her the courage to stand against evil.

Moses Freed would write no more.

But Charity Sinclair would never be silenced.

Chapter 10

Charity adjusted the cushion beneath Aunt Stella's leg, which was propped on a bench in front of her chair. "Are you sure you're comfortable?"

"Stop fussing over me and join your young man. I'm fine."

Charity followed Aunt Stella's gaze to the rail of the boat. Tavish had his back to her, his focus on the men standing on the loading platform. Elisha and Jesse Lowe, Judge Langford, and Gerald Marsh.

"He's not my young man."

"Isn't he?"

Not as long as he receives lilac envelopes from Syracuse.

Charity kissed her aunt's cheek. "I'm glad you're with us. But you can't stop me worrying."

"With everything that happened, I couldn't stay behind."

"I know."

The captain shouted a command, and a moment later the boat moved forward. Charity gave an encouraging smile to Sina Anne and David. The siblings sat close together, their shoulders tense despite all the reassurance they'd been given.

After the hearing, Elisha had worked out the details of their arrangement with Judge Langford and Marsh. Sina Anne and David spent the night at the hotel in the room next to Aunt Stella's, but Charity doubted either one had gotten much sleep. They wanted—they needed—their mother.

Elisha hadn't lied to Judge Hodges. Neither he nor Charity knew where she was. But others did. In a few more days, the family would be safely reunited.

"Charity," Tavish called from the rail. "It's time."

She joined him and raised her parasol to shield her eyes from the sun.

"The name." Marsh's voice boomed across the narrow strip of water separating the shore from the boat.

At Charity's nod, Elisha drew a folded piece of paper from his suit pocket and handed it to Marsh. Even at this distance, she sensed his gloating. He unfolded the paper, then his head jerked up. His stunned expression turned to an angry glare.

Charity smiled and waved as the boat floated farther away from the landing. "It says 'Charity Margaret Sinclair,'" she told Tavish.

"You're Moses Freed?"

"I am."

"So that's your family secret." His eyes narrowed, and she sensed his puzzlement. "But that doesn't explain your reluctance. . ." He held her gaze then nodded. "I should have known. The post office is a stop on the Under—"

She placed her hand against his lips. "Shh. Someone might hear you."

"Do you have any other secrets I should know about?"

A flurry of butterflies unsettled Charity's stomach. She couldn't postpone asking him any longer. "Do you?"

"I don't think so."

She stared at the shoreline where honeysuckle edged a stand of trees and tumbled down the slope to the towpath. For a moment, she breathed in the sun-warmed fragrance of the tangled vines.

"Charity? What is it?"

"I can't say without breaking postal regulations."

"Can you give me a hint?"

She lifted her chin and met his gaze. "Your correspondent has lovely taste in stationery."

"My correspondent? You mean my cousin?"

The butterflies in Charity's stomach rested in a tight knot. "She's your cousin?"

He drew her into an embrace and bent his head toward hers. "You were jealous."

"Only curious."

"Um-hm."

The butterflies danced as Charity basked in the delightful sweetness of love's first kiss.

Chapter 11

Charity and Tavish stood at the rail of the canal boat waving goodbye to Aunt Stella and Papa. They'd said their vows that morning and, after a reception in the gardens of the never-renovated post office, were on the first leg of their honeymoon trip.

The newlyweds planned to travel north on the Ohio-Erie Canal to Lake Erie then take the Erie Canal to Syracuse where Charity would meet Uncle Ned and his daughter, Tavish's cousin with the lovely taste in stationery.

But before heading east, they intended to take a slight detour to visit a small homestead in Canada where the Webster family lived free from bondage.

"We have a long journey ahead of us," Tavish said.

"We do," Charity murmured. A journey by boat. A journey into the future. A journey of two hearts.

Acknowledgments

I knew next-to-nothin' about the Erie Canal system when I was asked to join this collection. Several people answered my plea for help on a Facebook thread. Thanks to everyone who responded, and especially to:

Robyn Michaels, who shared newspaper articles and other links on odd and unusual events related to the Ohio canals; and

Shirley Bandy Cassidy, who shared historic photos of Circleville after I chose that small town—where my mom's extended family held Christmas potluck dinners during my growing-up years—as my setting.

When I got lost near the end, I called on my sister, Hebe Alexander, for brainstorming help. After a ninety-six-minute conversation and a near-sleepless night, all the details fell into place at exactly 3:39 a.m. (I know, because I checked the time.)

Special thanks too, to Sally Roach, a vivacious college student who didn't get weirded out when I tapped her on the shoulder, introduced myself as a novelist, and asked to take her photo. I've never done anything like that before—I rarely even "cast" my characters—but I noticed Sally's spark at a missions banquet and immediately saw her as Charity Sinclair.

A hug and thank-you to Rose McCauley for thinking of me when she got the go-ahead for this collection; to my fabulous agent, Tamela Hancock Murray, for her calm encouragement and guidance; and to the terrific team at Barbour.

Love always to my kids and their kids: Bethany and Justin Jett; Jillian and Jacob Lancour; Nate Donley; Jeremy, Jedidiah, and Josiah Jett; and Kaydi-Paris and Presley Lancour. You all add shine to my sun and tie the bow on my rain. (LOL!)

Johnnie Alexander is an award-winning author who creates characters you want to meet and imagines stories you won't forget. She writes contemporaries, historicals, and cozy mysteries, serves on the executive boards of Serious Writer, Inc. and the Mid-South Christian Writers Conference, co-hosts a weekly online show called Writers Chat, and interviews inspirational authors for Novelists Unwind. She also teaches at writers conferences and for Serious Writer Academy. Johnnie lives in Oklahoma with Griff, her happy-go-lucky collie, and Rugby, her raccoon-treeing papillon. Connect with her at johnnie-alexander .com and other social media sites via https://linktr.ee/johnniealexndr.

Pressing On

by Rose Allen McCauley

Dedication

To our youngest daughter and her husband, Amanda McCauley Thornberry
and Daniel Thornberry. My Amanda did become a dentist,
and Daniel once worked on a boat (a shrimp boat in Florida)
and now owns two businesses and two farms. Love you both!

Acknowledgments

Special thanks to:
My husband, Chester, who reads all my manuscripts aloud with me
to help find my mistakes and make my stories the best they can be.
Tamela Hancock Murray, for always believing in
me and guiding my writing career.
The other authors in this collection who joined me in this endeavor. I couldn't
have done it without your encouragement and help along the way. And Joy
Liddy who also encouraged and helped in the plotting of my story when
I first began. All the people at Barbour, especially Becky
Germany and our editor Ellen Tarver.
My critiquers who made this story much better than my original version—
Sherri Wilson Johnson and Kristy Horine. I thank God for both of you!
Great research help from the people of Zoar, Ohio, many of whom are
descendants of the original Zoarites and continue their tradition of helping
others: Steve Shonk, Diana Culler, Chuck and Ruth Knack, and Gayle
and Joe, the owners of the lovely Zoar School Inn where we stayed
while there (the food is great too!). Any mistakes are my own!
Many friends who pray for my writing. And ACFW for all the
writing instruction I've garnered over the years and all the
friendships that will last throughout eternity!
Most of all to my heavenly Father for giving me the privilege of writing
and now for letting my seventh story be published! I pray my words,
both written and spoken, will always bring Him the glory
and draw my readers closer to Him.

*I press toward the mark for the prize of the high
calling of God in Christ Jesus.*
PHILIPPIANS 3:14

Chapter 1

Zoar, Ohio
November 1856

Amanda Mack edged her way toward a window of the Assembly House to see if the rain still held off. Since this was her first day this week not on duty at the Zoar Hotel, she hoped to receive an outside task. "Miss Mack."

Her head snapped to attention at the sound of the trustee's voice. Mr. Grotzinger nodded in her direction. "You will be making the trip to the canal with Leo Kern to drop off some of our wares and pick up items our store needs."

Thank You, Father. Her heart fluttered at the answer to her silent prayer.

When all the jobs had been assigned, Leo Kern approached her. "Are you ready to go, Amanda?"

"*Da.* A trip to the canal sounds wonderful."

Mr. Kern handed her the list. "I thought you might want to look this over while I drive." She smiled at her friend Sabina's father.

He helped her into the loaded wagon parked in front of the store, and they were soon on their way.

Her mind roamed over the list. Lots of items, but the order for ten bolts of fabric caught her interest the most. Would all the women be sewing new dresses for this fall? Would there be any choice of fabrics?

They crossed the bridge and headed toward the dock, arriving in less than ten minutes. They couldn't see the boat yet. Mr. Kern helped her down. She walked around, enjoying the scenery while he tended to the horses.

Soon he called, "The canal boat's in sight."

Amanda stood as close as she dared to watch it dock. *Much more interesting than cleaning the hotel.*

As the boat approached, she saw a few passengers milling about on deck. The people unloaded first and climbed into a buggy to take them to the Zoar Hotel.

The captain of the boat appeared, and she recognized him as the same man who had piloted the boat the one other time she had been here. Tall and muscular with sandy hair. And, as he approached, she remembered his clear blue eyes—clear as a summer's sky. "Captain Daniel Jeremiah at your service, ma'am."

She bit her lip, not used to speaking to men she didn't know. *But I'd like to get to know him better.* If only her mother were still alive to discuss these things.

The man jumped off the boat and held out his hand to Leo, who met his shake. "I'm Leo Kern, and this is Miss Amanda Mack. We're here to deliver some goods and to collect supplies ordered for the Zoar store."

After the men transferred the wares from the wagon to the boat, Captain Jeremiah nodded at Leo then smiled at Amanda. "My men and I will bring your supplies up and help load them on your wagon. Do you have your order with you?"

Did men smile at all women like that? She had no idea as she spent her days surrounded by other Separatists in their own tiny community of Zoar. She lived in a beautiful piece of God's creation, with plentiful green pastures and trees, but it didn't help her understand the nuances between men and women.

◆•———————•◆

Daniel watched Miss Mack fumble in the pocket of her apron before holding out a piece of paper. Their hands touched as she gave it to him, and she startled. *Had she felt the same tingle he'd experienced?*

Glancing at the list to give himself time to recover, he then passed it on to one of his workers. Nodding at Miss Mack, he touched his hat in salute before jumping back onto the boat.

He remembered her from a previous stop at this dock. *I'd sure like to get to know this woman, Lord, if it's Your will.* But who was he to ask God for such a gift, after forsaking his father's ambitions for him.

On to the task at hand. Canal boats ran on a tight schedule. Who knew when he would see her again, if ever?

His deckhand helped him lift the wooden crates onto the dock then went back for another load. Daniel jumped again onto the dock, all the while searching for the young woman, but only saw the driver of the wagon. "Would you like me to hand you the items so you can pack the wagon yourself?"

"Da. Thank you." The man climbed into the back of his wagon and began to move the items around as Daniel lifted them.

The deckhand brought up the last load, and a feminine voice rang out, "Oh, what beautiful material. May I see a bolt of the green, please?"

Daniel lunged for the material and almost fell into the canal. It was worth it to see her smile when he handed the cloth to her. She held it against her face, making her eyes sparkle. "That material is the exact color of your eyes, Miss Mack."

"Thank you." Her face reddened, and she walked away.

With three men helping, the second load was soon finished—too soon for Daniel. He wished he could slow time down or make it stop, but knew as the captain it was his duty to keep things on schedule.

He positioned himself by the passenger side of the wagon, and it seemed as natural as breathing for him to offer his hand to help her up. Again, as their hands touched, it shot sparks clear up to his shoulder. As he looked into her eyes, he believed it had happened to her too.

Mr. Kern clucked to the horses. "Thank you for all the help. Hope to see you again."

Not as much as I do.

Daniel prepared the boat to depart, but his attention remained on the wagon until it disappeared out of sight.

* * *

Amanda was glad Mr. Kern didn't talk on the way back to the village. She wanted to enjoy the tan waves of the undulating grasses in the fields, to breathe in the heady autumn smells. To imprint everything onto her mind so she could remember what Captain Jeremiah looked like and how he talked, and how her hand tingled when it touched his. She couldn't wait to get supper over so she could sketch his face. Maybe she would dream about him.

When they arrived at the store, Mr. Kern set the brake and hollered, "Whoa." Amanda disembarked and began carrying things in.

The storekeeper's wife, Mrs. Wiebel, liked to stock the material. Amanda wanted to help but knew she should let the older woman do that while she brought in heavier items.

When they had finished, Mrs. Wiebel called out, "Amanda, come and see this new cloth. I think it's some of the prettiest we've ever had, don't you?"

"Yes, I do." Amanda's eyes twinkled with the memory of the captain's remark about the material matching her eye color—and her embarrassment.

Until closing time, she restocked the shelves at the store then went to her family's house, which she now shared with Mary and Elizabeth. No single person lived in a private house in Zoar. Her parents and the other original founders had agreed to have everything in common.

So, after her parents died from diphtheria, the trustees told her and her sister Johanna to invite two other single women to live with them. They all took turns with cooking, cleaning, and other chores, and were company for one another. Amanda appreciated Mary and Elizabeth's companionship after her sister left two years ago to earn money to attend Oberlin College in northern Ohio.

Amanda needed to answer Johanna's latest letter, and tonight she would look forward to retiring to her room early. She couldn't wait to start a sketch of the canal boat captain named Daniel Jeremiah. She might even send Johanna a small sketch.

* * *

Way after midnight, Daniel stretched out on his bunk while his more experienced hand spelled him at the wheel for a few short hours.

He couldn't sleep for thinking of the brown-haired beauty he'd seen today. How could he make sure he saw her again when he went through Zoar? He'd heard the Zoarites called a peculiar people, so would he even be able to speak to her if their paths did cross again? Who could he ask?

The same answer his parents always gave him popped into his mind. "Ask the Lord about it, son." He did then drifted off to sleep hoping he would dream of the beautiful Amanda.

At first light, the sun shining through the tiny window in his cabin woke him. He stretched, trying to remember if he'd dreamed of Amanda. He couldn't recall dreaming of anything. It would be at least a week before he had a chance to see her again. Better "rise and shine" as his mom called up the stairs each morning.

The day passed like many others, but the scenery on the canals always stunned him with its changing seasons. He loved the buds of spring, the greens of summer, the many-hued leaves of fall, even the sparkling ice and snow of winter when the boats would stop for several months. He loved being out on the water during all the seasons except the bitter winters, which would be upon them soon enough.

At least he had a chance of seeing Amanda again in the next few weeks. But once winter came, he didn't see how he would have any chance at all. It would be another long, lonely, cold winter.

Unless he went home. But he didn't know what good it would do. He and his father would only argue again, and his mother would cry, and he would leave. *Better to let sleeping dogs lie.*

He poured himself a cup of coffee then wished he hadn't when he tasted the bitter, cold brew. "Johnny, do you think you can make a decent pot of coffee if I take over?"

"I'll try, sir. If we had some eggshells I'd put them in like my ma always did."

"Go ask Cook for some right now if you think it will help any."

As the young pole-pusher left, Daniel's musings about Amanda turned into a prayer. He asked God to work it out for him to see her on his trip back through the Zoar part of the canal if it was His will.

That settled, he looked forward, toward the front of the boat. Another thing his parents had taught him—to always keep going forward, pressing on, whatever the task. Why had it taken him so long to realize the wisdom his parents had imparted to him over the years? Why hadn't he contacted them more often the past three years? He'd left, barely a man at twenty-one. Now he was twenty-four, and still a disappointment to his father.

Chapter 2

Two weeks later, Daniel woke with a throbbing jaw despite the cloves Cook had given him to pack around the ailing tooth last night. None of the men on the boat would attempt to pull it. He rolled out of bed and tried not to think about it, but the pain got so much worse he couldn't even concentrate on keeping the boat straight in the water. He hollered for Johnny to take control.

As he started back to his bunk, he hollered over his shoulder to Johnny, "Tie the boat off at the next town. I've got to see a doctor or barber or someone about taking this tooth out."

"Yes, sir. We should be at the Zoar dock in another half hour."

Zoar? His pain-filled brain registered the name. Would they have a doctor or a barber? Or neither? Would he see Amanda again?

Amanda had spent the last two weeks working in the hotel, doing laundry. At least today her assignment was to clean and dust instead. Her hands were raw from scrubbing the sheets with lye soap to keep them white.

She had given up hope of seeing the tall, handsome canal boat captain ever again. When she wrote Johanna last week she enclosed a small sketch of him, but it didn't do him justice. She didn't know how to show his height and muscles without adding herself to the picture, which would be too vain. But his size was one of the qualities that had attracted her to him. Many of the boys she'd gone to school with matched her height, some even shorter. Amanda stood five feet eight inches in her stocking feet. Standing next to the captain made her feel tiny and almost dainty, which she'd never experienced before.

Starting on the third floor, she worked her way down the hall, through each room. She stripped the beds, swept, and dusted, whatever the room needed. She piled the sheets at the top of the stairway for some other poor soul to scrub in the laundry room, then descended the staircase to the next level.

The second floor was a little cooler than the third, but it would heat up more as the sun continued to rise. This must be the last of the Indian summer that happened most years. She continued her tasks on that level, looking forward to arriving on the first floor soon.

As she started down the spiral staircase, a commotion at the front door caught her attention. Two men entered. Moaning came from a tall man with something white wrapped around his neck and head. Another man with him hollered out, "Is there a doctor here? My friend needs a tooth pulled."

No one else answered, so Amanda rushed to the men. "I believe the doctor is next door. Let me show you." She led them out the back door to a smaller building then opened the door and called out, "Dr. Peterman, are you here?"

The doctor poked his head out an inside door. "What is it, Miss Mack?"

"This man needs a tooth pulled."

"Bring him in here." He opened the door wider.

When Amanda turned around to help, the cloth slipped off the hurting man's face. *Captain Jeremiah?*

She steadied him with her hand as the younger man helped him onto a couch the doctor pointed to.

"How long has this tooth been hurting?" the doctor asked.

The captain held his hand against his jaw. "A-out a eek."

"The doctor chuckled. "About a week?"

The captain nodded.

"Amanda, please open the drapes for us." He peered in Captain Jeremiah's mouth again. "Still not enough light. Can you get me a lantern from the kitchen?"

She rushed to obey, not wanting the captain to be in pain any longer. Carrying a lantern in, she asked the doctor, "Do you have any matches?"

He patted his shirt pocket. "I always carry them, even when I go to bed."

Doctor Peterman lit the lantern. "Can you hold this steady for me, Amanda?"

She did as he asked.

"Tilt it a little toward the wall. . .good. Right there. Now hold it as still as you can."

The doctor poured a small amount of potent, sweet-smelling liquid out of a bottle onto a handkerchief and held it over the captain's face for a few minutes until he lost consciousness. Then he grabbed a pair of pliers off his shelf. "Pray I get it all on the first pull."

She followed the doctor's orders and prayed.

Her arm was as heavy as if she were holding up two full jugs of maple syrup.

"All right, you can put the lantern down now, Amanda. Good job." Dr. Peterman held up the pliers holding a discolored, bloody tooth. "I couldn't have done this without you."

Amanda watched the captain. After a short while, he started to stir then tried to sit up. The doc pushed him back down. "Not so fast there. I still have to pack your jaw to keep it from bleeding, and we'll need to put ice on it to slow the swelling. Amanda, can you get a bucket of ice from the icehouse?"

She shrugged. "If I can stop by the hotel and explain where I'm going and why."

"Of course, I wouldn't want you to get into any trouble with the Grotzingers. In fact, tell Mrs. Grotzinger I need you for several hours. I want you to ride in the back of the wagon with this young fellow to make sure he keeps the ice on his jaw."

Amanda rushed out to do the doctor's bidding. When she explained to the hotel manager why she would be gone for several hours, the older woman said, "Of course. That's the Separatists' way—to minister to anyone in need. And I'll have our kitchen help fix a lunch for the three of you to eat when you get back to the canal boat."

The bucket of ice weighted down her arms as she carried it back from the icehouse, and she was glad she could put it down every few minutes. But she didn't linger long, as she had the wagon ride with Daniel to look forward to. Plus, she was doing something she would choose to do instead of what the trustees told her to do for a change.

Thank You, God, for this beautiful fall day, and the opportunity to spend time outdoors—with Daniel. When had she changed from calling him Captain Jeremiah to Daniel? She better be careful to not say it aloud.

◆—•—◆

With help from Johnny, Daniel settled in the wagon bed they'd brought from the dock, and Amanda sat beside him. He closed his eyes to rest as the doctor had recommended, but every now and again he would try to snatch a glimpse of her when she wasn't looking. The coolness of the ice on his jaw reminded him of his mother's touch whenever he'd had a fever as a boy. Amanda's touch felt even better—because she wasn't his mother.

She shifted the ice lower on his jaw. He opened his eyes and stared into her beautiful green orbs. They were so close he could see flecks of gold in them.

"Sorry if I woke you, but the doctor told me to not leave the ice in any one place longer than fifteen minutes."

"I'm just sorry to take you away from your duties."

"It's my pleasure. I'd much rather be outside than cleaning in the hotel on a beautiful day like this."

Did this mean she liked being outside, but it had nothing to do with his company? "It is a beautiful day, but my favorite part is your company. I hope we can get to know each other better today and in the future."

A frown crossed her face.

"Did I say something to upset you?"

"No. . .yes. . .maybe." Her eyes clouded with doubt. "Do you know much about our group of Separatists?"

"No, but you and the others I've met have all been very kind to me."

"True. . .but our name means we are separated from the world at large, although the canals and now railroads are making inroads into our lives. But I could not pursue a relationship with you or anyone unless you joined our group."

He raised his eyebrows. "I don't understand. You can't get to know me unless I became a Separatist too?"

She nodded then hung her head, but not before he could see a tear in the corner of her eye.

Not knowing what to ask next without offending her, he remained silent for a couple of minutes. Then, because his time alone with her was about up, he blurted out, "Is this like Jews versus Gentiles or something like that?"

"No, it's not so much about religion as it is the type of community we belong to. We have all things in common, so I work wherever the trustees of our town assign me. I don't get paid for my work but receive a place to stay and food to eat and whatever else I need."

He had never heard of anything so strange. "And I could not come to see you unless I became a member of your group too?"

She shook her head.

Johnny called out, "Whoa," and the wagon lurched to a stop.

Daniel's heart thudded as he tried to take this all in.

Johnny came around to the rear of the wagon. He first helped Amanda and then Daniel down.

Amanda carried a basket the woman at the hotel had sent. How could the people of the town seem to want to help but then want nothing to do with him if he didn't follow their rules? He couldn't wrap his mind around this conundrum.

Amanda spread a blanket under a tree then began to unload the contents of the basket—several sandwiches, fruit, and a jug of lemonade, plus some cookies. They knew how to tempt a guy.

Daniel turned to Johnny. "This looks like enough for the whole crew, so you could ask the others to join us, Johnny, if it's all right with Amanda."

With a nod, she agreed, and Johnny went to fetch the others.

When they had all assembled, Daniel asked a blessing. "God, I thank You for this food Amanda's people have sent for us and ask You to bless them and bless us as we eat of it. In Jesus' name, amen."

They ate in silence, everyone hungry since it was now midafternoon.

Cook stood. "Guess I can go snooze now instead of fixing supper, since no one could be hungry later after eating that spread."

The other men left also, leaving only Amanda with him. "Tell the woman at the hotel how much we all appreciated the food. Can I send her and the doctor some money with you? I didn't think of it earlier."

"No need. I told you, a Separatist always helps those in want."

"Who can I ask besides you about the Separatists?"

"I don't. . . . Wait, I thought of someone. Did you know that Dr. Peterman, who pulled your tooth, is also known as Captain Peterman on the canal? He sometimes takes our wares up to Cleveland."

"So where would I find him?"

"At the village if he's not captaining the *Evening Star* or one of our other boats."

"All right. I'll be looking for the *Evening Star* docked in port somewhere so I can try to connect with him to understand more about your village."

"I. . .I'd like that." She stooped to gather any leftovers and stowed them in the basket. "I better leave now to have time to walk back before supper."

"Thank you, Miss Mack, for all you did today to help me."

"You're welcome. Goodbye." She turned and headed toward the village.

"Miss Mack?"

She swung around.

"I'll try to get back before the first deep freeze, unless the owners of the boat shut it down before then. If not, it may be next spring before I see you. Let me know if you ever need a job as a dentist." He winked.

She giggled and waved, and then turned and left.

Daniel watched her until she went around a bend. He didn't feel quite so forlorn as before. At least he had a plan to look for Captain Peterman and the *Evening Star* on the canal. Or he would go to the village of Zoar and find him later. He would not give up without doing everything he could to see Amanda Mack again. The first hard freeze could hit any time now. He would need to work fast.

❧————·——❧

Amanda strolled along the quiet canal path as she traveled back to Zoar. She needed time to sort out all the things that had happened today. A whippoorwill called for its mate. Would she someday have a mate?

When she'd started the morning out at the hotel, she could never have imagined that soon the doctor would commandeer her help with a dental patient. Then she would take a wagon ride to apply ice to the patient's jaw, plus a picnic lunch with Daniel and the other men. And, before their parting, Daniel would ask permission to come to see her.

What an amazing day. But how could a relationship between them play out? She couldn't imagine Daniel would want to become a Separatist or that they would let him visit her if he asked. She'd had to ask for permission to correspond with her sister when she moved to Oberlin. Maybe she and Daniel could write each other, but she didn't know his address. *Help me know what to do, God.*

Chapter 3

A manda had spent most of the past month praying about seeing Daniel again, but her prayers hadn't been answered. . .yet. Her mother had taught her God always has an answer—either yes, no, or wait. So she would continue to pray and wait.

Today was the morn of Christmas Eve, so there was plenty to do. The men had gone to the forest to cut branches from the larger fir trees. They cut various lengths and sizes, so each tree they assembled would be round like a good German tree should be. They placed the branches in holes bored in old broomsticks standing in the middle of a wooden base. Like a giant Christmas puzzle. They did it this way so they wouldn't be destroying whole trees in their forest.

Amanda had been assigned to candle-making duty today as she had done for the past several days. She was to make all the extra candles they would need for the trees, besides the ones for daily use. As she dipped each added layer of wax onto the candles, she thought about Christmases of her past.

The Separatists had always worked on Christmas Day like any other day, until about ten or eleven years ago. That day, the old earthen horn used for decades to summon workers each morning cracked when Trustee Ackerman blew it. The breaking of the horn appeared to many as a sign that they should no longer work on Christmas Day, so they never had since.

She recalled how she and Johanna danced around their parents after hearing the proclamation. She'd been almost eleven and Johanna twelve. It had seemed like a gift from God to have a silent Christmas morning with no horn and no jobs to rush to.

Ah, Johanna, I miss you so, and would love to hug you this Christmas and dance around again like we did then. But she would rather have Johanna at Oberlin College, where she would be able to study what she wanted, than here with her. Especially with the many restrictions they had grown up with, which still shackled Amanda's life. Even though she would like to see her sister again, she could never wish her back.

As she wrapped another finished candle in paper, she chose to remember more happy times. The light from the candles reflecting in Johanna's eyes.

Decorating the tree with cookies and popcorn. The Christmas morning they each got a rag doll Mother had made placed in a wooden crib made by Father. Singing carols around their own tree and the one at church.

Amanda and her friends who shared her house didn't have a tree this year. Many adults had given it up if they had no children to share it with, but Amanda still missed the glow of the candles, the smell of the branches, and the Christmas cookies.

An idea popped into her head. It was quitting time, so she put the wax and molds away then dressed in layers to head back to her house. When she arrived, she measured out the flour, sugar, and spices to make Christmas cookies. Even if they didn't have a tree to hang them on, they could still eat them.

Finding her mother's old recipes in her familiar handwriting brought another nostalgic but happy moment to her heart. Christmas should be a time of peace and goodwill. She would do her best to see that she and her friends celebrated the Christ-child's birth in the right way. She would write to Johanna about it tonight so her sister would never forget their memories or their love for each other.

Would she ever have a child of her own? Did she want to if she had to raise her child as a Separatist? What had brought all these musings to the forefront of her mind?

Her breath caught in her throat. *Daniel.*

◆◆———◆◆

Daniel could feel the chill in his bones. The temperature had dropped at least twenty degrees from yesterday. He tried to hurry his men so they could get home to their families before the Christmas freeze he knew was coming. And he hoped to get to Zoar and park the boat in a boathouse there. He wouldn't even mind being snowbound if it meant he could see Amanda more often.

He stared out the glass on the front of his boat. It had clouded over again. He might as well wait until he heard the horses being led out before he scraped it.

At the jangle of the horse's harnesses starting up the unloading ramp, Daniel jumped up and ran out the side door. Sometimes they needed some coaching from the sidelines but not today. The horses acted as eager as he was to get going.

Daniel grabbed hold of a rein. They didn't have time for a horse ending up in the canal today as had happened before. He pulled back on the reins as he led the horses down the ramp and onto dry land, followed by Sylvester.

The wizened horse driver winked. "Thanks, boss. They're a handful today. Must be the weather."

Daniel nodded. "I agree. The sooner we get started, the sooner we can stop and all get to our Christmas places-to-be."

The man shot him a toothless grin. "Boy-howdy. Don't that sound good?"

"Yep. Sure does to me too, Sylvester."

Johnny and the other poleman, James, came out on deck.

Daniel gave one last scrape to his windshield. "Everybody's in position, so let's get going."

The first couple miles went as usual, but soon Daniel had to slide the viewing glass out of the way. Much colder this way but easier than cleaning the glass every minute or two.

He could see small pieces of ice floating in the canal but not enough to worry about. After a couple more miles, large chunks of ice floated by. How much farther could they go?

CRACK!

What happened?

Daniel knew as soon as he saw the broken pole in Johnny's hand and the look on the young man's face. He hollered "Whoa!" then grabbed the emergency pole from the floor of the cabin and handed it out the window to Johnny.

Everything went off without a hitch, and soon they had regained their normal speed. They were halfway to Zoar by now. Would they make it before the river froze over? Only time would tell, but a prayer wouldn't hurt. *God, please get us each to where You want us to go. In Your Son's name. Amen.*

What should have taken one hour had taken more than two, but at least they had made it to the boathouse outside Zoar. Now, if he could only find his way to the village of Zoar and to Amanda without freezing to death.

The other men all had nearby places to go, and a couple encouraged him to come stay with them until the temperatures thawed. He declined, not wanting to wait any longer than necessary to see Amanda again. "Remember to keep an eye on the weather, and plan to meet me back here the day after it starts to thaw in case we can get an early start this year." *Although I doubt it.*

It took another two hours to get the boat stored and locked in the boathouse. Then the men took off together for Bolivar where there were a couple of taverns and also a hotel where they could stay the night. They would continue on their way home on Christmas morning.

Daniel headed south toward Zoar. Anticipation in his heart speeded up his steps. He was glad he'd grown a beard for the warmth and protection it gave from the cold, but didn't know what Amanda would think. Would she even be happy to see him?

He'd wanted to see Amanda that evening, so had walked straight from the boathouse to the hotel where she sometimes worked. He ordered some supper but never saw any signs of her in the hour it took him to eat his meal. How could he see her without getting her in trouble? He decided to book a room and take a long, hot bath, then he would come down and look around the town some more.

The warm water relaxed him so much he fell asleep and then woke with a chill. How long had he been here? Shadows bathed the room, so it must be dark outside. He climbed out of the tub then dressed in his warmest clothes before climbing into bed. Amanda was surely in bed. Their long-awaited meeting wouldn't take place tonight.

God, please give her a merry Christmas.

With memories of Christmases past flooding his mind, Daniel pulled out the New Testament his father had given him when he'd baptized him at the age of twelve. He read the second chapter of Luke, since he knew that's what his parents would be doing tonight, then fell asleep.

The next morning, Daniel couldn't believe his watch read almost ten o'clock when he woke. No wonder his stomach felt like it gnawed his backbone. He brushed down his hair then descended the spiral staircase. He'd never stayed in a place this nice before. He had quite a bit saved up since he never spent his pay on drink or other things Father had preached against. He wanted to buy Amanda something but didn't know her well enough to know what to get her.

He saw the same man who had checked him into his room last night. He remembered his spiel: "Meals are thirty cents. Breakfast at seven, dinner at twelve, and supper at six."

"Have I missed breakfast?"

"Most days, yes, but since today is Christmas, and everyone is on a different schedule, we will serve our meals throughout the day."

"Thank you. I look forward to whatever you place before me." Daniel followed the man to the nearest table. He turned over his cup. The man brought a pot of coffee and served it steaming hot. Then he set before Daniel a tray with a pitcher of rich cream, fresh butter, apple butter, rolls, hot pretzels, and cold meat and bread.

When he had finished most of the tray, a young woman brought by a plate with two stewed doves and two foot-long pickles in brine. She smiled down at him, and he nodded. Wanting to ask about Amanda, he decided to bide his time. If she worked at the hotel today, he would see her for certain, since he planned to eat all three meals here.

He left a nickel tip then climbed the staircase to his room to fetch his coat. When he came back down, he took his time on the stairs and used the high vantage point to search the ground floor for Amanda. No luck, but most of the day remained ahead of him.

When he came out the front door, the Zoar Store sign stared him in the face. It wouldn't be open today, but he could look in the windows to see if they might have something he could purchase tomorrow for Amanda. After several minutes, he didn't see anything he liked, but he would come back when they would be open.

Continuing down Main Street, Daniel passed a cobbler shop, then the town hall, before coming to the house marked No. 1. It was huge and had a large summer kitchen off to the side of it. He wondered who lived there.

Crossing Third Street, he noted a house labeled ASSEMBLY HOUSE next to a tin shop. On up the hill he could see a church and decided he would come back to it this afternoon or tomorrow.

Across Main Street he could see the garden, which took up an entire block. Several passengers on the boat had spoken of it when they traveled through this area. They had told him he should go there, so he strode across the street and found one of the gates to enter. First, he stared up at what the Zoarites called the Tree of Life in the center of the garden.

Many paths led out from the huge tree, like spokes on a wheel. Daniel counted eight spokes as he walked around the entire perimeter of the garden. Several other smaller spokes also fanned out, but they all led back to the Tree of Life. He noticed a greenhouse off to one side. It was closed, but he could see much greenery inside the glass walls. He walked past a gardener who was raking leaves into piles for composting.

He couldn't believe that after such a big breakfast he could be hungry again, but his stomach growled, so he walked back to the hotel. This time they served an even larger meal of roasted turkey, fried potatoes cooked in cream, rice, and bread with apple butter and molasses. After the server cleared the table, and he prepared to leave, the young woman came out smiling with sauerkraut fritters, which were quite tasty.

Another good meal, but not the treat he wanted—to find Amanda again—so he asked if he could come to eat later again tonight, and the girl said, "Da," with a twinkle in her eye. "As long as you are here by eight so we can do cleanup before nine."

"Thank you." He nodded at her then went out the door and turned right on Second Street to see a part of town he hadn't been to before. The building prowess of the Separatists amazed him. And, the cooking. The wondrous aroma of cooked apples told him he had passed by the old cider mill before he ever saw the sign.

Next, he turned onto Foltz Street and checked out the schoolhouse then the girls' dorm and boy's dorm. Then he passed the Bauer House where the farmworkers stayed. That made sense when he smelled the tannery and granary close by. Everything in this town seemed to be built for economy of movement.

He saw a tall man exit a house on the corner at dusk then watched as he carried a lantern and placed it into a glass globe atop a pole. "*Gute nacht*," the man said in a raspy voice.

"Good night to you also." Daniel nodded to the man and walked back to the hotel. The day had been tolerable while the sun shone but now had a definite chill to it. Would this freeze thaw out soon, or would he be stuck in Zoar for a while?

He'd enjoyed seeing more of the town by lamplight but was disappointed to not find the one he had come to Zoar to see. Since she had to be up so early, he figured she was in bed by now, so he headed back to the hotel. He enjoyed a meal of turkey and noodles then turned in for the night. As he prayed in bed that evening, he asked again for God to show him how to find Amanda. That night he dreamed of the old church on the hill.

Chapter 4

On the day after Christmas, Amanda's assignment was in the barn to help feed and milk the cows in the morning. She would rather do this than clean the hotel after all the festivities the past couple of days. But she also had been assigned supper duty at the hotel so would have a long day.

Why did the trustees have to make all the decisions? Her mother used to tell her to use the brain God had given her. Why had her parents stayed with the Separatists so long? Was it easier to let someone else make all the decisions? She knew they'd felt indebted to Joseph Bimeler and the others who had led them there. But did she?

She slipped her feet into the wooden clogs stored inside the barn. Next, she dipped out some warm water from the iron kettle to wash the cows' udders. After cleaning each one, she began the rhythmic squeezing her mother had taught her. Her mother's sweet voice rang in her head. "Not too hard or too soft. Not too fast or too slow. We want the cow to stay relaxed to give more milk."

A barn cat meowed. Amanda squirted a stream of milk into its waiting open mouth then whispered, "Go on with you now. We don't want to spook the cows."

She moved from cow to cow, following the same procedure. At the end of the row, she stood and stretched out her back and hips. Before sitting down again, she carried the full milk buckets to the vat where they stored it until someone came to take it to the cellar to keep cool.

As she started on the next row of cows, her friend and housemate, Mary, seated herself on a stool on the row next to hers. "Good morning."

"Good morning to you too, although I hope the morning is about over."

Mary giggled. "Not quite. We still have an hour to go before the noon meal."

"What kept you so long?"

"I had to do our wash first thing so the hotel could use the laundry room the rest of the day, then when the laundry became too crowded, they sent me here."

Amanda sighed. "I'd rather be here anyway. Cows don't argue with you."

"But you don't get very much conversation out of them either."

"True, but I prefer the quiet."

"I don't think you would say that if your captain was here. Have you heard from him yet?"

"No, and it's getting so cold I'm afraid the canal will freeze any day now, so I may not hear from him until spring."

"The water was already freezing in the puddles on my walk to the barn." A glint gleamed in Mary's eye as she shared, "The ladies from the hotel said a man came in there yesterday with icicles in his beard. Does your captain have a beard?"

"He didn't the last I saw him, but that's been a month ago." *I doubt it's Daniel, but wouldn't it be nice if it were? But. . .what would I say? I hardly know him.*

Daniel awoke to the seven o'clock winter bell and went downstairs for breakfast. He gladdened at the dish of potatoes in cream he had enjoyed so much the day before with a thick slice of ham, plus the usual bread and apple butter.

When he finished, he glimpsed a familiar face in a group across the drawing room. He approached the man he hoped was the doctor who pulled his tooth and waited for a break in the conversation. "Pardon me, but aren't you Dr. Peterman? You pulled my tooth last month."

The man peered over his glasses at him then grinned and offered his hand. "Nice to see you, young man. Is everything all right with you?"

"My teeth are fine, thanks, but this cold weather has stopped my canal boating for a while. I hope to get back out on the canal before too long if it thaws soon."

Dr. Peterman shook his head. "I hate to be the bearer of bad news, my friend, but that's not likely to happen. The last time we got an early freeze like this, we were snowed in until March. We couldn't get on the water until April. I hope that won't be the case this year, but we have to be prepared."

How could he prepare for that? He might already be in trouble with the owners of his boat for deciding to park it in the Zoar boathouse. He needed to find a way to contact them. Soon. "Could you tell me where I could go to telegraph a message to my boat's owners? I don't want them to worry."

Dr. Peterman smiled. "The closest telegraph office is in Bolivar. It's about three miles northwest of here. But I'm not even sure if it will be in operation with all the ice coating the lines. You could try renting a horse and riding over there though."

"Thank you again, Dr. Peterman. I'd also like to talk to you later on when I get back from Bolivar."

Dr. Peterman smiled and gave him his address.

Daniel donned his coat and gloves and hat, glad he had run into the man again. He left for the three-block walk to the church God had placed on his heart. By the time he got there, he was frozen. He hoped the building would be accessible so he hadn't walked here in the cold in vain.

His heart gladdened when the door opened without any trouble. The warmer temperature inside shocked him. Had someone built a fire today? *It isn't Sunday.* He discarded his coat and sat on a bench.

Two ladies walked through the door and came to an abrupt stop when they saw him. "Hello," the taller one called out. "May we help you?"

Neither was Amanda, so he didn't think so. "No, ma'am. I just came in to pray awhile, but if I'll be a bother, I'll get out of your way."

The shorter one smiled. "No bother. Some of us ladies wanted to undecorate the tree today, but we can come back later."

"Why don't you let me help you? If my mother were here, that's what she'd tell me to do."

The women looked at each other. The short lady cocked her head. "I think God must have sent you to help us since you are taller than either of us. Can you bring in the stepladder from out in the hall and take down the higher decorations? We can manage the ones below five feet."

"I'd be happy to. I love to decorate a Christmas tree, but it's been years since I've undecorated one. It will be a privilege to help you ladies." He went out the door where she had directed him then came back in with a stepstool. He set the stool on the floor near the back of the tree since the women had already started in the front.

"Do you have a box I can put the ornaments in as I remove them?"

"Yes." The taller lady carried a box around to him. "I am Mrs. Sturm, and my friend is Mrs. Ruof. May we ask your name, sir?"

"Of course. I am Daniel Jeremiah, a canal boat captain who had to hold up in Zoar because of the ice."

"Do you know Dr. Peterman?" Mrs. Ruof cocked her head again.

"Yes, ma'am, I met him the last time I came to Zoar. And again this morning in the hotel restaurant." His answers seemed to make them more at ease, so they all continued to work with little chatter for several minutes.

Joseph took a sniff of a star cookie. "Mmm. This gingerbread cookie smells good enough to eat. Or do you all keep them from year to year?"

"No, we make them fresh, and there are plenty, so eat any you'd like. The leftovers we'll save to take to the school for the children later."

All the Separatists he'd met had been very kind. "Did one of you build this fire before I got here?"

Mrs. Sturm laughed. "No, my husband Jacob built it up for us, but if you don't mind checking it if it starts to cool down in here, we'd appreciate it."

"It still feels pretty warm, but I'll go check it."

"Thank you, Mr. Daniel Jeremiah. With two Bible names, you would make a good Zoarite. Now all we have to do is find you a nice young woman."

Daniel walked out of the room so he wouldn't have to answer, but he knew he had already found a nice young woman. If only he could find her now and talk to her about the Separatists.

He reentered the room. "The fire was still burning, so I didn't add any wood to it. I think we can be through in another hour or so, don't you agree?"

Mrs. Ruof smiled. "Da. With your help, we should be finished in no time."

They continued on in their work, and true to his prediction, they were putting on their coats to leave in an hour. Daniel helped carry the boxes to the church attic and the cookies out to Mrs. Sturm's buggy. As they left she gave him a smaller bag of the treats. "We've had an enjoyable day with you, Mr. Jeremiah. Hope we will see you again."

He nodded. "Thanks to both of you for making me welcome." As he walked back in the church, he thanked God for the women and all the good people he had met in Zoar. *God, are You trying to tell me something? Please make it clear to me, and Amanda also, what You would have us to do. Please help me to follow You wherever You lead.*

He dropped to his knees on the hard wooden floor and cried out to God for clarity and wisdom. Next, he added what his parents had taught him was always the best prayer, "Not my will, but Thine." Then he stilled his heart to listen to what God had to say to him.

He arose an hour or so later, his mind buzzing with the words "*cow barn*" and "*hotel*" and "*trust Me*." He didn't often get "words" from God, so decided he'd better give feet to his trusting by going to the barn and the hotel.

He put on his coat and headed to the cow barn, stopping by the hotel on his way. The six o'clock dinner bell rang, so he asked one of the young servers if they would prepare him two turkey sandwiches to eat while he walked. They did, and he soon left. Since all he'd had to eat since breakfast was cookies, he ate one of the sandwiches before he arrived at the barn. He opened the door and hollered out, "Anyone here?"

The door was unlocked, so he hoped someone would be around. Or maybe the milkers had gone home for supper and then would come back for the night. *What now, Lord?*

Hay falling down from the loft startled him. Then a cat jumped down, scaring him with its loud, "Meow."

As the cat ran away, Daniel followed his trail then jumped back when he saw a dark hand and foot stuck out of the hay a few feet in front of him.

"H–hello?" It was a human body, but he couldn't tell if it was alive or not. "Are you all right?"

He held his breath while awaiting an answer.

Some more hay moved, and a leg then the rest of the body of a dark-skinned man appeared. "Sorry, suh, if I scared ya."

"It would have scared both of us if I had stepped on you."

"You sure right about that, suh." The man gave a deep chuckle as he sat up.

Daniel joined the man, thankful they could both find some humor in the situation to ease the tension. "Do you live here in Zoar?"

"No, suh, just passing through."

"Are you hungry?"

"I'se always hungry."

Daniel pulled the turkey sandwich from his pocket and placed it in the man's hand.

The sandwich disappeared in a few bites, so Daniel withdrew the gingerbread cookies in his other pocket. He offered them too. "My name is Daniel. What's yours?"

"Samuel."

"A good Bible name. We both had good Christian mothers."

"That's right. My mama says I was named from the Holy Book." Samuel took a bite of gingerbread. "Are you an angel, Daniel? Did God send you to feed me?"

Daniel laughed. "I've never been asked if I was an angel before, but God did send me here. And He provided this food through the hotel and some ladies who gave me the cookies earlier today."

"It sure tastes like angel food to this empty belly."

"I'll have to see about getting you some more then, and some warmer clothes." The man wore only a short shirt and pants, both ripped and worn.

"You done enough, suh." Samuel dropped his head but not before Daniel saw tears glistening.

"Are you safe here in the cow barn?"

"Yes, suh, until the bell rings in the morning, then I gotta run out of here off to another place."

"How will you know where to go?"

"Ain't s'posed to tell, but God'll show me the way."

"I know He will." *Just like He showed me.* "I'll bring you some more food and some warmer clothes before the morning bell, then you can get out of here before first light. Sleep well."

Samuel rubbed his belly. "I will, suh, thanks to that sandwich and the gingerbread."

"Good night, Samuel." Daniel turned to leave.

"Night, suh, and I'll be thanking God for you and praying for you as I go to sleep."

"And I'll do the same for you." *God, please bless Samuel, and lead us both on the path You have for us—wherever it is. And thank You for letting me minister to this runaway slave. Please keep him safe.*

Chapter 5

The clock hands pointed to eight o'clock. Amanda took off her apron and hung it up then stretched out the kinks from her shoulders. It had been such a long day. And it got worse when she found out from her house-mate that she had heard of a young stranger in the hotel that morning. Had it been Daniel?

Amanda had been here for hours and still hadn't seen him. Had he already left again? She wanted to go home and climb into bed. But first, she had to ready the dining room for the breakfast crew.

Mrs. Grotzinger hung up her apron then blew out the lamp in the kitchen. "I'm going to turn in for the night, Amanda. Can you finish the dining room for tomorrow?"

"Yes, ma'am. Good sleep." She slipped into the dining room and inspected the tablecloths to see which ones needed to be washed. After stripping the dirty ones, she put them in a laundry bag for the morning crew to launder. Then she went to the linen closet to get some clean ones.

When she walked past the kitchen, she caught a glimpse of someone walking around in the dark.

Fear clogged her throat. Who would hear her if she screamed? Summoning her courage, she called out, "Who's there?"

A tall figure loomed in front of her in the door. She couldn't see his features in the shadows of the dark room. "Amanda?"

She recognized the voice and exhaled. "Daniel?" What was he doing in the kitchen of the hotel this late? Was something wrong?

He stepped into the hallway and held a finger to his lips. "I thought I might never see you again."

"I thought the same."

"What. . . ?" They both blurted out at the same time.

He grinned and beckoned her to speak. "Ladies first."

"What are you doing here?"

"Can you keep a secret?"

She nodded.

"I needed to find some bread to make a sandwich for a runaway slave I found in the cow barn tonight."

She covered her mouth with her hand. "Oh, I can help you." She went past him into the kitchen and lit the lamp. She carved off four slices of bread and added ham to make two sandwiches. Next she found two apples and stuffed them and the sandwiches all in a cloth bag before handing it to him.

"Thank you. What are you doing here?"

She giggled. "I work here, remember?"

"Yes, but I've been here two days and hadn't seen you yet, so I wondered where you might be."

"This morning I worked at the cow barn. This afternoon they sent me to work the supper shift here when another girl took sick."

He smiled. "God answered my prayer."

She cocked her head. "Your prayer? For someone to get sick?"

"My prayer to see you again."

Her eyes grew big. "Oh."

He laughed. "This is the first time I've ever seen you speechless, Amanda."

Her cheeks warmed.

"Are you finished here now?"

"I need to take the clean tablecloths to the dining room first."

"May I accompany you there and then for a short walk in the garden? We'll walk fast to keep warm."

At the sight of him her weariness had vanished, but what if she was caught out with a stranger? "Maybe, for a few minutes, but then we both must be in by the nine o'clock bell. There is a lot you don't know about the Separatists and our ways."

He frowned as he looked at his watch. "It's after eight now, so let's hurry."

Amanda turned off the lamp before heading to the dining room. There she laid the clean tablecloths on a bare table where she or one of the other morning workers would be sure to see them. She donned her coat, gloves, and scarf before heading out into the cold.

They walked in silence. The one-block walk chilled her toes. If they could get to the overhang of the tree, it would block the worst of the wind, causing the temperatures to warm a bit.

Daniel followed her lead, and when they reached the tree, he said, "I walked all around the garden this morning. It's beautiful in daylight but even more so in the moonlight, or perhaps it's the company."

She was glad he couldn't see her blush this time. "Let's stay on one of the inside paths, so we can end back at the tree to sit and talk a little."

They did as she suggested, and the walk warmed her some. "You're staying at the hotel?"

"For a few days. Tomorrow morning I need to ride to Bolivar to see if I can send a telegram to my boss. He needs to know where I am and that the boat is all right. It's covered in icicles, but I was also by the time I arrived." He chuckled.

"Ah. I heard a stranger had arrived in town with icicles in his beard."

"The colder it got, the more my window on the boat would steam up, so I left it open much of the time. The hair on my face gave me a little covering from the wind and weather."

"Smart idea."

"Amanda, please tell me more about your Separatist ways. I don't understand why you can't choose what job you do or where you live or anything."

She lowered her head. "When my parents and the others who first settled here came over in 1817 from Germany, they decided to live as a commune and share everything in common. Each person did the work they were able to do, and they were given the food they needed and a place to stay, but no say in either one. My parents were youngsters in school then, but by the time they wished to marry, the building of the canal had already started. The Separatists agreed to separate the men and the women so there would be no childbearing during those years, so the whole workforce would be able to work on the canals." She looked at Daniel. "You know our people built the seven miles of the canal that run through our land?"

He nodded. "I knew the Separatists built one lock and several miles of canals through your territory, but I had no idea the women helped with the building."

She continued, "My mother helped watch the babies for the working mothers at the beginning of the building, but during the latter years she became one of the young women who helped dig. She told me how they dug with spades and shovels or even their hands until they were red and bleeding. Only a few had wheelbarrows, so the women toted most of the dirt in their aprons, or pockets, and even on their heads in baskets. My mother knew of several women who had huge bald spots on the top of their head from the weight of the dirt."

"I've never heard anything about this. It's hard to believe."

"After the trustees paid off the land with what they made, people wanted to marry and live in their own homes, so again it was voted and passed to allow everyone to marry and live in houses they built, although sometimes several families lived in each house. But they never changed the part about working where the trustees wanted you to or dividing the food by the size of the families, so it's still in effect today."

"So, you're like a slave to the trustees?"

She shook her head. "No. We are not mistreated, and we all have enough to eat and to wear and warm houses to sleep in. But we have no say in what we choose to do or when we do it. Our lives run by the same bell you woke to in the hotel today. We awaken at seven in the winter and six in the summer. A noon bell rings to tell us to go fix and eat our lunch, then another bell at one tells us to go back to work. A supper bell rings at six and a sleep bell at nine. We need to have all our evening chores done and lights out by then." She jerked her hand from his and stood. "What time is it?"

"It's fifteen minutes until nine. Do we need to start walking to your house now?" He reached for her hand again.

"Yes, we better. But I hope we can talk again soon."

"If the work in the barn begins at seven, what time do I need to be there to give the man his food?"

"Before six, as the barn manager will be there before everyone else."

"I'll do that, and then I need to go to the livery barn to rent a horse to ride to Bolivar, so I won't be back until later in the day. Where do you work tomorrow?"

"We often don't find out until the morning meeting unless it is for multiple days, so I won't know until then."

He frowned. "So you'll get off at six and go to your house unless you work at the hotel and don't get off until eight?"

"Yes."

"All right. I'll plan to be at your house a little after six. If you don't show up by then, I'll come to the hotel to eat and we can make plans from there."

"That should work. I also need to tell you I have two housemates—Mary and Elizabeth. I will tell them about you tonight." She stopped at a gate. "Here's my house. Looks like my friends are already here." She pointed to two windows with glowing lamps. "Good night."

"Good night. Until we meet again."

Amanda entered the door of their home to find both her housemates staring at her.

"Was that a young man who walked you home?" asked Elizabeth.

Mary smiled. "Who was he? Someone from Zoar, or the stranger from the canal boat?"

Amanda took a deep breath then exhaled as she took off her gloves and scarf. "Daniel from the canal boat, and yes, he did grow a beard this past month to protect his face from the cold."

"Oh, I thought he was so handsome," gushed Elizabeth.

"Not only handsome but very nice." Amanda couldn't stop the smile from forming on her face.

"When will you see him again?" Mary raised her eyebrows.

"Tomorrow."

Elizabeth looked at the clock on the wall. "The lights-out bell will ring in five minutes, so let's all put on our nightgowns then meet in Amanda's room to talk."

They did as she suggested and stayed up talking and giggling for hours like schoolgirls in the dark.

Amanda hadn't had this much fun since before her sister left for college.

Chapter 6

Daniel had left a window open in his hotel room so the cold would wake him early to go meet Samuel. When he awakened he checked his grandfather's watch to find it read four thirty. He searched through his meager clothes satchel to see what he could give the man. He decided on a warmer pair of pants and a long-sleeved shirt plus a pair of wool socks his mother had knitted for him.

He knew she would approve of his gift to this one who had so little. Daniel only had one pair of boots and one coat, but he also had a sweater he could wear until he could get to the store to buy another one. Taking the bag of food Amanda had packed last night, he tiptoed down the stairs and out the back door.

The night was cold and still, and so dark he had to wait for his eyes to adjust. After a minute, he stepped out the door and trod through the large frozen field toward the cow barn.

He only tripped once over a rock, but righted himself, and then continued on. No lanterns shined, so he crept around outside until he reached the door at the back of the barn.

The barn door creaked as he pulled it open a few inches to go through sideways.

He whispered, "Samuel." It reminded him of his mother whispering the name as she told him the story of God whispering to the boy Samuel in the Bible.

He stood still but didn't hear an answer, so he whispered a little louder. "Samuel."

"I's here, suh, under the hay." Samuel sat up, scattering the straw, then stood.

Daniel approached him and held out the sack of food. "Do you want to eat this now or take it with you for the road?"

"I'll wait a little while until I get away from town. I travel better in the dark. Thanks again to you, Mr. Daniel."

"You're welcome. I'm only glad God brought us together last night." He pulled the clothes from his coat. "I also brought you some warmer clothes to wear. I know I'm larger than you, so I brought a piece of rope to tie up the pants if they are too big."

"You'se sure a smart man, suh."

Daniel laughed. "Not everyone would agree with you, Samuel, but I hope you can use them." He pulled the sweater out of his coat pocket. "Now I need you to decide between this sweater or the coat I have on. They both can keep you warm, but which do you think will be more serviceable for you on the road?"

The man's eyes shone like two big white buttons in his face as he shook his head. "I. . .I couldn't take either one, suh. They're too nice for the likes of me."

"You have to take one, or I'll leave both."

Tears streaked down the man's face. "I never had such fine clothes in all my born days." He looked from the sweater to the coat then said, "I'll pick the sweater, if you'se sure." He lifted the sweater and pulled it over his head. " 'Snug as a bug in a rug' is what my happy mama would say."

"I'm also sure my mother will be happy when I go visit her soon and tell her why I need a new sweater and socks. I wish we were closer to my home so I could take you there to meet her. She'd put some meat on your bones." A rooster crowed, and Daniel glanced toward the barn doors.

Samuel looked too, and they both saw the lightening of the sky. "I best get on my way. I pray God bless you and yor kin, Mr. Daniel."

"I pray the same for you and yours, Samuel." He enclosed the man in a quick hug and then released him into the hands of God. "I'll never forget you."

"Me neither, suh."

Daniel waited and prayed for about five minutes before going out the door again. Next, he moved east through the open field, past the hotel, and toward the stable. He wanted to see if he could get a horse this early, then he would eat breakfast in Bolivar.

Daniel heard a horse snort as he approached the livery in the semidarkness. A young lad was in the stable when he arrived. Daniel waited, and soon a man in a loose gray smock topped by trousers and leather suspenders entered and took his money for a one-day horse rental to ride to Bolivar. "If you come in past six o'clock tonight, you'll owe an extra half day."

"I should be back in plenty of time to eat supper at the hotel." *And to see Amanda.*

Daniel rode off on a bay horse. It kept a steady pace the whole trip to Bolivar, arriving before eight. He first stopped at the Bolivar stable and paid a stable hand a nickel to water and feed his horse and told him he planned to be back by noon or a little after.

The ride had been what he needed after so many months on a canal boat where he had to keep the boat in strict lanes at all times and watch out for dangers in the water. Riding, and letting the horse do most of the work, left his mind free to wander to more pleasant things, like Amanda Mack. She seemed to be the answer to his prayer for a godly wife, something his parents had also taught him to pray for.

His encounter with Samuel had caused him to end and start his day with prayer, so he did some more praying during his ride. When he told his parents of all God had taught him along this journey, he knew they would be happy to see him when he returned.

Daniel walked to the Bolivar Hotel and ordered their biggest breakfast. He had been up four hours now, so he knew he could eat it all.

He needed to go to the telegraph office. Next, he would check out the town and what it might hold as a gift for Amanda.

At the telegraph office, he wrote out the message to his boss trying not to go over ten words. After the name and address where it would be delivered, he wrote,

CANALS FROZEN. BOAT IN ZOAR BOATSHED. PLEASE ADVISE. ZOAR HOTEL. DANIEL JEREMIAH.

While there he decided to splurge on another one to his parents. After their name and address, he wrote,

CANALS FROZEN. SAFE ZOAR HOTEL. KENTUCKY TRIP SOON. DANIEL.

He would have to wait until the boat owner shut down the canal boats, but in the meantime, he might as well check here in Bolivar for stagecoaches or other means of travel. He had enjoyed the horseback ride today but didn't think he wanted to go home on a horse, not in the dead of winter.

He set off on foot to explore the town and ask around. Soon, he came to the general store where he saw some pretty jewelry but couldn't remember if Amanda even wore jewelry. He settled on some embroidered handkerchiefs with flowers on them, which his mother always liked receiving.

While walking down the street, the wonderful smell of apple cider wafted out a shop door, so he went in and sat down at one of the tables. A young lady came to the table, and he ordered a cup of the cider and a cookie. The cider was too hot, so he nibbled on the molasses cookie and waited for his drink to cool.

While waiting, he couldn't help overhearing a man and woman at the next table.

"It looks like we may have a long winter ahead of us," the man grumbled.

"Why do you say that?" The woman took a sip of her drink.

The man picked up his cup then set it back down. "The latest weather forecast for the state has below freezing temperatures from now through the end of January."

"And then. . . ?" She frowned.

"It could stay frozen until April."

"April?"

"When the canal boats will start back up. I heard the canals north of here are already freezing over."

"How do the workers on the boats live with no paycheck for months?"

"They better be good savers or find somewhere else to work until the weather warms up next spring."

I've got money saved, but will it last four or five months?

Daniel downed his semi-cooled cider before leaving to face the cold again.

He went by the livery and checked on his horse then strolled the rest of the main street of Bolivar before finding a stagecoach office. He checked out the closest place a stage could take him to a train that traveled to Cincinnati, Ohio, or Maysville, Kentucky. He would have to make several layovers and switches, but it looked doable all the way. He could be home in a week or maybe less.

Daniel continued walking until he came to a place to eat that gave off smells like his mother's fried chicken, and where a lot of people had gathered. He'd learned a crowd often meant the food was good, so he waited in line a few minutes.

He found a seat at a long table. A waitress came by and asked, "Do you want the special? It's half a fried chicken, mashed potatoes, gravy and biscuits, plus a piece of pie, for a dollar."

A little more than his Zoar Hotel meals, but he didn't do this often. "Sure. If it tastes half as good as it smells, it'll be worth it."

She smiled. "I can guarantee it is, because my mom is the cook."

Returning a few minutes later, she set down everything except the dessert. "What flavor pie do you want? We've got dried-apple pie, or lemon or butterscotch."

"I'll take the dried-apple pie, thanks."

The chicken and potatoes filled him up, but once he tasted the pie, he knew he would have to eat all of it. He hadn't been this stuffed since his last Thanksgiving at home, three years ago. How could he have let three years pass without seeing his parents?

The memories of his last night there flooded back. The big, delicious meal his mother always made, which soon turned to bile when he and his father started arguing again.

"I don't know why you can't follow in my footsteps and your grandpa's and become a preacher. Can you think of anything any better?"

Daniel wiped his mouth with his napkin. "I've thought about it and prayed about it, but still I'm not sure what God is calling me to do."

"We could trade off Sundays and give you a chance to grow into it while giving me more time to help you on the farm."

He stood. "I'm sorry, Father. I know that would make both you and Mother happy, and I might do it someday. But right now, I have the feeling God wants me to do something else—go somewhere else."

"Let's please stop talking about this. You know we don't want you to leave." His mother began to cry into her handkerchief.

"I have to go, now. I planned to wait until after Christmas, but perhaps it's better if I leave now."

"Please, no. Stanley, talk some sense into him."

"I don't know what else to say, Garnetta. He'll have to make up his own mind." His father walked out the back door.

It was the last thing his father said to him before Daniel left. He carried his suitcase downstairs. His mother sat at the kitchen table, her head in her hands. "Your father has gone to the Andersons' to pray with Mrs. Anderson's mother who is dying."

"I'm sorry to hear that, but it doesn't change my mind. It may be better this way. At least we won't argue again."

The waitress laid his bill on the table, pulling him out of his thoughts. "Are you all right, sir? Did you like the pie?"

"Yes, in fact, tell your mother her meal reminded me so much of my own mother's cooking that it made me think of her. I believe it's time I paid her a visit very soon. Thank your mother for me, please." He left a dollar plus a quarter on the table then stood. "And ask her to pray for me too."

Daniel had a lot to think and pray about on his ride back. He hurried to the stable, paid the fee, and then headed back to Zoar and Amanda.

◆—·—◆

Amanda couldn't wait to see Daniel that evening and tell him what Mary had passed on to her in the hotel kitchen where they both had been assigned today. The men had determined the fishpond east of town was frozen solid so had given permission for anyone who wished to go ice skating tonight after supper.

Mrs. Grotzinger had even asked older women to fill in for the younger ones for the supper shift. She hoped Daniel would go with her but decided she would go with her friends, if not. Last winter she'd missed Johanna so much she didn't want to go without her and hadn't skated at all. The giggles in her bed last night had enlivened her to want to live more, laugh more, dream more.

But how would she meet with him to tell him if he didn't come in soon? They would have to leave for supper at home and then prepare for the skating party. An idea came to her. She would write a note and keep it in her pocket until she left at six. If he didn't show up before she had to go, she would leave it under his door and hope and pray he would see it and respond.

She finished the dishes, did the cleanup, and then made sure everything was set for the supper meal. At five minutes until six she ran up the stairs to his second-floor room and slipped the piece of paper under the door. She scampered back down the stairs and into the kitchen to say goodbye to Mrs. Grotzinger and the other ladies.

"Thank you so much for making it work for us to go skating tonight."

"Thank you for always being such good help, Amanda. Everybody needs a little fun sometimes. I still remember the nights Mr. Grotzinger and I went skating on the same pond. Make sure you dress warmly."

"I will." She waved then opened the front door and ran into tall, handsome Daniel. She closed the door then motioned for him to follow her away from any watching eyes. "I left a note under your door that the town is having a bonfire and skating party at the old fish pond tonight. I hope you can come."

"I wouldn't want to miss anything with you, so where can I meet you?"

"Be at my house at seven, and I will introduce you to my housemates, then we can walk over there together."

The evening meal bell rang. He grinned at her. "I best go eat my meal and dress for the cold then. But I don't know where I can get any skates."

"Some people bring extras, but I'll look in our old shed and see if I can find my father's skates."

"I'll see you at seven. And I hope it's not too forward of me to say you look beautiful tonight."

Warmth spread across her cheeks again. "Thank you."

"Thank you for inviting me." He winked at her.

She hurried away, not knowing how to respond.

Chapter 7

Amanda hurried to her house. She opened the door and hollered, "Mary, Elizabeth, are you home yet?"

Elizabeth came out of her bedroom. "I'm here, but Mary went home with Mae and will meet us at the pond. Is anything wrong?"

"No, but I need to go look for my dad's old skates for Daniel, so can you fix us ham and bread for supper tonight? I'll do it one night next week for you."

"Ohhh, so we get to meet this Daniel in person. Do you think any of the trustees will mind?"

"I hope not, but I refuse to live my life in fear of what the trustees think."

"Good for you. I'll go get ready then start a quick supper." Elizabeth went back into her bedroom.

Amanda bundled up to walk to the shed in back of the house. She hadn't seen the skates since the last time she and Johanna went skating, and that had been nigh on three years ago. When Johanna had told her of her desire to move to Oberlin to go to college the next summer. She wanted Amanda to move with her, but Amanda had been afraid of life outside the village. Could she live somewhere else? A small bit of hope told her heart now she could.

In church her first Sunday in Oberlin, Johanna had met an elderly woman who offered her room and board for companionship and light housekeeping. She still had time to work elsewhere part-time, so she could save enough money to attend college. She would take her first class after Christmas. Amanda was so proud of her sister. Oh, how she wished she had gone with her.

What had she come to the shed looking for? Her ice skates and also her dad's skates. She pawed through wooden boxes of an assortment of things, but no skates. She prayed for God's help in finding them then opened her eyes and saw two pair hanging on a hook on the wall.

She retrieved the skates with joyful memories filling her. *Mother and Father's skates!* Her mother's looked like they would fit her now, so she would take them to the house and try them on over her boots. First, she would need to give them a good cleaning.

Her mother's skates fit like they'd been made for her. *Thank You, Father, for the reminder that You are always with us, and my parents are with You too.*

Elizabeth looked up from the kitchen table. "What time is Daniel getting here?"

"Seven, why?"

"You have fifteen minutes to eat before he arrives then."

Amanda hurried to the table. "Thanks for fixing this for us, even though it was my night to prepare, Elizabeth."

"You would have done it for me. That's what friends are for." She squeezed Amanda's hand.

They both jumped at the knock at the door. "Come in."

A cautious Daniel stuck his head around the door. "I wanted to make sure I had the right place."

"You do, so come on the rest of the way in and shut the door." Amanda laughed then swallowed her last bite of ham. "This is Elizabeth. Our other housemate is meeting us there."

Daniel nodded. "Nice to meet you, Elizabeth."

"Do you wish to try my father's skates on before we go or wait until we get there?"

In answer, Daniel held them next to his large foot. "I think they'll work. Do you have some oil we can rub them with to shine them up?"

"I forgot Father used to do that. It's been about three years since I've skated."

Daniel cocked his head. "Why? Were you injured last year?"

"No, but my sister left a few months before, and I didn't feel like skating without her."

"I didn't know you had a sister, but I'm glad you are going tonight. Maybe you can tell me about her."

"Sometime. Elizabeth, are you ready to walk with us?"

"I don't want to be a bother."

"You're not a bother, you're my friend."

They bundled up then stood, skates in hand. Daniel looked from Amanda to Elizabeth then back again. "May I have the privilege of escorting you two beautiful women to the skating party?"

"Handsome and gallant too," Elizabeth teased as she locked arms with his.

"I agree." Amanda put her arm in his also.

◆—•———•—◆

Daniel didn't ever remember being this happy before. He had liked a couple of girls back home, but had never felt this strong feeling of love and connection he had for Amanda. She seemed to complete him in a way no other girl ever could or ever would. Now, what could he do about it?

First things first. He would escort them to the skating party and spend every moment possible with Amanda. He looked at her face shining in the moonlight. How he wanted to kiss her red nose. What was he thinking? *God, please keep me from doing anything stupid or something that will scare her. I don't want to lose her.*

"How much farther to the pond?" he asked.

Amanda pointed. "See the fire over there? It's about another block. Looks like the crowd is growing.

Elizabeth hollered, "Mary, wait up." Then she excused herself and ran to join two other girls. Amanda had explained a little of the Separatist ways last night, and he hoped she would tell him more tonight. Their strange customs kept him on tenterhooks all the time.

Amanda led him to a place close to the fire where some stacked hay and a log served as seating. "Ready to put your skates on?"

"Yes, please allow me to put yours on for you." He slipped her skates over her boots then tightened the screws with a tool he carried in his pocket. Then he buckled the leather straps. "How does it feel?"

"Very firm. I should be able to stay on my feet."

He sat to put his own skates on and tightened them. "I always loved to skate on our farm pond, but I haven't skated for over four years, so I hope I don't embarrass you."

"Don't worry. I may embarrass you if I fall down." She waved at several people, calling their names. He noted a few watching them, some older men with frowns on their faces.

"We'll have to hold on extra tight to each other then." *And I won't mind that at all.*

No one skated yet, as several still swept the surface, but it looked almost cleared now. Most of the skaters were teens or young adults, but he noticed several adult couples also. The moon shined on the ice, making it feel even colder but also more romantic. *I'm a goner. I don't usually think like this.*

They both held their hands out to the fire to warm them. It was chilly, but the skating would soon warm them. People began to venture onto the pond, so he stood. "May I have the first skate?"

"Of course, you may have as many as you want."

He took her hand and pulled her up so they could both keep their balance. As they walked out onto the ice, he felt like a king escorting a queen. He wanted her to be his queen.

The first time they circled the large pond they only skated around the outside perimeter. The next time, he asked if she knew how to skate backward. When she shook her head, he spun around and faced her, and then said for her to help push him so they could skate facing each other. After they had circled the pond again, he asked if he could push her this time.

She looked at him with trust sparkling in her eyes, and said, "Yes."

His heart thumped as he spun around. He had to keep her mind off her skating backward so he tried to get her talking. "Tell me more about your sister."

Amanda chewed on her lower lip for a second. "Johanna is only a year older than me, but she got all the bravery in the family. She was a better student than I, and mother always said she could do anything she put her mind to. So it shouldn't have surprised me when she announced she wanted to move to go to college."

He winked at her. "I think you are very smart too, so perhaps you could go to college someday, maybe even practice dentistry like you did on me."

She laughed. "I could never be as brave as she is. It made me happy when the trustees said I would have to share our family house with Mary and Elizabeth. I had never stayed in a house by myself before and couldn't imagine doing it."

Daniel grinned. "A few minutes ago, you had never skated backward before, but look how well you are skating now."

A look of joy swept over her face. "I am, aren't I?" She tripped, but he caught her.

"Do you want to stop to rest or get something to drink?"

"No. I like this feeling of bravery at doing something I never thought I would do, so let's do it again."

He threw back his head and laughed. "You are full of surprises tonight."

She joined him in laughter, and they skated around several more times before stopping to get something to drink—hot apple cider cooked in a huge pot over the bonfire. He took her back to a seat on the log then skated to get them each a cup.

When he returned, Dr. Peterman and a woman stood next to Amanda, conversing with her. He hoped he hadn't done something against their rules—anything to get her in trouble.

As Daniel approached, Dr. Peterman called out, "Daniel, my wife would like to learn to skate backward. Do you think you could teach her like you did Amanda?"

Daniel bowed before her. "Would you give me the honor of skating with me?" The woman giggled into her hand.

"Do you want me to go backward first like I did with Amanda?"

She nodded, so he took her hand and led her to the pond.

He positioned himself in front then spun around to face her. "Now, I need you to push me across the ice."

The lesson proceeded as it did with Amanda. Mrs. Peterman seemed to tire faster, so they soon returned to the others.

Mr. Peterman stood waiting with Amanda. He helped his wife down onto the log and removed her skates then turned to Daniel. "Thank you so much for granting my wife's desire to learn to skate backward, Mr. Jeremiah. I would like to invite you and Amanda to our home tomorrow night for supper."

Daniel looked to Amanda. She nodded with sparkles in her eyes, so he turned back to the other couple and said, "Miss Mack and I both accept, sir. Thank you so much for inviting us and allowing me to skate with two lovely women tonight."

Mr. Peterman glanced around the pond. "It appears this gathering is breaking up. It will soon be nine o'clock, so we best be going back to our homes. See you tomorrow evening at six."

"Yes, sir," Daniel replied. He bent over to take off Amanda's skates then his own. Carrying both pair in his right hand, he offered Amanda his left arm and escorted her back to her door.

"Thank you for a wonderful evening, Captain Jeremiah."

"It was my pleasure." He pulled a package from his coat pocket then handed it to her. "I picked up something for you in Bolivar this morning, but I couldn't find anything as pretty as you."

Her eyes widened as she unwrapped the gift. "These are the most beautiful handkerchiefs I have ever seen. Thank you."

"You are very welcome, and I look forward to escorting you to the Peterman house tomorrow. Will you have any trouble being ready in time to get to their house by six?"

"No, it is only a couple blocks away. If I tell whomever I work for tomorrow about the Peterman's inviting me to supper, I don't think there will be a problem."

"So, I will meet you here around a quarter to the hour?"

"Yes, good night." She slid into the house before he could reply.

But his heart responded for him. *I'm in love with you, Amanda Mack.*

As she entered, Amanda's friends enveloped her in a quiet bear hug.

Mary gave her a kiss on the cheek. "You looked wonderful out on the ice. When did you learn to skate so well?"

"Tonight. Daniel's a great teacher." Amanda sighed.

"Yes, we saw how he even taught Mrs. Peterman to skate backward." Elizabeth lifted her eyebrows.

"I wish we could talk again tonight," Amanda said, "but I'm afraid I'm too tired after all the exercise to stay awake tomorrow if I don't get some sleep."

"Me too." Mary tried to stifle a yawn, and they all laughed.

"Pleasant dreams, Amanda." Elizabeth added.

"Pleasant dreams to both of you," Amanda replied.

The bell rang before they had changed into their nightclothes. Mary extinguished the lamp, and they all padded around the house by moonlight.

After Amanda said her prayers and crawled into bed, sleep evaded her. Her heart still raced at the excitement of skating backward in Daniel's arms. She hadn't been scared at all with his strong arms holding her.

She hadn't felt so safe since Father had carried her home from an ice-skating trip where she'd fallen as a young child. Or the times Mother rocked her and Johanna together in the big rocker when she used to read to them. She had so many happy memories as a child. And now, Daniel had awakened a desire to raise children of her own, but she didn't think she wanted to do it in Zoar with all its rules and regulations.

Help me know what You want me to do, heavenly Father.

Chapter 8

Amanda went to the laundry behind the hotel to start the water boiling. Next, she went to find the manager of the hotel. "Good morning, Mrs. Grotzinger. I've already put the water on to boil this morning. I need to ask you if I can leave at five thirty this evening. At the skating party last night, the Petermans asked me to dinner, so I told them I would have to ask your permission to be there by six." Amanda didn't know what she would do if the woman wouldn't let her go.

Mrs. Grotzinger frowned and planted both hands on her hips. "You know many of us older ones don't agree with all this partying that's started since our leader's death a few years ago. We don't like all the changes we see. But I know you are a good girl and a hard worker, and I think dinner at the Peterman's house would be a fine time for you. So, you may leave at five thirty. Will that be enough time?"

"Yes, ma'am. I already laid my dress out, so all I have to do is get dressed and polish my shoes."

"You're always prepared, so go on with you now, so you can finish early and not keep the Petermans waiting."

Amanda nodded. "Thank you, Mrs. Grotzinger."

The Petermans had been friends with her parents before they passed away. Was that the reason they had invited her and Daniel to supper, or was it because Daniel also piloted a canal boat? She would have to wait until tonight to find out. She went upstairs to pick up the linens that had been changed so she could wash them.

She wouldn't even mind the job today since she hadn't done laundry at the hotel for a while. After getting the laundry from the third floor, she went down to the second to retrieve their bedding also. The bag had grown too full to handle, so she only did one side of the floor. Then she carried it down to the first floor before returning to the second to complete her gathering.

Raised voices came from Daniel's room. The noise seemed jarring in the normally peaceful hotel. What could it be about? His door opened, so she slipped from the hallway into another room behind a door that stood ajar. She peeked through the opening between the door and the doorjamb and saw two men depart. Daniel came out a minute later and hurried down the front stairs then out the door.

After collecting the rest of the linens from the second floor, Amanda carried them out the back door of the hotel to the laundry. She shaved the lye soap and mixed it with one of the tubs of water she had put on to boil earlier. She couldn't wait to see Daniel tonight and ask what had happened.

Her mother had always told her not to borrow trouble, so she hummed a hymn while she scrubbed each sheet and pillowcase. After rinsing them in another tub of clear water, she wrung them out and hung them on the line to dry. Then she repeated the steps until she got the first half of the sheets done before stopping to eat her lunch. Her day continued with the other half of the bedding, doing load after load. After she got them all hung outside on the lines, the first sets were usually dry on a sunny day like today.

By four o'clock Amanda was ironing the sheets with the flatirons heated in front of the fireplace. She switched out each iron as it cooled to replace it with a hot one. She had done this so many times she could do it in her sleep.

At five thirty, Mrs. Grotzinger came in to check on her. "Look at how much you've done today, girl. Now go on home and get ready for your time with the Peterman family."

After thanking her, Amanda dressed in her outerwear for her walk home. A niggle of guilt washed over her for not telling Mrs. Grotzinger about Daniel Jeremiah. Would the lady have been so kind if she'd known he would be there too?

Amanda walked at a fast pace, arriving home early enough to wash the sweat off her face and neck. Then she donned her new Sunday dress, a dark green one. The one Mary and Elizabeth told her made her eyes look even more green than usual. *I wonder if Daniel will recognize this dress material as what I picked up at his boat the day we first met.*

Her shoes were still wet from the trip home, so she dried them off as best she could and polished them before changing her damp socks out for a dry pair. Now she was warm and ready, except for her hair. She'd hoped to have time to do something besides pull it back in a bun, but the knock at her door signaled Daniel's arrival.

She opened the door, coat on and gloves in hand, as it wouldn't be proper to invite him in with no one else around. "Hello, I'm ready."

"You look more beautiful every time I see you, Miss Mack." He smiled. "Is that dress you're wearing from the material you picked up on the boat? I knew it would look lovely on you."

She nodded.

"Would it be all right for me to call you Amanda when we are alone since that is how I think of you?"

"Yes, as long as we are careful not to do it around others, especially the trustees." She lowered her eyes. "I already think of you as Daniel." Her cheeks warmed again. Would she ever outgrow this?

◆━━━━◆

Daniel hoped she would never stop blushing at his comments. His mother still blushed when Father gave her compliments or did things for her. He wanted to have a strong Christian marriage like they did. But he vowed to never try to make his son or any of his children follow in his career.

"Where are we going tonight?"

She pointed. "See the lantern light in the house on the next block? That is the Petermans'."

"Yes. It won't take us long to get there. Can we walk slowly and talk fast?"

She looked at him and nodded.

He continued. "I need to tell you about a visit I had from two of your trustees this morning. They visited my room and told me they'd heard I was courting you but that it wasn't allowed here in the village. Either I would have to go, or you would have to leave, because no Separatist could marry an outsider. Is this what you've been trying to tell me?"

"Yes, but I'd hoped they would change their minds. Several things have changed since our leader Joseph Bimeler died over three years ago. But it seems the trustees want to keep things going the old way. I'm sorry I haven't had a chance to tell you more. It seems like I don't have any private time."

Maybe that's one of their ways of keeping things from changing. They'd reached the Petermans' home. "We're here now. I hope we can discuss it more later after we leave."

"Yes, me too."

Daniel knocked, and the door opened.

Mr. Peterman waved them in. "Please come in, Amanda and Captain Jeremiah." *Why was the man frowning?*

Mrs. Peterman joined them. She hugged Amanda then held out her hands. "Please let me have your wraps and such."

They obeyed, and when she returned, Mrs. Peterman said, "We are so pleased to see you again tonight. Please come and sit down in the living room while I take things out of the oven."

Amanda offered, "May I help you, Mrs. Peterman?"

"Yes. Another pair of hands is always welcome, dear."

"Two sets of hands are better than one, my mother always said."

"Yes, I can remember your mother saying that very thing." She smiled. "I remember your mother with such fondness. I have missed her often since she passed on."

Their voices trailed off as the ladies left the room.

Mr. Peterman cleared his throat, and Daniel sat up straighter.

"So, you had a visit from two of our trustees at the hotel this morning?"

"Yes, sir. I have to say, it shocked me how vehemently they wanted me to leave town, after all the courtesy and help I've received here before now."

"Yes, and I'm sorry, but we have many strange ways here, and courting by an outsider is forbidden."

Daniel stood speechless for a minute at the man's candor, so he composed himself before speaking. "I met a negro slave a couple mornings ago in the hay barn. Abolition is a noble cause, one with which I agree. Your community and I have many values and principles in common. Yet the Zoarites will not accept me as a suitor for Amanda?" He spoke with restraint, but his blood boiled.

Mr. Peterman stood and paced. "I agree with you, Daniel, in many ways, and if you want to join our Separatist group, I would be glad to put in a good word for you. But you would have to live with us and give up any worldly goods you have and take orders from the board of trustees like the rest of us do."

Daniel stood. "Become a slave, in other words."

"No, because we do not own one another or own anything, we just share everything with one another."

"Sounds like being a slave to me. I want to work hard and earn a living for the family God blesses me with. And make my own decisions about where and how I live my life, as God leads."

Mr. Peterman gave him a sorrowful look. "And if I were younger, I might join you myself, but being a Separatist gives us security for the future. We always take care of our own and others."

"But at what cost?" Daniel asked as the women joined them.

Mr. Peterman continued, "Believe me, my wife and I have asked ourselves the same thing. The trustees kept our daughters from going on many of our canal boat trips in their younger years. Our girls later told us some of the people who cared for them did not treat them kindly. Now, one of our daughters has married an outsider and moved away. The other stays here but misses her sister."

Mrs. Peterman joined the conversation. "I have been telling Amanda of our sorrow at losing our daughter and now any grandchildren since they will be so far away from us. But please join us in the dining room, and we can continue our discussion while we eat."

They followed her into the next room where Daniel held out Amanda's chair for her while Mr. Peterman did likewise for his wife. Mr. Peterman asked a blessing then began by passing the food to Amanda.

"I hope you enjoy chicken and dumplings." Mrs. Peterman passed bread to Daniel. "I love to cook and miss cooking for our girls when they lived at home."

"Yes," Amanda said. "I remember how sad you were when Carolina left Zoar and moved away."

"We don't get to see Carolina often, but Wilhelmina still lives in the village and helps with the sheep. Carolina is expecting our first grandchild in a few months, so I plan to go stay with her to help for several weeks after the birth."

Amanda grinned. "Oh, how nice."

Mr. Peterman cleared his throat again. "We haven't been given permission yet to go."

"I have to, dear. It's my duty as a mother and soon-to-be grandmother."

He frowned. "I know she will enjoy your pampering and cooking for her again."

No one spoke as they finished passing the platters of bread and vegetables around then tasted their food. "These dumplings are delicious, Mrs. Peterman. They remind me of my mother's."

She smiled. "Thank you, Captain Jeremiah. And did your mother make dried-apple pies too? That's what we're having for dessert."

"No, but I have tried them, and I look forward to yours." Daniel smiled.

They chatted as the rest of the meal progressed.

Amanda insisted on helping clear the table while Mrs. Peterman brought out the pies.

She served Daniel first, then her husband, then Amanda and herself. "I'll be certain to take some dried apples to Cleveland to make some pies for Carolina."

"These pies are wonderful, and better than the one I had in Bolivar the other day." Daniel smiled and took another bite.

His hostess placed another one on his plate. "Here, and I'll send you home with a couple also."

Daniel nodded his thanks then turned to Mr. Peterman. "Does your wife try to fatten you up like this too?"

The man raised his eyebrows. "I'll never tell."

They all shared a chuckle as they finished their supper, ending the meal on a happy note.

Amanda again insisted she help Mrs. Peterman clear the table and wash the dishes while the men retired to the parlor.

Mr. Peterman motioned Daniel to sit close to him. "I do hope things will change around Zoar, but I know the two trustees who are in power right now, and I don't think it will happen anytime soon. So, I advise you to leave Zoar as soon as possible and correspond with Amanda by letters. Perhaps you two can work something out by mail."

"After my visit from the trustees, I am making plans to take a train to Maysville, Kentucky, near where my parents live, to stay the winter with them. But first I need to hear word from the canal boat owner if we are shut down for good this winter."

"I can guarantee they are shut down. I got a telegram delivered by a friend in Bolivar yesterday saying the main canals have already shut down for the winter. I don't think you could get very far."

"I wanted to have some more time with Amanda before I leave, so perhaps we can walk to the garden tonight and talk there."

Mr. Peterman chewed his lower lip before speaking. "I have a better idea. How about my wife and I leave the lamps on down here then retire upstairs to get ready for bed early? We both like to read for a while before we go to sleep. Then you two can sit down here and talk until a few minutes before nine."

The ladies reentered the room, and Mr. Peterman rehearsed his plan for them.

His wife had one thing to add. "I think my husband will need to come back downstairs around a quarter till nine, in case anyone is watching our house. Then he can let you out the front door before turning off the lights downstairs."

Amanda had tears in her eyes. "It's so sweet of you all to do this for us."

"I agree," added Daniel. "This is a wonderful opportunity you've given us to spend time together before being apart for several months. I promise you we won't take advantage of your kindness, and we won't forget it."

The older couple departed, and then Daniel took her hand in his, and they sat on the settee side by side, holding hands. *Thank You, God, for letting us have this time together. Help us to use it well.*

Daniel spoke first. "Since Mr. Peterman said all the major canals in this area are shutting down, I'll have to shut down my boat too. So, I'm going to Bolivar tomorrow to make plans to catch a train to a town near my parents' farm. Then I will spend the winter in Kentucky writing many letters to a Miss Amanda Mack."

Amanda wiped tears away before answering him. "I knew this would happen, but you still won't be able to come to see me in the spring if the trustees have their way. I've been thinking about this for a long while and have decided to go live with my sister in the spring. Perhaps you can visit me there."

"Does she live close to Kentucky?"

"No, she lives about ninety miles north of here. She wanted to move there ever since she read an article in a newspaper that said the town has one of the few colleges that admitted women. But since she had to work to earn enough money to go to college, she will be starting her first semester in a couple weeks."

"Where?"

"Oberlin, Ohio."

"At Oberlin College?"

"Yes. You've heard of it?"

I'm getting the message loud and clear now, God. "My dad told me about the college several years ago. He knew they taught Bible classes and they had admitted Negroes, both things he agreed with. A few people along the canal boat line had mentioned it as a great school also. I'd never thought much about it until I spent this afternoon in prayer at the church, praying for God to direct our paths. The name Oberlin College stayed in my mind every time I prayed—where to get a job. . .where to go to college. . .where to live after we marry."

She gasped, and he fell to his knees in front of her. "I think I'm getting a little ahead of myself." He laughed and took her hands in his again. "Amanda Mack, I know enough about your sweet spirit and Christian ways, that I am sure I want to marry you. I don't have a ring yet, but I will by next spring. So will you consider marrying me in May, after we write and know each other even better by then?"

She nodded, tears flooding her eyes. "Yes, yes, I will."

They sealed it with the exchanging of addresses to write each other and something Daniel would never forget—his first kiss.

Chapter 9

Amanda could still feel Daniel's gentle kiss on her lips when she wrote to Johanna the next night. Daniel had said it might take him a week or more to get home to Kentucky, so she knew it wouldn't matter if she waited one night to write him. Johanna would be happy for her to be coming to Oberlin and to be getting married to such a fine Christian man.

January 1, 1857

Dear Johanna,

    I know we have both missed each other so much these last two years, so I am eager to share with you my good news. I am planning to leave Zoar and the Separatists this coming spring. I hope to see you, dearest sister, in four months or less if things go as planned. I can't wait to hug you in person and stay up all night and talk and share when I get there.

    My other big news is I plan to marry riverboat captain Daniel Jeremiah sometime in the spring. He is the man I sent you a sketch of a couple of months ago. Daniel also hopes to attend Oberlin College and couldn't believe it when I told him I have a sister attending there!

    Daniel and I ate supper last night at the Petermans' home, and I had a good talk with Mrs. Peterman in the kitchen while helping her clean up. I believe she will help me any way she can, although I want to be careful not to get her in trouble with the trustees.

    Time for lights out. Please write soon and tell me if all this will work out with you or if I need to find somewhere else to stay for a few weeks.

Love,
Amanda

P.S. Will you be my maid of honor?

✦━━✦━━✦

Daniel couldn't wait until he got to Kentucky to write to Amanda, so he purchased a pad and pen and several stamped envelopes from the post office in

Bolivar. He wasn't sure how she could purchase stamps to write to him, so he planned to send one each time he wrote to her.

January 3, 1857

Dear Amanda,

I hope you are well, and as happy as I am. You have made me the happiest man in the world to have your love and your acceptance of my proposal. I am on a train heading to Maysville, Kentucky, although I will have to make several transfers to get there. It may take over a week, with some stagecoach rides in between, since most of these smaller rail lines don't go very far. In Maysville, my parents will pick me up in the farm wagon and take me to our house and farm outside the little town of Washington. In the future, I hope you can come with me to see the farm and the beautiful state of Kentucky.

My parents farm one hundred acres of rolling land with beef cattle, grain, hay, and two dairy cows for our own use—milk, butter, and cottage cheese my mother makes. My father also preaches at the local church although they aren't able to pay him much money. But he loves the job so much he would do it for free.

My mother is the second-sweetest woman in the world, after you, my dear. I cannot wait until you two meet. I know you will love each other. She has always wanted a daughter, since they only had me. I am thinking of asking my parents to accompany me on my trip to Oberlin, if it is all right with you. Then they can meet you and your sister and be there for the wedding. I would also like to ask my dad to perform the ceremony, but I won't say anything to them about these arrangements until I hear if both ideas meet with your approval.

I want us to always consider each other's wants and wishes above our own, or anyone else's. As God's Word says in Genesis 2:24, "Therefore shall a man leave his father and his mother, and shall cleave unto his wife."

Looking forward to that day,
Your fiancé,
Daniel Jeremiah

P.S. Until you tell me not to, I plan to insert a stamped envelope in case you have trouble obtaining it in Zoar. And I will plan to write every couple of days so we will both have something to look forward to until we can be together again.

◆━━◆

Mrs. Grotzinger sent Amanda to the Zoar store later in the week to pick up some items for a guest. She asked Amanda to also collect any mail while she was there since the post office had space in the same building. Amanda was shocked to hear from the postmaster that she had a letter awaiting her. Could Johanna have received her letter and written back so soon? Was something wrong? Her heart beat like a hummingbird flapping its wings so fast she couldn't count the beats. When she saw the handwriting on the envelope was Daniel's, she feared the postmaster would hear her pounding heart. She hoped he hadn't put any address on the envelope to let anyone know it came from him. She stuck it in her pocket until she got home.

January 6, 1857

My dearest Daniel,

Imagine my surprise when I received this letter from you at the post office. You had said it would take a week or more for you to reach Kentucky, and then I hear from you in five days. You are so thoughtful to send me a letter on your way. I loved hearing about your parents and can't wait to meet them. I am excited that you want your father to marry us and also for them to be there for their only son's wedding. Tell them I hope and pray they will both come.

And how sweet of you to send me this stamped envelope. I meant to ask for two stamps when I mailed this letter, but now I won't have to ask as often and make anyone suspicious. I only write my sister once or twice a month.

You are the most thoughtful man in the world. I'd resigned myself to waiting two to three weeks to hear from you after you got to Kentucky. Now I won't be so lonely at night with your letters to look forward to. It will help pass the evenings when I read and reread your letters.

The weather here is frightfully cold. The papers say the whole state of Ohio is setting record low temperatures. Of course, as I told you before, the paper is always a week or more old before I get to read it. Hope you are staying warm on the train or in Kentucky or wherever you are.

With all my love,
Your Amanda

Amanda waited two days until stopping by the post office again. She didn't expect Daniel to be able to write and send a letter every day. But she found no letter that day or the next. Maybe he had lost his stamps and envelopes along the way. She knew he wouldn't have forgotten to write her, but there had to be a reason. It took her hours to fall asleep, but she forced herself out of bed the next morning when the bell went off. Her assignment was at the cow barn again. She wished the other milker in her section would arrive soon so she would have someone to talk to. Even then, she couldn't share her thoughts with anyone except Mary or Elizabeth, and then only when no one else was around.

The rhythm of the milking almost lulled her to sleep. What song could she sing to keep awake? She sang the only fast song she could think of. "Joy to the world, the Lord is come. Let earth receive her king."

Elizabeth joined her and added an alto. "Let every heart prepare Him room. And heaven and nature sing. . ."

They were both laughing by the time they finished the song. Elizabeth held her stomach she laughed so hard. "Why are you singing Christmas carols in here? Do you think the cows will give more milk?"

Amanda peeked to make sure no one else heard. "No. I didn't sleep well. I haven't heard from Daniel in a week, and he said he would write every other day. I don't know what to do."

Her friend gave her a sympathetic look. "I hate this for you, but I do trust Daniel, so I guess you'll have to wait until he writes to find the reason."

"Oh, I trust him too, which is why I can't understand why he hasn't written again. He always has done what he said he would do." Amanda sniffled.

It was Elizabeth's turn to cook supper, and she made ham sandwiches with creamy potatoes, and green beans. Mary made a plate of Amanda's favorite cookies for dessert to try to lighten her mood.

"Thanks for the great meal, friends. I know both of you are trying to cheer me up."

Elizabeth smiled. "You're welcome. Daniel will write soon. Wait and see."

Amanda went to her room to write to Daniel so he would have something to read when he got to Kentucky. It had been a week since he left, so he might even be there by now.

January 9, 1857

Dearest Daniel,

I wish you could have been here tonight for supper. My housemates fixed a wondrous meal. They even made snickerdoodles to try to cheer me because I have not received any more letters from you after the very first one. I trust you are well and will be able to write soon.

It seems like each day is the same without a letter from you to look forward to, so I'm not sure what to write. I am well, and also my housemates. Oh! The cat in the barn had a litter of kittens this week. Wish you were here to see them.

We received more snow this week, so we are all sludging through it.
Praying for your health and safety and for you to be able to write again soon.
As always,
Your Amanda

◆— · —◆

Amanda vowed to not go to the post office again unless Mrs. Grotzinger sent her. She could not bear to set herself up for more disappointment. On Friday Mrs. Grotzinger again had need of Amanda to pick up something for a boarder. When she saw the postmaster, Mr. Wiebel, he frowned. "Sorry, still no mail for you, Amanda. But Mrs. Grotzinger did get a paper, so here it is." He handed her the newspaper and the item for the boarder.

Carrying the paper back to the hotel, she gave it to Mrs. Grotzinger, who stuffed it in her cloth bag. Then Amanda went about her day, cleaning the rooms and stripping the beds. When she entered Daniel's room for the first time since he'd left, she wanted to cry, but bit her lip to hold back the tears.

She'd never been inside the room with him, but just thinking about him spending over a week in this room made her heart ache even worse at all they had promised each other. Amanda knew she hadn't lied, and she couldn't believe it of him either. She had to pray and trust in God to bring them back together.

◆— · —◆

Daniel awoke from a deep sleep and looked around. A strange place. He had never been here before but knew he lay in a hospital bed. Where? How long had he been here? And why? He tried to raise himself to a seated position but didn't have the strength, and he collapsed back on the bed. As he gave way to the overpowering sleep again, he prayed one prayer: *God, help Amanda, and help me.*

◆— · —◆

Amanda knew it was only by God's strength she had been able to go through her days without breaking down. Now, two weeks since she had last received word from Daniel, she was back on duty at the hotel again and couldn't wait for her shift to finish. She had written Johanna to ask her to pray, and she knew Mary and Elizabeth also prayed. And the Petermans. Since she didn't know what had happened, she didn't even know what to pray, so she asked God to help her.

Mrs. Grotzinger met her at the door as she left. "You've seemed down the past couple of weeks, Amanda, so I thought I would share my newspaper first with you. I hope you can read through it tonight and bring it back soon so I can pass it on down the line."

"Thank you, Mrs. Grotzinger. I'll bring it back in a day or two. Is it all right if Mary and Elizabeth read it too?"

"Of course. It is wonderful you girls have each other to look out for one another. Happy reading."

"Goodbye." Amanda waved as she stepped out into the chilly air to begin her walk home. The sludgy snow had frozen into uneven piles and ruts, so she had to watch her step. When would this winter end?

It was her turn to fix supper, so Amanda sliced and set out a plate of cheese and bread then opened a jar of pickles. Next, she opened a jar of peaches and placed them in a bowl before sprinkling some cinnamon and sugar on top then set three plates. She admired the look of the blue pottery against the white cloth.

The others weren't home yet, so she sat at the table and began to read the newspaper from Mrs. Grotzinger. It was a weekly paper, the *American Lancaster Gazette*, with a drawing of George Washington's head on the cover. She thought Lancaster was in the middle of the state near Columbus but would have to check an atlas to be sure. There were several poems and stories on the front page, with lots of local news articles.

When she opened it to the second page, she saw a letter from George Washington written in 1778. She read all of it since she'd always liked history in school. Another article listed the local cattle and sheep market prices the men in the community always showed interest in. Page 3 contained much of the same with sales and announcements made. The final page held the district court news and ads for every sort of ailment you could imagine.

She folded the paper back up then noticed a small piece in the local news on the front page about a stagecoach robbery outside of Lancaster. She would usually skim over an article like that, but since Daniel was taking several coach rides, she thought she would read it in its entirety. Her heart squeezed as she read the title.

Stagecoach Robbed Last Week
Three gunmen on the road to Lancaster killed wagon master Robert Fuller in a robbery attack last Tuesday, January 06, 1857. A passenger, Mr. Daniel Jeremiah, tried to intervene and was knocked in the head with a gun. He is presently in Lancaster Hospital in a coma. No injuries were suffered among the other passengers. The thieves got away with a metal box containing several thousand dollars' worth of bank shares.

Daniel injured in a robbery? Dear God, please save him and heal him.
Amanda jumped when someone touched her shoulder. She looked up to see her housemates. "I. . .I didn't hear you all come in."

Elizabeth stared at her. "You look as white as a sheet. What's wrong?"

Amanda opened her mouth, but no words formed. She pointed to the article on the paper. Mary lifted it and began to read the paper aloud. "Wagon master. . . killed. . .robbery attack. . .passenger, Daniel Jeremiah. . .in hospital in a coma. . ."

Mary wrapped her arms around Amanda. "Oh, my dear, how awful. What can we do?"

"I don't know what any of us can do. Perhaps Mr. Peterman could help us. Let's eat supper, then I'll walk over to their house." A tear leaked out of Amanda's eye.

"We'll both go with you." Elizabeth patted her back.

"Thank you. I'm so glad you are here."

Mary began to set the table and pour glasses of milk. They all sat, and Elizabeth asked a blessing on the food, and on Daniel, and for God to show them what to do.

After supper Elizabeth placed the dirty dishes in the dishpan in the sink to soak. "I'll wash them when we get back."

They all bundled up for the cold walk to the Peterman home. Mrs. Peterman answered the door with a smile then asked, "What's wrong?"

Amanda had thought to bring the newspaper, so she handed it to her. Mr. Peterman read it over her shoulder. "The accident took place two weeks ago. Daniel could already be out of the hospital by now."

Mrs. Peterman ushered them all to seats in the living room.

As soon as they were seated, Amanda asked, "Can you help me find out how he is?"

Mr. Peterman tugged on his beard for several seconds. "If you give me his parents' address, I can ride to Bolivar tomorrow and send a telegraph to them and to the hospital. I'll also send one to the sheriff in Fairfield County to see what else we can find out. I have a friend in Bolivar who will deliver any return messages we get, so we can hope to hear something back soon. Until then, we wait."

"And pray," Amanda whispered.

Chapter 10

Daniel woke up again. He had no idea how long he'd been out, but long enough to have a powerful thirst and hunger. He opened his eyes and focused on a nurse in the room. "Miss, could I get a glass of water, please?" Was that his own rusty voice speaking?

She hurried to his bed. "Certainly, Mr. Jeremiah. We've all been praying you would wake up soon, and here you are awake and talking and wanting something to drink." She touched his forehead. "No temperature. You must be on the mend." She poured a glass of water and handed it to him.

He gulped it down and asked for more.

The nurse shook her finger. "No more until I tell the doctor you're awake." She walked out of the room then returned with a man in a white coat.

The man smiled. "I'm Doctor Frazier, and I'm very glad to see you awake. How did the water taste?"

"Like more," croaked Daniel.

"Good answer, young man. Get him another glass of water, Nurse Bailey. If it stays down, then we'll try him out on some soft food tonight for supper." The doctor turned when he reached the door. "Is there anyone we need to contact to let them know where you are?"

"Yes, my parents and my fiancée." *I love that word. Thank You, God, for keeping me alive to see Amanda again. Help her not to worry about me.*

"All right. Give the information to Nurse Bailey, and we'll try to get the telegrams sent tonight."

The nurse went to his locker and took out his jacket then brought him his wallet.

Daniel found the slips of paper with Amanda's and his parents' addresses. "There is no telegraph near my home or Amanda's, so maybe I should write a letter to them."

"I'll help you do that tonight. Sometimes when the telegraph is from a victim of a crime, the police will take it to the sheriff to take it to the family, so let's try anyway."

Daniel agreed then fell asleep again.

When he awoke a little later Nurse Bailey came to his bedside and sat. "What would you like the telegram to your parents to say?"

"Put the name and address of this hospital at the top then say, 'Recuperating from accident. Will send more later about new arrival.' For Amanda, do the same thing at the top then say, 'Recuperating from accident. Will write soon. Love and miss you.'"

The aides brought the supper trays around, and Nurse Bailey helped feed him. He couldn't believe how weak he was. He vowed to eat as much as they would give him to hasten his recovery and regain his strength.

After supper he wanted to fall asleep again, but asked Nurse Bailey to find his satchel. When she returned with it, he asked, "Can you find my paper, stamps, envelope, and pencil, please?"

She handed the supplies to him. "Do you want me to write it for you?"

"No, I want to try myself. Amanda won't worry so much if she sees my handwriting."

"All right. Holler if you get too tired and need assistance. You are doing great for your first day back after being in the coma so long."

His head jerked toward her. "How long was I out?"

"Your accident occurred on January 6th, and today is January 12th, so you've been in a coma for six days."

No wonder I'm so weak. He picked up the pencil and began to write. His hand shook, but his writing was legible.

January 12, 1857

Dearest Amanda,

I am sorry it took me so long to write you again. I was injured in an accident on the stagecoach outside Lancaster, Ohio, and lay in a coma for six days. But I am getting good care and hope to be able to travel on to Kentucky from here soon.

I had forgotten much of the robbery details until I started to write to you. When I saw a gun in the hand of one of the robbers, I remember praying, "Dear God, please keep him from shooting me so I can marry Amanda." The next thing I knew was blackness and then waking up here.

My hand is getting shakier, so I have asked the nurse to finish what I tell her.

They say I am making good progress and should get to go home as soon as I have the strength to walk to the train station. I know I can trust you to pray for me to recover and get home soon so I can get back to you even sooner than we had planned. Maybe we can move the wedding to the middle of

April if you can get everything done on your end. Life is too precious to spend more time apart from the one I love.

Please send any other letters to my parents' address because I don't plan to be in the hospital long enough to get mail here.

With gratitude to God and all my love to you.

Your fiancé,
Daniel

He had insisted on signing his own name. Then he fell asleep and slept like a baby.

✦━━━━━✦

Amanda stayed on pins and needles all day while waiting for Mr. Peterman to return from Bolivar. As the day passed, she figured it would be suppertime before she could visit them to hear what he had found out.

At the six o'clock bell, she hurried home from the cow barn, cleaned up, and then went to eat with the Petermans. Mrs. Peterman ushered her into their living room where Mr. Peterman waited. He rose to greet Amanda with a smile. "I'm sorry I couldn't rush to the barn with my good news, but I didn't want to let anyone else know what was going on. God prepared the way for us, Amanda."

"Please, tell me what you found out."

"I'll do better than that." He pulled a piece of yellow paper from his pocket and handed it to her. "Read it yourself. It's addressed to you. Mr. Samuels at the telegraph office asked me to convey to you his deepest apologies. Daniel's telegram was sent over a week ago but Mrs. Samuels was very ill last week and some telegrams got misplaced. I didn't think you'd mind if I read it first in case it held bad news."

Amanda opened the telegram with shaky fingers.

To: Amanda Mack
Recuperating from accident. Will write soon. Love and miss you.

"He's alive!" she sobbed. "Now that I know he's okay, I can allow myself to cry tears—of joy." *Thank You, Father.*

"Mr. Jeremiah kept his wits about him, as he still held the telegraph word count to ten words." Mr. Peterman chuckled.

They all laughed, then Mrs. Peterman asked Amanda to help her in the kitchen. She hugged Amanda. "I'm so glad to hear the wonderful news. And I wanted to tell you I've come up with a couple of ways you can earn money from me to earn your ticket to Oberlin."

"What can I do to help you?"

"For now, you can take the corn bread out of the oven." Mrs. Peterman looked at her. "But later, I'd like you to take home and darn some of Mr. Peterman's socks. Your mother always said you could darn better than she did."

"I'd be happy to do it for you without pay."

She laughed. "Silly girl, I'm trying to give you jobs to earn money."

Amanda nodded. "Yes, ma'am."

"Now, help me dip the soup while I pour us some milk, and I'll call my husband in while I tell you my other idea." She raised her voice a notch. "John, dinner is served."

He entered the kitchen and helped both ladies into their chairs. When seated, he offered a prayer giving thanks for the food and for the great news of Daniel's recovery.

Mrs. Peterman passed the corn bread around to go with the steaming bowls of soup already on the table. As they ate, she unfolded her plan for Amanda to earn some more money. "I'd like you to help me make a layette for my soon-to-be-born grandchild. I know there are store-bought ones to purchase, but I would like to make the same kind I sewed for my own daughters. If you come over next Sunday afternoon for lunch, I could get us started, and then you could finish some of the pieces at home at night. Our daughter sent me more than enough money to travel with."

Amanda smiled. "As I said before, I'd love to help you without pay, but since you insist, this will be a fun activity to do together. I can think of no one else I would rather teach me how to make a baby's layette. It's the next best thing to having my own mother teach me."

Mrs. Peterman nodded with tears in her eyes. "And having my best friend's daughter help me is like having my own daughter here."

Mr. Peterman stood on the stoop in front of the house to watch Amanda walk home. She turned and waved as she reached her front door then opened it with a joyful heart to share with her friends what God had done.

＊━━━＊

Daniel continued to gain back his strength once he was able to eat and walk around. The doctor released him to travel home on January 15, so that evening found him boarding a train toward Cincinnati. It would still take two days or more to reach the Maysville train depot, and he was looking forward to seeing his parents and apologizing to them.

And to tell them more about Amanda.

Daniel had written a letter all in his own hand to her this morning before leaving the hospital, asking her to move to Oberlin earlier if possible. But even if she could arrange to meet him in Oberlin in April, that was still three months away.

He'd also enclosed a newspaper clipping he had read while at the hospital about the first female dentist in the United States—Emeline Roberts Jones. He told Amanda she could go to college to be the second female dentist since she already had experience.

Pulling the little New Testament from his pocket that his father had given him, he began to read in Matthew. *Wonder how far I can read before I reach home?*

The reading passed the time and excited his heart. The miles clipped by as he read about the life, death, burial, and resurrection of his Lord. In Acts he was there in Jerusalem when the first church began.

Looking around, he saw everyone else had their lights out. When he checked his watch, he couldn't believe it showed 1:00 a.m. He tucked his Bible away but also tucked all he had learned on his journey into his heart and soul to share with others.

He continued his Bible reading the next morning after eating breakfast. When the conductor announced "Cincinnati" around noontime, he knew he would make it home by that evening. How good it would feel to have his father's hand on his shoulder and Mother's kiss on his cheek.

Daniel had begun reading the book of Revelation when the conductor called, "Maysville, Kentucky. All departing for Maysville, please take your bags. We have a ten-minute loading and unloading time here."

As the train slowed, Daniel saw his parents awaiting him at the station. They had aged some, and he knew he was part of the reason. As soon as the train stopped, he grabbed his satchel and walked to the door to be the first one off.

His mother saw him first and raised a hand to her mouth, and then Father came over and instead of shaking hands, enveloped him in a long hug. They broke apart so he could hug Mother, another long hug. *Why did I stay away so long?*

"Is that all you brought?" Father pointed to Daniel's satchel.

"Yes, sir. Canal boat captains travel lightly."

His father scowled. "I see. So is that what you plan to return to doing?"

Mother jumped in. "We can have this conversation tomorrow morning at the hotel."

The word shocked Daniel. "Hotel? I didn't know you two ever stayed at a hotel."

"We haven't," said his mother. "So what better time to try it than now when our son has returned after being gone over three years?"

His father pointed to their old farm wagon. "Let's all get to the hotel, so I can take Betsy and the wagon to the livery before it gets any darker."

They climbed onto the board seat in the front of the wagon and soon arrived at the hotel. "Let's let Mother out here, and I'll go with you to the livery stable, Father."

His mother nodded. "I agree, and I can sit right here in this beautiful room."

Daniel climbed down then escorted his mother into the hotel. "Are you sure you'll be all right?"

"Yes. We came early and already checked in this afternoon."

Daniel's head spun at all the changes in his parents. He waved to his mother then climbed back onto the wagon seat with his father.

The livery wasn't far, but Daniel was glad he had come with his father when they walked the three blocks back to the hotel. They had to pass a loud tavern, and Daniel breathed a sigh of relief to see the hotel nearing then to spot his mother sitting and conversing with someone.

They were soon in their rooms and agreed to eat breakfast in the hotel lobby at seven to get home in time to milk the cows. His father had paid a neighbor boy to milk them tonight. Another wonder.

The next morning they ate, and Daniel went to the livery to pick up the horse and wagon while his father checked their things out. Soon they started on their way home. *Home.* The word had never sounded so good.

Seeing the old place brought a lump to Daniel's throat. He offered to help his father milk, but he refused his offer. "Maybe tomorrow. Stay in and talk to your mother today."

His mother stood at the sink, so he hugged her then sat at the kitchen table where he'd eaten all his meals until three years ago. "The past three years have been harder on your father than me," she said. "I have my friends, but he's always been a loner. I think he doesn't want to choose one church member over another."

"I understand. When I had men under me, I had to be careful not to show favoritism, so I treated them all the same. But being a preacher would make it even harder."

"Is that why you left? You thought it would be too hard for you?"

"No. I'm not against hard work, but as I told Father, I didn't know what God wanted me to do. I still don't know exactly, but I do believe I'm supposed to marry Amanda and go to Oberlin College and take classes. I checked, and they have religion and Bible classes, but I want to go there with an open mind and see what God calls me to do. I'm leaning toward teaching, perhaps even teaching Bible classes."

His mother looked at him and smiled. "I never told you this, but before we married I wanted to be a teacher, but it didn't work out."

"You were the best teacher I ever had. I still remember the Bible stories you taught me. In fact, a few weeks ago I met a slave named Samuel. When I whispered his name it reminded me of you whispering the boy Samuel's name when God called him." Daniel smiled at her. "I gave him my brown sweater and a pair of wool socks you made me, so I hope you don't mind."

"Of course I don't mind, and I'll have plenty of time to knit this winter." Mother fixed two cups of coffee and sat at the table. "I want to hear all about this slave."

Daniel spent the next hour telling her about Zoar and how they aided others. He also shared how strict they were with some of their rules, like lights out at nine o'clock and not courting or marrying an outsider.

When his father came in, Daniel continued to talk about what he liked and didn't like about Zoar. He was proud to share how Amanda planned to leave Zoar and get married as soon as he arrived in Oberlin where her sister had also enrolled in college. Later, he took both their hands in his and apologized to them for all the worry he had caused them. Then he repeated to Father all he'd already shared with Mother.

"I can't wait for you both to meet Amanda. We hope to marry in April. . . ."

His mother jumped out of her chair like a mouse had climbed up her leg, then ran to the hall table. "I forgot. You got two letters a couple days ago." She handed them to him.

"They're from Amanda. Do you mind if I go to my room to read them?"

"Of course not. I need to get our lunch ready anyway."

He kissed her cheek then nodded to Father. "I can't wait to read them and then come back and tell you what she said."

Daniel's fingers shook as he opened the letters. He read the latest letter first and grew so heartsick at her sad spirit he could tell she was trying to cover up. Oh! He would have to write to her tonight and send it out tomorrow. He prayed she had received his telegram. He read the longer letter next then read it again before shouting, "Hooray!" He ran down the stairs two at a time. His parents were waiting at the bottom with questions on their faces.

"Amanda wants you both to come to our wedding and she also agrees with me. . . ." He looked from his mother to his father. His eyes locked on Father's. "We want Father to marry us."

"Glory be to God!" Mother shouted.

Epilogue

At the first note of the organ, Amanda started down the aisle on the arm of Daniel's uncle at First Church in Oberlin. Her eyes searched for the one for whom she had traveled all this way. The one for whom she was leaving all that was familiar, all she had ever done or known, to wed—her Daniel.

Six months ago, they hadn't even known each other, and now they would be pledging their love and faithfulness to each other for as long as they both would live. Only God could have given her a groom who encouraged her to press on in her dreams of whatever she felt God was calling her to do, just as she would support him as he sought his calling.

She would now have a companion to press on through life with, to share her joys and sorrows, her weaknesses and strengths, and be her forever family.

Rose Allen McCauley has been writing since she retired from teaching school and joined American Christian Fiction Writers (ACFW). She is thrilled for this to be her third collection with Barbour. She and her spouse just celebrated their golden anniversary with their three children and spouses and now six grandchildren! She loves to hear from her readers. You can reach her through her website www.rosemccauley.com or twitter @RoseAMcCauley and on Facebook under Rose Allen McCauley.

The Bridge Between Us

by Sherri Wilson Johnson

Dedication

To all the "bridges" out there. May God use you in mighty ways.

Acknowledgments

To my Lord and Savior, Jesus Christ—thank You for giving Your life for me
and for giving me a love for spreading the good news through my writing.
To my husband, Dan, thank you for believing that I can write more stories.
To Kayla, Seth, and Thea, thank you for being the
best kids a mom could ask for.
Rose, thank you for inviting me to be a part of this collection
and making some of my publishing dreams come true.
Tamela Hancock Murray, thank you for representing me on this project.
Laura, thank you for researching with me and for finding my setting.
Susan and Scott, thank you for being my heroine and hero in this fun story.
Christy and Brandy, thank you for "masterminding" with me.
To all my family, friends, and Bible study ladies,
thank you for your love and support.

Chapter 1

September 28, 1859
Albion, New York

The aroma of boiled peanuts and fried dough traveled along the crisp September breeze and tickled Susannah Higley's nose as exhilaration over the day's events delighted her heart. She had never experienced a Wednesday like this in all her twenty-three years. Waiting for the results of the wax flower contest and hoping a blue ribbon and prize money would be hers, she stood on the three-arched, iron Main Street bridge with hundreds of other townsfolk ready for the tightrope artist from Brockport to walk across the Erie Canal.

Susannah adjusted her white crepe bonnet and stuffed in a few unruly curls then sighed. The fearless young man would do on this fall day what she could never imagine mustering the courage to do.

For months, she had lived under the shadow of abandonment. Richard had declared his love for her, but when she had refused to go to California on a quest for gold, he hopped on a train and broke her heart. Although she longed for unforgettable experiences, eloping and leaving behind her widowed father was not among them. She should have known entertaining the idea of love with a drifter who had worked his way to Albion on boats traveling the canal would not be wise.

Since Richard's departure, Susannah had devoted her time to Pa's sawmill as the bookkeeper, a position Mama held before her passing. Once she balanced the ledgers and completed the household chores each day, Susannah fashioned flowers from wax and dreamed of one day sharing her creations with merchants in New York City.

The black metal box containing her patterns, brushes, tints, and wax was the last gift Mama gave her. Every time she formed the red roses, yellow geraniums, and purple and white violets from wax Mama had loved so much, she felt her presence.

Winning a ribbon at the Orleans County Fair not only increased her chances of someone discovering her but would also confirm to her this pastime brought as much joy to others as it did to her. The long-awaited day was finally here.

Mr. Smith pulled his team of horses and lumber wagon along the southbound pathway of the bridge and gave a shout-out to Mr. Thayer, who stood next to Susannah in his dark suit and shining black top hat. The bridge groaned under the added weight, and she gripped the railing even tighter while shifting her full skirts of brown taffeta a bit, giving little Laura Baker a better view.

Pa must be somewhere on the crowded bridge. But where?

How lively their supper conversation would be tonight. For once. Most evenings, they talked about their lack of provision or how they missed Mama. No matter how often Susannah shared with Pa her ideas for increasing their earnings or encouraged him to court Mary Waterbury at the bakery, he always grumbled, too unwilling—or perhaps afraid—to take a risk.

Susannah smiled and felt a twinkle touch her brown eyes as leaves of red, gold, and brown floated through the air. Yes, tonight their discussion would be filled with talk of the tightrope walker and, hopefully, her accomplishments as a flower designer. Maybe Pa would follow her lead after today and make changes in his life.

Laura pushed between Susannah and Mr. Thayer and ran to her mother, who stood on the towpath with an infant swaddled against her. Susannah redirected her attention to the second floor of the Mansion House and giggled when the brave man started his journey toward the second floor of the Pierpont Dyer's building.

She had never experienced such anticipation racing through her. Covering her mouth with gloved hands, her glee uncontainable, she lifted onto her tiptoes and never moved her gaze from the acrobat. He teetered and balanced on the line as clouds muted the sun's warm glow.

Then the bridge creaked and lurched, groaned and popped.

Susannah gripped the railing and questioned Mr. Thayer with a raised eyebrow.

He shrugged and patted her hand, but piercing screams erupted midway across the bridge.

They plummeted through the collapsing railing and crashed into the chilly water with a bone-jarring impact.

Susannah pinched her nose and held her breath seconds before someone landed on top of her with a hard thud and dragged her below the surface.

Despite the murky water's attempt at hampering Susannah's vision, the late afternoon sunlight illuminated her surroundings enough to discern the direction of the surface and avoid the pieces of the still-falling bridge. Releasing her nose, she used both hands to heave her way to the surface of the seven-foot-deep water, tugging against the weight of her bulky skirt and cape and the flailing arms of the people joining her in this watery death trap.

Susannah reached the surface and gasped for life-giving air but could not make her way out from underneath the bridge's fallen trusses.

People screamed and cried for help while thrashing in the water. Men on the towpath whistled and yelled instructions. Surely someone would rescue them before they drowned.

If Susannah could swim, she would let go of the iron beam and save herself then rescue someone else. But her lack of swimming ability mattered not right now. No matter how hard she tried inching closer to the bank and increasing her chances of someone lifting her out of the water, she could not move. Either her saturated dress was too heavy because of her steel-hooped cage crinoline or it was snagged by bridge debris.

How long would she wait before someone pulled her out of the water? Would she freeze before then? Would she slip under from the exhaustion of hanging on to the beam? With closed eyes, she whispered through chattering teeth a prayer to her heavenly Father.

Then someone grabbed her right hand. "Release the beam, miss." After another tug, the gentleman repeated, "Ma'am? Let it go."

Opening her eyes, Susannah stared into the warm, coffee-colored eyes of a bearded stranger on the other side of the wreckage. "I—I can't. I'll—I'll drown."

He shook his head as he held on to the beam above him with his left hand. "No, I've got you." He patted her hand. "You won't drown. I will not let you. Give me both your hands, and I will pull you free. I promise."

Did she have a choice? If she did not let him free her, she would freeze to death in this water.

"Ma'am, hold your breath and go under enough to slide through this opening."

"No. You'll let me go."

"I won't. I've got you."

Fear rumbled through Susannah, as a gust of wind took her breath. With reservation, she nodded then slid one hand from the beam. The gentleman clasped it with great strength, then she slid her other hand off the beam and grabbed his taut forearm.

"Go ahead. You will come up on the other side of the truss—on the same side as me."

Susannah did as the stranger directed. In seconds, he whisked her through the opening and popped her back to the surface. They both held to the beam and rested a moment.

As Susannah studied this kindhearted man treading water next to her, a smile spread across his face. Her gaze roamed from his eyes to his smile and back to his eyes again.

"John?" What was John Hawkins doing back in Albion? After the town ran his family away seven years ago, Susannah assumed she would never see him again.

"Yes? Do I know you?" He squinted in the afternoon glow and examined her face.

Of course, how would he recognize her when she must look like a half-drowned rat, bonnet drenched and curls in disarray? But then he arched an eyebrow and nodded, and her heart leaped.

"Susannah? Susannah Higley?"

A smile exploded across her face. "Yes, yes, it is me."

He moved closer to her. "I guess I picked the right day to return to Albion."

"The right day and the right place at the right time, I'd say." She shivered, her teeth chattering again. "Now, do you think you can finish rescuing me? My dress is caught on something. I cannot move."

He glared into the green water. "Maybe it's cumbersome because it's soaked."

Susannah kicked her legs then shook her head. "No, I am stuck. I cannot pull my dress through the opening."

John squeezed the back of his neck and shifted closer to her as someone bobbed to the surface beside him. "I will go under and check."

"Please stay here."

He smiled. "I'll be right back." Sucking in a breath, he dove under the surface.

When John yanked at her skirt, Susannah squealed and clutched the beam as tight as her frozen hands would allow so he would not drag her under. All around her, crying people struggled to stay afloat while men in small boats came to their aid. Thankfully, Laura Baker joined her mother before the bridge collapsed.

With a splash, John emerged, shook his head to remove the water from his hair, and ran his right hand down his bearded face. "You are free. Your skirt was caught. I am afraid I ripped it though. I will purchase a new dress for you or buy you some new fabric."

Susannah shook her head at his ill-timed declaration. "Sir, you do not have to purchase a new skirt for me. You saved my life. How can I ever repay you?"

"No repayment necessary except that you not call me sir ever again. I am but a few years your senior. Besides, I haven't completely rescued you yet."

"Where is Pa?"

"Let me get you to the bank, and I will come back to look for your father."

"No, he cannot know you are here."

John bowed his head and sucked in a breath. "We cannot worry about your father's reaction to me being in town right now, Susannah. Can you swim?"

"No."

He sighed. "Okay, do exactly as I do." Inching one hand at a time down the beam, John guided the way to the sloping bank.

Within minutes, they had reached the shallow part of the canal. Susannah allowed John to tug her to her feet and accepted a rope that someone tossed down to her. Despite her weakened legs and water-laden clothing, she walked her way up the rocky embankment and straight into a warmed blanket.

"Susannah! Is that you?"

Susannah turned her attention to Pa, who ran toward her with an intensity in his eyes she had never seen. "It is me, Pa!" Thank the Lord he was safe.

He threw his arms around her. "Are you hurt? Do you need a doctor?"

"I am fine, Pa. Cold and wet, but I am glad I am back on land."

"Who can I thank for fishing you out of the canal?"

Pivoting, Susannah faced the canal and searched for John. Where was he? Maybe he had seen Pa and decided he would not make his presence in Albion known. At least God had given her a few moments with the man she once thought she would marry.

"Susannah?" Pa urged.

"Someone from out of town rescued me. He must be here for the fair."

"I will forever be grateful to him."

"Me too, Pa. Me too."

◆━━━━◆

Susannah pulled her rose-colored velvet cape closed and tried to block the wind as she made her way down the boardwalk to the dry goods store on Canal Street to collect her blue ribbon and prize money. A crowd stood near the canal at Main and Alley probably buzzing about the bridge collapse, injuries, and deaths. Everything on the canal had come to a halt after they drained it to secure the bodies and clear the wreckage. Once they refilled the canal though, people could board boats and enjoy sites all the way from New York City to Buffalo. But months would pass before they rebuilt the bridge. At least the bridge at Ingersoll Street still stood for crossing the canal by wagon if necessary.

Although chills and coughing spasms had plagued Susannah since her plunge into the Erie Canal two days earlier, thankfulness filled her soul today. Fifteen of her townsfolk had lost their lives, yet God had chosen to let her live with the help of John Hawkins. Because of that, she would not waste another day fretting over Richard and the regrets and disappointments of the past.

The thrill over winning the wax flower category and her name appearing in the Orleans County newspaper for her accomplishment was irrepressible. The prize money equaled a day's wages. Oh, the timeliness of this prize.

As she stood here on the street, her red and pink roses and geraniums traveled by train to New York City for the state fair. This win gave her the confidence she needed to plan her travels to the big city to speak with merchants about carrying her flowers in their stores.

"Good morning, Susannah. Are you feeling better today?"

Susannah pulled her gaze from the dry goods store before entering and smiled at her former schoolteacher, whose approach had gone unnoticed while her mind drifted to the days ahead.

"Yes, Mrs. Peterson. Much better, except for this nagging cough. Were Mr. Peterson's injuries from the bridge mild or severe?"

Mrs. Peterson nodded, and her deep-blue bonnet, which hid her vibrant red waves, slipped down her forehead. After repositioning the bonnet, she answered, "He received a deep cut on his shoulder, but he will be fine." She adjusted the bell-shaped sleeves of her black silk dress and folded her hands across her stomach.

"Good." Susannah cast her gaze down Main Street toward where the bridge once stood. "I hate we lost so many people but am glad it was not more."

"Yes, dear. I told Mr. Peterson that. The whole ordeal stresses him. He wishes he could have done something to prevent the bridge from collapsing, wishes he could have saved lives."

"My pa says the same thing, but we can have no regrets. Everyone did the best they could." Susannah shivered, her lungs tightening from the cool air. "I had better get inside and out of this wind. My cough will worsen if I stay out here much longer."

"You take care. And congratulations on winning first prize."

"Thank you." Susannah ducked into the store. Her mouth watered as the aroma of warm cinnamon rolls reached her nose. Mrs. Adams usually baked something fresh each day for her customers. If two cinnamon rolls remained after Susannah received her ribbon and made her purchases of coffee, tea, and salt, she would take them home and enjoy them with Pa over a cup of coffee.

Mr. Adams and his wife were nowhere in the store, so Susannah peeked through the doorway into the storage room. *Where could they be?*

"Good morning," boomed a voice from behind her.

Susannah lurched and stepped backward into a crate of potatoes. Her weighty skirt of gray grenadine tipped the crate over, and the potatoes spilled all over the wooden floor. Face aflame, she pivoted, to find John Hawkins smirking, arms crossed and brown eyes glimmering.

"Mr. Hawkins, you startled me," she huffed, triggering a coughing spasm.

John removed his boiler cap and clasped it against his chest. "Miss Susannah, I did not intend to frighten you or send you into a fit." He placed his hat atop his head again and collected a few potatoes off the floor.

She sucked in a deep, raspy breath and exhaled. "Well, you did, Mr. Hawk—"

"John." The twinkle still sparkled in his eyes.

Susannah stooped and picked up the remaining potatoes. Maybe she could avoid locking gazes with John. Even when he teased her, she found his kindness and attentiveness difficult to resist. "Fine. John, if you insist. You should not have startled me so."

"Please accept my apologies. Are you looking for something or someone?"

"Yes, Mr. or Mrs. Adams. I came to get a few staples and the prize I won."

"I heard about your success in the competition. You must be quite proud of your accomplishment."

"I am honored, yes. Especially since I nearly died and could have missed ever knowing about my success. I am grateful to you for saving me." How John appeared right where Susannah needed him after falling into the canal, she may never know, but she owed him her life.

"Always a pleasure to save a friend."

"Welcome back to Albion. Are you here for a long visit?" Mr. and Mrs. Adams must have stepped out for a meal. Or could they be upstairs in their room?

"Depends on if I get everything done I came to do."

"You came on business then?" Susannah peeked into the back room again. She needed to get her supplies and prize and return to the office before Pa worried about her.

"In a way. Would you like to hear about my plans? I'd like to know how you make the wax flowers. Perhaps I could pay you a visit this evening?"

Susannah jerked her attention from the back room and onto John, yanking a knot in her neck. "No! Pa would not welcome you into our home, John. I am sorry."

"But what happened with our families happened long ago. Does your father still hold a grudge?"

Susannah massaged the side of her neck and winced. "It is more than a grudge, John. It is true, heartfelt pain of the betrayal. Do not come."

"Very well. I respect your wishes, Miss Higley." He shoved his hands into his front pants pockets and shuffled his feet. "Would you walk with me down to the canal? Perhaps I can explain the reason for my return?"

As much as a walk down by the canal would refresh her, her responsibilities thwarted her consent. "I am sorry, but I must get my supplies home and then return to the office to help Pa."

"Can you not spare a weary traveler a few minutes of your time?"

"You are more than a traveler passing through, John. But I cannot."

"Miss Susannah, is that you down there?" Mrs. Adams hollered from upstairs.

A flood of relief washed over Susannah. If she had spent one more minute alone with John, she would have accepted his invitation. "Yes, ma'am. I came for my prize and a few staples."

"Dear, your ribbon and money are in the bin underneath the counter. Go ahead and take them and whatever you need. I am giving Mr. Adams a shave, and I cannot come downstairs right now."

"Thank you, I will." Susannah made her way behind the counter, careful not to knock anything else over with her skirt. "John, I cannot join you today. I must get these supplies home and return to the office. Good seeing you." She nodded and then busied herself with getting what she needed.

"Good day then." And with that, John departed.

If she could, she would run after him and devote her entire day to him, begging him to regale her with stories of the big city, soaking in his warm voice as he recited his plans while in Albion. But doing so would involve her heart and jeopardize her harmony with Pa. Besides, John planned to leave again, and no one could protect Susannah's heart better than she could. She had to guard it.

Chapter 2

John stomped away from the dry goods store headed south on Main Street toward the Albion Hotel. With each powerful punch of his boots on the sidewalk, he imagined himself boxing with an opponent in a ring. If steam could burst from his ears, it would do so now.

Susannah's loyalty to her father and her characteristic knack for all things proper and right provoked aggravation in him akin to that of a splinter wedged underneath a fingernail. Without her help, John could not reconcile with Chauncey Higley and repay him what his grandfather had cheated him out of when they worked together on the canal in its early days.

Being this honor-bound to her father, she might refuse his request. But if she would listen and cooperate, he could be on his way and out of her life forever. By all appearances, she wanted that.

Even though she had expressed her gratitude for saving her life—he would do it a thousand times more—he did not need a genius to figure out that being around him embarrassed Susannah. Why else would she have shooed him away like a pesky fly in the store?

Maybe she had a fiancé and did not want to raise her neighbors' suspicions by associating with him. Or maybe being a Hawkins was the problem. Susannah, his longtime friend and the young woman who had captured his heart when they were youngsters, had changed.

If she would not hear him out, thereby reducing his chances of reconciliation with Higley, he might as well sign out of his room at the hotel and hop the train now. Even though New York City was not home to his ostracized family, it welcomed him more than Albion had thus far.

Speaking with Susannah's father would serve no purpose anyway. If Higley had held on to the grudge all these years, like a tick on a hound, he probably would not let go now. Good thing John abstained, or he would stop off at the tavern on the way to the hotel and wash away his cares. But he had learned from his grandfather's life that drowning one's sorrows in a bottle only made problems worse, and he had enough problems.

"Excuse me, sir?"

John halted in front of a robust woman in a dark blue dress, a young boy about the age of ten standing beside her in an ill-fitting, worn suit. "Yes?"

"I am Mrs. Fleming." She smiled and nodded, her oversized, peacock-green hat nearly knocking his hat off his head. "You're the man who pulled my son out of the canal when the bridge collapsed." She tugged the lad closer and kneaded his shoulder with her gloved hand.

"I am?" John grinned and winked at the boy. His answering smile brought warmth to John's heart.

"Yes, sir. I'd recognize you in a crowd of a hundred people. Thank you for rescuing him."

"My pleasure. What's your name, sir?" John knelt in front of the spindly fellow with golden hair and bright green eyes.

"Daniel, sir."

John reached out his hand. "Glad to make your acquaintance."

Daniel accepted John's offered hand. "Yours too."

Mrs. Fleming interjected, "My husband passed six months ago. Now my son, who is only twelve, is the man of the house. I could not live without him."

The boy was twelve? His small stature made him appear much younger. "Ma'am, I am glad you will not have to find out what life would be like without him."

"I am blessed indeed. Are you new in town, sir?"

John pushed to his feet. "Just passing through. I had intended to leave the day after the bridge collapsed, but my business was delayed."

"Let me be the first to welcome you, providing no one else has. I hope you'll consider making Albion your home." The kind widow moved past him on the sidewalk, and her son wriggled away from her grasp and joined a group of boys playing marbles in front of the store. Carefree. John used to be that way.

"Thank you, ma'am. Your welcome is the best I have had here in Albion."

Maybe he would stay a little while longer after all and see if he could arrange an appointment with Higley—even if Susannah thought poorly of the idea.

John twirled a red maple leaf between his thumb and forefinger and studied the activity on the drained canal from his seat on a bench by the towpath. A policeman blew his whistle and gave the call to the workers that they had retrieved the last body. Now they could open the gates and send word to the towns east of them, so they could open their gates. Once the water level returned to normal, everyone could resume their activities on the many boats that traveled along the canal.

As a boy, and all the way up until he turned eighteen when the townsfolk ran his family out of Albion, John would sit by the canal after his daily lessons avoiding going home to do chores. Instead of milking the cow and tending to the pigs, he preferred watching the boats filled with all sorts of ruffians and travelers coming from and going to locations he had never imagined visiting at that age. He would dream of stowing away on one of those boats and living an adventurous life unlike anyone in his family before him.

Now, at twenty-five, he had been to Buffalo, Albany, New York City, and every city in between along the canal and the Hudson River. He had been out on the open ocean testing the expansive ships built by his father and grandfather after they relocated in the city. Today he missed the salty air of the Atlantic and the piercing calls of seagulls flying overhead when he and his crew set sail. The horns and whistles of merchant ships and steamboats would forever call his name. But he had a job to do while here, and he needed to stop his reverie.

"Mr. Hawkins, might I have a word with you?"

The hairs rose on the back of John's neck and not from the cool September air. The velvet-smooth voice of Susannah Higley came from behind him. He would know that voice anywhere, even if he had not already spoken with her twice since arriving in Albion.

He jumped to his feet, removed his hat, and faced her. She held a small crate that contained her supplies from the store. Her blue ribbon peeked out over the edge of the crate. John could only imagine how hard she had worked on her wax flowers to get them as perfect as possible. And now, her hours of labor had accomplished one of her dreams. Her faithfulness to the task encouraged him not to give up on his quest.

"Miss Higley, it is a pleasure to see you again. And so soon." The blush on her cheeks matched the heat in his heart at the mere sight of her lovely face and dark curls attempting to hide her fawn eyes from him. Why did the woman who had earlier cast him away like the evening meal's scraps produce a knot in his chest tighter than a hangman's snare?

More importantly, why did she stand here before him now, looking flustered?

"May I?" She nodded toward the bench.

John replaced his hat and took the crate from her then stepped aside. "Yes, yes, of course. Please sit."

Susannah pulled her skirt close to her after sitting and made room for John to join her. "If you insist I call you John, then I must insist you call me Susannah."

John placed the crate on the ground and sat beside her, inhaling her refreshing lavender and rose fragrance. "Very well. What can I do for you, Susannah? You seemed in such a hurry at the dry goods store."

"Please forgive my rudeness earlier. You caught me by surprise and, frankly, I pretended you were not welcome out of desperation."

"So I am welcome?"

"John, what kind of Christian would I be if I treated you as our parents and grandparents treated each other? We are friends, are we not? I am afraid I let my fears of Pa's reaction to you being in town affect the way I behaved toward you."

"Thank you, Susannah. Are you well? Your cough gave me reason to worry about your health."

"Your concern is sweet. I'll be fine. I am afraid getting soaked in the canal chilled me a bit too much."

"I'm glad you will recover." He tapped his fingers on his knees and tried to hide the jitters, which ran through him being this close to her.

"The cough will go away. I only hope the nightmares I have had of falling into the water will go away too." Susannah looked toward the canal and shivered.

"I do hope they will."

"You asked me to let you explain your purpose here. If you have time now, I would love to hear what you have to say."

John removed his hat and kneaded it with shaking hands. "Susannah, my father recently passed."

She placed her hand on his forearm, and a shiver of pleasure scurried up his arm. "I am sorry for your loss."

"Thank you."

"Did you bring him for burial in the Albion cemetery with your mother?"

"No, I buried him in New York City where he wanted. He left instructions in his will for me to return to Albion though, and give your father the money my grandfather owed your grandfather. Had he paid for the lumber he ordered instead of stealing it in the dead of night, this feud would have never happened. I want to make amends for my grandfather's deception."

"I see. How honorable of you." She folded her delicate hands atop her lap.

He gazed into her eyes a moment then cast his focus on the bridge wreckage. "My father wanted this. Would you help me make things right with your father?"

"What could I possibly do?"

"You could prepare the way. Let him know I am here and I want to talk."

Susannah covered her heart with her hand and sighed. His request must be too much. "You would ask me to face the brunt of his anger in your stead?"

"It is a great deal to ask, Susannah. You would only have to tell him I want to speak with him." He did not want her to feel like a pawn. This was not a game. John's family's reputation was at stake, and only Susannah could pave the way for restoration.

"John, I am afraid you'll regret talking to Pa about the feud. He wants nothing to do with any of the Hawkins people. If you want to talk to him, you will have to do it without me."

"Why would he feel anger toward me? The business between our grandfathers had nothing to do with me. Or your pa."

"I know. But he was instructed to avoid all people who go by the name Hawkins. Everybody in town knows how crooked your grandfather was. They want nothing to do with the Hawkinses."

John groaned. "I cannot believe no one in this town would accept me here. We left a long time ago. The numbers have doubled since we left. No one knows of this feud."

Susannah pushed to her feet and strolled to the edge of the waterless canal. She folded her arms and hugged her waist. Was she considering helping him?

John waited on the bench. If he pushed her too hard, she would not only refuse her help, but he would possibly lose her friendship forever.

Susannah pivoted, and by the grim look on her face, she was not acquiescing. "John, I cannot involve myself in this matter. My allegiance is to Pa. Since Mama passed, I am all he has. We struggle to get by, and we depend on each other."

John joined her by the canal's edge. "But this repayment could be the answer your pa needs."

She shook her head. "I must remain unbiased. Whatever you do, you will have to do it without my help." A tear slipped from her right eye and slid down her cheek, then she turned away.

He moaned and reached out, grasping her wrist. "I had nothing to do with that feud, yet they forced me to leave behind the life I wanted."

Although she halted, her gaze landed on the bench instead of on him.

"Why must I suffer for what my forefathers did? Where's the fairness in that?"

She pulled away from him and picked up the crate. "I am sorry, John. I truly am. But you must see I have to do as Pa says."

Without giving him the chance to plead his case further, Susannah scurried away, carrying with her the last of his hope.

Chapter 3

Susannah grabbed her gray shawl off the hook on the wall and flung the door open. The crisp afternoon air tousled her curls and nipped at the back of her neck as she darted out before John reached the porch steps of her family's white Victorian on Madison Street, southeast of town.

"John, what are you doing here? I told you not to come." She jammed her hands onto her hips. When her heart raced, and her breath quickened at the sight of him, denying the renewal of her love for John proved futile. Her feelings for Richard had only replaced it for a short while. The town—or at least Pa—might not welcome him, but she wanted him here. Encouraging him to stay though meant trouble for them both.

John removed his hat and gripped it against his chest. A flurry of autumn leaves swirled around him. "Please forgive me for going against your wishes. I did not want the last time we saw each other to involve you dashing away from me as you did this morning."

Her breath hitched. Seven years ago, they had said their last goodbyes. Would this now be the last time she would see his charming smile and glistening eyes? "You are leaving Albion already?"

"I see no reason to stay if I cannot conduct my business." He snapped his hat on top of his head and adjusted his checked, double-breasted vest at the waist. His black trousers and long jacket fit him well, hiding the muscles that had rescued Susannah from the bridge debris.

"John, I—" She paused. No words could heal this predicament.

"I did not want to leave without saying my farewells. You are too good a friend to leave that way. May I come in for a cup of coffee?"

Susannah pulled at her collar. How she would love to bring him inside for a visit, but proper etiquette forbade unchaperoned calls and certainly so did Pa's house rules. "My pa is away."

John moved closer to her but remained in the grass, not breaching the imaginary boundary line she had drawn. "Then allow me to sit on the steps with you?" He shifted his way closer, placing one foot on the bottom step.

Susannah chewed on the inside of her cheek and studied his face. "I am not sure. If Pa comes in from town and finds you here, you'll have a mess of trouble on your hands."

Shrugging, he stepped closer. "I'll take that risk." A gust of wind ruffled his coat.

With John's bearded face, Pa might not recognize him. No neighbor peeking out a window would identify him as a Hawkins. Maybe they could steal a few minutes together without being discovered.

Susannah nodded, as willing as John to risk Pa finding them together.

After he took the second step from the bottom, she sat on the top step and tucked her skirt to the side. Although autumn dominated their surroundings, spring butterflies fluttered inside her stomach. Never had she imagined being this close to him again.

"Susannah, I came here hopeful. I wanted to repay your father and then see if I could make Albion my home again. With my father now gone, nothing keeps me in New York City." He leaned over and scooped a dozen or so leaves into his hands, the gathered reds, yellows, and browns making a fall bouquet.

"What about your business? Do you not have work there? What about acquaintances?" Did he have a fiancée he would bring here to Albion? Susannah dared not intrude into his private affairs lest she spoil the fleeting bliss found in his presence.

"We build ships. Someone recently offered to purchase the company from me, but I haven't decided yet. I suppose I wanted to see if Albion would welcome me home first. I have some friends but none I would not leave if more awaited me here." He kept his gaze focused on the leaves, but Susannah sensed his attention directed at her.

"I am sure being gone has been difficult for you. We have all missed you."

John chuckled, the dimple on his right cheek barely visible beneath his beard. "I doubt that."

She snickered then cleared her throat. "Well, your true friends have."

"Like you?"

She smiled. "Like me."

John offered her the leaf arrangement. They were more beautiful than any bouquet of roses.

"Thank you, kind sir." She received the leaves and placed them on her lap. "As a shipbuilder, you have probably seen more adventure than you ever saw here in Albion."

"I have been to England. I have seen castles and dolphins and mountains. But none of them replaced the sadness in my heart that I could not be here."

"Why? If you can see beautiful things like the ocean and foreign lands and anything other than the Erie Canal, why would you ever want to come back?"

"Do you dream of leaving?"

"I have dreamed of seeing something other than this town, yes. I want to see New York City. Shop in Manhattan. Find my wax flowers in their storefront windows. See the ocean and the crashing waves."

"You could take a boat down the canal with some friends to Albany and see all the stops then go down the Hudson to the city."

"Pa would never allow it. Nor could I afford such a trip."

"Maybe one day."

"Perhaps. I had the opportunity not long ago to go out west, but Mama had recently passed, and I could not leave Pa." Susannah organized the leaves by color on her lap and sighed, trying not to regret letting Richard leave without her. "So why have you really come today, John Hawkins?"

He scratched his beard and stared at the ground. "I came to see you before I leave." Raising his gaze to her eyes and sending sparks to her heart, he continued, "However, it is vital I make amends with your pa first. Would you help me make things right with him?"

A train whistle blew a couple blocks away. If Susannah could hop on that train right now and escape this impossible predicament, she would. She wanted John here, but she wanted to please Pa. Obeying him meant dissatisfying John. However, satisfying John meant disobeying Pa. Being pinned between these two hard places crippled her.

A curl fell across her forehead, and she brushed it aside. "We were young when all of that happened between our grandfathers, too young to understand everything. Even if unfair from our perspective, the Higleys have reason to dislike the Hawkinses." As she spoke the words, she rebuked them in her heart. Not forgiving, harboring resentment, seemed wrong.

"Let me explain to you about the ill blood between our families."

"John, my father has already explained everything to me."

"Did he tell you my father tried to repay your grandfather, but he refused? That he would rather hold a grudge and soil our family name than to accept the goodwill gesture and make amends?"

"Well, no. But your grandfather's actions made my grandfather look poorly as a businessman in the eyes of the town because he could not fulfill his obligations."

"Yes, but my father tried to settle it, and your grandfather refused. Your father refused as well."

Susannah's face flushed. Her father could have ended the feud but did not? Anger brewed from deep within her. John could have stayed in town all these years instead of losing everything he had ever known?

This situation lacked fairness. Why did a feuding family's grudge obligate the children? Could they not forgive and start anew?

She shook her head. "How does that matter now? What is done cannot be undone. It is best to look into the future and not the past."

"Your future still includes the home you have known most of your life. They did not run you out of town and force you to begin again."

Susannah placed her hand on John's shoulder. "I empathize with you, but can you not see my position?"

He squeezed his hands into fists. "Your position? What about my position? I was forced to leave behind the woman I thought would be my wife."

She gasped and faced him. "John?" He had wanted to marry her? Long ago, she had hoped one day to marry him but never imagined he wanted the same.

"I am sorry, Susannah. I could not leave without telling you how I feel."

"I—John, you—"

In the distance, Pa appeared, marching down the street whistling.

"John! My father!" Susannah bolted off the step, scattering the leaves everywhere, and pulled him by the coat collar until he stood. "Here he comes! You must go. He will explode if he sees us here together—if he discovers you are in town."

"No, I want to stay and talk to him." John locked his knees, keeping Susannah from budging him off the step.

Her heart raced, and she could not swallow the terror in her throat. "John, please! I will talk to him for you. I will tell him you want to repay the debt. Just go." She shoved him off the step. "Go around the back of the house and down Temperance Street to Main."

John jammed his hat onto his head, plopped a kiss upon her left cheek, and was out of sight when Pa rounded the picket fence in the front.

◆——·——◆

Susannah stirred the beef stew after sampling the broth and adding more salt and pepper then slid the iron skillet with the corn bread batter into the oven. The savory meal would be perfect for a chilly night like tonight. After wiping crumbs and stew drippings from the stovetop with a soapy cloth, she tossed the cloth into the wash pan.

Leaning against the cabinet, she wiped her forehead with the back of her hand and sighed. As her hand slid down the side of her face, her fingers rested on the spot John had placed his kiss. Echoes of the tingles she had felt from his kiss remained.

How could she look at Pa tonight during dinner without telling him about John?

Thankfully, when he returned home earlier, he sought only a fresh shirt before his meeting with a potential customer. Because business occupied his mind, he overlooked Susannah's panic over his near collision with John.

399

But once he slowed down for the day, he would know she was hiding something from him. He always knew.

When he returned this evening from the train station after sending off the lumber order headed for Manhattan, she would cut the corn bread into slices and give him the hearty meal he deserved. Then if he inquired about her day, she would distract him with her apple pie.

Susannah grabbed the broom and swept the heart pine kitchen floor. Would that it could be this easy to sweep her cares away.

Did Pa have to know of John's presence? That he had rescued her?

She stopped sweeping mid-stroke. Yes, she should tell Pa everything, especially that John had come to their home. If not, one of the neighbors most assuredly would, and Pa's heart would break over her dishonesty and secrecy. Plus, she had told John she would speak on his behalf to Pa.

That settled the matter. If Pa inquired, she would tell him the truth. If not, she would wait until the time was right to speak for John.

She leaned the broom against the wall and sauntered down the hall to the front door. A good sit on the porch before Pa came home would cool her off from cooking and clear her thoughts.

◆━━━━━◆

"Pa, you are right on time. I was heading inside to check on the corn bread."

The swaying of the porch swing and the breeze created by the fan from Mr. Barker's funeral had done a perfect job of returning Susannah to her usual calm demeanor.

Pa joined Susannah on the porch in silence. His furrowed brow and crumpled, bushy eyebrows spoke volumes about his state and made him look much older than his fifty years.

She gazed into his blue eyes, which resembled a stormy summer sky tonight. "Are you hungry?"

Pa scratched his chin and ran his hands through his sandy-blond hair. "I was, but now my appetite is gone." He yanked open the door and marched into the house.

Susannah's body went hot. Had someone told him about John? She sprang from the rocking chair and followed him into the house, tossing the fan on the foyer table then chasing after Pa. He tossed his coat on the stair rail and discarded his hat onto the post cap.

"What is the matter, Pa? You always want dinner. I made your favorite stew with beef, carrots, potatoes, and onions."

A heaviness settled into the parlor as Pa plopped into the armchair beside the fireplace. "I received news in town, and it drove the hunger right out of me."

Susannah's heart fell to her feet. Pa must know about John. What else could trouble him in such a way? She sank into the settee and braced for Pa's chastisement.

He remained silent with his head buried in his hands. Was he waiting on her to admit her secrets? No good could come of her hiding anything from him. She might as well tell him now. "Pa. . ."

Pa jerked his hands away from his head and slapped his knees. "Susannah, I am distraught."

She bit her lip and waited for him to finish.

"I have the chance to fill a substantial order for a company in Buffalo. If I can produce all the lumber they need by their deadline, I can pay the loan on our home, and we will not worry over our future any longer."

"Such wonderful news, Pa." Susannah relaxed her shoulders. When had she tightened them? "Why are you out of sorts?"

Pa scrubbed his face with his hands and groaned. He reached into his tobacco box on the table beside the fireplace and pulled out his pipe.

"Now, Pa, do not let this drive you to smoking. You know Mama hated when you brought out that pipe. What do you always say about vices? 'If you reach for them in troubling times, you'll have an abundance of trouble.'"

Pa sighed and returned the pipe to its box.

"Come, let us eat. You can tell me why this order is causing you strife later."

She stood from the settee and motioned for him to lead the way to the kitchen. Telling him about John could wait until he felt better. Although Pa's worry pained her, at least his concerns had nothing to do with John.

After dinner Susannah and Pa retired to the parlor and sat beside a toasty fire with chamomile tea and butter-lemon cookies. Now that the house had cooled from cooking, the warmth of the embers in the fireplace brought serenity into Susannah's heart instead of causing her discomfort. She kept her fingers busy with pressing wax onto the pattern for making violets. Once the wax set a bit, she would brush purple and white tint onto her creation.

"Pa, why is this large order troubling you so? You have done large ones before, have you not? The order you sent to Manhattan today was quite large."

Having eaten more stew than usual tonight, Pa adjusted the waistline of his pants. "These people own half of New York's finest establishments. If I do well by them, they will do well by me. But if I fail to meet their expectations, they'll ruin me. Do you know how long it took me to undo the damage the Hawkins family did to us?"

Susannah halted her fingers. A burning rose from her stomach and set her throat on fire. She gulped and tried to keep her dinner from rising into her mouth.

"We cannot afford anything like that disgrace to happen again. They will laugh us out of town and send us westward to start over."

"Pa, the townsfolk respect you. Nothing will cause them to push us out of here."

Pa drummed the fingers of his right hand on the tobacco box. His anxiousness would take over soon, and he would probably smoke his pipe after she retired for the evening.

"Here, have a cookie." She offered the plate to him.

Pa lifted a cookie from the plate and raised it to his lips. Before he took a bite, he declared, "They did it to the Hawkinses, and they can do it to us." He crammed the cookie into his mouth and chomped it, disregarding the crumbs that landed in his beard.

"But you say the Hawkins family deserved their fate. The same fate would not apply to you."

"I doubt they'd be that unbiased."

Susannah dropped the unfinished wax flower onto the table. One of her brushes rolled to the floor. "Well, I refuse to live any place that kicks hardworking businessmen out of town if they make a mistake or fail in some way."

"Susannah, Albion is your home."

"I know, Pa, but home should be safe and forgiving. I cannot be proud of a place that would abandon its own like a cow who rejects its calf. I just cannot."

"Why are you on the defensive so? I think you could use a cookie worse than me." Pa offered her the plate, and she slid a soft cookie into her hand.

Now was her chance. A more perfect time to defend John may never come. Pa might not think she should rebel against a town that shoved out its own, but surely he would agree John belonged here. She swallowed her bite of cookie and straightened her shoulders. "People judge others unfairly for their mistakes and even for the wrongs of their loved ones."

"I agree."

"What if I stole something from the dry goods store? Would you want others to blame you for my actions?"

"I would not want it, but I am afraid they would, Susannah. A parent is directly responsible for the actions of the children. It is a reflection on how well the parent has taught the child."

She scooted to the edge of her seat. "I do not agree completely with you, Pa, but say you are right. What if the parent stole something from the store? Should the child be punished?"

"I do not think so. But I am afraid my opinion would not matter. The town would judge, Susannah."

"Pa, any town that would form a judgment against you if you make a mistake is unfair. People make mistakes, and they sometimes cannot meet the expectations of others. There is no shame in that."

"I suppose."

"I would not—or should not—be judged if you fail to produce what this large company wants from you. Right?"

"Right."

Susannah could not stop herself from smiling. Pa had contradicted his own case against the Hawkinses.

"Why are you smiling?"

"John Hawkins should not be judged for what his grandfather did all those years ago."

Pa slammed his teacup onto the table, splashing tea on his cuff. "John Hawkins? What do you know of that situation?"

"I know what you told me. And I know what *he* told me."

"When? Seven years ago, before the town asked his family to leave? He was barely a man then. He knew nothing about what happened between your grandfather and his."

"Yes, seven years ago." She paused then jumped in feetfirst. "And today."

Pa glared at her, and if she could crawl underneath the settee, she would. "Today? You spoke with him today?"

"Yes, Pa, I did. And I saw him two days ago."

"Two days ago? You are only telling me now this man is in town?"

"I am sorry, Pa. I thought telling you served no purpose and would only upset you. I thought I would not see him again."

"You saw him at the fair?"

She folded her hands on her lap and squeezed her eyes shut. "Yes, sir. He rescued me after the bridge collapsed."

"Look at me! You said someone from out of town rescued you."

She opened her eyes, Pa's anger constricting her. "He *is* from out of town."

"You lied to me."

"No, I did not. I simply did not tell you it was him."

"Time for bed, Susannah. Go on up to your room. I cannot talk about this anymore." He bolted from his chair and headed for the front door.

Susannah ran after him. "Pa, please let me explain why John is here."

He forced open the door and pivoted toward her. "No! I do not want to hear the name Hawkins mentioned in my home or my presence ever again." Pa stomped out to the porch and slammed the door behind him, shutting Susannah and her plight to defend John out of his world—for now.

Chapter 4

The evening glow of the sun glimmered off the canal while John stood west of Higley's Sawmill and Lumberyard on his third day in Albion, his coat pulled shut and his hat pulled down blocking the wind. Boats once again traveled along the waters, passengers chattering and laughing from their seats, their happiness over resuming their leisurely activities obvious.

He had come here tonight because Susannah failed to contact him with her pa's answer. She must have had a good reason. Maybe Higley had forbidden her from seeing him.

If John could cross paths with him accidentally—accidentally on purpose, that is—on his way home for the evening, perhaps he could explain his presence in town.

Three days ago, John rode into town on the train with every intention of paying Higley, visiting Mama's grave in the Albion Cemetery, and riding the rails back to New York City. He never imagined when he stood on the banks of the canal that evening that he would save Susannah from drowning, much less lock hearts with her again. If someone had told him on Wednesday that today he would desire to stay, he would have laughed. Who would want to live in small-town Albion when New York City awaited him?

John chuckled, not caring if bystanders heard him. Albion had one lure the city did not: Susannah. How had he fallen for her without intention?

The result surprised him not. He learned growing up on the canal that life always brought surprises and rarely offered guarantees. Here he stood, wanting to stay and as unwelcome as a skunk at a picnic.

Ready to receive no for an answer but hoping for a yes, John stepped away from the edge of the canal and marched his way down the towpath to the sawmill. An absence of the saw's ear-splitting roar let him know the end of Higley's workday drew near.

John opened the entryway door, the front glass sparkling like crystal and the leather furniture reminding him of his childhood horse's saddle. A rush of heat flowed through his body when his gaze landed on Susannah sitting behind a desk and writing in a ledger. Adorned in a purple velvet dress, her rosy cheeks and full lips welcomed him, even though the spark in her eyes told him his presence was not prudent.

"John Hawkins," Susannah whispered while darting out from behind the desk, her boots hammering the pristine wood floors and her dress swishing as she hurried to him. "What are you doing here? First, you come to the house uninvited and now here? You need to leave before Pa sees you." She pushed at his shoulders and tried to turn him back around toward the door.

John pushed against her attempts. "Susannah, I must see your father. Just let me tell him why I am here, and I will go back to New York City. I know you do not want me here."

"Why would you say that? I never said anything of the sort."

He shrugged. "Every time I've seen you, except for the night at the canal, you have acted as if you wanted me to leave. You did not tell me of your talk with your father on my behalf. I assumed you were letting me return home without saying a word to me."

"John, you are mistaken. I do not want you to leave. I tried telling my pa about your return to Albion. He refused to let me speak of you. He all but sent me to my room as if I were a child."

He crumpled his brow. "So he does not know I am here?"

Her eyes bulged. "Oh, he knows you're here. He knows you rescued me. He knows I think the townsfolk are cruel for running your family out of town."

"What doesn't he know?"

"That you came to the house. . .and he does not know *why* you are here."

"Very well. I will tell him myself."

"No!" she half-whispered, half-yelled and pushed him toward the door farther. Beads of sweat glistened on her upper lip. "You would be wise to leave and keep the money. I know your intentions are good. I promise to do everything I can to help rebuild your family's name. But you must leave."

"No. I am not going until I speak with your—"

"What's all the commotion out here?" Higley stormed into the office from the back room. He paused, looked John square in the face, and jammed his hands onto his hips. "Hawkins? John Hawkins? Is that you? What are you doing here? Get away from my daughter now!"

John stepped forward despite Susannah's attempts to stop him. "Mr. Higley—"

With eyes as sharp as an eagle's and teeth clenched, Higley bellowed, "Do not speak to me. Regardless of why you are here, you are not welcome."

"Mr. Higley, please let me explain."

Higley crossed his arms across his stomach, glanced at Susannah's worried face, and sighed. "I'll give you thirty seconds."

John cleared his throat, removed his hat from his head, and squeezed it like an orange. "Mr. Higley, I came to Albion because my father asked me to come. He passed away not long ago, God rest his soul, and he left a will. He put me in charge as executor and asked me to repay you the money my grandfather owed you."

"That money is tainted. You can take it and go back home."

"Sir, my father tried to repay you years ago, and you would not accept. His dying wish was to make amends, so I could return to my home and the woman I love."

Higley fumed. "Do you mean *my* Susannah?"

"Yes, sir."

"Absolutely not! Get out!" He pointed toward the door.

"Mr. Higley, sir, I cannot leave. I promised my father I would make amends. Surely, you understand the importance of keeping promises."

"I do. I promised my father on his deathbed I would never forget what your family did to us."

Susannah jammed her hands onto her hips. "Pa! I cannot stand here a moment longer and listen to you speak in such an unforgiving way. Mama would fall on her face in tears right now if she heard you spew such hatred."

"You listen to me—"

"No, Pa, you listen to me. I love you with all my heart, but I do not respect you much at this moment. If you cannot forgive the Hawkinses like a good Christian man, then I will have to rest my head elsewhere tonight."

"Susannah, what is this nonsense you speak?"

She folded her arms across her stomach and stamped her foot on the floor. "Pa, I cannot live under the same roof with such ill will. I simply cannot. I have heard this drivel my whole life, but I will not listen to it anymore." She burst into tears and collapsed into a chair.

John's gaze flashed from Higley to Susannah and back again. Causing another family feud had not been his intention in trying to make amends. Instead of Hawkins versus Higley, now two Higleys erupted all over each other.

Higley pointed a crooked finger at him. "See what you've done? You have upset my daughter. Now get out."

"Sir, I am not leaving until you accept my apology and allow me to repay my grandfather's debt." John took two steps closer to Higley.

Susannah tugged on her father's arm, tears staining her cheeks, but Higley yanked away from her and closed the distance between them, the look of a rabid fox in his eyes.

Then John's head snapped, Susannah screamed, and pain shot through his face and neck. He stumbled backward into the paneled wall while shocks ran through his arms and legs. After he steadied himself against one of the leather chairs in the waiting area, he recognized the metallic taste of blood in his mouth.

Had Higley really punched him in the face? John wiped away the blood from his lip and held out his hands in surrender.

Susannah bolted from the chair. "Pa, John is not the cause of my discontent. It's you—and this feud that will not go away."

Higley buried his bloodred face in his hands and paced to the north side of the office. He leaned against the glass and glared outside toward the canal.

John pulled his handkerchief from the inside pocket of his suitcoat and dabbed at the blood on his lip while he waited for his opportunity to speak again. From this viewpoint, the cattails and sparkling water offered a calming effect even now in the midst of this chaos.

"John, maybe you should go. I will come to you at the canal in a few minutes." Susannah waved at him and joined her father at the window.

If not for Susannah, he would leave and never return. But something quaked inside John. Would Higley lash out at her when he left? If so, he could not bear being responsible for that. He could not leave her in this distraught condition with her angry father. He could not leave her ever. "Susannah, I would rather stay and make sure you are all right."

"I am fine. I need to see that Pa is calmed, and then I will come to you."

John nodded and took a step toward the door, yielding that she would be fine.

"Hawkins, wait." Higley's booming voice pulled John out of his momentary peace.

The hairs on the back of his neck bristled, and his arms went numb. Was he ready for this fight with Susannah's father? He twirled around and faced him where he remained by the window.

Susannah backed away from her father, almost as if she anticipated his fists would flail again at any moment.

"John." Higley said his given name for the first time. "You were not old enough to understand how your grandfather wronged my father. You could not have known the embarrassment my father felt when he nearly lost this company because your grandfather did not pay him for the wood he ordered. Then he and his men came into our lumberyard in the middle of the night and stole the wood. My father could not pay his men, and he lost his reputation in this town as a good businessman."

"I am sorry that happened, Mr. Higley. I came to apologize on my father's behalf because of that. He could never forget what his father did to your family."

Higley turned away from the window as Susannah slipped into a leather armchair in front of her desk. Her face held a paleness John had never seen. Was she afraid of her father or humiliated for him?

Higley took a few steps toward John and halted. He ran his hands through his hair and looped his thumbs through his suspenders. His gaze blared at John, eyes seeking—what did they seek? "I have lived under the shadow of this shame for seven years."

"As have I, sir. And so has Susannah."

"Yes, you both have. I am surprised at myself for saying this, but keeping this grudge causes worse suffering than the wrong done to my father. Had our family forgiven your grandfather and parted ways with each other amicably, the last seven years would have looked different."

"Yes, sir."

"Pa, what are you saying?"

"I want to put this feud behind us, to forgive. I hate what it has done to me. To us. Susannah is right. A good Christian man sets an example for his family. I should have demonstrated forgiveness."

John smiled. "Thank you, sir."

"No, thank you for coming back to Albion and for waiting on me to accept your apology."

"My pleasure, sir."

Higley looked at Susannah then back at John. "Thank you for rescuing my dear Susannah from the canal. If not for you, she could've drowned."

Susannah popped out of the chair and joined her father in the center of the office.

John longed to take Susannah into his arms, to grab Higley into a bear hug. But he restrained himself.

"John, will you forgive me for being such a mule and for taking out my anger on you? I am not a brawler. I do not hit people. I was blinded by years of hate."

"Yes, sir, Mr. Higley." John reached out his hand to him and felt like clicking his heels together.

"Please, call me Chauncey." When Chauncey accepted John's hand and pumped it a few times, John's soul soared, unencumbered for the first time in years.

Susannah wiped tears from her cheeks and grinned. "This feels better than a watermelon on a hot summer day."

The men joined her in laughter.

"Chauncey, sir, will you allow me to repay the debt?"

Chauncey puckered his lips. "No, I will not hear of it."

"Sir, my father truly wanted you to have what my grandfather owed your father."

"I will not accept it. It is tainted."

"Pa, must you be so hardheaded?" Susannah scoffed. "We need the money."

Chauncey groaned, and the tension returned to the room. "Susannah, refrain from talking about our business matters in front of John. We are fine without the Hawkins's money."

"I understand, sir. I suppose I can give it to the church or to the children's home. Would you allow me to take a walk down the canal with Susannah, sir?"

"Now?"

"Yes, sir."

"I am afraid I cannot allow it."

John picked his hat up off the floor and returned it to his head. "I am sorry. I forgot it is close to dinnertime. Another time, perhaps?"

Chauncey shook his head. "Making amends for the wrongs done years ago and allowing friendliness between the families now are two different things. No one in town would appreciate me welcoming a Hawkins to Albion, even if he did save my daughter. I am afraid you'll need to move on or go back to where you came from. It is better this way."

"Pa!" Susannah's mouth gaped.

"Susannah, I have said all I am going to say on the matter."

John inched forward. "Sir?"

"No." Chauncey stopped him with raised palms.

"Sir, I plan to court your daughter even if you do not approve of me doing so."

"I forbid it."

"Pa, you cannot stop it. I give my consent, and that is all that matters." Susannah stepped away from her father, looped her hand inside John's bended arm, and pulled him toward the door.

While Chauncey yelled, they exited the sawmill and headed toward the canal. They may have just rekindled the spark between them, but they also rekindled the fury inside her father.

Chapter 5

John's strong arm encircled Susannah's waist as they strolled along the banks of the canal, an owl hooting in the distance and herons fishing for an evening meal. The evening sun dipped behind the canal, bringing their time together to a close. If Susannah never again shared a moment like this with John, she would never forget it.

Never had anyone made her feel this safe, this valued, and this wanted as John had today. Her fears of being near the water had subsided—and all because of him and his reassurance that Wednesday's tragedy was not an everyday occurrence and would not happen again to her. He had reminded her that the Lord always watches out for His children. How could she forget he had confronted Pa and fought for her?

But could she trust her heart to him? Had he not said he would return to the city once Pa accepted his offer? Yes, he had said that on her porch steps, but then he had declared his desire to court her straight to Pa in their office. Surely, he planned to stay in Albion.

If the townsfolk ran him out of town like they had done his family, Susannah could face the worst heartbreak of her life.

If...

She shook her head and scattered the confusing thoughts out of her mind. She could not think of any of that right now.

John squeezed her waist—more so than was proper—but she did not mind. "Are you cold?"

She sidled up as close to him as her dress would allow, his earthy scent swirling around her in the fall breeze, and the heat from his body driving away the chill. "A bit."

"I should get you home."

Her heart plummeted. Did this night have to end? "Not yet. Please, can we stay awhile longer?"

Once John walked her home, she would make amends with Pa, if he would let her. Although she had threatened to live elsewhere, she had never made another place her home. Hopefully, Pa would not hold her to her threat.

"If you wish, we shall." John smiled down at her, the swelling still lingering on his bottom lip.

She frowned. "I am truly sorry Pa split your lip."

John dabbed at the corner of his mouth and dismissed her concerns with a crinkle of his nose. "He was protecting you."

A couple wrapped arm in arm passed them, and they nodded and exchanged greetings.

"No, he was angry. He had no excuse to treat you like a criminal."

"In his eyes, I am a criminal because he sees my grandfather that way. But he has forgiven that wrong, and we can be thankful."

She shrugged as a heron zoomed across the water with a fish in its mouth. "He still does not want you in town or near me."

"He may change his mind soon. I intend to show him and the people of this town I am a good and trustworthy fellow despite what they think of my grandfather." John stiffened his neck and held back his shoulders, his confidence adding an inch or more to his height.

Susannah craved that confidence. "I do not see how that will change Pa's mind about letting you court me—if you really do want to court me." Thankfully, the evening had fallen upon them, and her blush would not be visible to John.

"I would not have said it if I did not want to court you. I do apologize for declaring my wishes to your father before asking you for your favor."

"John, no need to apologize."

They continued down the street, their steps in sync with each other. Everything Susannah had ever liked to do—picnicking in the park, ice skating on the frozen pond, picking wildflowers in the fields on the other side of the canal—all paled in comparison to walking with John.

"You may have a beau already."

She nudged his arm with hers. "Would I be here walking with you now if I had a beau? No, I would not." She giggled. "I had a fiancé once though."

"A fiancé?"

"Yes. Richard. He worked the canal and charmed his way into Pa's company then into my heart. But he decided the hunt for gold out west was more appealing than staying here."

"He left? Something must be wrong with him to leave such a resplendent woman as you behind. He already had gold."

John's flattering words, while they might be empty, boosted Susannah's hope for the future. "You are too kind. Richard asked me to go with him, but I did not want to leave Pa. I guess if I had thought his love for me was genuine, I would have gone with him."

"But you didn't."

"No, I did not. I am glad I stayed." With Susannah's left arm still looped inside John's right arm, she placed her right hand on his upper arm and patted it.

"I am glad you stayed too. I would not have seen you again if you had left." John tucked his chin and sighed. "Best get you home. Your father might send the sheriff out after you if you are not home soon." When he raised his head and looked her way, a sweet smile graced his bearded face.

Susannah reluctantly let him change the direction of their walk toward Main Street and toward her home on Madison.

"Your father asked you not to talk about your business situation with me, but I wonder how you are getting along. You said you struggle."

If Susannah shared with John about the sawmill, she would betray Pa for the second time in one day. Would letting John know about their struggles of late hurt?

"You do not have to tell me. I should not have asked."

"No, it is fine. Pa worked diligently for years to recoup the loss from your—well, to recover from everything. Then two years ago, we had a fire in the lumberyard that took out over half our stock. That next cutting season, we had twenty-two inches of snow that stayed on the ground for over a month. Pa could not replenish his stock fast enough and could not keep his men working. Many of them went to work for his competitors who had not suffered the same losses. Others took to the rails and headed west."

How Pa had survived all that, Susannah did not know. He said his faith in God sustained him, and that must be true.

"Then Mama died."

John cupped her hand with his. "Your father has had hurt after hurt heaped upon him."

"Yes, he has. And now I have gone and caused him pain."

"Susannah, your father is being unreasonable. It is natural he would want to protect his only daughter—his only child—but he has to let you go and let you make the choices that are right for you."

"Why do the choices have to mean either Pa or you? Why can I not have both?"

"Give him time, Susannah. He will soften."

"He might, but I doubt he will ever accept your money. It is best to give it to the church or to the children's home."

John leaned into her a bit. "Would you accept it? You are the bookkeeper. He would never have to know."

Susannah halted, yanking her hand away from the crook of his arm. "No!" She arched her eyebrow and crinkled her forehead, even if the dimness kept him from seeing her expression. "I cannot believe you'd ask me to do such a thing."

"I am sorry."

"John, to do something that unscrupulous would taint everything we have accomplished today."

He held up his hands. "I know, but I want to repay that debt, especially since your father needs the funds." Kicking a rock out of their path, he groaned. "You do not think poorly of me?"

"No, John. We cannot speak of this again though."

"Very well. Shall we?" John started walking, and Susannah joined him.

She fought hard against the feelings that John kept close to her only to repay the debt. Why else would he continue to push the repayment on her? Would he leave as soon as he found a way to return the money?

Although doubt trickled into her heart, Susannah refused to let it drown her hope that John's presence in Albion had reason. He had appeared at the perfect time to save her and declared he wanted to know her better.

She slowed her pace, delaying their farewell. "John, if you think spending time with me will help you repay my father, you are wrong. If that is why you remain here, I see no cause for you to stay."

"Susannah, how can I prove my feelings for you have nothing to do with paying your father?" He stopped at the corner of Market and Madison and took her elbow in his hand. "Three days ago, I wanted to pay your father, make amends, say hello to you, and leave. Then I rescued you. Seeing you again made me want to stay. A fire lit inside me. After that, I could not imagine not seeing you every day."

Susannah studied John's face in the subdued glow of the gas streetlamps that graced the intersection.

"Susannah? Please believe me." He captured her hand in his.

Warmth spread up her arm and into her heart. Would this moment of pleasure disguise something about John she should notice? Seven years was a long time of separation.

While Susannah's life had remained the same most every day, she had no way of knowing who John really was deep inside his heart, or what he had done while he was gone. She needed more than flattering words and potentially empty promises before she trusted him completely.

"John, I do not doubt you genuinely care for me, and I understand your desire to end the feud. I believe you believe those two things are unrelated. I hope they are not, but I cannot rush into a courtship with you, no matter how much I would like to."

And she would like to.

"I understand. You are scared to trust me. I have been gone a long time. We know little about each other. I can wait. I am a patient man." He led Susannah across the intersection of Ingersol and Madison, her hand once again tucked in the crook of his arm.

That was acceptable for Susannah for now. She forced herself to appear reserved. She couldn't let him know how his declaration stirred her heart. She must wait and see how things with Pa transpired.

"Shall I walk you to your door?"

"No, not tonight. Pa is probably sitting on the front porch waiting for me. Thank you for offering though."

"I will watch you from the corner and make sure you arrive safely."

Before Susannah turned away, John stooped and pecked her cheek, the manliness of his beard and firmness of his lips sending fireworks through her entire body. Not succumbing to the charms of John Hawkins would take every ounce of her willpower.

Susannah pushed on the front door after turning the handle, fully expecting that Pa had barricaded the door, preventing her from entering. Relief flooded her when the door opened. Would anger pour from him because she had left the office with John against his will? Because she returned home too late for dinner?

Inside, she found the sitting room dark and the kitchen as well. Pa had retired and not waited up for her. He must believe she was not coming home.

After a snack of ham and bread, Susannah retired upstairs to her room down the hall from Pa's. His lamp was extinguished; he must have already fallen asleep. Sunday morning was but seven hours away, and facing Pa's mood in the morning with courage and love required that many hours of sleep and more.

She removed her hat and her hairpins then brushed her hair, unfastened her dress, and hung it inside her wardrobe. Her gown awaited her in the top dresser drawer. As she slid into the gown, the cool linen caressing her skin ever so gently, she whispered her prayers for protection and provision then climbed into her grandmother's carved walnut bed.

Morning came all too quickly. The savory aroma of coffee, eggs, and bacon drifted into her room and wrestled her from her slumber. Susannah washed her face and dressed in her blue poplin walking dress trimmed with white bows and soft blue lace. After brushing her hair and twisting it into a bun, she powdered her face and neck, fastened her locket necklace, and grabbed her white bonnet off the chair.

Pa rarely cooked breakfast. Did he believe she had stayed elsewhere last night and wasn't home this morning to cook?

Susannah descended the stairs, sucking in a breath to prepare for his reaction when he saw her. Then she blew out her breath and rebuked the ridiculous thoughts. Pa loved her, and he cared what happened to her. He would not have rested well last night until verifying her return. And he would never refuse her a pillow for her head.

She tossed her bonnet next to her Bible on the entryway table and headed down the hall to the kitchen. "Good morning, Pa. It is early for you."

Pa sat at the table and buttered a biscuit. "I could not sleep."

"I am sorry." She kissed the top of his blond head and collected a plate from the cupboard and a fork from the drawer beside the sink.

"Why are you sorry? You did not stop me from sleeping."

After scooping a spoonful of eggs onto her plate, she added two strips of crispy bacon and licked the grease from her fingers in a most unladylike way. With plate and fork in hand, she slid into the chair across from Pa. "No? Yesterday did not upset you?" She did not mention John's name or her stormy departure from the office. Both knew what she meant.

"Susannah, you are a grown woman. . .and a godly woman. Your heart is bigger than Lake Ontario, and your love flows mightier than Niagara Falls. If you trust John Hawkins, then I trust him."

She cocked her head and arched her eyebrow. Did he have a fever? The only thing he did more rarely than cook was shower her with compliments. "Pa?"

He laughed while buttering another biscuit. "It's me. No one came in here last night and replaced your father with a double."

Susannah hooted. "Pa, thank you for those kind words. I am still determining if I can fully trust John. I believe so, but I have been wrong about people before, as you know. But we must forgive, and we must love. Thank you for giving John a chance to prove himself."

"How could I not?" His eyes, which had burned like hot coals of unfairness yesterday, sparkled with love and kindness this morning.

"Then what kept you from sleeping last night?" Now at the sink, Susannah sank her plate into the pan of soapy water and turned to face him.

Pa washed down the last of his bacon and biscuit with a gulp of coffee. He wiped his mouth with the linen napkin then kept it there for a moment, hiding his expression. But the heaviness on his face spoke of the trouble that flickered in his heart. That, he could not hide. "My conscience. I could not forgive myself for how I treated you and John."

"Oh Pa!" She crossed the room, wrapped her arms around his neck, and squeezed him. As John had expected, Pa had had a change of heart.

❖━━━ ━ ━❖

On the way to church, Pa carried Susannah's Bible for her and kept his pace slow, so she could keep up with him. They walked instead of taking the wagon today because the sun shone bright, and the air remained still. Pa enjoyed walking on days like this.

"Thank you for the fine breakfast this morning, Pa. I love how you add cheese to the eggs."

"You always did favor that as a child. You know, I did not cook often. Your mama would not let me near her kitchen." He chuckled. "She disliked cleaning up after me. Mama was particular about her kitchen." He shook his head and grinned. "I could not rest well for another reason."

"Oh?"

"I kept wrestling with making a decision about the order from Carmichael Building Company. Prayed all night long."

Susannah waited. Pa responded best when not rushed.

He raised his brushy eyebrows and sighed. "I am going to accept the order. We need the business. I want to pay the bank and get the deed back to our house."

Susannah squeezed his arm. Now that was her *real* pa. The man who conquered difficult things. "That is a wise decision. I am proud of you for your boldness."

"Maybe stupidity. We will have to wait and see how things unfold."

"Pa, you taught me God helps people do big things when they trust Him. If you put your faith in Him and not in your ability, this will go right. He will help you."

He nodded. "I am concerned, though, about my lack of workers. But there are plenty of men around town who might help with the cutting and splitting."

A gust of wind ripped across them, and Susannah snuggled up close to Pa. The aroma of his coffee and bacon still clung to him. "I can help. I am not stout, but I have a willing heart."

"I know, dear, I know. Continue working the ledgers for me. That will help."

"Yes, sir. Remember, John's still here in town. I am sure he would help if you asked him."

"I don't—" He cleared his throat and stiffened. "I will find plenty of help and will not need him."

Susannah refrained from poking at Pa's obvious avoidance of John. Sunday should be free of arguing, and given yesterday's turmoil between them, she would avoid causing a fuss today.

They had fewer than ten paces before arriving at the church front steps when John sauntered up beside them, hat in hand. "Good morning, Mr. Higley, Miss Higley. How are you both on this fine Lord's Day?"

Susannah gulped and nearly tripped over her feet at the sight of John in his dark blue morning coat, striped vest, and gray tie. The boldness that flowed through that man matched or exceeded any she had ever seen in Pa. If she could somehow get these two working together instead of chewing on the bones of the past, they could conquer Albion and all of New York.

"Good morning," Susannah muttered. Would Pa show politeness this morning or hurl offenses at John again?

Pa pulled away from Susannah and glared at John. "Hawkins—John, what're you doing here at our church? Your family always attended the one two blocks over on Market Street."

"Sir, I want to spend my Sunday with your daughter."

"Uh, well, I am not so sure—"

"Good morning, Higleys," Reverend White interrupted. "Who do we have here with you today?" He held his hand out, and John accepted it.

Pa cleared his throat and sputtered over some incomprehensible words.

"Reverend, this is my friend John," Susannah interjected. "He is visiting from New York City."

Reverend White nodded, not seeming to notice Pa's discomfort. "Well, good to have you, John. I hope you receive a blessing today."

"I already have, sir." John winked at Susannah, and she giggled all the way to her toes.

Pa took her by the arm. "This is not the place for flirtations."

"I am sorry, sir." John followed them up the steps and into the church, greeting everyone who acknowledged him. "Would you share the Sunday meal with me at my hotel after service?"

"Dinner is on the stove already waiting on us. Besides, we do not patronize restaurants on the Lord's day," Pa growled, scooting into the fourth pew on the left-hand side of the church.

"Thank you for the invitation. I would love to join you." John slid in next to Susannah, and she stifled a giggle.

"That was not an invitation, young man."

"Pa." Susannah whispered, encouraging Pa to lower his voice.

"Oh, very well. You can join us for dinner."

Chapter 6

"Mr. Higley, I cannot express my gratitude enough for the invitation to your afternoon meal." John wiped his mouth then tucked the napkin into his shirt collar.

"I dare say, I didn't exactly invite you."

"Pa! Where are your manners?" Susannah faced John with an obvious apology in her eyes. "John, would you like apple pie?"

"Yes, Miss Susannah." John laughed inwardly at the pain on Higley's face as he endured John's presence in his house. He was not accustomed to barging his way into another man's home, but Chauncey's discomfort was too entertaining to resist. If Susannah had not challenged her father, he would have exercised more respect of Chauncey's boundaries, but knowing she entertained the idea of them courting permitted John a few liberties.

"When you finish your pie, I suppose you will head back to the hotel. Planning to catch the train to New York City soon?"

"Well, sir—"

"John, would you like coffee with your pie?" With gentle hands, Susannah served him and her father both generous slices of warm, golden pie, sugary filling oozing from underneath the flaky braided crust. Her cheerful determination to ignore her father's behavior gave him courage.

"Indeed. Then I will take my leave, so you can enjoy the rest of your Sunday."

"Don't let me slow you down." Chauncey dug into his pie and shoveled a double serving into his mouth.

John did the same, as Susannah partook of one small bite after the next.

What she must think of him for barging his way into their home, giving himself his own invitation. Did she even want him here? She had said a courtship with him would take time.

Father had taught him to be aggressive in business, to make sure he stuck his foot in the door, so the door could not shut on him. Was he wrong for taking this approach with Chauncey?

Susannah sipped her coffee, peering at him over the top of her cup.

His face burned hot from her flirtation, and thankfully his beard disguised it.

"To answer your question, I will stay another week. Maybe ten days."

Susannah lowered her cup. "Will you return?"

"Yes, once I settle my business matters."

Chauncey dropped his fork onto his plate, several bites of pie remaining there uneaten. "You are coming back? I thought you only came to make amends and then you would return."

"Sir, I want to stay. As I stated yesterday, my intentions are to court Susannah. I cannot very well do that from New York City. . .sir." John winced and expected Chauncey to throw him out of the house.

"That is not wise. The town hates the Hawkins family."

"I plan to stay and make my presence known. I will see Susannah as much as I am allowed. If the people of this town, as you presume, will not welcome me, and I cannot do anything to change their minds, I will have to—well, I am not going to speculate what I will do, because I trust that God is with me in my decision to stay."

Susannah smiled, and John nearly bounded from his chair and kissed her square on the mouth right in front of her father. Instead, he contained his joy and resisted his urges.

"I will go to New York City one day soon. My wax flowers are on their way there now. If all goes well, a merchant may want them in a store in Manhattan or Brooklyn."

"You would fancy New York City. I do hope you get to go someday."

"Nonsense. Just because your flowers are going to New York City does not mean you will ever go," Pa groused.

Her eyes flashed. "Why not? What is wrong with wanting to go on an adventure to New York City?"

"People who go off like that do things they were taught not to do. The big city is no place for you, Susannah. I would never let you go."

"Pa, I am not a child. I will not always live here. The day will come when I am keeping my own home, and I can travel when and where I want." She huffed.

"See what you have done?" Chauncey pointed at John. "My daughter never had a spiteful bone in her body or ill tone in her voice until you walked back into town. You are corrupting her good morals. The Bible says bad company does that."

"Sir—"

"Pa!" Susannah jumped from her chair and took a position behind John's chair. She placed her hand on his shoulder.

"Not a word more from either of you. This meal and this visit are over." Chauncey pushed up out of his chair and stormed out of the dining room and down the hall.

"John, I suppose you should leave. I am sorry for Pa's rudeness." Susannah averted her gaze and busied herself with cleaning up the dishes.

John did not need a certificate from the university to understand Susannah's feelings. Her hands trembled, her shoulders shook, and she chewed on her bottom lip. She must be fighting with everything she had to keep herself composed.

"Let me help you put these dishes away."

"No, I can do it." Tears glistened in her eyes.

"Susannah, do not cry. It will be all right."

"I am not sure about that. My father's heart is hardened. Even though he said he forgave your grandfather and settled things with you, he is not being kind. I have never heard him say such hurtful things."

"His behavior could be worse, Susannah. He has loads of anger built up in him, and I am the first Hawkins he has seen in years. Let him say these things until his heart settles. I will survive."

Susannah set the stack of plates on the table and looked up into his face. "John, you are the most patient and understanding man I have ever met."

"I have had time to prepare for this moment. Your father hasn't. Besides, it is easy to be this way when I stare into your eyes. You are worth waiting for no matter what hardship I must endure."

Chauncey returned to the dining room as John took Susannah's hands in his.

"Get out of here and let me take my nap in peace, or you will endure that hardship right now."

John whipped around and faced Chauncey. "Yes, sir. I'm leaving." The kiss he wanted to give Susannah would have to wait a little longer.

❖————❖

Without Susannah, the canal held no beauty and no meaning.

On Wednesday, when John arrived in Albion, he had dropped off his traveling bag at the hotel after getting off the train and followed the crowd to the canal where everyone shouted and whistled. He had soaked in all the sights and sounds of home.

Water lapping against the bridge.

Boats filled with partying people.

The aroma of boiled peanuts and fried donuts filling the air, his mouth watering in response.

Fall leaves—always his favorite—blanketing the ground.

Such a full heart he had that afternoon.

Then the bridge collapsed, and he jumped in and saved Susannah.

Since the rescuing, Susannah filled his every thought, every decision based off what she would do or say. No matter how hard he tried, he could not stop thinking about a future with her, seeing her every day for the rest of his life akin to walking on clouds.

John shoved his hands into his front pockets and planted his feet in the grassy section between the towpath and the canal. A blue packet boat cruised past him led by a mule up ahead, Sunday evening leisure at its finest. The passengers had no way of knowing his life had fallen apart like the Main Street Bridge.

Susannah and his future may as well be on the north side of the canal—or more likely, he might as well be stranded on the other side. Chauncey would like that. If he had his way, John would be on the train right now headed far away from Susannah.

John straightened his shoulders and stiffened his neck then clenched his jaw. Father had not raised a coward, had not allowed him to back down from a worthy fight. He would not act like a coward now.

Chauncey had accepted his apology for Grandfather's actions, but Susannah was right. He had not embraced the forgiveness. Her father wanted him out of town so he could hold on to his comfortable grudge.

Change never came for free or without work. If Chauncey truly forgave the Hawkinses, he would face possible ridicule in town for forgiving and for letting his daughter be with John. He must prefer his rut of unforgiveness, or he did not see forgiveness as something worth effort.

John pulled his hands from his coat pockets and rubbed them together. He would find a way for Chauncey to trust him with Susannah, to truly forgive and forget the wrongs of the past. How he would do that without raising Chauncey's anger or his suspicions, he did not know. But he would figure something out.

"John! John!" Susannah screamed from behind him.

John zipped around and dashed toward her. "What is it?"

She grabbed his forearms and gasped for breath, her cheeks rosy like the redbirds he had seen foraging for seeds outside her house.

"Pa. . .he fell. . .down the attic stairs." She bent and grabbed her side.

"He fell? Is he okay? Where is he?"

"He's. . .I. . .he is lying on the floor by the stairs. He hurt his shoulder and his ankle, split his head open."

"Did you go for the doctor? Is anyone with him?"

She nodded and gasped again before straightening. "Mr. Wagner from next door is with him. I ran as fast as I could to the doctor's house, but he is not home. Someone probably invited him to Sunday dinner. I hoped to find you here."

"We can ask around while we make our way back to your house. Maybe someone knows where the doc is."

Susannah nodded, wiping her face with the handkerchief she pulled from inside her sleeve.

"Are you cold? You ran out without your shawl."

"No, running all the way to the doctor's house and then to you kept me from catching a chill."

"Well, let's get you home. One chill this week is enough." John clasped Susannah's forearm and led the way home. Her trembling quaked through to his body. "How did your father fall down the stairs?"

Susannah brushed a few curls out of her face and exhaled. "After you left, he stomped around the house like a stallion in search of a mare. I could not console him. He believes you are here under false pretenses."

"Me? How so?"

"He thinks you only used your grandfather as an excuse to steal me away to New York City." She massaged her side and blew out a few small puffs of air. Several coughs followed, and John's concerns heightened.

As he led her down Main Street toward Madison, searching for the doctor or anyone who might know his location, his lunch rose from his stomach, burning his chest and throat. How could Chauncey think these things about him? Why could he not trust that John had not intended to fall for Susannah?

"Susannah, you know the truth, don't you? You know I came to town to make amends and leave. But then I rescued you and haven't stopped thinking about you."

"I know. I have not stopped thinking of you either."

"I believe God brought me here at this time. My motives are not evil."

"I know." She patted his hand and smiled.

"I am glad. I couldn't bear it if you doubted me. I would leave right now if you withheld your support."

John stopped in front of the feed store where a group of men played checkers and whittled. "Excuse me, sirs. Do any of you know where the doctor is?"

A gray-haired man snapped a light-colored piece onto the board and looked up at John and Susannah with deep-set dark eyes. "I seen him head to the Higley house. Somebody passed the word along that Chauncey got hurt."

"Yeah, a hysterical woman ran through the streets cryin' out fer him." The freckle-faced man with orange hair sipped water from a mason jar. "I suppose somebody heard her commotion and knew where Doc was."

"It was her." A scrawny man in blue overalls pointed at Susannah.

A strange snicker bubbled from her. Was she embarrassed about running through the streets in panic or maybe offended by this man's description of her? It did not matter. At least Doc was helping Chauncey.

"Thank you, kind sirs. Enjoy the rest of your day." John wrapped his arm around Susannah's waist, and they continued their walk home, albeit a bit slower than before. "So finish telling me how your father fell."

"Pa was beyond angry when you left, and he stomped his way up to the attic, marched around in there for a bit, and then missed a step coming down and tumbled all the way to the landing. He could have died. I'd never be able to forgive myself if something bad happened to him." Susannah's sobs choked her words.

John halted and took her by the shoulders. "Look at me." He gently shook her until she gazed at him. She seemed like a frightened child. "Your father's inability to control his rage is the reason he fell from the attic. You didn't do anything. Nor did I. He does not want to lose you and sees me as the culprit behind your adventuresome ways."

"That is not true. I've always wanted to travel."

"Well, we need to help him understand it is okay for you to dream and to travel—to marry. You are not a villain for having dreams."

"And you are not a villain for helping me realize my dreams."

"Thank you. Maybe we can convince him I am not on the wrong side of the canal."

Chapter 7

In her black walking dress, Susannah carried an apple pie to Mrs. Henry's house and expressed her condolences for the loss of her son, Harry, who died when the bridge collapsed. She had attended school with him until he quit to work the farm.

Afterward, Susannah stopped at the bakery. Mary Waterbury should know of Pa's condition. Perhaps she would pay him a visit while Susannah handled the day's business.

Then on the way to the sawmill, she mailed a letter to Aunt Eleanor in New Hampshire, whose birthday was a month away. Pa wanted his sister to receive his well wishes in plenty of time. Susannah suspected he wanted her to know he had fallen down the stairs, in case she might come for a visit.

Could Pa's fear that Susannah might leave him be the motive behind the letter's urgency?

Susannah agreed with Pa that his sister might want to know they fared well after the bridge collapse. Since the story hit newspapers all over New York and probably even the whole country, Aunt Eleanor had no doubt heard of the disaster by now and must be worried about them.

When the doc visited, he examined Pa then listened to Susannah's lungs again, making sure she was well. He ordered Pa to stay in bed for a minimum of three days, so they'd closed the office yesterday and rested. Closing two days in a row, however, might give Pa's competitors reason to suspect problems with the company, so Susannah would open it herself on this Tuesday morning and see what she could do with the order from Carmichael Building Company.

John had visited and offered his assistance, but Pa refused it and asked him to leave. Pa's anger over John's presence had caused the fall, and he would not soon forget it. But his soreness would not go away in time to fill the order, so Susannah would have to convince him to let John solicit men from town for cutting, loading, and delivering the lumber to the train station.

Susannah unlocked the door, stepped into the office, and found a folded piece of paper at her feet. She shut the door and scooped the paper off the wood floor.

SOMEONE WHO BEFRIENDS A HAWKINS IS NO FRIEND TO ALBION!

Susannah gasped and crumpled the note. Who would write such a thing to Pa? He had only associated with John at church. Had someone in their congregation written this note? How had anyone recognized John with his beard after being gone since he was eighteen?

Susannah locked the office door behind her and collapsed into the closest chair, its padded leather offering no comfort to her. She tossed the note across the room.

As Pa had suspected, Albion rejected anyone from the Hawkins family. What did that mean for her? If she chose to let John court her and eventually move into marriage, they would not be welcome here.

Choose between Pa and John? How?

Susannah swiped away tears as they drained from her eyes.

"Lord, I don't understand why—I do not understand anything. John came here on the day I needed rescuing. You chose him as my rescuer. How can I convince this whole town he is not his grandfather? His father lived with shame over his own father's actions until his death. His grandfather never had the opportunity to make things right with my grandfather or Pa. John wants to do what they could not do. Pa said he would forgive, but at what cost? His business? His standing in the community? How can I convince Pa to defend John? Doing the right thing should be better than holding a high position in town. Better than having a thriving business. Lord, give me the wisdom to know if I am supposed to do something."

Susannah wiped away the remaining tears and sniffled. She felt the same after praying as before, but sometimes comfort and direction took awhile. God always faithfully answered her though.

Would He call her to some action? Would He ask that she defend John to the whole town?

Two men wanted and needed her. But this feud forced her to choose between them. If she defended John, she made her father an outcast. If she defended Pa, she would lose John.

A heaviness came upon her heart, and dizziness threatened to knock her out of her chair.

"What is it, Lord? Are You telling me something?"

Ever since the bridge collapsed and John saved her, something remained unsettled in her heart. What significance did the bridge—

"The bridge! I have to rebuild the bridge—not between the north and south sides of Albion, but between the Higleys and the Hawkinses."

No! She *was* the bridge.

Like Nehemiah in the Bible, whom God had commissioned to rebuild the wall around the city of Jerusalem, she would rebuild what the town had destroyed.

"First, I need to help Pa with this order. That's the best place to start." She stood, straightened the bodice of her dress, and went to Pa's desk.

After a few minutes of sifting through Pa's unorganized piles of paper and coughing from the dust her search triggered, she found an envelope marked with Carmichael's stamp.

"Thank You, Lord."

Later she would make sense of the chaos on Pa's desk. For now, she would see what they needed, check inventory, and figure out how to fill the order.

Someone jiggled the door handle and pounded on the door, producing a squeal in Susannah as she lunged forward in Pa's chair. Papers scattered to the floor including the ones for the Carmichael order.

"Goodness! Frightening people is so rude." Susannah bolted from the chair, marched to the door, and peeked outside into the street. No one was there, but another note lay at her feet.

❖ — · — ❖

Susannah sat in the leather chair beside the door as she had done earlier, holding the second note and trembling. Whoever had sent these threatening messages and attempted to scare Pa had instead terrified his daughter and knocked her courage into the canal.

If Pa knew these notes had come, he would rage beyond control. His anger, Susannah feared, would not only be at the bullies but also at John for trying to associate with him and his daughter.

If John found out about the notes, what would he do? He did not seem to have a cowardly bone in his body. While kindness exuded from him, he also believed in justice. He had fought for it every day since arriving in Albion and probably for many days before. Yes, he would stay and fight these people with her, even if Pa refused his help.

Getting word to John without leaving the store proved difficult. She had no guarantees someone would not attack her.

Susannah brushed her curls out of her face and cleared her throat. She refused to sit frozen in this office until someone figured out she was missing. She slid out of the chair and inched her way to the door, her throat dry and her heart pounding stronger than the invasive pounding on the door an hour ago. She blew out a breath and closed her eyes, whispering a prayer of protection over herself and Pa and John.

Pressing her face against the glass door, she studied the street, which bustled like on any other day. No one seemed to notice she was imprisoned in her own office, unable to leave but too scared to stay.

Then she spotted Daniel Fleming, Effie's son. The little scruff of a boy kicked a tin can down the street, dodging wagons and horses. Susannah unlocked the door and flung it open. Before the idea of changing her mind crept in, she rushed outside and called him.

"Daniel, please come here."

He did not respond and continued kicking the can.

"Daniel!"

Daniel whipped his head around and ran to her when she summoned him. "Yes, ma'am?"

With clasped hands, she attempted to appear calm. "Good afternoon, Daniel. Why aren't you in school today?"

"My mama's helping Mrs. Jones have her baby. I came with her, so I could run for the doc if need be."

Susannah kneaded her hands and watched the street like a hawk. "Do you think your mama would mind if you did an errand for me? It will take but a few minutes."

"Miss Susannah, what if they need the doc sudden like and I am not here?"

"I understand. Go ask your mama. I need you to go to the Albion Hotel and get someone for me. It is an emergency of sorts, so you would help me more than you know."

Daniel pursed his lips and adjusted his cap. He glanced across the street at the boardinghouse and then back to Susannah. "I will run across and ask her."

When Daniel returned with permission from his mama, Susannah sent him to fetch John. He came back a quarter of an hour later with John in tow.

John, once again in his dark blue morning coat, striped vest, and gray tie, paid him ten cents, and the boy ran off with a spring in his step and resumed kicking the can. "What is wrong, Susannah?"

Susannah yanked John by the arm and pulled him inside the office, locking the door behind them.

"Susannah? What's the matter? You are shaking like an autumn leaf that is ready to fall off a tree." His minty breath drifted toward her and calmed her a bit.

Rather than collapsing into his arms, she hustled to Pa's desk and retrieved the crumpled note off the floor. Returning to his side, she pushed both notes into his hand.

John studied the second note then read it aloud. "If you associate with the Hawkins boy, we will burn your place to the ground."

Susannah grabbed her throat and tucked her chin.

John frowned but remained calm. "Susannah, do not let these threats frighten you."

A groan boiled up from inside her. "Do not let them frighten me? Too late for that, John."

Someone had threatened their livelihood. Was this because John wanted to court her? No one knew but Pa. Was it because they thought Pa had welcomed him back to Albion and into their home? If so, they were mistaken. Pa had done neither of those things.

"Susannah, I am sorry. I know this is frightening. But do you really think someone would resort to burning this place?"

"We had a fire a few years ago. Remember, I told you about it? Pa always thought a competitor did it."

"Could that be happening now?"

"I doubt it. This is about you. Although. . .he recently accepted the order I told you about. A competitor might try to sabotage Pa, so he could get the order instead."

"Do you think that's it?"

Susannah sighed and pulled at her collar, which felt like a yoke today. "No."

"Me neither."

"So what do we do?"

"Convince your pa he needs me on guard here at night. Persuade him to let me supervise the entire order. The quicker we can put it all together, the better."

"Will your help make things better? Or worse?"

"Susannah, I will do anything I can to help your pa. The sooner he trusts me, the sooner I can court you."

"You still want to? Even with all this turmoil?"

"More than I did yesterday and the day before and the day before that. How do you feel about that?"

Susannah leaned up and placed a kiss on John's cheek. "Does that answer your question?"

Chapter 8

The crackling fire in the parlor fireplace seemed to warm everything but Chauncey Higley's cold heart. His pride would choke him to death. If it were not for Susannah, John would give up hoping he'd ever change his mind.

"Mr. Higley, please be reasonable. You need help with this order. You should still be in bed. You cannot use your shoulder or stand on your ankle. This order—"

"What do you know of my order?"

"Susannah told me everything when she summoned me to your sawmill."

Chauncey's face flushed. "Susannah, why did you involve him in our affairs?"

"Pa, I told you twice already. Someone left two threatening notes, and I was afraid to stay at the office alone."

"You did not have to tell him our business."

Susannah cocked her chin and arched her eyebrow. "Well, I did, and I cannot change that."

"Hawkins, if you were not here in Albion, I would do this myself or find my own help. Why do you think you can do it any better than I can?"

"I don't, sir. I want to help. I want to prove you can trust me."

"You are worse than a pesky fly on a slice of watermelon, son. Do you know that?"

John laughed, encouraged for the first time in days by Chauncey's teasing and his term of endearment. "Yes, sir." He took a bite of a sugary tea cake made by Susannah and nearly forgot his purpose there. The cookie brought almost as much delight to him as Susannah did.

"Pa, John is not trying to wrong you in any way. Do you remember accepting his plea on his father's and grandfather's behalf Saturday?"

"Of course."

"Even after you bloodied his lip, instead of harboring ill will against you, he sought to make amends in its stead."

"Well, yes, I remember."

"John is a good man. He wants to help. You refused to accept his money. While you say you accept his apology, you have not quite dissolved your grudge against his family. Your behavior toward him is embarrassing."

"It is okay, Susannah," John interjected.

Susannah held up her hand to John. "It is not okay. My father is a kind man. He loves God. But he is withholding the love and kindness you deserve."

John smiled and allowed his heart to fill with hope over Susannah's defense of him.

Chauncey shifted in his chair and rubbed his stubbly chin. "My father built this business from the ground up when he came to Albion the year I was born—fifty years ago. He befriended your grandfather when they worked on the canal together. They dreamed big dreams together. I spent my childhood with your father. He was a good person. Your mother and Susannah's mother quilted together, took care of the churchwomen together, and raised the two of you together. They used to say you two would either marry, or you would tire of each other and never see each other again once you were grown."

Both John and Susannah laughed in response. Then John glanced at Susannah in the armchair beside the fireplace. The golden glow of the fire radiated on her ivory face, giving her an angelic appearance. She turned her gaze to him and graced him with a smile then returned her focus to her father.

"I am a smart man, John Hawkins. You haven't grown ill from my daughter's presence."

"No, sir."

"I do not want to presume you intend to marry her, but I believe your desire to help me could be related to your desire to win her heart."

"Sir, I do want to win her heart, but I am not showing kindness toward you just to earn her favor, nor am I doing so to gain your blessing."

"Then why?"

"You were one of my father's most cherished friends. He always spoke well of you. Even when you refused his offer of repayment, he never spoke ill of you. In fact, he said on numerous occasions that if he were wronged like your family was, he might behave the same way."

Chauncey drummed his fingers on his tobacco box and seemed to consider John's words. The fire hissed and crackled next to Susannah while her father tapped his foot on the oak floor.

John recalled many times when Father sat next to a blazing fire making decisions that affected their future. The wintry night the town banished them brought with it long hours in front of the fire planning their departure and relocation.

No matter how hard the fight, he would do everything in his power to help Chauncey and bring their families back together. Even if the town never accepted him back home, he would sleep well knowing he had done right by the Higleys.

Susannah stood and moved to the table in front of the settee. "More tea, John?"

"Yes, thank you. Your tea cakes are delicious."

"Thank you." She poured his tea and returned to her chair by the fire.

John rapped his fingers on his knees and tried to think of something to say while Chauncey contemplated. But nothing seemed important enough to mention in this moment.

Chauncey pushed out of his chair and limped over to Susannah. Backing up to the fire, he stared at John. "All right. You can help with the order."

John sprang from his seat and joined them, extending his hand in offering. "When's the order due?"

Chauncey accepted his hand then winced at the pain he must have felt in the opposite shoulder when they shook. "We've got two and a half weeks to get it there, so we need to have it at the train station by the nineteenth. They need 110,000 board feet. That's between 150 to 160 trees."

"Do we have that in the lumberyard?" Susannah spoke through a wide grin and with sparkling eyes. She must feel as thrilled as John.

"Oh, we have it. Because our orders of late have decreased, my stock has stayed the same."

John clapped his hands together once and bounced on his toes. "Good."

"This wood will be rough sawn, and we will need lots of hands."

"You leave that to me, sir. I have some old school friends who would be more than happy to help us. We'll work around the clock in shifts."

Susannah nibbled on her finger and creased her brow. "What about the threats?"

"Chauncey, may I?"

Chauncey nodded and limped to his chair. "Sure."

"We need someone watching the sawmill and lumberyard at all times because of the fire threat."

"I agree." Chauncey massaged his shoulder.

"And I believe once we start sending everything over to the woodshed at the train station, someone should watch the wood there too."

"I agree."

"Well, sir, if I have your permission, I'll start tomorrow."

Chauncey sighed, the relief in his voice tangible. "I am blessed to have you working with me. Thank you for your patience while I softened up to you. You are a good man, John Hawkins. Just like your father."

Because of the late hour, John said his goodbyes to Susannah at the front door and whistled all the way to the hotel. He needed a good night's rest because tomorrow would begin many days of hard labor and much adversity. Finally,

John knew why God had brought him to Albion when He did.

◆━━━━◆

Five days of lifting, cutting, and stacking timber put kinks in John's neck and back, and each night, he fell onto the cot in the back room of the sawmill in agony. Since Chauncey had offered the cot, John no longer paid for a hotel room. Every night, when the next shift of men arrived, his reprieve was but a few steps away.

Threats were nil since the first two, and Susannah finally seemed relaxed at the office, not jumping at every closing door or dropping of a log onto the carriage.

Ten men worked around the clock, stopping only to sharpen the saw blades or make deliveries to the train station. John's oldest childhood friend, Matthew, worked at the train station and secured a storage spot for the prepared lumber.

Although a few of John's old friends needed convincing to work in secret without telling anyone about him, the others willingly offered their help and were glad to have John back in Albion.

He planned to split the money from his father between the men. They would probably argue with him, but he would find a way to repay them for defending him and for helping Higley.

"Hey, Hawkins, which one of the misses is bringing dinner tonight?" Matthew helped Thomas load another log onto the carriage and set the guard.

Sawdust spewed into the air as the blade screamed its way through the pine log two feet in diameter. John stood on the receiving end and guided the new board onto the wagon as it exited the sawing area.

"Susannah." Mentioning her name sent excitement down his spine.

"What will your lovely lass bring us?"

"She's not my lovely lass." John pushed the end of the carriage back to Matthew so he could run the log across the blade again and cut another board.

"Oh, is that right? So you would not mind if I asked her to the husking bee later this month?"

"The husking bee? What makes you think she would go with a rogue like you?" John laughed, but inside, sharp pains shot through him. He could not let Matthew take Susannah to the barn dance and cornhusking, yet he had not officially declared his desire to court her, because of their work here at the sawmill.

Matthew fed the last section of the log through the blade, and John caught it on the other end and guided it onto the wagon. He motioned for Matthew to hold off before starting another log. Wiping the sweat from his brow with his handkerchief, he scooped a ladle full of water into his mouth and let the coolness refresh him.

"Way I see it, she's not spoken for, so I can ask her to accompany me."

"Now, Matthew, Susannah—well, she is. . . I mean to say. . ." John yanked his hat off his head and ran his fingers through his sweaty hair. How had the afternoon grown this hot? October was usually cooler.

"John, save your words and your heartache. Your eyes are set on Higley's daughter. We've all known it since our days in the schoolhouse as youngins." He laughed. "Right, Thomas?"

Thomas gulped water from the ladle. "Always knew you'd come back for her. Always knew she would wait on you."

"But she did not wait. What about that Richard gent she almost married?"

"She wouldn't have married him."

"How do you know that, Matthew?"

"She never had *the look* in her eyes for Richard that she has for you." Matthew pulled another log onto the cutting area with Thomas's help.

"*The look*?" What did his friends see that had escaped him? As the blade ate into the log, John tried to focus on the board when it spit out to the bench.

"The look a woman gets in her eyes when she sees the man she wants to marry. You know *the look*, right?"

"I am not sure."

Matthew laughed over the buzz of the saw blade. "Peer into her eyes, and you'll see it. She has it for you."

◆━━━◆━◆

"John, is everyone ready for dinner?" Susannah's sweet voice rang through the back room. Her dress of white and pink silk ruffles made her look like she was ready for a picnic in the park. If he could stop working now, he would steal her away for a picnic without delay.

"I believe they may be. We are over halfway through with the order after only five days of labor."

She grinned. "That is delightful. Thank you for making sure Pa meets the deadline."

John motioned for Susannah to step inside the office so they could speak in private without the roar of the saw, hiss of the steam engine, and without his friends' listening ears.

After he shut the door behind them, John removed his leather gloves, swiped his face with the handkerchief again, and licked his lips. Why was he this parched?

"What is it? If we tarry, the pea soup and turkey and vegetables will get cold."

John licked his lips again and sighed. "I have been preoccupied this week with business."

"Yes, you have."

"But I have not been too busy to notice you here every day. You are always quite lovely in your dresses and hats."

"Thank you."

"I, uh, well, I have contemplated my plans for when this order goes to Buffalo."

"I am surprised you have had more than a moment to allow yourself the luxury of thinking of the future. I have barely had more than a moment myself."

"Susannah, when I wake up each morning, I am already thinking of you."

"That is so sweet, John." Susannah brought her hand to her collarbone and played with her necklace.

John gazed into her eyes searching for the look Matthew mentioned. Would he recognize it?

"John?"

"Yes, sorry. I not only wake up thinking of you, but I lie down at night thinking of seeing you the next morning. It may be inappropriate for me to tell you this, but even as painful and exhausting as it is working all day at the sawmill, it is not nearly as grueling as you leaving me at the end of the day."

Susannah smiled, and her eyes moistened. "That is the nicest thing anyone has ever said to me, John." She lowered her gaze for a moment and then looked into his eyes.

Was that *the look*? He could not tell.

"John, I must confess, even though I know it is not proper—"

Matthew bolted into the office from the back room. "John—" He halted. "Oh, here you are. Miss Susannah, good seeing you today. Did you bring dinner? The men are shutting everything down now." He gazed at them, seemingly without a clue of his interruption.

"Yes, I brought dinner. Tell them to wash up, and we will bring it out in a few minutes."

"Anything I can carry?"

Susannah sighed. "Sure. There are a few baskets on the wagon out front."

Matthew blazed past them like a man on an important mission. He opened the office door and disappeared outside, but he would return any moment heavy-laden with food baskets.

John grabbed Susannah by the forearms. "Susannah, will you go with me to the husking bee? I don't know when it is, and I hope it is not until we finish this order, but I want to ask you to accompany me before someone else asks you."

Susannah broke into laughter. "That is the oddest request I have ever heard, but yes!"

"What if you get another offer?" John dropped his hands.

"I won't. And if I did, I would say no, because you are the only one I want to go with to the dance." Susannah leaned closer to John with fiery eyes, his emotions hitting the ceiling. She twirled a curl beside her ear with her forefinger and breathed a raspy breath.

Was that *the look*?

John took a step and closed the distance between them. He grabbed her face with his grimy hands. Without allowing for a chance to second-guess himself, he seized her lips with his.

When Susannah wrapped her hands around him and returned his kiss with an urgency, John did not worry if the dirt from his hands soiled her. He only drank in her loveliness and hoped they never parted again.

"Hawkins!"

John jerked away from Susannah, almost pulling her to the floor.

"What are you doing violating my daughter?" Chauncey stood in the entrance with a basket of food propped on one hip and the hand of his injured shoulder propped on the other. His eyes glowed like pieces of hot coal, and his face looked like it would explode at any moment. "I didn't give you complete freedom with all my property. Only my business and only for this order. My daughter was not part of the deal."

Someone might as well have poured cement down John's throat. No words came out, even though he tried. His chances of Chauncey accepting him? Ruined.

"Get your hands off my daughter!"

Matthew stood beside Chauncey with his mouth agape and nearly dropped the food basket when he bellowed.

John gulped. When had he caressed Susannah's shoulders? "Sir, I—"

Susannah tugged free of John's hold. "Papa, I am not your property."

"What?"

"You called me your property. That, I am not. I'm your daughter."

"Well, I—"

"And I let John kiss me. I would not stop him if he does it again."

"Now listen here—"

Matthew ducked behind John and into the back room. John entertained the idea of following him.

"Susannah, it is not appropriate. The two of you in here unchaperoned carrying on like—well, it is just not appropriate."

John cleared his throat. "Sir, I am sorry. I should not have kissed Susannah without your permission." He glanced into her face and bent forward in laughter.

She frowned. "What?"

His grimy hand marks graced her cheeks. "Your face is smudged with my hands. Even if your pa had not caught us this way, he would have figured something out."

Chauncey let loose a laugh like John had never heard. "Susannah, my daughter, wash your face, and then help me and your favorite fellow serve these hardworking men."

"Yes, sir." She turned toward the back room then faced John again. Her eyes twinkled, her smile brighter than the day. "I would love to go with you to the husking bee. I would love to go with you anywhere."

"I love that you want to go with me. And—" John glanced at Chauncey for a second then back at Susannah. "And I love you."

Susannah beamed, her lips slightly parted.

Ah, that was *the look*! "I love you too, John Hawkins. I always have."

Chapter 9

S ecrets did not often stay secrets forever, Susannah knew all too well. But for sixteen days, they had managed to hide John's presence in Albion and his involvement in the Carmichael order. Against Pa's better judgment, John had attended church with them the last two Sundays, the only days they had closed the sawmill, but no one seemed to recognize him as a Hawkins.

If everyone was cordial at church, then who had written the frightening notes? And why had they now stopped?

Susannah strolled the canal on this Friday morning, her smile uncontainable. Maybe the threats were over. Maybe someone had seen John's goodness and spread the word that Albion could use a man like him.

They would finish the order tonight, then tomorrow night she would dance at the husking bee with the man she'd grown to love over the last three weeks. Maybe then John would finally feel welcomed in Albion.

After her stroll, Susannah stopped at the post office to see if a letter from Aunt Eleanor had come. Although her aunt had not written them yet, the postmaster told her that a telegram awaited her at the telegraph office.

Susannah stepped next door and retrieved her telegram. She held the paper in gloved hands and almost jumped out of her boots when she read the message. Unsure she had read it correctly, she read it again.

CONGRATULATIONS. YOU HAVE WON FIRST PLACE IN THE WAX FLOWER CONTEST. YOUR RIBBON AND PRIZE MONEY ARE ON THEIR WAY. MERCHANTS FROM NEW YORK CITY WILL CONTACT YOU SOON ABOUT SELLING YOUR FLOWERS.

Susannah squealed and then cleared her throat when a few passersby gave her odd glances. With a stifled giggle erupting from her throat, she bounced her way to the sawmill, ignoring proper etiquette.

"I cannot believe I won! Merchants want to speak with me? Thank You, Lord, for blessing me in this way."

Susannah arrived at the sawmill to find John and Pa huddled around her desk in the office with grave looks on their faces. She stuffed the telegram into her purse and joined them. "What is it? Pa? Is everything okay?" Was there an injury? Had a piece of equipment broken, thereby rendering them unable to complete the order? "John? Speak to me."

John shook his head, walked to the window, and cast his gaze toward the canal.

Pa dropped into the desk chair.

Susannah placed her hand on Pa's hand. "Tell me, Pa."

Pa sighed. "I received a note today threatening to burn down my sawmill and all the wood stored at the train station if I associate with John."

"What? I thought these horrible people had given up trying to control you."

"I thought so too."

"What are you going to do?"

"John said he will return to New York City and let his men finish the job. He does not want to endanger us or our property by his presence."

Susannah jerked her head to face John, still comforting Pa with her touch. "John, you cannot let them run you out of town. We cannot let them win. We need to send for the sheriff."

"They will persist until I am gone, Susannah."

"John, I have learned something from you the last two weeks. It is to never give up. To always fight. We cannot give up now."

John pressed his forehead against the glass and seemed to surrender.

The saw roared out back and men shouted orders to each other as they worked.

The sawmill had not seen this much life in years. "Pa, do you hear that noise out there?" She pointed through the back room toward the lumberyard. "That's life. Progress. You took this order because you wanted to secure our home. John helped make all of this happen. You cannot let a few threats wipe all of his hard work away."

She crossed the room and joined John at the window. "John, how close are we to finishing the order?"

"Maybe an hour or two. Then we will load everything and deliver it to the woodshed. The train for Buffalo comes in the morning."

"Okay, see, we are so close. We will not let these people threaten us." She faced Pa. "We will not let them exile John again."

Both men mumbled their complaints and arguments.

"Where are my strong and determined men?"

With that, John smiled and pushed his shoulders back.

Pa joined them by the window and whacked John on the back then landed a peck to Susannah's cheek. "I am willing if you are, Hawkins."

"I suppose one more night could not hurt."

"Wonderful! Now what do I do to help?"

John glanced at Pa then at her. "Perk some coffee. We have a long night ahead."

◆━━━━━◆

Susannah held on to John's arm and enjoyed the fading light of day with him, confident he would let no harm come her way. This nightly walk along the canal refreshed them from the long hours at the sawmill and drew them closer to each other.

The canal was the same tonight as every night since John had plucked Susannah out of it. Katydids sang and frogs croaked, owls called to their mates, and water lapped at the shoreline.

Yet tonight things were different.

John's stay in Albion had hinged on Pa's forgiveness and acceptance of him. From the first day here, he had been willing to return to the city. But Pa had forgiven. Would everyone else?

After the husking bee tomorrow night, John might find the opposition proved more of a struggle than he cared to face, and Susannah might suffer one of the greatest heartaches of her life.

With her head on his shoulder, she closed her eyes while John led the way along the towpath, and prayed he would stay if God allowed.

"Susannah, you are anxious. What troubles you?"

John knew her well enough now to discern her nervous twitches and quick answers as signs of her unsettled spirit. He could read her discomfort better than Pa, and he had only had a couple of weeks to study her.

"I am concerned about the watch tonight. Will the person who's threatening us attempt to destroy the sawmill and the order? Or is it a threat of no value?"

"You needn't worry about tonight. Every one of my friends will either be at the sawmill or at the train station guarding the woodshed. Their wives and fiancées will be with you at home."

Susannah stopped cold. "I will not sit at home tonight. I will be there with you and Pa. . .all night long and until that order is safely on its way to Buffalo."

"Susannah—"

Susannah stomped her foot on the towpath. "John, I will be there, and I will not hear another word about it. This business is mine as much as it is Pa's. And you are—well, I will be by your side too."

"I am what?" He tapped her nose with his forefinger. "Am I your beau?"

"Would you like to be?"

"I would love to be."

Susannah giggled and dipped her chin. "Then that you will be."

John led Susannah to the office and left her with a room full of women—the women who later would have been at her home had she agreed to stay there—who chatted about the impending danger of the night as if another tightrope walker planned to walk across the canal. The companionship did not bother Susannah though. They chatted about their gowns for the husking bee and the preparations they had made for the holidays, which would be here in a month.

Looming in Susannah's mind, however, was tonight's uncertain events and John's potential departure.

After a short break of bread, ham, boiled eggs, and apples, the men loaded the last of the lumber onto the wagons and made the delivery to the train station. An hour later, half the men returned, and the night watch began.

＋＋━━━━━━━━━━＋＋

Susannah startled awake at the sound of broken glass and women screaming. She had fallen asleep in her desk chair, facedown on the desktop. In the middle of the office floor sat a blazing lantern. As quickly as she could move in her hooped dress, she bounded from her chair, ran to the back room, and returned with a bucket of water. She doused the flames and tossed the bucket on the floor by the cloud of smoke.

Pa and John charged into the room followed by several of the other men; the women surrounded them with tales of the event.

"Susannah, you put out the fire?" John stomped to the center of the room and joined her. "Are you all right?"

Her unruly curls had slipped from their pins during the commotion and now framed her shoulders. "Yes, I did, and yes, I am. I could not let someone burn this place down while I am on watch." Of course, she had not stayed alert. She had slept. But at least she had acted quickly and extinguished the fire before it spread.

"John! Mr. Higley! Out here." Matthew hollered from the street.

Pa joined them in the center of the room, and they all ran outside to the sidewalk. There, a wagon blazed, and heat radiated all the way to the doorway.

Susannah coughed and covered her mouth with her hand. "Who would set a wagon on fire right in front of our sawmill?"

Pa crossed his arms across his chest and shook his head. "I cannot believe this much hatred exists in Albion. I sure hope they catch whoever's doing this and they give me the chance to confront him."

"There!" John shouted while pointing across the street. "See that man running with the torch?"

"Get him!" Pa yelled.

Before Susannah considered her actions, she yanked up her skirt above her ankles, ran alongside John and Pa, and chased the culprit.

As they ran through the streets, people bolted out of their homes and joined them on the chase. They ran all the way to the train station, then John burst in front of them and tackled the man to the ground, the torch landing by him.

Matthew stomped out the flame with his boot.

John flipped the offender onto his back, beads of sweat dripping on the man's face. "Who are you? Why are you threatening Mr. Higley? Why do you care about my presence in town?"

Susannah threw her hands over her mouth and screamed, her voice piercing the night air. "Richard! What are you doing here?" Although the dark night blanketed the details of Richard's face, she recognized him.

John shoved Richard's shoulders into the dirt. "This is Richard?" He gazed at Susannah and then back at Richard.

"Yes." Susannah shifted her gaze toward Richard as the crowd dissipated. "What are you doing here? Why are you threatening my pa and John?"

Richard shrugged and tried to free himself from John's hold, but John tightened his grip.

The sheriff sauntered up to them and pulled John off Richard. "I'll take over now. What do you have to say about your actions here tonight?" He pulled Richard to his feet and held his arms behind his back.

"Richard, answer him." How could he do something like this to her family?

Richard tucked his chin. "I didn't strike gold in California. I struck nothing but misfortune. I came home seeking your forgiveness, but I saw you with *him*." He motioned toward John with his head. "I kept watching you two grow closer, and I dreamed up a plan to run him out of town. At the barber, I overheard somebody say who he was and that he was here in secret. So I decided to run him out of town for good by turning folks against him."

Susannah closed the gap between them. "Richard, I would never let you court me again, and it is not because of John. It is because of what you have done."

Pa stepped up and explained the evening's events to the sheriff, who jerked Richard by the arm and carried him off toward Market Street to the jail. He would spend the night there waiting on the judge to determine his sentence.

Richard would not be welcomed here, but John would, and Susannah's heart soared.

Chapter 10

One month ago on this day, Susannah's life changed in ways she never thought possible. Her wax flowers won a prize and brought awareness of her talent to merchants in New York City, and the collapse of the bridge afforded her a second chance at life.

As John steered the small dory along the Erie Canal, Susannah pulled her shawl around her shoulders. Once again, she put her life in John's hands and trusted if the boat overturned, he would rescue her.

"You all right?" The tenderness in his dark eyes melted all cares away.

"I'm perfect."

"My dear, I have known you were perfect for a long time."

"Now, John, I am far from perfect in that way."

"You are perfect for me."

"I am?"

He nodded and scrubbed his beard. "Susannah, would you be my wife?"

She gulped, and the chill from the late October air left her as her heart pumped blood furiously through her veins. "Your wife?"

"My wife. I've planned on asking your father for his blessing ever since last week when we completed the order, caught Richard, and charmed the whole town at the husking bee."

"Charmed the town? I am not sure you could call it that." She chuckled.

"I would say winning the title of Mr. and Miss Bee proves not only that the feud is over and that Albion accepts me but that everyone likes us together."

Susannah shifted her gaze to a pair of mallard ducks swimming together on the canal. They stayed side by side and took turns dipping their heads in the water searching for food. They were a perfect pair, the female as lovely as the male, although the male's iridescent-green, white, and blue adornment were more fetching than her brown, spotted feathers.

"Susannah?"

She tugged her gaze away from the ducks and lingered on his kind face, warm eyes, and sweet smile.

"Would you be my wife? I understand if you are not sure about me yet."

Like the surety of the next morning's sunrise, Susannah's answer could not be anything but yes. She would not feel complete until she married John.

"I will wait as long as it—"

"Yes! I will be your wife."

"Yes?" John jerked his hands off the oars and clapped them in the air, frightening the ducks away and making the boat teeter.

Susannah grabbed both sides of the boat and squealed. Would she go over into the canal again?

John quickly steadied the boat, and laughter broke forth from them both. Life would always be an adventure with John Hawkins.

"I am the most privileged man in all of Albion. No, in all of New York. In all—"

"John, please. Your compliments are far too generous. After all, I am quite the privileged one."

"How so?"

"God made sure I did not have to choose between you and Pa. I get to have you both."

"He did indeed. I am amazed at how your father has softened over the last few weeks."

"Yes, and now he courts Mary Waterbury at the bakery."

"Shall we marry in the morning?"

She crinkled her nose. "The morning? John! Have you lost all reason?"

"I have. My love for you has blinded me to all things that make sense."

"Why the morning?"

"The train's coming through on the way to New York City. I could take you with me to sell my business and gather my things."

"And I could see the merchants about my flowers?"

"Absolutely. We would ride in the passenger car on velvet seats and eat cakes and pies, or we could take a packet boat down the canal and stop in every city. Once in New York City, you will see the new Central Park, Manhattan stores, theaters, and—"

"The ocean?" Susannah clasped her hands in front of her heart.

"The ocean, yes."

Susannah pretended a moment of consideration, although it was not necessary. Marrying John and traveling to New York City on a honeymoon was her idea of perfection. Now that Pa's business was safe, and the house secured once again, nothing stopped her from going. "I will marry you in the morning."

"You have made me the happiest man on earth. I promise I will make you the happiest woman on earth."

"You already have!" Susannah leaned forward, and John did the same.

He placed the sweetest kiss on her lips, the promise of good things to come.

Sherri Wilson Johnson is a multi-published inspirational romance novelist, speaker, and virtual assistant. She lives in Georgia with her husband and her Chihuahua-Beagle puppy. She loves spending time with her adult children and friends or curling up with a good book or her current work in progress. Sherri enjoys doing jigsaw puzzles in the winter, watching Bob Ross painting videos (although she can't paint), and counts the days every year until she can take another trip to the beach. You can find Sherri on Facebook, Instagram, Twitter, and Pinterest. Find out more about Sherri at her website: www.sherriwilson-johnson.com!

More Great Romance Collections from Barbour...

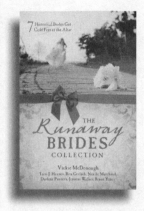

The Runaway Brides Collection

What is a woman of the 1800s to do when she feels pressured to marry without love to protect her family, to gain wealth, to fulfill an obligation, or to bend under an evil plan? *Run!* Seven women facing the marriage altar make the decision to flee, but who can they now trust?

Paperback / 978-1-68322-817-2 / $14.99

The MISSadventure Brides Collection

Seven daring damsels don't let the norms of their eras hold them back. They embrace adventure whether at home working what is considered a man's job, or leaving the city for a rural assignment, or by completely crossing the country in pursuit of a dream. And while chasing adventure, romances overtake them.

Paperback / 978-1-68322-775-5 / $14.99